"Bradley doesn't disappoint with the second in her Runaway Brides trilogy, which is certain to have readers laughing and crying. Her characters leap off the page, especially little Melody, the precocious 'heroine,' and her three fathers. There's passion, adventure, nonstop action, and secrets that make the pages fly by."

—*Romantic Times BOOKreviews*

"When it comes to crafting fairy tale–like, wonderfully escapist historicals, Bradley is unrivaled, and the second addition to her Runaway Brides trilogy cleverly blends madcap adventure and sexy romance."   —*Booklist*

DEVIL IN MY BED

"From its unconventional prologue to its superb conclusion, every page of the first in Bradley' ̶ ̶away Brides series is perfection and joy. ̶ ̶ ̶ ̶ ̶ ̶mor that never overshadows ̶ ̶ ̶ ̶ ̶ ̶ ̶ ̶led with remarkable c ̶ ̶ ̶ ̶ ̶ ̶ ̶us Melody who will s ̶ ̶ ̶ ̶ ̶ ̶ ̶ ̶ ̶."

̶views

"Part romantic come ̶ ̶ ̶ ̶ ̶omantic suspense, and wholly entertaining, *Devil in My Bed* is a delight!"

—*Romance Reviews Today*

"Laughter, tears, drama, suspense, and a heartily deserved happily-ever-after." —*All About Romance*

DUKE MOST WANTED

"Passionate and utterly memorable. Witty dialogue and fantastic imagery round out a novel that is a must-have for any Celeste Bradley fan." —*Romance Junkies*

"A marvelous, delightful, emotional conclusion to Bradley's trilogy. Readers have been eagerly waiting to see what happens next, and they've also been anticipating a nonstop, beautifully crafted story, which Bradley delivers in spades." —*Romantic Times BOOKreviews*

THE DUKE NEXT DOOR

"This spectacular, fast-paced, sexy romance will have you in laughter and tears. With delightful characters seeking love and a title, [this] heartfelt romance will make readers sigh with pleasure." —*Romantic Times BOOKreviews*

"Not only fun and sexy but relentlessly pulls at the heartstrings. Ms. Bradley has set the bar quite high with this one!" —*Romance Readers Connection*

DESPERATELY SEEKING A DUKE

"A humorous romp of marriage mayhem that's a love-and-laughter treat, tinged with heated sensuality and tenderness. [A] winning combination."
—*Romantic Times BOOKreviews*

Also by
CELESTE BRADLEY

And Then Comes Marriage

CELESTE BRADLEY

St. Martin's Paperbacks

This is a work of fiction. All of the characters, organizations, and events portrayed in this novel are either products of the author's imagination or are used fictitiously.

AND THEN COMES MARRIAGE

Copyright © 2013 by Celeste Bradley.

For information address St. Martin's Press, 175 Fifth Avenue, New York, NY 10010.

ISBN: 978-1-250-01613-3

Printed in the United States of America

St. Martin's Paperbacks edition / August 2013

St. Martin's Paperbacks are published by St. Martin's Press, 175 Fifth Avenue, New York, NY 10010.

10 9 8 7 6 5 4 3 2 1

Chapter One

ENGLAND, 1818
*If only I dared, I might be the most blissful of women—
although tiresome good sense rushes to assure me I might
well be the unhappiest, with a lifetime of regret ahead of
me and only sweet memories behind.*

*I think I might take either future rather than live one
more day in this tedious shelter of "unloved" and "over-
looked."*

If only I dared. . . .

Mrs. Gideon Talbot strolled sedately down the walk. Miranda was without her maid today, for poor Tildy had a
bad cold and was nestled up in her attic bedroom with a
hot pot of tea and a crock of broth.

Miranda liked feeling unfettered by company. Why
exactly did a lady need to be accompanied by a maid at
all times? Tiny Tildy could hardly protect her in a crisis.
Nor was Tildy needed to carry parcels, for Miranda
merely gave the vendors her address, and everything she
purchased was delivered promptly and without fail.

When one was a wealthy, respectable widow, the world

tended to do as it was told. Such a position was quite refreshing, to tell the truth.

So instead of making her usual round of shops and vendors, Miranda directed her hired hack to let her off in an unfamiliar neighborhood.

It wasn't as though she actually expected to see *him* here. She was simply curious. She knew he resided nearby and wished to know a little more about the man she could not stop thinking about.

And then, ahead of her, as if summoned by her thoughts, a tall, brown-haired fellow stepped out of an alleyway and ran across the street, dodging carts and riders and piles of horse apples.

Miranda knew that man. She knew the breadth of his shoulders and the way his hair curled down over the back of his collar and most especially she knew that hard, muscled horseman's bottom.

It had sat upon her sofa for most of the last month of afternoons, while she plied its owner with tea and conversation.

Mr. Pollux Worthington.

Mr. Worthington was a handsome fellow indeed, but his primary attraction for Miranda was his easy smile and his wicked sense of humor. After her dry, lifeless, loveless marriage had turned to a quiet and dusty widowhood, the heat and light generated by Mr. Worthington's calls had become the climax of her days.

It was entirely proper for her to have a gentleman caller or two, she reminded the harsh voice echoing in her mind from her past. She'd completed her half mourning, and she'd allowed only two entirely respectable fellows through her very respectable door. Their calls took place in the bright light of afternoon and rarely lasted more than a congenial half-hour.

If her mind sometimes wandered to Mr. Worthington's

wide, capable hands, or if her eyes lingered on his lips, or if her imagination waxed eloquent on the probable feel of his muscular buttocks in her hands, well, no one had to know what went on behind her demurely downcast eyes, did they?

Mr. Worthington had not called upon her in the last few days. Miranda told herself that she wished only to determine that he was well . . . although perhaps a broken bone or three would most gratifyingly explain his strange and abrupt absence after he'd been so attentive!

So it was merely out of friendly concern that she now strolled in the vicinity of his home. She hadn't followed him there; truly she hadn't.

However, since he was there and, by random chance, so was she, and they happened to be dawdling on the same street . . . well, she could go on all day in her mind on how she wasn't tracking the man like a hound on a scent, but the fact remained that she was doing exactly that.

Now, even after so brief a separation, the sight of him made her smile.

I believe I am giddy. Impossible! I am much too mature and respectable to become giddy.

Thirty-one years of age and a widow, to boot! How could the mere sight of a certain fellow transform her into a mooning schoolgirl?

This is unbearable. I refuse to participate in this—this preposterous state of affairs for one more moment.

Didn't he look fine, though, with the early summer sunlight pouring over him like golden honey, gleaming his light brown hair and creating that intriguing shadow just beneath his chiseled cheekbone? He was so handsome.

Giddy! And dreamy! Intolerable!

Panic set in. What should she do? Should she be casual and assured and greet him nonchalantly?

Should she stand here like an empty-headed bit of plaster statuary and hope he spotted her?

Miranda bit her lip as she considered her dilemma, or was she considering Mr. Worthington's bottom? It was muscled and hard, clad in tight riding breeches and just the right shape and form for a man.

After all, too little bottom, and a fellow's back fell directly into his legs, like rain down a gutter. Too much bottom, and a fellow bore an unfortunate resemblance to a duck, including the tendency to waddle.

No, the derrière in question was without a doubt a superior specimen.

And it belonged to her.

Or, it could belong to her if she dared. That very bottom had sat upon her parlor sofa for many afternoons in the past few weeks . . . day after day of visits and cups of tea and delightfully witty conversation. To Miranda, good conversation was more heady than wine. Her late husband had never been much of a talker . . . or a listener.

Gideon had been a highly regarded gentleman, a catch, really, for a plain girl like her, with her gawky elbows and knees and that unfortunate tendency toward flatness in the bosom.

It wasn't Gideon's fault that he'd not realized she wished to talk. She'd been virtually ordered to silence by her grandmother while he courted her.

That harsh voice rang from the mists of the past once again. "You'll sit silently and you'll keep good posture and you'll nod but not too much! Mind you, smile but not too widely!" The echoes of her grandmother's ranting rang as fresh as ever. "You'll not shame me like your wild mother, that hussy! That my pathetic son should have dishonored himself for her—"

Well, the rest of that was better not thought on.

Time and maturity had finally gifted Miranda with a bit of bosom and she'd learned to manage her elbows and knees with grace, mostly by keeping her movements slow and flowing.

Yet she'd never truly been able to stop her mind from coming up with odd things to say. She'd only learned to keep her mouth from uttering them.

The derrière—er, the man she'd been observing—left the building that he had briefly entered, only to dart across the street and back down the alleyway opposite.

Curiosity, while unbecoming in a sedate and mature widow of thirty-one years, mewed piteously and scratched to be let in.

Frowning slightly, Miranda could not resist pausing in her perfectly innocent and not-at-all-unseemly stroll to peer down the alleyway when she came abreast of it.

She could see very little but dingy cobbles and shadowy rubbish bins. The morning sun did nothing to illuminate the narrow lane between the tall brick buildings.

Tilting her head, Miranda listened carefully, but heard only a few strange banging noises, amplified oddly by the narrow passage.

Ladies, especially not sedate widows of a certain age, did not trot down dark alleyways after men.

Yet the unfettered sensation caused by dutiful Tildy's absence gave a gloss of freedom to Miranda's thoughts, a sheen they'd not had for so many, many years.

I can do as I please. I am no one's wife, or charge.

Besides, Mr. Worthington was a nice, respectable fellow, prone to amusing conversation about books and current events. Perhaps he had a perfectly good reason to be in such an odd location on a weekday morning.

She opened that figurative door, and curiosity strolled in, tail high and crooked in a question mark at the tip.

Without really allowing herself to ponder the question further, Miranda began to pick her way down the dim, narrow alley, careful to avoid soiling her hem on any of the many wads of nameless really-rather-not-know on the damp, slimy cobbles.

She lifted her skirts with one hand and used the other to trail along the brick wall to her right, as if by keeping a few fingertips on something solid, she could prevent being swept away by her own curiosity. She kept close the wall, stepping away from it only briefly to avoid something especially noxious at her feet.

The distant clanging noises increased in tempo and volume. Now it sounded as though a machine were grinding away. She could definitely distinguish the grinding gears, pistons pumping, steam whistling.

Curiosity swiveled its ears and quivered its whiskers.

What in heaven's name could lie ahead?

Pollux Worthington turned to his companion and smirked. "I told you it would work!" His green eyes gleamed.

Castor Worthington, who looked a great deal like Poll— being his identical twin, after all—only frowned as he pondered the giant contraption that took up most of the space in this crook in the alleyway. It was so large, they'd had to do most of the secret final assembly here, in this canyon of brick and stone, with bad light and the constant chance of discovery.

It was a steam engine, at heart. All the other many parts and functions had been added along the way to suit Poll's evolving design. Now it was meant to be a steam engine, a water pump, a pressure boiler, a home-heating device, and of course, a work of art worthy of gracing the palace of the Prince Regent himself!

Cas wrinkled his brow. Just like many of Poll's very worst ideas, it had all sounded most interesting at the time. Now Cas wondered how long this test run would take. He had pressing matters to attend to. "Well, it runs . . . sort of. As for actually *working* . . . "

Poll rolled his eyes and raised his voice over the noise of the engine. "You still doubt me? Didn't I get all of it down this alley after you said the cart wouldn't fit?"

"Well . . . yes, but—"

"And didn't I get it fired up after you said the coal was too damp?"

Cas shook his head. "I didn't say damp—"

"And isn't it, right this very moment, running like a top?"

Once more, Cas gazed at the gusting, clanging—and, let's be frank, hideous—creation. "I still think coal is a poor choice. It burns too hot. The steam pressure will—"

"Wood heat would never get the pressure high enough! Just wait, you'll see!"

Just then, the whistle they had affixed to the meter blew shrilly. Poll grinned triumphantly when it shot a neat plume of steam into the air as it trilled.

"Ha! Listen to that!"

Cas listened as the whistle squeaked. Then it screamed. Then it popped a rivet, detaching itself to blow off the stack and sail across the alley, its trill weakening in a sudden, pathetic whimper.

Poll's grin faded. "Oh, damn."

The twins stepped back at once, Cas down one side of the alley, Poll down the other. After a brief alarmed glance at each other through the growing clouds of steam that really shouldn't be there, they stepped back again. And again.

A movement at the edge of Castor's vision caught his attention. He turned his head to peer into the dimness of the alley that ran from the street. A woman? Who—?

The stack itself shook from the pressure building up

inside. The rivets holding it in its tubular form commenced to pop off in sudden, bulletlike haste. The twins threw themselves away from the machine, scrambling over the cobbles, intent only on getting as far from imminent death as possible.

Then Cas remembered the woman. He twisted half about to see that she had come closer, her appalled gaze on the wheezing, screaming, buckling machine.

Opposite him, Poll threw an arm over his face. "We need to get out of here!"

Cas pointed Poll toward the door to the safe interior of the building. "Run!"

He turned back to where the woman stood, her face pale and her hands held before her. She was finally backing away, as it was now quite obvious that the machine was about to explode like a Chinese firework, but she wasn't moving fast enough.

Cas ran at her full-out, diving into her, wrapping his arms about her, and throwing them both back into the narrow, angled safety of the street entrance.

Just as they hit the hard, slimy cobbles, the monster behind them groaned into a roar.

Chapter Two

Miranda lay with a heavy weight upon her; a hard, cold lumpy surface beneath her; and a great ringing in her ears.

Through it, she could barely detect Mr. Worthington's rather gratifying tone of concern. "Oh hell. Oh damn. Are you all right? Are you hurt?"

She remained still, a little surprised that she was, in fact, quite well. Her heart was racing and her bottom grew colder by the moment as the dampness of the ground seeped through her gown, but she felt nary a single bruise on her flesh.

His arms were wound about her, so very little of her had impacted the cobbles at full force. His large hand was wrapped around the back of her head, protecting her from the stones even now. She remembered that as they had fallen, he had tucked her face into the hollow of his neck and shoulder and rolled with her quite enveloped in his hold. It had been a splendidly athletic move and really a most gallant rescue.

Now he remained wrapped about her, lying fully upon her, his knee pressing her own apart. If anything, her pulse increased. He shifted his weight from her and knelt by her side. "Damn it, I've killed her!"

Opening her eyes, she couldn't help smiling up at him gazing worriedly down at her. "A most graceful rescue, sir. Perhaps I should keep you at my side for all future explosions."

He let out a gusting sigh of relief and grinned ruefully back at her. "No future explosions, I promise. In fact, let us pretend that one never happened!"

He stood easily and bowed to her, extending his hand. Taking hers, he lifted her to a standing position, steadying her as she staggered.

His arms were strong, keeping her easily on her feet. He took her shoulders in his hands, stepping back while yet steadying her.

"My deepest apologies! Are you quite sure you are all right?"

Miranda nodded, blinking back the sudden wave of heat that had apparently come directly from contact with Mr. Worthington's iron-hard body. Goodness, he might have a taste for awful, foppish weskits, but there was nothing of the soft, doughy dandy about him!

Her feminine obsession with his bottom instantly expanded to a new fascination with that muscled chest.

I am incorrigible!

The notion rather pleased her, even as she smiled breathlessly up at Mr. Worthington. Imagine her—shy, awkward Miranda Talbot—incorrigible!

Mr. Worthington took her hand to bow over it. "Lovely lady, might I plead my heroism as cause to sidestep the proprieties just this once? I am Worthington."

Miranda smiled, completely charmed. *Let us pretend that one never happened.* He meant to start over indeed, for those were the very words he used the day they had met!

On that afternoon a month ago, she'd been crossing a busy street in Mayfair and had caught her heel between two cobbles. Tildy, toting packages, had fallen a little behind.

Miranda knew she'd been silly to lose sight of the on-coming traffic in her worry over a shoe, but thankfully a handsome man—Mr. Worthington!—had simply stepped into the street, wrapped an arm about her waist, and plucked her from danger—and the offending shoe!

Now, just as she had then, Miranda dipped a curtsy and said, "Gallantry is its own reward, sir, but your actions were most heroic. I might allow that the act of intro-ducing yourself—while shocking and forward of you!—is a just and proper reward for such valor."

When she straightened, she found her own reward in the warmth of his smile. Goodness, she'd never seen his eyes gleam so at her! Previously warm and friendly, like spring sun on green grass, his eyes now promised heat and light and shadow and all manner of wickedly playful possibilities!

It must be that he'd been affected by their brief inti-macy on the cobbles as well!

Miranda's pulse became more rapid. She loved the spring sun but the flame of a midsummer bonfire might warm one twice as well, might it not? Fighting her own timidity, she gazed right back and continued the game. "I am Mrs. Gideon Talbot, Mr. Worthington. However, my hero may address me as Miranda."

Would he say it again? Would he say the words that had made a fiercely circumspect widow, the very model of propriety, begin to remember that she was a flesh-and-blood woman as well?

His lips curled up at the corners. "Miranda, lovely daughter of Prospero. 'O you, / So perfect and so peerless, are created / Of every creature's best!' "

Miranda's jaw dropped slightly. *Oh my.*

The first time, he had smiled teasingly and recited, " 'The very instant that I saw you, did / My heart fly to your service.' " She'd been flattered, impressed by his

Shakespeare-at-the-ready compliment, and charmed by his relaxed impertinence.

Now, with his leaf green eyes gleaming wicked promise and his lean, broad-shouldered form leaning close over hers, she found herself thrilled by the breathtaking notion of being seen as "perfect and peerless" by such a man!

She struggled for a light laugh. "You've studied up on your *Tempest*! Very good! But are you my Ferdinand or simply a Caliban?" She pretended arch indifference. "That remains to be seen, does it not?"

Cas stared down at the pretty widow, perplexed. She ought to be weak-kneed and simpering by now, not teasing him so pitilessly. He'd been quite proud of yanking that handy Miranda quote out of his memory.

Of course, his father, Archimedes Worthington, Shakespeare scholar, had strolled around the house quoting that bloody play for months. There was nothing so likely to drive a fellow off Shakespeare as an elderly man wandering the house at midnight in his baggy drawers stentoriously spouting Ferdinand's lines from *The Tempest*!

Mr. Castor Worthington, confirmed bachelor, appreciator of all things feminine, stepped back to take a better look at the delightfully soft object of his sudden collision.

She seemed rather poised. Was this the same woman he'd just tackled and flung onto the cobbles—after very nearly exploding her?

She looked a mess, actually. Her fine straw bonnet, dyed to match her spencer, was a smeary ruin, as was the spencer. Beneath the short jacket, her gown was sullied with more alley slime, especially about the er . . . arse.

The damp fabric clung to her flesh, and Cas took a moment to appreciate the delightful shape revealed beneath it. Then he firmly returned his gaze to her face to find her assessing him expectantly.

Hmm. His smile warmed. *Pretty.* Perhaps even beautiful, properly gowned in something that would set off that nicely structured bosom and that alabaster skin. Not that she wasn't well dressed, just a bit understated.

Widow? Who else wore that weary shade of lavender gray?

A pretty widow with a wayward sense of adventure, if he was not mistaken.

His very favorite kind.

He smiled in return, a slow, lazy grin that had stripped many a woman right down to her knickers on the spot. He might need to flee the scene of the crime in the next few moments, but that didn't mean he would pass up a chance to flirt with a pert young widow!

He was yet breathing, after all.

Miranda inhaled, her mouth going dry. Why, all of a sudden, was he smiling down into her eyes as if she were a present he'd very much like to unwrap?

Oh, yes. Please unwrap me.

Miranda closed her eyes and stilled her body against the heat that shot through her at that outrageous, wayward thought and the vague, disturbing, and delicious images that followed.

"Mrs. Talbot, I do believe I ought to take you—"

Miranda's eyes flew open and her lips parted. In addition, her hands went completely numb with shock and parted ways with her reticule, which plopped to the filthy ground.

"—home. You'll want to change out of these . . . er, damp things."

Removing her revolting gown would be . . . "Wonderful," she breathed. Then she caught herself up. Yes. Home. Changing into something that didn't reek of best-not-ask! Good plan.

She reached out to awkwardly shake his hand. "It was lovely to . . . well, not really, but . . ." Don't blather, girl! She straightened and curtsied sedately. "Home. Yes. I really must be heading home. I should not like to leave it too late, for it is becoming quite chilly out, isn't it?"

He smiled down at her. Such a bold little thing! "Is it?" He bent his elbow and offered it to her, his busy schedule entirely dismissed from his thoughts. "Then I must continue my gallantry and accompany you home."

He tucked the pretty hand of the pretty widow into his arm and allowed the lady to turn their feet toward the street, a hired cab, and this fascinating destination.

With those sea green eyes and those enchanting lips, not to mention a smashing figure, she was lovely, sultry, and altogether enticing.

What a grand way to pass the afternoon.

In the hired hack, Miranda found herself very nearly speechless in the company of the man she valued for his sparkling conversation! Yet something was different now. There was a new element, a tension between them that perhaps came from the way their bodies had mingled and warmed to each other.

And when he looked at her with that teasing, appreciative glint in his eyes?

I feel almost . . . alluring.

Now, that was a word she'd never thought to apply to herself.

Ever.

She was a widow, attractive enough, but no raving beauty. Mr. Worthington was tall, broad-shouldered, fit as a horseman should be, and possessed of a handsome chiseled face, brilliant green eyes, a devilish smile, and charmingly wayward brown curls.

And a truly outstanding bottom. Her fingers twitched with a nearly overwhelming desire to explore further.

Miranda sighed. She had never once thought of running her hands over Gideon's bottom. She'd never seen her stoop-shouldered, scholarly late husband without his frock coat or his nightshirt. Even marital copulation had been most decorous, in the dark with only the most necessary bits of muslin shifted to allow for the act. She'd done her duty to Gideon, as overseen and supervised by the ever-present Constance, Gideon's strict elder sister, but she hadn't loved him.

Nor had he loved her. He'd provided. She'd done her duty, all but for bearing a child. Gideon had found that flaw in his plan a tad disconcerting, but eventually allowed that children were a disturbing element in a house of cerebral pursuits, and magnanimously forgave her. Miranda had comforted herself in her barrenness with the thought that a houseful of little Gideons might have been a bit more than any sane woman might tolerate.

She'd kept her husband's house in good order and his cerebral work uninterrupted. In return, he'd doled out just enough funds to keep her looking respectable, in gowns subject to Constance's vision of respectability—that is, plain and demurely Quakerish. She'd not gone hungry, nor been beaten, nor actually deprived in body at all.

She'd simply been ignored to tiny little bits. She'd actually felt those bits falling off her, like flaking paint on a neglected house, shreds of her mind and soul drifting invisibly down to the carpet, day after day, year after long year.

Then Gideon had died, and shortly afterwards, miraculously, came the retirement of the repressive Constance, leaving Miranda most satisfactorily alone.

It was odd how being alone with oneself was so much less tedious than being alone with others.

Her year of true mourning was long past, and her year of half mourning had ended a month prior. She still wore her lavenders and grays, but that was only out of habit.

The hack pulled onto her square. Miranda's gaze, unable to meet Mr. Worthington's, went with relief to the neat, respectable facade of her own address.

Satisfaction slowed her pulse, calming her. It was her house, her very own, where she might do precisely as she pleased. When she died, she supposed the property would revert to Gideon's family, if there were Talbots left by then. Constance was twenty years Miranda's senior and she had no children, maintaining her rigid spinsterhood with pride, as though loneliness were a virtue.

Miranda didn't think loneliness was virtue. She thought it a great bloody waste of existence, when the bright world beckoned to anyone brave enough to take it.

With a series of brief glances, she contemplated the man seated across from her. *If only I dared.*

She wasn't bold, not really. Gideon had chosen her because she was timid, had preferred her timid.

Yet she didn't wish to be, not in her dreams, not in her mind—and not in the recent and delightful company of Mr. Worthington.

Now, shutting the door firmly on her past marriage, Miranda contemplated her current freedom with serenity and even some eagerness. No one owned her. Her parents were naught but sketchy memory, her harsh, overbearing grandmother gone on to her long-desired reward.

She ran the tip of her tongue over her lips. *I am a widow of means. I can do anything I like.*

And I like Mr. Worthington.

Chapter Three

It was, without a doubt, the fastest bath Miranda had ever taken in her life. Without Tildy to oversee the right and proper sequence of scrubbing and shampooing, Miranda found herself in and out of the tub in mere minutes.

Dressing was not much of a challenge, for she'd dressed herself all her life until recently. She dithered a moment between one drab half-mourning gown and another, finally decided that they were both equally awful, and chose the one that did the most for her finally adequate bosom. She pulled her still-damp hair up into a loose knot, thrust a few tortoiseshell pins into it, and declared it good enough.

As she ran full speed for the stairs, she reminded herself that ladies didn't run down halls, ladies didn't pound down the stairs, and most important, ladies did not arrive at the parlor door breathless and red-faced.

Smiling demurely while attempting to control her panting, she opened the door to see that Mr. Worthington had waited for her.

Her butler, Twigg, had assisted Mr. Worthington when they arrived. Now Miranda could see that his coat and trousers had been sponged and brushed and that his hair curled damply over his collar.

And she'd thought her bath was a swift one!

At her entrance, he turned from peering at the array of truly horrible ceramic dogs squatting on the mantel and smiled warmly at her.

Cas was surprised at how young the pretty widow looked, all freshly scrubbed and pink from her bath. She'd seemed rather more withdrawn on the way home in the carriage and he'd wondered if she regretted allowing him to accompany her here.

He was a bit astonished that he'd wanted to, and not simply out of duty to see to her well-being. Furthermore, he'd found that he wanted to remain, to wait for her to bathe and change.

Looking at her now, her eyes bright and her cheeks pink, clearly happy to see him still present, he felt a strange sensation in return. She was obviously a bold creature, inviting a strange man back to her home—although she was not the first widow in Cas's extensive acquaintance to do so!—so he'd half formed an intention to call on her for mutually nefarious purposes.

Yet as she smiled shyly at him and took a seat on the settee, waving him to the chair opposite her, he wasn't so sure.

He ignored the chair and settled next to her on the settee. She only sent him a startled glance and then leaned forward to tend to the covered tea tray that sat on the table waiting for them.

Widows had a great deal of freedom, as long as they were fairly discreet. Cas had indulged many an appealing lady with an afternoon here and there.

Yet this creature was something else altogether. She seemed entirely disinclined to flirt. Where was the coquettish giggle? Where were the knowing glances that traveled up and down his body? Where were the parting of full lips and the widening of dark-lashed eyes?

She straightened with a cup of tea in her hand, preparing to hand it to him. When she glanced up to see the intensity of his gaze on her, her full lips parted and her dark-lashed eyes widened.

Aha. Testing her a little, Cas leaned closer, then closer still. She did not back away, but she blinked in surprise and a tiny pink tip of her tongue flicked out to dampen her lips.

Something warm and tender bloomed in the vicinity of Cas's middle when he saw that vulnerable motion. He backed away, although he was not usually known for his mercy.

He was wrong. She wasn't bold, not really. He found himself confused—and Cas had not been confused by a female since the age of fifteen. Who was this creature, this sweetly bold, shyly tempting goddess in widow's weeds?

"Mrs. Gideon Talbot," he said softly. "Where did you come from?"

She blinked again. "I have always been here," she said faintly. "It is you who have just arrived."

He laughed. She was quite winning, in an off-center way. "So I have. Am I welcome?"

She shook her head and laughed at herself. "I beg your pardon, Mr. Worthington. Of course, you are a welcome guest."

Miranda returned to pouring the tea. Pity there were not twenty cups to fill, for she could truly use a moment to think!

Excitement and confusion twined through her belly. Mr. Worthington had always been so . . . so gentlemanly! Calm and respectful and really, truly, irritatingly circumspect!

She thought she'd done her part. She'd always smiled warmly. She'd tried to do interesting things with her hair. She'd made sure that every afternoon, there was a plate of lovely things for tea.

Wasn't that how one caught a man's attention?

What had she done today so differently to make him behave so familiarly? Why was he unexpectedly leaning in close enough that she could feel the warmth of him on her cheek?

Perhaps it was simply that he'd come to know her and to think she was a bit attractive, and now when she'd very nearly given up hope, he was finally longing for her as well.

"I am longing . . ."

Startled by his warm voice near her ear, Miranda dropped the sugar tongs on the carpet beneath the table.

". . . for a little milk."

"Oh!" Embarrassed, she rose quickly to snatch them up—just as Mr. Worthington himself bent to fetch them for her.

To avoid knocking heads, she stepped back swiftly, catching her heel on a wrinkle in the rug. As she lost her balance, she also lost all hope of Mr. Worthington thinking her anything but a complete ninny.

Every embarrassing, clumsy moment of her girlhood paled in comparison to the sure conviction that she was about to flail into the tea table and land right on her shattered dignity.

A single strong hand reached out to wrap sure fingers about her elbow. She regained her balance, and calm descended once more. She let out a breath of relief and raised her gaze to meet Mr. Worthington's amused and sympathetic one.

His green eyes twinkled. "Bloody carpets. They constantly trip one up."

She raised a brow at his insouciant vulgarity, but she

couldn't help the smile that tugged at the corners of her mouth. "You are most gallant, sir. I fear I would have looked most ridiculous on the floor!"

His gaze heated. "You," he said huskily, "would look lovely on the floor."

Shocking! Tawdry!

And entirely riveting. She stared at him as the breath left her lungs and her heart pounded. Then, swallowing hard, she managed to tear her gaze away. She sat once more, blinking down at the tongs that had rematerialized in her hands. "Sir, I—"

Her not-so-very-forceful remonstrance went unsaid, for he leaned forward quickly to press his mouth upon her parted lips.

Her heart stopped, failing her entirely, as her body erupted in a steamy explosion that outdid the one in the alley.

To be kissed—at last, at long, aching, forever last!

The hot jolt that had pierced Cas's gut had no name. It was something other than want, something other than simple masculine need for a willing female partner. It was the feel of her soft, vulnerable mouth beneath his—or possibly it was her soft squeak of astonishment that vibrated against his lips.

No, it had to be the way that her sweet, tea-flavored mouth melted into his, as if he were the answer to a lifetime of aching lonely dreams.

The jolt hurt. It expanded within him, blazing like wildfire, threatening his carefully constructed walls, which turned out not to be stone after all, but dry and brittle as driftwood, more than ready to be burned down.

No. Such an invasion was unwanted and unnecessary and quite frankly to be avoided at all costs in the future.

Cas pulled his lips reluctantly from the astonishing

mouth of the rather pretty, strangely shy, highly tempting widow.

With all his will, he removed his hands from where they had somehow slid up to caress the silken skin of her upper arms. He stood abruptly and stepped away, his fists closing over the last sweet warmth of her flesh on his palms.

"My apologies, Mrs. Talbot. I—I just realized that my time is in much demand today. I really must bid you good day." There was somewhere else he ought to be. Now.

He started to rush from the room, but a glance at her confused, crestfallen expression held him at the door for a moment. "I truly am glad you came to no harm today," he said softly.

Then he ran for his life from the confusing widow with the astonishing lips and the wide, sea green eyes.

Miranda sat very still on the settee, wondering why the cushions were shaking. It wasn't the stuffed velvet upholstery at all. It was her hands, her knees, and her assumptions.

Mouths were for talking. Lips . . . well, lips were for no more than smiling, were they not? Tongues . . . .

She shivered, remembering the way Mr. Worthington's hot mouth had parted and his tongue had escaped just long enough to trace the seam of her lips and to dip ever so slightly between. Nothing forced, just a soft, slick, quick invasion that had shattered her like a battering ram.

She pressed trembling fingertips to her lips, which were now for so much more than simply talking. A good thing, too, for she'd been rendered utterly speechless by the wave of liquid heat that had flooded her veins at the taste of him. Even now, her body shimmered with a new, sweet awareness of the man she'd thought she knew.

How could a simple press of mouth on mouth convey so much? How could she feel his hidden heat? His secret need? And, shockingly—and surely born of her imagination flamed by her own isolation—his buried loneliness?

Was that the real man, the man underneath? Was she mad, to think that she could understand someone's inner thoughts just by the touch of their mouth on hers?

She dropped her hands to her lap and clasped them there, her grip more desperate than firm. *Pull yourself together! So your very nice friend has decided to see you as a woman at last.*

What of it?

I am in such trouble here. No, nothing so minor as trouble. Danger. The promise of catastrophe only made it all the sweeter. Danger and risk and sweet, delicious possible reward.

Perhaps she was mad, or had at least been driven temporarily insane. Or perhaps she was merely completely mistaken.

It had been her very first kiss, after all.

Cas waited in the smallish—for a palace—receiving room he'd been shown into by a white-and-gold-liveried servant who had sized him up and labeled him with perfect accuracy with one lift of one brow.

Not titled. Not moneyed. Not politically significant. Yet has an appointment for a quiet moment with the Prince Regent.

Therefore, old acquaintance. Possible drinking companion, or worse. No need to be respectful. No point in being rude.

Cas just grinned at the man and blew him a kiss.

When the servant bowed and left the room, Cas inwardly chided himself for his cheeky act, then shrugged off his concern. He had come to speak to Prinny about something that was so important to him, he'd not breathed a word about it to another living soul. Even Poll knew nothing of the idea that had been swirling about in Cas's mind for months.

The time had come to take action. Enough fiddling about with toys and gimcracks! If he and Poll were ever to be taken seriously as inventors, they must put their combined ingenuity on one path and pursue it like rational—or at least coherent!—men of science.

However, he was still a Worthington, and Worthingtons were intimidated by no one. *With a family tree as old as Stonehenge,* Archie Worthington liked to say, *we've outlasted invasions and kings aplenty.*

So when the Prince Regent entered the room, moving as briskly as his bulk and his age allowed, Cas bowed with deep irony but didn't bother to fawn any further than that.

As he rose, Prinny snorted. Perhaps not the serious attention Cas sought, but Royal Amusement was preferable to Royal Boredom. Amusement he could work with.

"Well, what is it, Square Root? I haven't got all day."

Cas grinned at the nickname, a derivative of Worthington Squared, one of Society's kinder sobriquets for him and Poll. "Why, what's your hurry, Your Highness? Is she pretty?"

Prinny grimaced. "Stout and bald, actually. The envoy from Brussels is in Our office, cooling his heels and drinking Our wine. Actual princely work, mind you. Tedious as hell and twice as annoying." He considered Cas cynically. "Almost as annoying as you lot. Amuse Us or get out."

Cas's grin faltered slightly. Then he stood straight and bowed a bit more seriously. "Your Highness, I have come seeking royal patronage."

"Ha!" The Prince Regent wheezed a laugh. "That's a new one. Shall We allow you a stipend to go womanizing? Or shall We subsidize your scholarly pursuit of drinking? A study of whiskey versus whisky, perhaps? Brandy Demystified for the Masses?"

"No, Your Highness." Cas stiffened. "I, along with my brother, am an inventor. I wish to pursue some of our more workable designs in order to—" *Hopefully, perchance, with any luck at all.* "—to *confidently* bring them into public use one day."

Prinny raised a brow. "Hmm. It seems I heard of some strange contraption exploding in an alleyway in the vicinity of your family's madhouse earlier today. Was that one of these alleged 'workable designs'?"

Cas gulped. "That was—" *Fast.* "—a mere glitch. We had hopes for it, but P—but we put it into operation too soon, without adequate testing. If we had research funds, we could bring our ideas into development more—ah—" *Rationally, safely, sanely.* "—sedately."

"Ha! That I'd like to see," the Prince Regent remarked, finally dropping into informal address. "A sedate Worthington!" Prinny folded his arms across his paunch and leaned one silk-clad buttock on the arm of a great wingback chair.

"So you're telling me that you, Castor Worthington—one half of the Double Devils, middle son of the most demented family in the history of the Empire—wish to be taken seriously?" The Prince Regent leaned back for a good laugh at the very notion. The Royal Belly quivered. Prinny drew out a square mile of fine lace from his satin weskit and wiped the Royal Eyes, still chortling. "Inventors of what? Pandemonium? Havoc?"

Cas cleared his throat. "Labor-saving devices."

The Prince Regent snorted another laugh, though Cas was relieved that the Royal Sense of the Absurd appeared to be winding down. Prinny dabbed at his eyes again and smiled wryly at Cas. "Ah, see? Now you have earned your keep! I haven't laughed so in months!" He tucked the Royal Hankie back into his sleeve and leaned an elbow onto the chair back as he regarded Cas with what Cas hoped was *fond* exasperation. "What does a Worthington know about labor? The lot of you live on the sufferance of befuddled merchants, your finances hanging by a thread, occasionally supplemented by random outrageous luck!"

Cas's smile became rather fixed. "I daresay I know as much about labor as . . . say . . . a prince."

The Royal Gaze grew sharp. "Clever. It is true none of you lack for wits, mad as you all are. Yet the only thing that ever seems to hold *your* attention is a woman, and even that for not long at all—which of course ends badly, upsetting the lady, her husband, and stirring up my court. Every time I run across a scandal, it seems that one of the Double Devils is in the middle of it!"

Cas lifted his chin. "My name is never in the scandal sheets!"

The prince waved a hand. "Only because you aren't rich enough for that sort of attention. It's always An Unknown Gentleman or A Secret Paramour, but I know it's you, or your slightly better half."

Cas flushed at that. Poll was a better man than he, true, but it wasn't very polite of the prince to say so to his face.

"However, should you two ever decide to turn all that considerable ingenuity and vigor to something other than climbing into the bedroom windows of married ladies, I daresay you would succeed indeed." The Prince Regent's smile remained, but his eyes glinted. "Think you have something good up your sleeve, do you?"

Cas gazed back evenly. "We have several—" *Mad, preposterous, dodgy.* "—*brilliant* notions at present."

"Hmm."

A discreet tap came at the door. Cas cursed inwardly, knowing his allotted time was up.

The Prince Regent clapped his broad hands together. "Ah! There we go, then. It's agreed." The prince straightened and dusted his spotless arse with one beringed hand, as if he'd been sitting upon the grass instead of a spotless silk cushion.

"Er, what is agreed, Your Highness?" Hope stirred within Cas, but he remained wary. Best to get the specifics down when dealing with Prinny. Weasel-minded old . . . potential Royal Patron.

Prinny smiled at Cas, and it wasn't a particularly nice one. "One month. That's the bargain. One full month without a scandal or an explosion or a screeching, wailing Society wife throwing herself at your coldhearted feet, and I shall grant your royal patronage. You two useless drones will have one year to come up with something useful, and I'll foot the bill. It will be worth it just to gain a little peace and quiet amongst Our courtiers."

A year! It was several times what Cas had hoped for! "Yes, Sire!" This time when he bowed, it was just this side of fawning, but he was far too excited to care.

Chapter Four

Pollux Worthington, or Poll, as he preferred to be called—prepared to back up that preference with force if necessary—stood before his mirror and frowned at his waistcoat. For some time now, he and his twin brother had leaned toward a festive sort of weskit, or, in the words of his sister Elektra, "poisonous and vile."

The little sartorial joke didn't seem quite so amusing as it once had. He switched out the blinding lime and puce jacquard for one of his eldest brother Dade's more somber ones in deep blue. No, better the forest green one, to bring out his eyes.

He sighed. "Cas is right. I am a girl."

Poll looked up to see his own face in the mirror and effortlessly translated it to that of his twin. All it took was a bit more of a hardened jaw, less tendency to smile, an arrogant tilt to the head.

Some might find it odd to look upon another and see oneself, and vice versa, but Poll had never known anything else. Cas was more than brother, more than friend. A twin was like oneself, except that private conversations did not make one mad.

They were partners in every crime they could think of,

and a few they'd made up. To Cas, women were simply meant to pass the time between one great adventure and the next.

Until he met Mrs. Gideon Talbot, Poll had subscribed heartily to that philosophy himself.

Until he met Miranda.

Nothing juicy had happened yet. The pretty widow smiled and blushed and rose to his every sally, but she seemed content with naught but amusing conversation. Poll found himself reluctant to press her, for she brightened more every day, even in her pale half-mourning gowns. Yet he was sure her smile came more readily when she saw him, and her laugh rang sweetly through the parlor more and more often. Seduction by humor was a novel approach, but he truly enjoyed making her laugh with tales of his family exploits.

She was particularly fond of Attie stories. His little sister would kill him if she knew that he'd used her as bait to gain a woman's interest. Attie was not a fan of anything that might draw her family members away from her. Why, she'd very nearly murdered Callie while trying to murder Callie's husband, just to get Callie to come home!

He'd left that bit out of his stories to Miranda. He wouldn't want her to think that true madness ran through their family.

It stunned him that it even occurred to him to care. After all, he and his brother ate madness for breakfast.

He had plans for the widow. From the first time he saw Mrs. Talbot, he'd wanted to do things, teach her things, show her all the things she'd been deprived of in her dry marriage to that desiccated husk of a man.

Pretty Mrs. Talbot had been simply perishing to do something; it was true. She'd been dying to talk to someone.

So he outdid himself. He'd never bothered to do much

more than trade jousts or bestow compliments. He managed to fly by the seat of his pants the first week with Shakespeare. For the millionth time in his life, he thanked the stars that the ladies loved the Bard!

However, by the second week, he found himself perusing the newssheet for interesting tidbits. By the third week, he was forced to read actual books, then casually lend them to her—"an old favorite of mine . . . perhaps you might enjoy it."

He'd never had to work so hard to get a woman on her back in his life. He probably ought to have moved on—after all, it had been a while for him and he could truly use a good rogering—yet he found himself there at her door, day after day, toting a gift—a book, a piece of sheet music for them to try out upon her pianoforte, a posy of simple country blossoms that he knew she preferred to the grandeur of roses or the severity of lilies.

"Weddings and funerals," she'd told him once. "Neither of which I am in any hurry to attend."

The deep green weskit looked too somber. He'd finally decided to make an evening call—one painstakingly calculated to be nothing more than a friend casually stopping by to bring a volume of poetry, "thought you might like to read them this evening," and so on. Carefully timed to be invited for dinner without being so late as to appear to be crashing dinner.

His smile returned as he recalled the day he'd saved her life on Bond Street. . . . Well, it hadn't been quite so dramatic, although the freight wagon was going a bit fast and she was preoccupied by the heel of her shoe snagging in between two cobbles.

Poll had simply swept her out of her shoe and onto the safety of the curb, and the wagon had clattered past. The offending shoe had been undamaged and he'd retrieved it with a swift move and returned it with a gallant bow.

Her shy smile had brightened the very day around him. He'd begged an introduction, pleading heroism as cause to sidestep proprieties just this once. She'd solemnly agreed that his actions had been most selfless and allowed that his introducing himself was only right in the way of reward. Then she'd laughed, a bright bubble of light that made him want to make her do it again.

And again.

Poll hadn't told his twin where he was disappearing to in the afternoons and Cas had not asked. It was understood that sexual adventures were to be savored over whiskey in the male retreat of the attic, a corner of which they'd carved out for themselves years ago in desperate retreat from the stern eye of their eldest brother, Daedalus, and the maternal exasperation of their eldest sister, Calliope.

Many a wicked plan had been hatched in that attic room. All sexual conquests were shared, analyzed, and mined for answers to that mystery called woman.

All except Miranda.

Castor Worthington sauntered into his family home, then paused in the foyer and listened absently. Off-key humming came from the family parlor. Mama was painting. He sniffed. Yes, turpentine. He reminded himself to sniff the tea before he drank. One never knew where Mama might clean her brushes.

A screech of pure feminine rage echoed down the stairs. His second sister, Elektra. Since he and Poll hadn't plotted against Ellie lately, it must be that their youngest sister, Atalanta, was at it again.

Next Castor listened for the brooding silence of Lysander. Yes, one could hear silence that deep, especially in a raucous household like this one. The black mass of it followed Zander around like a cloud, leaching away the noise until it weighed the house down like lead. Castor loved his brother, but it was high time Zander dealt with whatever it was that had happened to him on the battlefield . . . or at least told someone what the hell it was so they could all understand!

Orion's study door was closed, which meant Cas's investigative-minded brother was busy extrapolating the mathematical patterning of scales on a snake or some such. Boring. Fortunately, Rion was bloody good at explosives, which made him rather entertaining company, if one could penetrate his abstraction long enough to gain his interest.

A fragment of *King Lear* drifted down the hall. Papa. Archimedes Worthington preferred to read the Bard aloud and at full volume. He claimed the words were meant to be decried from the stage. Castor had known every word of every sonnet and play by heart since he was nine, whether he liked it or not. Mostly not.

Raising his head, he sniffed the air. Philpott was doing something delicious with pork for dinner. At least the family wasn't pinching pennies any longer. Callie and her well-heeled husband, Sir Lawrence Porter, had made sure that there was food in the larder and coal for the fire, slipping them to Elektra past Iris and Archie's insistence that such generosity wasn't necessary, that everything was fine.

With his family mostly accounted for and no impending explosions apparent—because they'd already done that today—Cas allowed his thoughts to drift back to his surprising afternoon.

Miranda.

Mrs. Gideon Talbot, of Breton Square.

And then, the astonishing interview at St. James's Palace. Cas felt inward to find that satisfying ember of accomplishment. In one month, he—and Poll, of course—would be more than just gossip fodder, more than the Double Devils, more than cocksmen-about-town—

The front hall was quiet. Too quiet. "Come on out, Rattie."

His youngest sister, Attie—as usual, a right mess from her scabbed knees to her tangled amber curls—crawled out from behind the coat stand. "You're clean."

He smirked. "I'm always clean."

She narrowed her eyes. "No, sometimes you come home clean like you've just had a bath and you sing that stupid song about the dancing maids. This time you're all clean and you're not singing." She scowled at him. "Poll came in filthy and smudged and wouldn't tell me a thing. What went wrong?"

"Later, Rattie."

She screwed up her face at the nickname given her by their brand-new brother-in-law. The entire family had begun to use it, particularly when Attie's behavior waxed most foul. Which was more often now, left as she was without Callie's commonsense guidance and attempted instruction in the ladylike arts.

"Where's Poll?"

"He's had a bath." Attie rolled her eyes. "Now he's primping in his room. I think he has a new girl."

I don't have a new girl. I don't. "He's likely using that newfangled invention of ours."

Attie brightened, which meant that her permanent scowl became slightly less frightening. "You've made something new?"

Cas grinned. "Yes. It's called a 'hairbrush.' You should try it."

Attie's scowl became truly fearsome and she stalked away down the hall, all pointy elbows and stormy mutterings.

Cas snorted. He'd best remember to check his sheets tonight before he climbed into them. Attie was a vicious prankster. After all, he'd taught her everything she knew. He climbed the stairs, whistling although he did not much feel like it. *Ye merry maids come dancing* . . . .

Dancing with Mrs. Talbot would be intriguing. She had a languid grace that soothed his own restlessness.

Not that he would be seeing her again. There was no need to allow her to think his stolen peck had been anything more than healthy male opportunism. All imagined sweetness aside, a kiss was just a kiss, wasn't it? Just one of hundreds, after all.

One month without scandal. No problem.

He entered his brother's bedchamber still whistling, then flung himself down on the worn chair before the fire.

"I see you escaped the alley unscathed," he commented without much rancor. He could hardly blame Poll for fleeing the scene, and he was glad his brother had not been apprehended by anyone interested in the prosecution of a little harmless inventing.

He tossed the brown paper parcel onto the dressing table. "I found that book you were going on about. Coleridge." Cas stifled a yawn. More poetry.

"What put you into such a good mood?" Poll frowned at him in the mirror, where he stood impatiently ripping out the knot in his cravat, probably in order to start over. "I'd have thought you'd be ready to toss me into the boiler after today's mess."

Cas smirked as he watched Poll struggle with his cravat. Poll was always becoming obsessed with some pretty creature and getting himself into a dither. Once in a while, he even waxed eloquent upon the alleged joys of matrimony. That simply wouldn't do.

However, Cas wasn't too worried. Passions swept Poll from time to time. He never managed to keep his heart entirely uninvolved, despite Cas's tutelage. Fortunately, those sweeping passions eventually swept right past, leaving Poll completely well and slightly mystified by his former craving.

Women had one purpose in the lives of the Double Devils, as they were known in Society. Women were for kissing if they could be convinced of it, and for more if they could be seduced to it. Oh, they expended no energy toward the despoiling of virgins. They were too aware of the evil of that, what with three beloved if irritating sisters.

However, bored wives, wicked widows, and lusty barmaids were readily available and easily charmed. Why bother with anything more complicated than that?

I don't have a new girl. Truly.

Catching Cas's grin in the mirror, Poll cocked a brow. "Seriously, what are you so happy about?"

Cas hesitated. He wasn't ready to reveal the bargain with the Prince Regent. He knew Poll wouldn't like it. Poll found their impudent existence to be highly agreeable. Bringing his twin around to a new, more serious status might take some time, and some thought.

However, he truly ought to share his afternoon escapade with the pretty widow. He and Poll always did. Women were wonders to cherish and pleasure—but they were also adventures to relate over a brandy. Debates would ensue, discussions of blonde versus brunette, of curvaceous versus slender. Neither of them had a true preference, it seemed. They were both equal-prospect lovers. Poll would enjoy the story of the pleasantly rounded widow rolling beneath Cas in the alley. And that kiss.

Except that it was just a kiss. Of course. Really, there was nothing to tell.

Cas just grinned and shook his head. "I'm looking forward to tonight, that's all."

Poll looked confused, then dismayed. "Oh hell. I forgot about tonight."

" 'Oh hell'?" Cas frowned at his twin, firmly putting his mixed afternoon behind him. "Our invitation to Mrs. Blythe's House of Pleasure rates an 'oh hell'? A posh and dissolute orgy—er, *ball*—is a subject of consternation?" For the first time the danger occurred to him. Need he worry about scandal? No. What happened at Mrs. Blythe's never made it past the doorman. Which was a relief, since the bargain had been struck barely an hour ago. He'd feel a fool if he could not even make it though one day!

Poll turned away from the mirror, his expression a bit mulish. "I had another plan for this evening."

No, Poll, you don't. You are going to stay where I can keep an eye on you at all times. "You had a plan more exciting than an evening of decadent entertainments provided by the most notorious brothel in London? What will you be doing, hunting tigers in Hyde Park?"

Poll narrowed his eyes. "No, it was nothing so fascinating. Just an interesting prospect."

Cas took his brother by both shoulders and gazed pityingly into his eyes. "Tonight is not a prospect. Tonight is not a gamble. Tonight is a houseful of beautiful, willing, and eager!"

Pol grinned. "But I like hunting tigers."

Cas grinned back. "I, as well." He released Pol with a little shake. "But since we are neither moneyed nor likely to ever be, we are fortunate just to be invited into this evening's bacchanalia."

Pol smirked. "Mrs. Blythe loves us. We keep things interesting."

Cas untied his own hastily knotted cravat as he graced the room with an angelic smile. "Well, we are lovable—"

"—and so imaginative—"

"—and twice as handsome as any other bloke!" They recited the old joke in unison.

"And the ladies are so grateful for a respite—"

"—from boring old statesmen and corpulent dukes!"

Cas tugged free his cravat and swept it into a deep bow like a flowing lace handkerchief from another era. "We aim to please."

"And please—"

"—and please—"

Their laughter was interrupted by an unholy screech from the floor above.

"Attie!"

Chapter Five

The Worthington brothers cringed.

"Ellie," Cas commented wryly, "has a lovely singing voice."

"Mm." Poll rubbed at his ears. "Truly a gift from the gods. Its splendor brings tears to my eyes. Look at me now. I'm already about to weep."

At that moment, a small skinny whirlwind blew into the room, slamming the door behind her. Attie pressed her back to the oak panel and assessed them thoughtfully. "If you hide me, I'll cry pax on you two."

Poll narrowed his eyes. "For how long?"

Laughing, Cas opened his hands. "I don't care how long. Take the deal. Even one day of safety from her would be worth it!"

Poll shook his head, his attention never leaving the glinting eyes of his youngest and deadliest sibling. "I'd do just about anything for a day free of pranks—except that if we do this, we'll have to suffer Ellie's wrath instead."

Attie huffed dismissal of her elder sister's fury. "Ellie's a featherweight."

Cas nodded. "Exactly. Take the deal."

"You must think she's in a truly bloodthirsty mood, or you wouldn't be here." Poll pursed his lips. "One month."

Attie scowled. "Two weeks."

Poll lifted his chin. "One month. We could hear her from here."

Thudding noises sounded overhead, as if heavy items were being tossed about the upper bedchambers. Attie tilted her head. "A short month. Twenty-eight days."

Poll looked upward. An animal shriek of pure rage penetrated the ceiling. Attie flinched.

Poll smiled at that flinch. "Long month. Thirty-one days. Beginning tomorrow."

Attie snarled.

Poll held up a hand. "You know the rules. Pax means no vengeance later. Clean slate."

"Never mind." Skinny arms folded and pointy chin lifted. "I'd rather face Ellie down."

It wasn't true and both brothers knew it. Ellie could definitely be considered a featherweight in the vengeance department—unless one were caught in the first, most intense explosion. No one wanted that.

Attie, on the other hand, might take months to develop the most perfect and devious retribution. For a child, she had a deep and true understanding of "Revenge should have no bounds."

Immediately through Poll's mind rang his mother's voice. *Hamlet, Act Four, Scene Seven.* He shook off the twitch-inducing pronouncement with a sigh.

"Attie, she'll be down here in approximately forty-five seconds. It's going to take at least thirty seconds to hide you properly. Agree or run for it."

Attie tried blinking back tears, throwing in a little lip tremble for good measure. Poll snorted. "Nice try."

Cas smirked. "Don't bother, Rattie."

Poll started counting down with fingers held up. "Thirty-five seconds."

They heard the swift patter of sure-footed Ellie racing full-speed down the stairs.

"Thirty seconds. Twenty-nine."

"Fine!" Attie growled. "Hurry!"

Poll smiled. "Cas?"

With a snort of laughter, Cas reached beneath Poll's bed to withdraw a medium-sized carpetbag. He stripped the buckle open and held it wide. "Get in."

Attie drew back. "I won't fit."

Poll grinned. "Yes, you will. We bought it for just such an occasion."

Cas put the bag on the floor and Attie stepped in. It took a moment to kneel and fit all her gangly limbs within, but Cas was able to fasten it closed over her folded form. He then stood and lifted it easily, holding it as casually as a man about to board a coach.

Just in time. The door flew open and Elektra stormed in, lightning flashing from her blue eyes and an unseen wind blowing her golden hair about her face. Well, not really, but very nearly.

"She's in here," Elektra stated with a snarl. "I know it."

Cas and Poll glanced at each other innocently, then turned back to Ellie. "Who is in here?"

Again, Ellie sneered. "The Queen, you arse. Attie, are you in here?"

Cas blinked. "Well, she'd hardly be likely to answer—"

"—having no history of suicidal behavior—"

"—nor lack of survival instinct—"

"—but we cannot help you—"

"—because we've been out all day—"

"—buying new luggage—"

"—although we're not sure this one is quite the thing—"

"—for it's a tad small. What do you think, Ellie?"

Cas held out the bag to his sister, who rolled her eyes and pushed past him. "I don't give a fig about your luggage! Where is the little monster? She's taken my new evening gloves—the ones from Lementeur meant specially for me to wear to the Marquis of Wyndham's Midsummer Ball!"

This was serious. Elektra, having grown weary of her parents' lack of interest in matchmaking, had arranged her own coming out. With grim determination, she had begged, borrowed, and stolen a Season for herself. Poll applauded how his resourceful sister had finagled her presentation to the Prince Regent on the basis of at least seventeen flat-out falsehoods, had responded to her growing list of invitations in Iris's name, and had even struck some kind of devil's bargain with Lementeur to keep her in gowns—heaven knows what she promised the man.

Fortunately, it wasn't likely to be her virtue. Elektra had plans for that virtue, plans that included snagging a title at the very least.

The twins waited while Ellie searched the room, checking all the obvious places and then a few that made the brothers exchange glances of alarm. Apparently, they didn't have as many secrets from their family as they'd thought.

Poll was beginning to worry that Attie might run out of air by the time Ellie climbed wearily to her feet and dusted her skirts, muttering in disgust. "Poisonous little elf . . . when I catch her." Dire threats fell from her lips, but it was obvious that because of her exertions, her rage was running its course.

She left with another suspicious glance at Cas and Poll, who shook their heads in commiseration. When the door slammed on Ellie's defeat, they each exhaled in relief.

Cas moved to open the bag. Poll held out a hand. "Wait."

It was a fortunate instinct, for just as Cas straightened, the door flew open yet again. Ellie, tight-lipped and blotchy-faced, glared at them both one last time, obviously surprised to find them doing nothing wrong.

"Hmph!" She turned on her heel and stalked down the hall.

Poll stepped forward and silently shut the door. This time he locked it, taking great care that the bolt slid noiselessly into place.

Cas let out another whoosh of breath and hurriedly ripped at the buckle of the bag. Poll worriedly bent over it as well. It wouldn't do to kill Attie. She was a righteous pain in the arse, but she wasn't a bad little beast.

Their little sister lay curled in the cramped space, unmoving. Still. Too still. Then, just as Poll's heart crawled right up into his throat, she lifted her tangled reddish mop from her face with one hand and grinned up at them. "That was bloody amazing!"

Cas sighed and closed his eyes. *"Worthingtons."*

Poll helped Attie clamber out of the bag. "That was a one-off, pet. We'll never be able to use it again . . . unless it's Mama. It's good for a half dozen times on her."

Attie shook out her gangling limbs as she straightened. Then she cocked her head and examined them in turn, her green-gray eyes sharp. "I smell secrets. You two are up to something."

Cas didn't look at his brother. "Haven't the faintest idea what you mean."

Attie snorted, then shrugged. Holding out her sticky paw, she pumped their hands in turn. "One month pax, as agreed." Then she turned and strolled from the room, though she did check the hall most carefully first.

"You, too." Poll laughed and shoved his brother from

the room as well. "Get out. Go dig through your own weskits for something to wear tonight."

"I'd thought to borrow one of yours."

"Go look in your wardrobe. I guarantee you that half of those *are* mine."

"Dandy."

"Thief."

Poll shut the door on his brother with a laugh, but sobered as he turned back to regard himself in the mirror.

Now he wasn't to see Miranda tonight after all. It wasn't as though he were disappointed. No, of course not. The evening promised to be famously satisfying—the sort of night one could relive for simply months, hashing out the details and delights with Cas over brandies during the chill February deprivations, when most of Society had had its fill of midwinter house parties and of extending invitations to useless but entertaining young men to fill out their table settings.

Not that Poll minded being a "place card." He and Cas made the most of their time in the country, being enthusiastic hunters—and, oh yes, there was all that shooting, too. Mostly they hunted for tigers, the women who'd married men twice their ages and now found themselves still vibrant and alive, yet dutifully attending to their doddering husbands.

That was Cas's specialty, anyway—mature women with time on their hands and well-honed sexuality to indulge. Women who most definitely were not looking for a husband!

Poll didn't gravitate toward any particular species, himself. World-weary wives filled the bill, but so did lonely widows and even the occasional saucy housemaid. What Poll looked for was a certain something he found hard to describe, even when laughingly pressured by Cas. It could be described as a grace, perhaps—a cleverness, to be sure. A . . . quality.

A quality that Mrs. Gideon Talbot held in bucketloads.

He tied the cravat again and donned a loudly colorful weskit, pulling on his best black surcoat over the ensemble. His gaze slid to the clock on the mantel. It was only seven o'clock. If he moved quickly, he could have his widow and his orgy, too.

With a single swift motion, he swept the book off the dressing table and grabbed up his hat. He paused outside the door to Cas's chamber.

No time for explanations—and no desire for them either. "See you there," he called through the oak door.

By the time Cas opened his door with his shirt off and his damp hair dripping onto his chest and shoulders, Poll was slipping out the front of the house with an expectant smile on his face.

Miranda.

Poll whistled happily as he sauntered down a street in Mayfair. It was a lovely summer's evening. He doffed his hat at a pair of slowly strolling ladies who shot him disapproving looks with betraying glints of appreciation in their eyes.

Women. Poll loved all women—from shy, twittering maidens to severely elegant creatures with silver hair and regal postures. His first lover had been two and half decades older than he and she had taught him the foremost important lesson of his life—that time spent on romance was never wasted.

He'd missed the courtship ritual over the past week while he'd been perfecting the steam engine . . . the one that currently lay in hastily scavenged bits in the workshop, the gears so welded together that they might never part ways again.

Oh, well. Eventually, one of his and Cas's inventions would pay off and then they would sit back and collect.

Currently, however, no one seemed to have a need for a rotating clothing-drying device, or a child's toy that careened wildly out of control, knocking into anything in its way. It was too bad. Poll rather liked that one.

It was a child's India rubber ball with a windup weighted clockwork within. It had been inspired by the epic failure of their wedding gift to their sister Callie last year. Well, best not think about that night. Their brother-in-law was still trying to bring that ballroom back to its former glory.

Philpott really liked the clothes dryer, though.

Poll smiled at another lady, who didn't even bother to hide her appreciation.

He kept walking, a smile on his face, knowing that the lady had stopped to catch the rear view. Tigers, indeed.

Although at the moment, he was surprisingly captivated by one single woman.

As he mounted the steps to Miranda's front door, Poll thought perhaps today might be the day when he would tease a little kiss from her. She really was coming along, and he felt it was time to make gentle advances. Nothing too forward, of course, for he didn't wish to frighten her.

With a smile and with the gift of a book of poetry under one arm, he knocked confidently on his sweetheart's door.

Yes, a kiss would be just the thing.

Matters commenced just as usual. They sat down over tea in the parlor. She rang for cakes. He bestowed the book upon her.

"Coleridge! Thank you, sir." She smiled in shy delight at the long, poetic inscription. Poll was rather proud of the sonnet, for he'd actually written it himself.

Poll watched her pour the tea, enjoying her feminine grace. "And how are all your children doing?"

She did not laugh at his little joke, for she took her responsibility to her favorite charity, a children's home near Newgate Prison, very seriously.

She regarded him soberly. "I fear I am failing them. I know there must be a way to assist the older children into decent employment, but there is so much intolerance toward them—" She looked away, not finishing her thought.

Oddly, the moment turned awkward. Poll considered Miranda. She answered his sallies congenially, although as the conversation went on, her replies became less and less expansive.

Then suddenly, she burst out. "I've spent all day thinking of you kissing me!"

Poll didn't need a second invitation. In a flash he was next to her on the settee, taking her hands in his, kissing her palms and wrists. She smiled at him then, her expression so open and passionate that she took his breath away.

Miranda tangled her fingers in his hair and lifted her face up to his.

"Miranda," he whispered. At last. He bent closer—

A perfunctory tap came on the parlor door and the little maid Tildy scuttled in. "Missus, it's Miss Constance come calling!"

Miranda sprang back from Poll so effortlessly that one might think she might have been engaged only in intimate conversation and turned to smile at her maid graciously. "Thank you, Tildy. I'll be along at once."

She shot Poll a pleading glance and, after giving Tildy a quick signal to clear away the tea things, went to the front hall to greet her late husband's sister, Miss Constance Talbot.

Poll straightened, willing his pulse to slow, ordering his

lust back into its cage of civility. It was a damned shame, for it had promised to be a most delicious first kiss.

Bloody bad luck, Miranda's sister-in-law dropping in at this hour!

Not to worry. Something had changed tonight. Poll was quite sure he would have many more such opportunities in the future. When Miss Constance Talbot entered the room, he smiled and made nice bows to the stout spinster who eyed him with trenchant suspicion, then made his escape as quickly as possible.

Another time, Miranda, I shall claim that kiss.

When Mr. Worthington left—and who could blame him for his speed?—Miranda inhaled deeply and turned to face her sister-in-law, Miss Constance Talbot. The name might conjure a sweet-faced young girl—if one had never met her.

Miranda was quite sure that Constance had never been that. Small and round and bustling even in youth, if the portraits in the upper hall didn't lie. Even as a girl, her snub features had held an expression of self-righteous disapproval.

The Talbot height and hawkish profile had completely passed Constance by, a fact that Miranda was sure Constance regretted.

Constance would have dearly loved to loom.

Instead, the Constance of the present was a petite, solid ball of thinly veiled animosity toward Miranda.

"You've let the house go," Constance snapped. "There's dust on the newel post in the hall."

Very thinly veiled. In fact, hardly veiled at all.

"Hello, Constance."

Remember to smile.

Why?

Oh, simply smile and get this over with. "What might

I do for you . . . this evening?" Miranda carefully implied that it was just a tad late for afternoon calls.

Constance sniffed, in her turn implying that Miranda had nothing better to do with her days than to wait on callers, since she surely wasn't doing her duty of monitoring the staff with eagle eye and pennypinching fingers.

Ah, the stealthy context between women who had lived together for too many years.

But Constance didn't live here any longer. The house belonged to Miranda, fair and square. If Gideon had wanted Constance to have it, he ought to have outlined that in his exhaustively detailed will. Miranda had scarcely been able to remain awake during the reading of the hefty, meticulously comprehensive document, in which every stock pin and pair of shoe buckles had been parceled out to acquaintances and favored retainers.

Not friends. Gideon had not had true friends. Colleagues, perhaps. Other desiccated men whose minds were wrapped up in debating the fine points of this document versus that record, this letter versus that missive, until the richness of history became as dry and lifeless as the dust of the past.

Dust that had unhappily ended up on her newel post the very moment Constance chose to make her call. Miranda's smile felt like paint on her face. If she wasn't careful, it would begin to chip.

Constance drew off her gloves and snapped them impatiently. "Well? Aren't you going to offer me tea?"

Not likely. If I feed it, it will never leave. Miranda blinked. "But it is so late! I know you drink nothing but boiled milk after six o'clock."

Constance narrowed her eyes. "I take tea on occasion. I will take some now."

She turned to Twigg, who straightened or perhaps stiffened in anticipation. *Oh no. I give the orders here.*

Miranda stepped smoothly between Constance and her former butler. "Twigg, please see to Miss Talbot's tea."

Twigg fled, probably reluctant to decide which mistress to obey, the one he'd known or the one who now paid his wages.

Constance tilted her head. "Too late for tea, but not too late for a gentleman caller, Miranda? If he'd stayed any later, I would have accused you of keeping company . . . and you still in mourning!"

"Half mourning," Miranda pointed out. Half mourning that had actually ended a few months previously, but Miranda didn't have the spinal strength needed to go through that argument again with Constance, who seemed to feel that any woman lucky enough to have wed a Talbot owed that husband a lifetime of black gowns and impenetrable veils. Nor would periodic bursts of weeping be considered amiss.

Not that Constance had wept. At least, Miranda had seen no sign of it. Constance had been very nearly smug, after the first shock of Gideon's sudden demise wore off. It was not until the reading of the will that Constance had realized that it was Miranda who would hold the keys to the kingdom, not her.

Miranda's smile firmed, thinking of that lovely moment.

Constance trailed the toe of her slipper on the carpet. "These look swept, at least. You mustn't forget to keep the draperies closed. The sun will fade the carpets." She reached into her sturdy, practical reticule. "I've made you out a list of the household matters. I suggest you attend to them at once."

Miranda's smile was definitely beginning to crack a bit around the edges. "How very kind of you when I know perfectly well that you have your own household to manage now." *Yes, yours, as opposed to mine!*

"My house is in perfect order, thank you." Constance

snapped. She drew in a breath, as if reaching for her deepest patience. She held out a folded piece of paper, the threatened list. "As you know, midsummer has always been an important time in our house. There will not be a better time of year to have the carpets treated with benzene. It will do wonders for their longevity—"

"Oh, but the smell." Miranda wrinkled her nose. Constance's insistence on this annual ritual nearly drove Miranda off to the soonest ship to the Americas. The stink of the chemical treatment was enough to kill fleas—and people!

Constance's jaw hardened beneath her round cheeks. "You think too much on your senses, Miranda. You always did. There is a proper way to attend to matters. See that you don't neglect it!"

Keep smiling. Smile until your face aches.

Miranda smiled and took the list, though she thrust it into her pocket without reading it. "Oh, dear, where is Twigg with that tea? Should I run down and see to it myself?"

Running was good.

Constance sniffed and cast her gaze scornfully about the room. "Lax, that's what it is. That's what happens when you coddle the staff."

"Hmm." Not that Miranda blamed Twigg for fleeing, but without the ritual of tea to serve, she had no idea what to do with the woman standing before her.

Offer her a seat.

Well . . . but then she might stay.

Miranda, knowing perfectly well that she was being very rude, simply stood there with the idiotic smile on her face and blinked her eyes. Childish, perhaps. Maybe if she projected empty-headed tedium for long enough—

"Oh, well, never mind!" Constance pulled on her gloves

with such force that Miranda half expected the kid leather to part at the seams.

The gloves survived. Miranda rather thought they dared not do otherwise. No such flimsy trimmings for Constance!

Miranda followed Constance to the door, nodding like a simpleton at the continuing list of instructions for the care and feeding of the house—*oh, for pity's sake, please leave*—and shook her sister-in-law's hand good-bye with decided enthusiasm.

Shutting the door at last, she closed her eyes. "Oh, but you didn't have your tea," she murmured, now that she was certain Constance couldn't hear her. "What a shame you have to go so soon." She giggled, too relieved to be quite sane.

As she turned from the door, she felt the list crackle in her pocket. Drawing it out, she opened it as she walked slowly down the hall.

Carpets. Benzene.

Chutney canning.

Silver counting.

The letter contained more in that vein. Constance was still trying to run the house, even while residing a mile away.

Miranda refolded the list with precision, then strolled into the parlor, which was laid, as it was every day, for callers. The coals glowed, for it was a damp, rainy day. The letter, somehow, ended up falling into the fireplace, where it immediately smoldered on the coals.

Miranda smiled to herself. "Oops."

Then she turned to ponder her personal little realm, where the carpets remained benzene-free and the days and nights belonged to her . . . and just possibly, Mr. Worthington.

"Constance, you really should take a lover," Miranda said out loud. "It would do wonders for your longevity."

"Ahem." She turned to see Twigg standing behind her, his hands full of a heaping tray of silver tea things and cakes and little triangle-cut sandwiches.

"Oh." Poor Twigg. She giggled again, helplessly. "Oh, dear."

Twigg merely glared.

Chapter Six

Poll was a bit late to the bash at Mrs. Blythe's House of Pleasure but no one noticed. The celebration of—well, whatever landed on the calendar this week!—was well under way. Liquor flowed freely, and there was plenty of food, which would come in handy when the patrons required fuel for further fornication. Mrs. Blythe's ladies were the loveliest, healthiest, most good-natured and enthusiastic in all of London.

Hence the exorbitant entrance fee charged to the male attendees. Poll, however, merely sent the madam's head guard—er, butler—a cheery salute as he sauntered in the front door.

All the Worthington lads had an open invite from Mrs. Blythe. Apparently, someone in the family had done her a favor once upon an age. None of the siblings knew the story and the elders weren't telling, but Cas and Poll had been delighted to sponge off that debt of honor many times over the past several years.

To Poll's knowledge, Dade had never visited the establishment. Do Dade good, it would. However, his eldest brother was wound a bit too tight for that.

Orion had come with the twins one time, years ago,

and had spent his night examining one bewildered but willing lady extensively. Mrs. Blythe had wisely suggested he go back to sticking bugs on a pin and leave her talented ladies for those who could appreciate their many charms.

Lysander had come once in while, before. Wild horses couldn't drag him to such festivities now, unfortunately. In Poll's opinion, a vigorous rogering would do Zander up right!

Tonight's event was created around the notion of a Roman orgy. Somehow, white plaster columns had been transported into a very English ballroom, then swathed in silk. There were piles of pillows in the corners, as well as velvet fainting couches where numerous people seemed in danger of losing consciousness. As Poll watched, a giggling buxom creature clad in the shreds of a diaphanous goddess costume was being chased through the room by a rickety old fellow sporting a cane and baggy drawers.

An unbearably curvaceous redhead in a swath of translucent chiffon that was intended to pass as a toga offered Poll a glass of champagne and, incidentally, herself. Poll took the champagne with a gallant bow, but merely kissed her hand. "Let a fellow catch his breath, will you, darling? Later."

She meandered onward after bestowing a sultry pout upon him. God, with a carnivorous mouth like that, she could likely kiss a bloke to death before he got his trousers off!

Lips made him think of Miranda's sweet mouth and the almost-kiss. *Bloody Constance.*

"There you are!"

Poll turned to see Cas approaching with—gasp—a twin blonde on each arm!

"Look what I found. This is Lily and this is Dilly." Cas grinned. "Mrs. Blythe has offered us a pile of gold to join these two to put on a show for the clientele. It broke my heart to turn her down, but Dade would make life unfit to live if he found out—not to mention what Callie would do!"

Not a very good example to Attie, either, but Poll didn't bother to say it. He knew Cas wasn't serious. No doubt he would mention the thought to Dade, just to wind him up—but Worthingtons were always honorable, in the end.

Well, mostly. Poll winced as a few best-forgotten moments slid through his memory. A long time ago, certainly far away. And Dade had never learned of those moments, which made them practically not happen.

Still, Poll raised his glass to the golden-siren beauty of the twins before him. "Ladies, no one would notice us next to you anyway."

One of them smirked. "You'd be surprised, you would, sir!"

The other laughed and trailed her fingers down the buttons of Cas's weskit. "If you lads are ever short of coin, there are those that would let you wear masks. We'd make a fortune, we would. A private costume *ball*."

They all laughed. "Clever." Poll pointed to her. "I'll take that one."

Cas handed her off to Poll willingly enough. "Be careful, Dilly. He bites."

Dilly didn't seem alarmed. "I bite back, but it'll cost him."

Poll smiled at the charming creature. "Dilly? I thought all of Mrs. Blythe's ladies had flower names?"

"'Tis short for Daffodil, sir." She pressed closer and breathed into his ear. "But you can call me anything you like, handsome."

Poll gave her his best smoldering look. "But will it cost me?"

She drew back and assessed him. Then she ran her

fingers through his hair, arranging it in a maternal fashion. "Not you, pet. Not tonight, anyway. You've already got some lucky girl, I think."

Poll blinked. "I—how did you know?"

Dilly laughed. "Didn't get into the business yesterday, for one. For the other, most blokes would've pushed me up against the wall after I blew in your ear. You're no tea leaf, so that means you're in love. Your hair still looks like a woman's had her hands in it."

Giving a sigh, Poll regarded her with a slight smile. "Altogether too discerning, pet. The loss is mine, for you're a sumptuous morsel indeed. I suppose you'll be wanting to go back to my brother, then?"

"Glory, no!" Dilly rolled her eyes. "He's worse than you, that one. He's got an edge on him like a razor tonight." She lowered her voice confidentially. "I think he got worked up by some sweet thing he can't properly get his hands on. Can't get his mind off her, either. Lily's about to toss him back. She can't do a thing with him."

"Oh-ho!" Poll twisted his neck to get a glimpse of Cas in the throng. He saw his twin with Lily, standing in a corner near one of the feast tables . . . *talking*.

Cas didn't talk to women. Talking was Poll's gambit. Cas didn't need to do much more than bestow his famous cynical, world-weary smile to get a woman to drop everything—including her pantalets—on a hopeless quest to help him regain his faith in love, beauty, humanity, and so forth.

It worked every time. Which meant that this time, Cas wasn't even bothering.

"I wonder who she is." Poll thought back over the past few weeks. He'd been so busy with Miranda that he'd scarcely seen Cas except when they were working on the steam engine. "She must be someone I haven't met yet."

Dilly snorted. "She must be a goddess on a mountaintop,

for Lily's the zestiest bit in the city and your brother's not so much as given her a good groping."

Poll, feeling guilty, turned to her at once. "You're a vastly zesty bit, Dills."

She considered him for a moment. "And yet, here I stand, ungroped as well." She went up on tiptoe to give him a kiss on the cheek. "Don't worry. I'll tell old Blythe that we had a rouser, we did."

"You're a true lady, Miss Daffodil," Poll said gratefully.

She parted from him with a little wave of her fingers and a bit of extra wiggle in her walk, just to show him what he was missing. Poll, his head tilted, watched with great appreciation. The view was magnificent. By God, just because he was courting Miranda didn't mean he was dead!

Yet, attending an orgy without lust was rather like going fishing without a pole. He might as well be one of the elderly codgers sitting on the sidelines, smoking Mrs. Blythe's excellent cigars and drinking Mrs. Blythe's excellent whiskey, talking politics in a room full of nearly naked girls.

Poll shuddered. Never.

Still, there wasn't much else to do, so he asked for his coat and hat from a disbelieving chucker-out—er, footman—who regarded him pityingly as he showed Poll the door.

Poll only smiled, thinking of Miranda's sweet lips.

Cas left the captivating Lily behind with mingled regret and relief. Regret that he walked away from what likely would have been one of the more memorable nights of his life. Relief that he might no longer be distracted from thoughts of his mystery woman.

Miranda Talbot.

Sedate widow. Breathless temptress.

Her house, while of good address and well kept, was oddly a bit on the elder-auntie side of decor.

Young. Old-fashioned.

Lovely. Lackluster.

Demure. Bold.

Prim. Sensual.

It must be the conflicting impressions that made her linger so in his mind. He'd had prettier women—although delicate Miranda had a certain quality.

Cas felt like knocking himself on the back of the head as he trotted down the steps of Mrs. Blythe's House of Pleasure and away—away from Lily, away from certain pleasure, away from drink and dance and carousel—to where?

Or to whom?

The time was well past three in the morning. He could hardly call upon the pretty widow at this late hour. In fact, he'd not actually been invited to call again at all.

He stopped in the middle of the walk, frowning in consternation. He'd walked out on her. What if she didn't like him anymore?

God, I sound like a girl. He shuddered. Such thoughts were mad, anyway. Unfinished business, that was all.

So finish it.

If he caught a hack, he could make it to that prim little house in half an hour.

If he walked, he'd not be there until after dawn.

Castor Worthington didn't rush for any woman. It was a fine night. He would indulge in a leisurely stroll through early-morning London. A constitutional, for his health, partaking of morning air, contemplating the awakening sky.

His pace quickened. No sense in dawdling, either.

Miranda had gone to bed at her usual early hour, and it hadn't done her a bit of good. She'd lain awake for hours.

Then sleeping fitfully, found herself prone to blurred, sensual dreams, tossing and turning, kicking the covers down and then pulling them up again.

Her flesh seemed to burn too hot for the summer night temperature. Her hungry, sensitized skin felt every irritating wrinkle in the bedsheets. Finally, unable to bear the twisting of her nightdress, she shucked it off and tossed it across the room and lay naked and aquiver in the cool room.

I want.

What did she want?

I want more.

Oh yes. More would do nicely.

His kiss. His mouth. His hands, warm and large and caressing on her skin.

She allowed her thoughts to go beyond such innocent things, since said thoughts would remain in the privacy of her own skull.

Him, naked and muscled and sweating against her, the two of them in this bed, rising and falling and rolling—

The place between her legs throbbed and ached. It hungered for him. Raising her arms above her head, she ran her fingers through her fallen hair and tugged restlessly on it as she remembered the feeling of his lips on hers.

Sliding one hand down her other arm, the way he'd slid his warm palm over her, she slipped it down and cupped her own breast.

Would he like her bosom? Her late husband never even looked at her, never touched her without a gown on. She thought she filled out her bodice well enough now, but she had the vague notion that men liked a great deal of bosom.

Her other hand slid beneath the blankets to where her thighs parted, damp and restless.

Tentatively, she touched herself. This was something she'd only done a few times in her life, mostly after

Gideon had left her so empty and unsatisfied. She'd given it up as a bad job, unable to help herself enough, feeling ashamed of her need to do so.

Not this time. She lay thinking of him, of the hardness of his body, of the weight of him on top of her in the alley, and the strength of him as he'd helped her up.

The taste of his mouth as he kissed her on the settee. She thought of the heat of him, of the warmth of his palms as they cupped her arms . . . his mouth, his lips . . .

Pleasure grew and quickened as she quickened her touch. Her breath came fast until she panted and moaned, carried away on the wave of her lust, reaching . . . reaching . . . .

She shattered, there, alone, at her own hand—a small burst of pleasure yet quite intense. She gasped loudly in the silent room, glad at her solitude, glad at the lack of judgment and constraint. As she lay sighing, sweating, soothing herself gently once more, she smiled to think of him—what would be his opinion of her if he could see her now?

She rather thought he would like what he saw.

The floating pleasure drifted away. Her body at peace at last, Miranda pulled her covers up high to her chin and snuggled into her pillow for a few hours of sleep. The sun would rise soon.

I wonder if I shall see him today?

Her eyes flew open, staring into the black darkness of her room.

I want more.

Oh, damn!

Cas loitered in the park across the street from Mrs. Talbot's front door. *Miranda. Mira.*

He ought to feel like a fool. The hour still lacked several minutes of dawn and he'd walked as slowly as he could force himself to. Which wasn't terribly slowly.

Yet somehow, he didn't feel foolish. He felt eager.

Now he lurked like some spy, hands behind his back, pacing restlessly in the shadow of a large oak. He witnessed the early deliveries of milk and vegetables to the houses around the square. He even witnessed a few husbands sneaking into their homes with the help of collusive servants, well past the hour that a fellow might wish his wife to know.

Now, there's an idea. Go home.

He ought to. The Cas of even a few days ago would have. If Poll ever learned of such antics, he'd never hear the end of his brother's mockery.

A movement at an upper-story window caught Cas's attention. It was the little maid—Tildy?—pulling back the draperies of her mistress's bedchamber.

She's awake.

Awake at dawn? Surely not.

Yet as he watched, he saw a slender figure move behind Tildy, in a pale green dressing gown, dark hair tumbled about her shoulders.

Mira.

He didn't think twice. He didn't think at all. His feet made up his mind for him and he was across the street, tapping at her door before he realized it.

After an excruciating wait, her door opened and Miranda's irritated butler glared out at him. "May I help you, sir?" came out with a bit of a snarl attached, and then the fellow blinked. "Oh, Mr. Worthington!"

The man obviously remembered him from the day before. Cas nodded. "I wish to speak to Mrs. Talbot."

The butler frowned. "But . . . the hour—"

A feminine voice came from behind the man. Cas leaned forward eagerly, then realized that he heard the uncultured accent of the maid. The butler turned away from Cas for a moment.

"Yes, but—truly? Now?"

Cas shifted on his feet, tempted to push past the officious fellow and make a break for Miranda's stairs. He'd actually stepped forward when the butler turned back to him, a look of profound disapproval on his face. "Mrs. Talbot will see you."

Cas stepped smartly into the house and tossed his hat and gloves to the annoying bloke in the livery. He looked about, thinking he'd await her in the parlor, as people did.

"Upstairs, sir."

Oh yes. Invitation to the inner sanctum!

Mira. Cas pushed past the butler and up the stairs, his eagerness more than he could bear. He found his way to her room and let himself in, opening the door in a rush.

She stood in the middle of the room. Her hair was a tangled mess, and she had dark shadows beneath her eyes. She looked like heaven.

She held her dressing gown clutched tightly closed, but her eyes . . . her eyes offered a vast ocean of invitation.

Cas stumbled to a stop before her. He ought to say something polite, make some apology for the inexcusable hour.

"I couldn't sleep." Her words came out in a rush. "I couldn't sleep for thinking of you."

Cas let out a sigh, all pretty stilted words swept from his mind by her breathless honesty. "I didn't even bother to try," he told her.

A smile started at the corners of her mouth and widened until it reached her eyes.

He moved forward slowly, unsmiling, intent on her skin, her voice, her tumbled hair, the sea green of her eyes. When he reached her, he took her hands in his.

"I had to come back to finish that kiss, Mira."

Her smile brightened even more, and something new tinted her sweet expression. He could see the gleam of awareness in her eyes—a first blooming of a new confidence, a fresh belief in her feminine powers.

Cas moved closer, enjoying her shy blush as her nervousness warred with her evident eagerness.

"No one ever kissed me before," she blurted.

What? Cas halted. "But . . . your husband?" Oh hell, she wasn't some kind of rare married virgin, was she?

She shook her head. "On the cheek only, after . . . ." She glanced away. "Afterward."

Cas considered the strangely innocent temptress who stood before him. Lifting one hand, he brushed back her tousled hair and looked into her eyes. "The very first kiss?"

She nodded, biting her lip in embarrassment. "It was so wonderful," she whispered. She blushed and looked away. "You surely think me simple."

He pulled her close, tucking her head beneath his chin. "I think you're delicious. Such honesty is a refreshing change, I must admit."

Honesty. She liked that. She twined her arms around his neck and sighed into his shirt. "I like you," she whispered, risking more honesty. "Now I think I like you even more."

He said nothing for a long moment. Then, very softly, "I like you too, Mira."

She smiled, sifting her fingers through his curls. Then she yawned, so deeply that her jaw popped. She ducked her head, mortified. He only laughed and bent to sweep her into his arms, lifting her easily. Then he carried her to the bed and tucked her in, dressing gown and all.

"Sleep," he said. "You are up much too early. My sisters would never be about at such an unholy hour."

She curled beneath the covers, smiling. His sisters . . . Callie and Ellie and Attie. She yawned again, this time without apology. He'd told her so much about them, she felt as though she knew them . . . and his brothers . . .

Dade and Zander and Rion . . . and the other one . . . what was his name?

"Sleep well. We'll have plenty of time for that kiss later," Castor whispered as he tucked the covers high under her chin. Such a beauty she was, with her slender legs and her long neck, like a swan or a Thoroughbred horse, shimmering with life and sweet honest lust.

Absolutely delicious.

Perhaps he did have a new girl.

Chapter Seven

When Cas left Miranda's house, it was still early morning.

She had fallen asleep at once and he'd not had the heart to wake her, for she seemed so tired. He'd stayed awhile anyway, sitting on the edge of the bed, watching her sleep with her forehead tucked down into the pillows and her long limbs curled up beneath the covers.

Before he'd left, and when he knew she was quite deeply asleep, he'd buried his face in her fragrant hair and breathed her in as he stroked his fingertips down her arm with a tenderness he did not remember ever feeling before.

Not only was it a relief to spend time with a woman who did not seem to know the concept of romantic strategy, but her bashful sincerity made him feel trusted. He felt a rare desire to be forthcoming in return, as though he might be able to share things with her that he'd never shared with anyone.

Not that he would truly spill his heart, of course. That was not his style. There were places inside him that he would just as soon not know about himself, much less share with a woman—a woman who might look at him differently after, or might not wish to look upon him at all.

Although, if ever there was such a woman, he thought she might be a lot like Miranda.

At the bottom of the steps, he had the good fortune to hail a hack right away. Swinging himself up into the taxi before it even stopped rolling, he called out his destination and settled back into the shabby velvet seat.

Poll stood on the grass of the park across the street. He'd cut across rather than try to hail a cab at one of the busiest hours of the morning. Now he stood openmouthed as he watched his twin ramble down the steps of Miranda's house and ride away.

Cas? And Miranda?

Snap. Poll looked down at the double handful of splinters in his palms. Splintered wood that had once been a pretty little carved hair comb. He'd begun it years ago, probably as a gift for his mother, but had finished it in the wee hours of the morning, inspired by Miranda's rich dark hair.

There was nothing left but splinters. Ruined past repair.

How could she? With his own brother? His twin— which was somehow worse, although he couldn't say precisely why.

How could she do such a thing to him?

Fury swept him, yet there was a single, dissenting voice in his mind.

Miranda is not the two-timing sort.

But Cas—with the rumpled hair—

Your hair still looks like a woman's had her hands in it.

No. Miranda was painstakingly honest. She simply wouldn't.

A horrifying thought crossed his mind. If Miranda

was seeing them both—yet was a woman who would not do such a thing—

That could only mean she didn't know she was seeing two men at once.

Which meant that bloody Cas was lying to her, sneaking in on Poll's sweet, innocent widow! The rotter!

And how is it that the lady you've been seeing for weeks does not know you are a twin? Everyone knows.

Her very conservative marriage had sheltered Miranda from Society for years. She was aware of only what was printed in the newssheets. The Worthingtons, unholy terrors that they might be considered, weren't rich enough to be truly newsworthy.

And you somehow neglected to mention it.

There was a very good reason why he hadn't mentioned his brother, other than in a general "I have scads of brothers" kind of way.

For some mystifying reason, there had never been a woman born who did not think longer on Castor Worthington, who did not linger more at his side, who did not listen more closely or gaze more longingly than she might at his identical twin, Pollux.

Cas, of course, couldn't care less, except to dally briefly and move on.

When Poll realized that sheltered Mrs. Talbot had never heard a single word of gossip or otherwise about the Worthingtons, he knew at that moment that he would never introduce her to his family and, most especially, would not introduce her to Cas.

Now he regretted that impulse. He should have told her—warned her—that his predatory brother would be circling her!

It must end. Now. If a bit of Worthington blood must be spilled to make it end, so be it.

This time it would be Cas who bled.

* * *

Poll strode through Worthington House, too furious to pause as usual to enjoy the marvelous mess that was his family home.

He found Cas sitting in their attic study, pouring himself a brandy and contemplating the afternoon city through the large-paned, leaky window that made their haven a challenging spot to linger come January.

Cas turned his head when he entered, and grinned. "Had a good time at Mrs. Blythe's, did you?"

For lack of any more deadly projectiles, Poll stripped off his coat and threw it at his brother. "You *poacher*!"

Cas drew back, his expression confused. "What? Poach? I did not! Dilly was all yours!"

Poll stood over him, fists clenched. He'd never hated his twin before. His more-than-brother, his other piece—at the moment, he'd like to tear that piece away and toss it from that grimy, smeared window and watch it fall to the street below!

Cas tossed the balled-up coat aside and peered at him a little worriedly. "Poll, you don't look well at all. Have a brandy." He held out the decanter, still uncapped.

Poll struck it from his hand. The crystal smashed on the floor, sending brandy splashing over both their boots.

Cas was on his feet in a flash. Not one to let something like that slide, not his brother. Good. Nothing would satisfy Poll more right now than to thrash Cas within an inch of his life. But first, a confession!

"You couldn't bear it, could you? You couldn't bear that I'd found a good woman, a widow who is a million times finer than your usual jades! You thought you'd slide in, tricking her, making her think you were me, and . . . and . . . ."

Poll couldn't say it. Cas had been in her house.

Cas had been in her arms!

It would not do to merely thrash Cas. Poll deeply and sincerely wanted him dead.

Cas held up a hand to halt his brother's threatening advance. "Wait . . . wait, Poll. Are you speaking of Mira—of Mrs. Talbot?"

Poll growled. "Of course I'm speaking of Miranda! I've been courting her for weeks, as you well know!"

"You have?" Cas's eyes widened. "Oh. Oh hell." He put a hand to his face, rubbing at his cheeks.

Cas didn't want to think it. He didn't want to know it.

However, it was terribly, horribly possible.

I suppose you've had time to perfect your Tempest*! Very good!*

She'd been speaking to Poll, not him.

I wanted to see you.

Cas didn't know why it had not occurred to him before. Why would a woman, even a free and sexually available widow, take a man home within moments of meeting him? When did a woman require no preamble, no dancing or flowers or pretty conversation?

All the things Poll was so very good at.

Cas took a step backwards, away from his brother. Guilt washed over him. He'd been so casual, so reckless.

He thought of lovely, honest Mira—who belonged to Poll.

I like you, she'd whispered to him as she sheltered in his arms. *Now I think I like you even more.*

Him, not Poll. "You courted her for how long?"

"Since the beginning of last month."

"Nearly four weeks. Four weeks before I first encountered her."

"Yes! You saw what I had and you wanted it for yourself!"

Cas shook his head. "No. Poll, no. It was a mistake.

She confused us . . . as people so often do. She must have followed me into the alley, thinking I was you." He explained his flying leap of rescue and that he had escorted the lady home.

Poll halted in his fury. "That's—but how could you let her think you were me?"

Cas shrugged. "It honestly didn't occur to me. She was pretty and bold and I thought she was just another widow with a taste for adventure."

Poll stared at him in sudden horror. "Yesterday?"

Cas looked up sharply. "Yes. I told you, she followed me into the alley. We nearly blew her up!"

It was Poll's turn to rub at his face. "I went to Miranda's last evening, before I attended the party. She . . . she was different, more open, more . . ." The remembered delight made his throat close now. "She almost kissed me, at last."

Cas's expression cleared. "Then I was first," he stated calmly.

"What?"

Cas folded his arms. "I was first to kiss her, so it is you who should step down."

Cas knew he wasn't making much sense. Yet as quickly as he realized what he'd inadvertently done, he decided he just didn't bloody care.

Mira was his and he was going to keep her.

Poll stared at his brother as if he were a stranger. "You . . . you can't! You know now—I am courting her! She is mine. You can't keep seeing her!"

Cas shrugged. "I don't know that she is yours. I don't know what would have happened if you had saved her yesterday instead of me," he pointed out. "You might have missed her meaning, you might have decided to wait a little longer." He lifted his chin. "But I didn't hesitate. I took her home and I kissed her first. She is mine."

"Yours! You stole her!"

Cas held up his hands in defense. "I didn't know—I swear I didn't!"

"I'm sure!" Poll scoffed. "You just happened to trip and fall onto her lips, I suppose. Have to watch out for those troubling carpets and all."

He saw anger flash in Cas's eyes. Good. Bastard.

Cas unfolded his arms and straightened. "It was you who couldn't get the merry widow to sign on the dotted line!"

Poll flinched. "I was building her up," he retorted. "Of course, now you've ruined all that work—"

"Done you a favor, you mean! I was the proud recipient of her first kiss," Cas taunted. "That will make a woman lean toward gratitude."

Poll frowned. "Her first? Ever?"

Cas grimaced. "Yes, poor thing. That husband of hers was too bound up to do more than peck her on the cheek!"

The fact that Mira had enjoyed his brother's attentions did not actually help. A red fog flirted with the edge of his vision. Poll's fists clenched. Then they eased and his eyes narrowed. "Ha. She has better taste than to settle for a bounder like you."

Cas snorted. "I'm a bounder? When every woman you get involved with ends up thinking you'll love her forever, only to see the back of you by month's end!"

Poll snarled. "That's right, they're begging me to stay. Yours are begging you to leave, or they would be if you ever stuck around long enough!"

Cas's face darkened. "Mrs. Talbot wasn't begging me to leave. She practically dragged me home yesterday!"

Again, Poll flinched. "She thought you were me! And you neglected to tell her differently!" Poll turned away, running his hands through his hair. The image of Miranda, lolling on the settee, her arms outstretched for him—

Not him. Cas.

For the first time since they were lads and figured out that they were stronger together, he rounded on his brother and swung his fist.

The fight didn't last long. They were too equally matched. Poll was a little faster. Cas was a tad more vicious. In a short time, they were tangled on the floor, each with the other in a stranglehold.

Cas felt his vision going a bit fizzy and tapped out. "Pax!" he wheezed.

Poll released him and rolled away. Standing, he brushed off his trousers. "I'm glad you see it my way, Cas."

"I said 'Pax,' not 'Uncle.' " Cas ran a hand through his disheveled hair. "While I was trouncing you, I had an idea."

Poll eyed him warily. "I'm listening . . . for now."

"We let her choose."

Poll wrinkled his brow. "If you think she'll choose you after one mistaken kiss—"

Cas shrugged carefully. It wouldn't do to let Poll know how important this was to him. He could barely admit it to himself! "So we confess all. We lay our suits before her and beg her to let us both court her." Cas wasn't terribly concerned that Poll would last long. His passions waxed and waned as quickly as the moon itself.

Poll frowned. "She might throw us out."

Cas smiled slightly. "Scared she'll choose me right off?"

Poll narrowed his eyes. Women professed their love to Cas on a weekly basis. "No. Let it be something harder. A challenge." He lifted his chin. "The one she agrees to marry."

It wasn't fair, for Poll knew from his weeks of actual conversation with Miranda that she considered marriage in the same way another might consider a wolf trap—as in, something she would gnaw off a limb to escape!

Poll kept the triumph from his face as Cas nodded. Of course, Miranda wasn't going to accept any proposals at all, but this way Poll knew that Cas wouldn't win while he, Poll, was working on a way to cut his brother out.

Cas's interest didn't last long. Miranda would be no different for Cas—not the way she was different for Poll.

Poll nodded. "I'll take mornings, then. I've always been an earlier riser than you."

Cas agreed. "I shall take the afternoons."

"Evenings for me, then." Poll smiled. It wasn't a brotherly smile.

Cas snorted. "Hardly. I'll take evens."

It was how they had divided the world since they were five. It was just another game, after all. One that Poll intended to win.

Poll bowed his head slightly. "I'll take odds." That meant tonight, actually.

Cas folded his arms. "Not that I shall need more than one."

"Ha," Poll said sourly. "The usual wager?"

In answer, Cas reached into his weskit pocket and withdrew a shilling. He held it up and tossed it onto the table, where it spun, ringing in the silent attic.

Poll matched it with a coin of his own. " 'The game's afoot.' "

Cas snorted. "*King Henry the Fifth.* Act Three, Scene One."

Poll didn't respond. He was already thinking of Miranda and the evening to come.

Perhaps if they had been raised in a normal household,

by ordinary people who didn't believe that the theater was real and life was but a stage—in other words, if they weren't Worthingtons—they might have realized that there was something wrong with such a wager.

Unfortunately, to a matched pair of Worthingtons, such an outrageous venture was just another bit of midsummer madness!

Chapter Eight

Poll slammed the door on his way out of the attic study. His jaw set, he trotted down the stairs, nimbly sidestepping the decades' worth of accumulated flotsam on the way. In his simmering anger, he didn't notice down the cluttered hallway in a book-lined cave carved out of the hoard, his baby sister's large alarmed eyes peering at him from the darkness.

As Poll continued on, Attie wrapped her arms about her bony knees and shivered. Cas and Poll never argued, never even disagreed.

Ever.

Mrs. Gideon Talbot, of Breton Square.

Attie peered down the bottomless divide that had suddenly appeared in her family and scowled. This Miranda woman had best watch herself. If this villainous vixen thought she was going to harm the Worthingtons, she had best think again!

First thing tomorrow, it would be time for reconnaissance. And, if necessary, a spot of sabotage—or even eradication!

Mr. Seymour called on Miranda that afternoon. Torn from her giddy musings on her early-morning embrace with

Mr. Worthington, Miranda had to force herself to smooth her hair and step sedately into the parlor to attend his call.

The poor man seemed a pale and insipid creature after the virile Mr. Worthington. It wasn't his fault that he was not a more memorable fellow, after all.

Miranda smiled sincerely, if a bit exasperatedly, at him when he presented her with his usual bouquet of roses.

"Oh, you shouldn't have!" He really shouldn't have. She'd mentioned more than once that she preferred other blooms, but sweet Mr. Seymour seemed to think that roses were the best of flowers. How could one argue with someone who believed one deserved the best?

She gave the blooms to Tildy to put in a vase. She would keep them here in the parlor, for that was where Mr. Seymour would be, and he did seem to enjoy roses so much. She kept the sprightly, more common flowers Mr. Worthington brought her in her bedchamber, for she enjoyed seeing them upon opening her eyes in the morning.

When they'd seated themselves, Mr. Seymour smoothed his unexceptional dark hair and fixed her with his unexceptional blue eyes. He was not a handsome man, although Miranda would be at a lost to explain why he was not attractive. He was of adequate height. He was neither fat nor thin. He had all the required symmetry of features and no specific unfortunate characteristic.

It was merely, she decided, a certain lack of life. Mr. Seymour wasn't attractive, because Mr. Seymour wasn't vigorous.

Mr. Worthington personified the word *vigorous*. Whether in a dark intense mood like recently, or a laughing, playful one like before, his life shone from him, heating her blood and warming her heart. He would attract her even if he were not so handsome.

Mr. Seymour commenced to speak in educated tones about current events that had been in the newssheets.

Interesting topics all—and, if Miranda was not mistaken, recited in the precise order in which they'd appeared in the London newssheets.

He'd memorized things of interest to provide interesting conversation. This was very thoughtful, for Miranda dearly loved interesting conversation.

So why was she not interested?

She stifled a yawn. It was nearly three o'clock in the afternoon. Mr. Worthington often came to her around three or four o'clock.

Her mind wandered to the memory of early that morning, when she'd done such a shocking thing, all by herself, in the privacy of her own bedchamber . . . would a lover touch her there? Would a lover touch her everywhere?

A lover like Mr. Worthington?

A fantasy bloomed in her mind of making love during the day, draperies wide open, sunlight spilling over them both as they rolled naked on the carpet . . . on her back, sprawled unashamed before him as he caressed her wet, throbbing—

"—crevice, but I hardly think that the Prime Minister should leave the condition of our streets to a committee. Mrs. Talbot? Is something wrong? You look a bit flushed. Is the room too warm? I shall ring for your maid to bring your fan."

Miranda focused her vision and saw, to her surprise, that it was Mr. Seymour, fully clothed (thank heaven!) sitting across from her. She pressed her palms to her hot cheeks. "My goodness! I. . . ."

Mr. Seymour's unexceptional eyes narrowed in concern. "I believe you must have caught a chill. My dear Mrs. Talbot, I recommend a dose of castor oil and a day in bed—"

Miranda choked. Bed, where Mr. Worthington had sat beside her, where he'd caressed her softly when he thought her sleeping—

"—you should have your man call a physician at once! A fever can burn for days—"

God, yes, let me burn for days!

Tildy entered the parlor with concern on her freckled features. Lost in an overwhelming wave of maddening, formless desire, Miranda shot her maid a helpless glance.

Tildy blinked, then rolled her eyes behind Mr. Seymour's back and set about fussing ridiculously over Miranda, going on about how her mistress needed her bed right away and goodness, with the illnesses rampaging through the streets of Evil London, it was a miracle they all weren't dead in their beds and she wasn't going to let her mistress move a muscle for at least a week and—

Mr. Seymour couldn't help but back away a few steps, visibly appalled at the apparently unrealized potential for contagion. Tildy ushered him out, thanking him earnestly for his heroic ringing of the bell before her mistress expired on the spot—

The door shut and the house went quiet. Miranda sat in her pretty feminine chair in her still-not-quite-to-her-taste parlor and covered her face with her hands. *He is right. I am ill. I am infected with lust.*

She remembered the heat in Mr. Worthington's eyes as he came into her bedchamber this morning.

And yes, Mr. Seymour, this fever does seem to be contagious—but you have nothing to worry about.

Cas didn't press Poll for conversation as they rode to Miranda's house on Breton Square. Poll alternated between obvious fuming and glum resignation, a state he'd been in since their agreement the day before.

As for Cas, he'd gone around and around the issue in his mind all night. Was this advisable? He meant to prove himself to the Prince Regent. Royal patronage, for pity's sake! Adding a woman to the matter certainly wouldn't help matters.

Cas tried to tell himself that he meant only to keep an eye on Poll's activities. He tried to convince himself that keeping a possible lady on a string for the next month would curb his own tendency toward fleshly distraction. Simply look at what had happened the other evening at Blythe's! He, Castor Worthington, had walked away from an orgy.

It still boggled his mind a bit.

However, even as he listed all the reasons why embarking on this odd wager with Poll would in fact further his ambitions, he did rather feel like both the master of misdirection and its willing dupe.

Mira.

Sea-green eyes and silken skin and lips that tasted like sin dipped in crystal sugar, all wrapped about a creature crafted of radiant decency.

The hack pulled up to the respectable address of the respectable lady.

Cas was the first one out.

Mira.

Miranda had been waiting for Mr. Worthington's call for the entire morning and well into the afternoon.

She felt like a nervous cat, unable to sit, unable to stop restlessly moving about the ornate, stuffy drawing room, rearranging horrid china dogs and adjusting paintings of insipid shepherdesses that were already entirely level.

Twigg followed her after a time, subtly readjusting the phalanx of china dogs so that their snouts aligned with military precision, putting tilting shepherdesses upright and replacing sofa cushions restlessly tossed aside.

Miranda ignored his aggrieved hauteur, preferring

instead the slightly petty enjoyment of making him fix everything in the room at least three times.

Twigg had not been her personal choice for butler. He was part of the previous era of the house and Miranda suspected where his loyalty truly lay. Unfortunately, one couldn't fire a member of one's staff simply because the individual had performed too well for their former employer!

Finally, she turned to him with her arms crossed over her bosom.

"Twigg, is that a china dog you hold in your hand?"

He eyed her warily, then nodded. "Yes, madam."

Miranda raised a brow. "Is it *your* china dog?"

Twigg drew back cautiously. "No, madam. The china dog belongs to Talbot House."

To Talbot House, not to her. Miranda lifted her chin. "Drop the china dog, Twigg."

His brows rose sky-high. "Madam?"

"You heard me perfectly." She tilted her head. "Drop—the—blasted—dog—now."

Twigg swallowed and looked down. Directly beneath the defenseless ceramic spaniel's little china feet was a long fall to a shattering death on the tile of the hearth. Twigg looked at Miranda, then back at the floor. She almost felt sorry for the butler—until she recalled his tendency to sneer at her callers and sigh heavily at her every request. And there was that little matter of Constance knowing her every move.

Twigg let go of the dog . . . after swinging his arm until his hand was over carpet.

China spaniels can really take a spill, Miranda thought sourly as she looked down at the entirely whole dog lying on the woolen rug. *Smug little monstrosity.*

Oddly, she wasn't sorry that the figurine was unbroken. Smashing things wasn't a constructive method of resolution, although she secretly suspected that it might be quite satisfying, at least in the short term.

Still, she ought not to let Twigg get away with his continual subversion. "Very ingenious. Once again, I am obeyed in the letter, if not in the spirit."

Twigg very carefully stared over her left shoulder. "Madam?"

"Pick up the dog, Twigg. Pack it in a box. Pack them all in a box and send a message to an auction house that I have an apparently endless supply of china canines I wish to part company with."

Twigg picked up the dog and cradled it carefully in his hands. "Miss Constance Talbot sets great store by her grandmother's china collection."

Miranda inhaled slowly. *Steady. Consistent. Fair.* And then, of course, she utterly lost her temper. "Twigg, if Miss Constance Talbot wanted to take her grandmother's pack of glassy-eyed curs with her to preserve for eternity, she had every opportunity to pack them off with her. Instead, she left them for me to tend! Now, box them up and dispense with them or you'll be sweeping shards from the hearth for the rest of the day. I refuse to run this porcelain kennel for *one more blasted minute*!"

From the doorway came a feminine cough. "Ahem . . . Missus? Mr. Worthington and—"

It was Tildy, poor thing, wide-eyed at Miranda's uncharacteristic fury. A tall dark form emerged from the shadows behind the little maid.

Oh, for pity's sake! Miranda turned quickly away to compose herself. *Not only does he finally appear to find me screeching like a fishwife, but I am likely the color of a blotchy beet as well!*

Before turning back to the door, she pressed her fingertips to her temples in an attempt to cool her bad humor and her pounding head. Then she turned with the best smile she could manage in her mortification.

Mr. Worthington entered the room, looking a bit embarrassed himself. Then Mr. Worthington entered the room . . . again.

Miranda gazed blankly at the second man, who gave her a wry twist of his lips in return. Then she stared at the first man, who widened his eyes and gave her an uneasy shrug.

She forgot all about tardy callers and china dogs and undermining butlers and her own peculiar outburst.

"You . . . he . . . I . . ." She blinked. ". . . seem to require a chair."

Miranda sat in her chair, like royalty on a throne.

I am Queen. In this house, I am Queen.

Except that at this moment, she felt more like a criminal on trial.

Resilience. She would not allow anything to rob her of her newfound confidence and stature. She was a wealthy, independent woman. She could handle anything that came down her road.

Even prepared as she was, when she raised her eyes at last to look at the two men seated across from her on her putridly puce sofa in her ludicrously dog-infested parlor, she gasped slightly.

One of them sardonically lifted a corner of his mouth at her small sound of surprise. The other only gazed at her earnestly.

She looked down again, pressing her damp palms to her lap, sliding them over her skirt, smoothing what did not need to be smoothed. *I need to be smoothed! I am feeling rather ragged at the moment!*

Because she'd known, of course. She'd realized it the instant she truly accepted that there were two of them.

She had kissed the wrong man.

Unable to suppress a small recoil at the notion, she twined her fingers together on her lap to keep them from flapping wildly in the air like wings broken by sheer mortification.

"What you must think of me." To her astonishment, her voice sounded low, smooth, and composed.

Then she frowned and lifted her head, her attention snapping from one twin to the other. "Or rather, what must I think of *you*?"

The earnest one held up his hands. "Miranda, it wasn't intentional, truly—"

"I see. One of you accidentally tripped and landed on my lips?"

The cool one raised a brow. "That's just what he said to me," he commented in a low voice. "Perhaps the two of you have more in common than I thought."

She watched as the earnest one—the one she was beginning to suspect was *her* Mr. Worthington—er, her first Mr. Worthington—oh, bother it—turned eagerly to his twin.

"That's just what I was trying to tell you! It is I who belongs here, not you!"

The cool one just looked arrogantly mulish—which seemed to be a rather well-set expression on his handsome features. Miranda suspected that it settled there often.

She decided she didn't like him at all. Yes, she much preferred the first one—the other one—

"Oh, *bother*!" She shook her head with impatience. "Will you please introduce yourselves properly before I am driven entirely insane?" *Because I am halfway there, I truly am.*

The earnest one, the first Mr. Worthington she was sure, confirmed her suspicions at once. He leaned forward. "Forgive us, Miranda. I am Pollux Worthington. Poll. I am the fellow who saved you from a snagged heel in the cobbles and I am the only one you encountered until yesterday morning—"

"—when I saved you from a steam explosion—" The Other Worthington cast his brother an arch glance, as if to claim the superior rescue—which, in all fairness, it had been. "—and you invited me back to your house."

She scoffed. "I did not! I wouldn't! I don't even know you!" She glared at him. Such nerve! "I—invited—" She pointed to his brother. "—*him.*"

Pollux nodded. "Yes, that's what I said."

The Other Worthington leaned forward to fix her with that peculiarly luminous green gaze. "You may have invited him, but you kissed *me,*" he said softly. Then he leaned back and spread his arms over the back of the settee. "And you know it, Mira."

Well, yes, her belly trembled a little and she might have pressed her thighs together ever so slightly beneath her full skirts, but she was sure that no sign of her disquiet showed when she lifted her chin. "Sir, we have not been introduced—and I certainly have not given you leave to address me by my given name—" Mira, he called her, as her mother had, disdaining the formality of Miranda. "—nor any versions of it!"

He only tilted his head as he boldly fixed his gaze on her mouth.

Poll elbowed his brother without the slightest attempt at subtlety. "He is Castor. Cas. He is insufferable—but in all honesty, he is still better than most of the blokes I know. And please do not let his general loutishness fool you. He likes you. We both do. Therein lies our dilemma, in fact. We both wish to court you."

Miranda drew back. She had not thought she would see either of them again after this horrifying revelation.

How could they even think she would wish to continue seeing either of them, much less both? It was unthinkable, absurd, absolutely insupportable!

So impossible was the very notion, in fact, that she'd already begun to imagine the endless, culturally enriching, politically educational, deathly boring afternoons with only Mr. Seymour for company.

Fortitude. She inhaled deeply. She ignored Cas Worthington's unconcealed appreciation of the general vicinity of her bodice. *Lout.*

Then she rose to her feet. Both men stood as one, in movements of such eerie, mirrorlike similarity that Miranda was momentarily distracted from her purpose.

Recovering quickly, she clasped her hands before her. "My most sincere regrets, Mr. Pollux Worthington, Mr. Castor Worthington, but I do not feel that it would be appropriate for a woman in my position to consent to such an outré arrangement. Now, I fear I must bid you good day."

She was gratified to see that the hand she extended toward the door did not tremble in the slightest.

Poll looked terribly disappointed, and sent her a deeply wounded glance as he turned toward the door. Regret pierced Miranda. She'd so enjoyed his company. Her life had been much brightened these last weeks by his humor and his kindness and—

"Wait!"

Miranda went very still as she realized that it had been she who had spoken. To be truthful, she'd very nearly shouted.

Both men stopped in the doorway and turned back toward her, Pollux standing slightly closer to her than Castor, who remained in the shadows of the hall.

Miranda smiled tremulously at Poll. "Sir, I do not

suppose it would be too difficult to put this untoward event behind us. You and I . . . we might continue our . . . our friendship, might we not?"

Poll brightened for an instant, but then his expression fell. "No."

Miranda blinked. No? *Oh, for pity's sake, why not?*

"Oh, for pity's sake, why not?" she asked sharply. Oh, dear. Her temper had not been improved by the day's strange turn.

She thought she heard a muffled snort from the man in the shadow of the doorway. Poll was not laughing, however. He looked entirely serious.

"Miranda, you must understand—Cas *likes* you."

The feeling is not mutual, she almost said, but that would be somewhat less than the truth, and after a lifetime of hiding her true feelings, Miranda had vowed to be as truthful as possible, especially with herself.

Instead, she limited herself to a single complete truth. "I do not understand."

Poll ran a restless hand through his hair. "I like you, so Cas cannot court you. Cas likes you, so I cannot court you. It is . . . it is an issue of honor, I suppose."

"It is an issue of life expectancy," murmured a deep, matching voice behind him.

Poll's elbow shot backwards, though his earnest attention never left her. Miranda was quite certain he was not even aware of his own motion.

She frowned, trying to decipher the variables of this "honor issue."

"So, if I am not mistaken, you are saying that one of you cannot court me . . . unless both of you court me?"

Poll looked relieved. "Precisely."

Since Miranda had been shooting wildly in the dark— the stormy, windy, flying-debris sort of dark—she wasn't at all sure she had been precise about anything. "If I de-

sire one caller—" Oh, why had she used the word *desire?*
"—then I must allow two?"

Poll nodded. "Yes, yes. You understand."

She sighed. "No, I don't."

Twin suitors? If she was scandalized by the notion, she was sure that the rest of Society would be agog. Constance would have kittens on the spot.

However, she had been very secluded until Mr. Poll Worthington came around . . . and Mr. Seymour as well, of course. She didn't care to think about going back to those long, dreary, endless days.

Yet, what of her reputation? What would the world think of her?

Do you mean the world that has forgotten you exist?

Who could blame it if it had?

I had very nearly forgotten that I existed.

She shook off that thought, forcing her mind back to the most important question of all.

What of all the many hard-won years of demure, circumspect caution? Could she risk all of that now?

She had guarded her respectability as if it would keep her company during the long days of her widowhood, a chill but self-righteous companion.

Just like Constance.

"Fine!" She threw her hands wide. "Mr. Pollux Worthington, I choose you!"

Poll looked sincerely flattered, but a glance at his brother had him shrugging in regret. "I'm sorry, Miranda, but I cannot accept your decision so quickly. In order for this to be a fair fight for your affections, you must give Cas a reasonable period of acquaintance."

He smiled at her so warmly that the back of her neck started to tickle.

"But I thank you for the honor of your preference." He shot a triumphant glance at his twin.

For his part, Castor looked irritated and a bit . . . hurt? Blast it, she was going to end up hurting someone, couldn't they see that?

Didn't they care that someone was going to get their heart broken in this mad scheme?

It might be me. . . .

She brushed that thought away. She had no intention of falling in love. What a ridiculous notion. She'd known several gentlemen in her life and she'd never been the slightest bit tempted to fall in love with any of them. Ergo, she did not have the disposition to fall in love.

She could not give a heart to be broken if she couldn't give her heart.

Entirely simple. Or at least, it ought to be.

Unsure, she frowned at her two tormentors. "I must allow both of you to call—forever? Or until one of you becomes bored? Are there some parameters to this odd arrangement?" Then a horrible thought struck her. "Have you done this before?"

"No!" Poll assured her—

"Well, yes, actually," Cas interjected.

Poll turned to his brother. "We have not!"

"Remember when Mama forced us to that dancing master—?"

"Yes, the one with the single hair wound seventy times about his pate—"

"And there were one too many fellows—"

"And we had to—oh, right." Poll turned back to Miranda. "We have done this before, once, when we shared the attentions of one Miss Leticia Montgomery."

"A porcelain beauty, with hair as black as night," Cas murmured. "She loved the attention."

Poll's smile became slightly fixed as he looked sheepishly at Miranda. "Yes, well . . . that was rather long ago."

Miranda narrowed her eyes at him. "How long ago?"

Poll turned back to Cas. "When was that? There was—"

"—that long winter when we—"

"—couldn't leave the house for the ice—"

"—and it was the year after that—"

Poll turned back to Miranda, who was fast losing patience with their strange method of conversing.

He smiled apologetically. "Eleven."

Eleven years ago. They would have been about nineteen or twenty, wouldn't they? Old enough to know better. Shocking. Miranda closed her eyes briefly. "Eleven years ago?"

"Eleven years of age." That was Cas's voice, arrogant and amused.

She opened her eyes. *Oh.*

Heavens, I'll wager they were adorable. I'll wager even more that they were terrors. Little raven-haired Miss Leticia Montgomery in dancing class hadn't stood a chance against them.

As the smile twisted the corners of her mouth despite her best efforts to remain cool and regal, Miranda was beginning to fear that she herself stood very little chance as well.

Oh no.

Oh yes.

Chapter Nine

Miranda answered her own door the next afternoon, positive that Mr. Poll Worthington would be standing on her step and not wishing to miss a moment of his presence. His brother she did not look forward to seeing again. At all.

Instead, there stood a skinny little girl of perhaps twelve years.

"Ah. Hello." Miranda cast a glance about the street for any sign of a governess, nurse, or mother. Goodness, the poor little thing was all on her own! "Do you need help, little one?"

"I'm not little. I'm twelve and three quarters." The girl strode into Miranda's house without invitation. Once in the entrance hall, she stood with her arms crossed, sharp green eyes taking in every detail of the house.

Miranda frowned at her little intruder. "Is there something I can do for you?" Although she would wager that this self-assured little person did not require anyone's help.

The girl turned to her. "I'm Atalanta Worthington."

"Oh!" Miranda smiled. "I should have known it by your

lovely green eyes. I'm delighted to make your acquaintance!" The little girl shot her a sour glance. Miranda tried again. "I've heard a great deal about you!"

Mr. Poll Worthington had perhaps mentioned that he occasionally feared for the life of anyone who made an enemy of Attie Worthington—but Miranda couldn't see how that was possible. She was just a wee little thing! Not very tall, and as thin as a straw. She looked as though she might break in a strong wind!

Miranda held out a hand, gesturing welcome. "Please, come and sit with me. I'll ring for some tea and cakes, shall I?"

Little Atalanta settled on the sofa with her gawky ankles askew beneath her slightly too long dress and her hair quite frankly a mess under that many-times-crushed bonnet. Miranda had to wonder who had the care of the child. To not only let her wander the streets of London, but to send her out in such a state as well!

Miranda's untapped maternal instinct bubbled up and she found her fingers absolutely twitching to take a hairbrush to the girl's untidy mop of amber-red curls.

"Have you any interesting news to tell of your family, Miss Atalanta? I've heard so many tales now, I feel as if I know you all."

Attie glared at her with such ferocity, Miranda fought the urge to scan the room for weaponry that might be used against her. She dealt with the children from the home often enough to know a sad, bereft child when she saw one, no matter how furious or frightening they might think they appeared to others.

Miranda wanted Attie to like her—she didn't dare ask herself why—but she sat opposite the child without the slightest notion how to get through to her.

* * *

Attie sat across from her enemy. She was quite horrible looking . . . in a pretty sort of way. The ladylike way she sat reminded Attie of Ellie when she was on her best behavior, which made Attie want to sit straighter and move more gracefully. Which urge, of course, made her want to squat like a frog and screech like a chimpanzee.

Callie said she was incorrigible. Orion said she was developing a large bump of antiauthoritarianism.

Orion was terribly smart, but he didn't know everything. He didn't know what lived inside Attie's mind. He couldn't know that she was frightened that her family might be ever so slightly broken and that Attie had no idea how to fix it.

He didn't know that inside she wasn't fierce or strong or dangerous, like they all thought. He didn't know she was really terrified. No one could.

"I recall being your age. I think I spent a great deal of time being quite frightened," Miranda Talbot said softly. "I know how lonely life can be, even in a house full of people."

Oh, no, you don't! Attie scrunched up her face and prepared to put a hex of hate upon Miranda's shining dark head.

It would be worth it, Attie thought, as she wondered what terrible thing was about to happen. *Except when the roof falls down, I'll probably be under it.*

Then Miranda's prune-faced butler came in with a tea tray filled with iced cakes and cream and early summer raspberries in a bowl—

Well, perhaps I'll hex her later, after tea.

Atalanta Worthington wasn't normally one to dawdle when it came time for action, which was why she astonished herself by waiting nearly an entire afternoon after her visit to the she-devil's house before climbing out from under her bed (Ellie was in a mood) and wrestling herself into her slightly too large walking dress (Ellie had grown a bosom at a very early age) and sneaking out through the kitchen while Philpott was in the larder, secretively concocting the blend of herbs for her evening "tea."

Attie didn't know what herbs the cook used in the teapot, but the one time she'd managed to sneak a taste, she'd felt like a piece of paper on the wind and had actually begun to write words on herself before she lost track of the thought in a sudden urge to eat pickles and cheese and chocolate cake together.

Once out on the street, she clomped confidently along the sidewalk, ignoring the astonished glances of strangers. It wasn't more than half a mile to her destination, though she did take a side venture for a stop at a confectioner's. She even paid for the sweets, for they were a gift and one couldn't give a gift if one didn't actually own it.

On the Strand, she lingered across the street from a discreet and tasteful doorway, sucking noisily on a sweet. Eventually, a lady left the establishment, escorted to her waiting carriage by a very handsome young man. His sharp eyes caught Attie's presence at once. With a twitch of his cheek, he told her to go to the back of the shop. Attie nodded and placidly made her way around through the alley.

Cabot let her in. "He's very busy."

"He's never too busy to see me."

Cabot didn't bother denying it, because it was quite true. Still, he eyed her sticky hands and face and sighed. "I'll be right back."

Since she adored Cabot, mostly because he never, ever treated her like a child, she waited with uncharacteristic patience. He returned with a bowl of steaming water and a towel. There was a very pretty little soap, pressed into the shape of a fish that Attie promptly dropped into the bowl so she could watch it swim to the bottom. Then she scrubbed her face and hands until even the grime under her nails was gone.

There was no point in rebelling against Cabot. He was the only person in the world who was actually more persistent than she was. And she felt sorry for him.

Clean at last, she dried off with the luxurious bit of toweling and handed it back to Cabot, grimy streaks and all. "It's really important."

He didn't seem impressed. "It always is."

Still, he led her down a silk-papered hallway to a simple painted door and tapped on it. "It's the littlest one," he announced through the wood.

In response to a murmur from the other side, Cabot opened the door and ushered Attie through.

The man at the small cluttered desk turned to greet her with a sweet smile. "Ah, the lovely Atalanta! What a fetching frock."

Attie looked down at her dress and plucked indifferently at the deflated bodice. "It was Ellie's."

The man tilted his head. "I imagine it was. I would be happy to make up one new for you, you know."

Attie shrugged and plunked herself down on the faded needlepoint footstool at his knee and happily contemplated the tiny, cluttered office of the renowned Lementeur, the greatest and most expensive dressmaker in all of England. "No need," she said. "I'll likely get a bosom eventually."

She loved to come here. Being in this little room, with its piles of papers and fabrics on the desk and bits of trimming pinned up on the walls that nearly covered the hundreds of drawings layered beneath them—why, it reminded her of Worthington House!

Wrapping her arms around her knees, she rocked gently to and fro. "I have a problem."

Lementeur, or Mr. Button, as he was known to the Worthington clan, nodded sagely. "I could tell the moment

I saw you. You must be extremely distressed to have forgotten—"

"Oh!" Attie sat up and dug into her pocket. "Here.
These are for you!"

Button beamed as if he'd been handed the Crown Jew-
els. "Ah! You did remember! How very kind!" With ut-
most care, he took the slightly grubby paper packet that
had gone just a bit sweat-soft in her pocket and untwisted
it with an expression of delighted expectation.

"Lemon drops! How did you know?"

Attie chuckled, for he always said that. When he offered her one, she graciously accepted and popped it
into her mouth. For several minutes they sat in compan-
ionable silence sucking on the sweet-tart hard candies.
Then, with a sigh of satisfaction, Button carefully redid
the paper twist and stored the gift carefully in the chaos
of his desk.

Then he dusted his hands in a businesslike fashion and
turned back to Attie. "Tell me everything."

Attie did, relating the fight between the twins, her visit
to Mrs. Talbot, confessing even her eavesdropping without hesitation, for Button understood that in a world of
misbehaving adults, a child did what a child had to do.

"Oh, dear" and "oh, heavens" were his only responses
as he let her tell the entire tale without interruption.

She really, truly loved Button.

When she finished with a sigh, Button nodded. "I see.
It is indeed a pickle." He leaned forward eagerly. "What
do you propose to do about it?"

Attie scratched meditatively at her nose. "Well, I
thought about poison, of course. I think I could really do
it properly this time."

Button pursed his lips. "Oh my. Is she so terrible?"

She wrinkled her nose. "No, actually. She's really
rather nice, as it happens. I mean, she must be removed

from between Cas and Poll, obviously, but this time I don't see any immediate need for murder."

Button let out a breath. "Well . . . that's a relief," he said faintly.

Attie nodded in agreement. Her last attempt at homicide had not gone very well at all. She really wasn't ready to attempt it again. Not that she'd lost her nerve or anything. Simply . . . not ready.

"I thought and thought, and then I had the answer. We must make her beautiful!"

"Ah!" Button brightened at once. "My favorite thing!"

Attie nodded quickly. "Yes! If she's beautiful, then she'll have lots of suitors—exceedingly good ones, with lots of money and titles and such—and she'll forget all about Cas and Poll . . . at least, I think she will." She frowned. "They are terribly handsome, though. And nice. And funny." She straightened. "You'll just have to make her really, truly gorgeous!"

Button nodded. "Yes. It is an excellent plan, truly an ingenious solution to an impossible fix. I should assume, I suppose, knowing the twins' tastes in the past, that she is already quite pretty?"

Attie scrunched up her face in thought. "Well, her dress wasn't much to look at . . . a bit dull. And she's quite modest. You'll have to do something about that. But she has a figure like Ellie's . . . and hair like Aunt Clemmie's used to be before the silver came . . . and her eyes are sort of . . ." She waved her hand in search of the perfect word. ". . . green-gold, like the sun shining on the sea."

Button made an impressed face. "That sounds promising."

"So you'll help?"

Button smiled and spread his hands. "Need you even ask?"

*   *   *

There weren't many invitations in Mrs. Talbot's post on a usual day—none, to be exact.

Until the next morning, when a subtly striped mauve envelope was brought to her door.

The deliverer of this mysterious epistle was a quite unbelievably handsome young man in an exquisitely fitted suit of gray superfine that perfectly matched his eyes. When Miranda stepped into the front hall in anticipation of her suitor, she found the fellow coolly refusing the protests of her butler, Twigg, who was accustomed to being the first to lay hands on the mistress's mail.

Twigg was very aware of his rank and defensive of his privileges. He was also on the managing side. Miranda stepped forward to resolve the stalemate.

"Twigg, I shall handle this matter. Please return to your duties."

Her butler-cum-guard-dog cast a dismissive sniff in the elegant young man's general direction and hustled away, perhaps intending to give the impression of much more important things to attend to. Miranda waited for him to be gone, then turned to her visitor with a smile.

"I suppose one cannot overdo on a virtue such as diligence."

He gazed down at her impassively. So tall. So very decorative . . .

"My master would likely say, 'Why do when one can overdo?'"

Miranda, who was, after all, on the brink of a rather "overdoing" adventure—twin suitors—oh my!—could only concur with that philosophy. "Your master sounds delightfully wise." She gestured with one hand. "Won't you come sit, Mr.—?"

He bowed with courteous precision. "Please, forgive my imposition, madam. I am Cabot. I am here on behalf of my master, who would like to extend to you this invitation. He desired that I personally place it in your hand."

He handed her the elegantly embossed envelope with another bow. Upon taking possession of it, Miranda was driven to caress the heavy, expensive paper ever so slightly with her fingertips. Goodness, her senses were becoming most unguarded, weren't they?

To her discomfort, she realized that Cabot had noticed her sensual tendency and, if the glint in his beautiful eyes meant anything, had drawn some conclusion from it.

He nodded toward the missive. "If it please you, madam, my master has requested that I abide for your reply."

"Oh! Of course!" Miranda opened the envelope then and there, for she was already perishing from curiosity. Merely the way Cabot spoke of his master, with the most peculiar hint of pride of possession in his tone—

"Oh!" The stationery was emblazoned at the top with a looping elegant *L*—a symbol every woman in London knew as well as she knew her own initials! "But—I don't understand—" She peered at the beautiful script. "Lementeur wishes to see *me*?"

Stunned, she looked up at Cabot in shock. Really, so very attractive . . . .

"But I have never even met him! Why ever should he wish to see me?" She drew back. "You cannot be in earnest. Is this some sort of jest?"

Cabot blinked at her, clearly set back by her doubt. Indeed, most women would likely shop first and ask questions later.

"Mrs. Talbot, I assure you that this is nothing of the sort. A mutual friend, who prefers not to be named, has asked Lementeur to assist you as you move past your mourning period. Many ladies find it difficult to keep up with the latest modes whilst in bereavement. It was merely meant as a kindness, I pledge to you."

"Oh." Miranda nodded, ashamed now of her suspicion. Mr. Worthington knew many people in London, did he not? What a lovely gesture. She had no doubt that it was Poll who had directed the famous Lementeur to pay her such attentions. "That is very kind."

She did most desperately need new gowns. The very plain one she wore at that moment had been ordered for her by her sister-in-law after Gideon's burial, of course without the slightest consultation with Miranda.

Abruptly, Miranda wanted to burn it, to burn them all. How presumptuous of Constance, to use Miranda's money to purchase unwanted gowns for her! If she wished gowns, she would buy them herself! Furthermore, she could afford to treat herself to Lementeur, if she wished!

She lifted her chin. "I shall be there, just as Mr. Lementeur has requested, this afternoon at three o'clock."

Cabot narrowed his eyes slightly and his lips twitched. A smile? Surely not. No more would a marble statue of a Greek god smile. He bowed yet again.

"Madam, it will be my genuine pleasure to see you then."

Miranda saw him out, then closed the door and leaned against it, running her fingertips over the invitation once more.

Lementeur.

Oh, Mr. Worthington, you are a darling!

Then she looked down at her gown, one of a nauseating array of bland-to-blander half mourning dresses that were all she owned, other than her black widow's weeds. Was there perhaps one of them in which she could manage to appear before the great arbiter of style himself?

Best to start at once!

She was halfway up the stairs, skirts in hand, desperately cataloging her lackluster wardrobe in her mind, when Twigg called for her.

"Madam, what should I say to the gentleman in the parlor?"

Miranda frowned. "What gentleman? Oh! Oh, dear! I completely forgot about Mr. Seymour!"

Again.

Chapter Ten

"Thank you for interrupting your very busy schedule to meet with me, Mrs. Talbot."

Miranda examined that gracious statement with wary care. This odd little man seemed to know a great deal about her.

The great Lementeur smiled gently at her. "It must be difficult to return to Society after such a long mourning absence."

"Ah. Well, yes, I suppose." Horrified, Miranda realized she was blushing, just thinking about her "busy" schedule!

Identical shoulders, identical hands, identical parts all about—

She turned slightly away, pretending to examine the mad collage of drawings on the wall of the surprisingly tiny cluttered office. The showroom in the front of the shop was spacious and elegant. This wee chamber felt like a closet.

Then her vision focused properly on the sketches papering the wall floor-to-ceiling and she realized that she stood in a privileged place where genius was born. In wonder, she let her fingertips trail over a drawing, tracing the curving high waistline of a screamingly modish riding habit.

"A design I recently created for the Duke of York's . . . er . . . dear friend," Lementeur commented from the vicinity of her elbow. "Shall I have one made up for you as well? In a fiery russet, perhaps. I shall change the collar for you, I think. It is a blessing to have such a long, elegant neck, is it not?"

Miranda, realizing that she was being a tiny bit rude, ignoring her host for his drawings, snatched her hand away and turned back to face the great dressmaker. "You are too kind, Mr. Lementeur."

His face crinkled into a gleeful smile and he chuckled. "Darling creature, Lementeur isn't my name. It is my calling! *Le Menteur.*"

Miranda's French was little better than schoolroom level. She frowned. "The . . . Liar?"

He bowed, sweeping a ridiculously low, pointed-toe pose that should have looked silly but didn't, instead calling to mind a hat feathered in plumes swept to his side. "At your service, my dear." He straightened and spread his hands to include the hundreds of sketches. "Now, how shall we lie today? You may choose anything you like."

Her eyes roamed around the room filled with beauty and style and something else—a depth of understanding of women, of their dreams, of what they loved and needed.

For her?

Abruptly, Miranda found herself blinking back tears. Horrified, she pressed her gloved fingertips to her leaking eyes. "I'm so sorry—I don't know what's come over me—"

Warm fingers tugged gently at her hands and she found herself gazing into sympathetic eyes.

"My sweet, you need a cup of tea." He shoved her gently into a deep soft chair. "Sit."

Suddenly Miranda was perishing for a cup of tea.

And a friend.

An hour later, she was laughing delightedly at the

exquisite double entendres which Button—as he insisted she address him—dropped as easily as flower petals into every sentence.

Several new sketches had emerged from their consultation, though Miranda knew she could not afford them all.

"Nonsense, my darling. I charge in indirect proportion to my affection for my clients—and I am fast becoming fond of you. Each Season brings me a new muse. You, I think, shall be one of my finest creations."

"I?" The offer took Miranda's breath away. "Button, that is . . . so alarming!"

Her frank assessment of his generosity surprised a new bout of hilarity from them both. Miranda felt drunk—intoxicated by silk and velvet and tea and friendship.

At last, she knew she could take up no more of his valuable time. As she made her good-byes, however, he stopped her with a warm touch to her wrist and a suddenly serious expression.

"My dear, this is very important. In one month, I shall unveil you at the Marquis of Wyndham's Midsummer Ball."

Miranda's jaw dropped.

Button dismissed her astonishment with a wave of his hand. "The marchioness is a dear friend and shall not mind extending an invitation." He pressed her hand intently. "Here is the point. Under no circumstances shall you discuss our arrangement with anyone."

Miranda nodded, a little perplexed. "Of course, if that is what you wish."

Button narrowed his eyes at her. "No one is to know, pet. Not even your . . . *dearest friends.*"

A tiny chill went through Miranda. Yes, this odd, endearing little man definitely knew all too much about her.

* * *

After placing Mrs. Talbot into Cabot's care to be returned to her carriage, Button strolled meditatively back into his office with his hands behind his back. "Most illuminating."

He bent to move aside an armful of silks in various lemony hues draping off a viewing stand. "Indeed, I see what you mean," he said thoughtfully into the space beneath. "She doesn't quite match one's idea of an evil seductress."

"I know." Attie crawled out of the glorious silken tent and stood, pushing her tangled hair out of her face. "But she wants both of them! Why would she do that? Why would she make them fight over her if she isn't an evil seductress?"

Button frowned, considering the problem. "Perhaps she likes them both and cannot choose between? They are very much alike, after all."

Attie scowled. "Everyone says that. It isn't true, you know. They're not very much alike at all."

"How so?"

"Well," Attie shrugged. "Cas is . . . well, he's Cas! And Poll is Poll! That's as much as saying Ellie and I are just alike, just because we're sisters!"

"I suppose you are right. Looking alike is one thing. Feeling alike—no one can feel precisely like anyone else, can they?" Button returned to his chair and thoughtfully stirred his tea.

This was Attie's favorite part—Button's thinking pose! She scrambled into the opposite chair so recently vacated by Mrs. Talbot and waited.

Presently the ringing of the spoon slowed, then stopped. Button absently took a sip of his tea. Then he grimaced. "It is cold."

Attie hopped up, ready for action. "I'll call Cabot, shall I?"

"No need for that, Miss Atalanta." Cabot backed into the office with another full tea tray, this time graced with iced gingerbread and chocolates.

"Ah!" Button brightened. "Cabot, you're a wonder!"

Attie watched as Cabot served the tea. Did Button ever notice that Cabot took special care with everything he gave his master? The handle of the teacup was spun to just the right angle for Button to grasp. The two chocolates precisely and beautifully placed across a mint leaf on the saucer he gave Button were the orange and cherry ones, for people who knew Button well knew that he most preferred fruity sweets.

Did Button ever notice the way Cabot looked at him when he thought Button couldn't see? It was a little bit like Button was a chocolate on a mint leaf.

Attie took the teacup handed her by Cabot, then hid her smile behind the first sip. It was awfully sweet—Cabot, not the tea—and Attie didn't understand why it was that Button never seemed to notice.

Button took a sip of fresh, steaming tea and smacked his lips. "Excellent! Whatever would I do without you, Cabot?"

"Melt into a multicolored puddle of mismanaged creativity, without a doubt." Cabot's tone was completely without expression.

"Most definitely." Button smiled sweetly. "I cannot think without my tea."

What wasn't so sweet was the blank desolation that crossed Cabot's perfectly symmetrical features when he turned away to take away the cold tea.

Which was why Attie could never bear to give Cabot any bit of bother.

Poor Cabot.

When Cabot had left the room, Button turned to Attie. "I believe your plan will work rather beautifully—this time. I applaud your personal growth and maturity in not resorting to firearms."

Attie smirked. "That was last year. I was just a child then."

Nearly a week has passed since that day in the alley. My two suitors—I should say three, for it would not be right to forget Mr. Seymour, even in my diary, except that I do always tend to forget Mr. Seymour—attend me daily. They have worked out some sort of schedule between them, for they never overlap in their calls.

Poor Mr. Seymour, however, does not appear to be in on the plan. A Worthington here, a Worthington there . . . they seem to pop up out of the woodwork just when he has a monologue in full steam, casting his opinion upon the waters of politics and tittle-tattle.

I swear I never saw such a man for gossip.

I find him by turns endearing and boring. Although I do not wish to be unkind, I cannot seem to attend to the words he is saying. I am all the while thinking of my identical Mr. Worthingtons.

Mr. Poll Worthington, my "old" friend, he of the clever books and easy charm, is my constant companion of the mornings. During hours that most of Society is asleep, he and I sit just a bit too close together on my settee, laughing and talking.

And that is all we do. Since my terribly embarrassing error, I have determined that I shall not kiss any gentleman who does not love me exclusively, and I him.

It is hard not to kiss Mr. Poll Worthington.

Mr. Cas Worthington, on the other hand, calls upon me in the afternoons. He chooses no regular time, instead seeming to prefer to stop in at whatever time suits him the best. He insists on calling me Mira, which is a bit disconcerting, as it constantly puts me in mind of my—of the past.

I am, of course, quite cool to him and his shameless teasing, especially when poor Mr. Seymour is present. I fear Mr. Cas Worthington is not kind to poor Mr. Seymour, although it is true that Mr. Seymour often brings it upon himself. . . .

Castor Worthington strolled into Miranda's drawing room as if he owned it. "Hello, Mira, my pet. Heigh-ho, Seymour."

Miranda watched Mr. Seymour stiffen as she tried to suppress her own sense of pleasure.

"*Mrs. Talbot* is not your pet, Worthington!"

Miranda bit back a sigh. When Mr. Seymour was not present, Castor Worthington was not inclined to call her any such thing!

"Please ignore him, Mr. Seymour. You were telling me about your new purchase? . . . ."

Mr. Seymour sniffed indignantly and pointedly turned away from Mr. Worthington, who had sprawled his length onto the sofa within reach.

"It is a curricle, dear Mrs. Talbot. Just the sort of vehicle to take for a drive through Hyde Park." He allowed himself a deep, indulgent chuckle. "Of course, I shall not alarm you with any races down Rotten Row! I know ladies don't care for great speed—"

"I've seen your nags, Seymour," Mr. Worthington drawled lazily. "I'm fairly certain the only speed you'll attain is when you flip over the traces when your vehicle stops due to sudden equine failure."

Mr. Seymour looked entirely stuffed, but could seem to find no ready rejoinder. Cas seemed almost discomfited to have won a battle of wits so easily. Had he believed his opponent to be more suitably armed?

Cas let his attention wander the room, then fixed it upon the mantel, which now gleamed with a proper waxing and sported only a pair of silver candelabra and a small clock.

"By gum, I knew something was different! Did the whole pack of them go hunting?"

Miranda smiled demurely. "Hunting new homes, perhaps. I will be auctioning the lot very soon."

Mr. Seymour took a bit longer, but eventually he gasped. "The dogs! Oh my, what a shame. Such an impressive collection!"

Both Miranda and Cas eyed him with some disbelief. He pinned Miranda with a disappointed moue. "Mrs. Talbot, you ought to have told me you were in such financial straits! I have a modest savings. I could have prevented such a terrible sacrifice!"

Miranda drew back. "Mr. Seymour, you are very kind, but I am not selling the—er, collection out of need. It is quite my preference to be rid of them, I assure you."

"There's no need to be brave, my dear Mrs. Talbot! You're amongst friends!" Mr. Seymour leaned forward to pat her hand. Since her hand was on her lap, Miranda hoped he hadn't intended that accidental touch upon her upper thigh. Surely the man was only being sympathetic to her ah, *straits*. Nonetheless, she moved her hand to the arm of the chair.

His sympathy might be kindly meant, but he surely wasn't listening to her at all. Still, she could hardly say, *"I loathed the damned things!"*

"She loathed the damn things," Cas informed Seymour irritably. "As should we all. She has the right to smash them all on the hearth if she likes." He didn't continue out loud, but his expression most clearly stated, *You pompous twit!*

Miranda cleared her throat and shot a glare Mr. Worthington's way. *I don't need you to defend my decisions.*

His response was a wry expression and a hand slightly opened, palm upward, in silent apology. Except that he didn't look rueful. He merely looked amused—at her, at her silly tantrum over the dogs the other day, at her silly Mr. Seymour and his silly, self-important ways.

She scowled outright at Mr. Worthington. Such an irritating fellow!

Her furious glare only made his smile widen.

God, she was delicious when she was angry! Cas thought her still a bit too refined, however. When a woman was angry, a man ought to feel the need to duck—even if she wasn't particularly inclined to throw large pottery objects!

Of course, perhaps that was only Worthington women. Other sorts of women seemed to resort to less direct methods of expressing themselves. Like that politician's wife he'd taken up with a few years back—now, she'd had very nearly a Worthingtonian sense of vengeance!

Mira needed a good dose of that forthrightness. The sooner, the better—for then she'd no longer suffer the likes of that prig, Seymour!

Not that he was here to rescue Mrs. Talbot from anything. He'd decided that he was interested only in a bit of distraction. The world had become quite dark some time ago, and Miranda's company did much to lighten it.

He'd not told Poll, but he'd grown tired of the game in the last year. Meet, seduce, leave. Again and again. Season after season. It seemed better to remain alone . . . or at least, it had until he'd flung himself at Miranda.

He didn't feel quite so jaded when basking in the glow of her shy honesty. He didn't feel quite so deathly bored when presented with her intriguing contradictions—her beauty versus her naïveté, her natural sensuality versus her decorum.

Someday, Mrs. Talbot was really going to speak her mind. Cas found himself looking forward to that day.

Seymour, having found the object of his affection had become distracted by shinier and more interesting things—namely, Cas!—stood and gave a stuffed bow and an even stuffier farewell to his hostess.

Cas leaned back in his chair and smiled, wiggling his fingers good-bye when Seymour shot him a black look that implied that he ought to leave as well.

Cas fluttered his eyelids in injured innocence. *But I only just got here!*

Frustrated and now obviously wishing he hadn't assumed any such thing, Seymour could only continue to leave, which he did . . . very slowly.

At last the front door closed on the insufferable twit. At once, Cas swiveled on his cushion and regarded Miranda with a challenging look.

"Papa's gone. Let's set fire to the nursery."

She drew back primly. "Mr. Worthington, I must request that you desist in—"

"Oh, don't worry about Seymour. He's too thick-skinned to pierce with a fork. By the time he gets home, he'll be convinced that he intentionally left me here so that I might embarrass myself before you—upon which you, of course, will immediately turn to someone more mature and responsible!"

She looked down at her hands in her lap, but he could see her lips twitch.

Leaning forward, he pressed his advantage. "I have a box at the opera this evening," he cajoled. He didn't, really. He had a friend who had a box—well, sort of a friend. A friend's wife, actually—who had promised to keep her husband home tonight, busy with other matters. So the box would be empty. Nature abhorred a vacuum, did it not?

Miranda looked up at him, unable to hide the excitement in her eyes. "The opera? You wish to take me *out* for the evening?"

She looked like a little girl getting a birthing-day gift for the first time in her life. *Damn you, Poll—did you think her a doll to leave on the shelf until you were ready to play with her again?*

Cas dropped his smirking facade and smiled warmly at Miranda. "Yes. You deserve to get out of this mausoleum tonight. This place looks like it was decorated by a committee of blind octogenarians on a slender budget!"

She pressed her lips together at that description, then smiled openly. "At least it no longer looks like a china kennel!"

Chapter Eleven

Less than week after he'd walked all night following Mrs. Blythe's festivities, Cas walked in the night again, but this time with the most beautiful woman in London on his arm; Mrs. Gideon Talbot, out about Town with him as her escort at last.

He only wished she were having a bit more fun.

It was a lovely evening. They'd had a wonderful time earlier. The opera they'd attended had been fairly good, but Cas had found more enjoyment in watching Miranda attend her first event after her mourning.

She'd never been to the opera, she confessed. She'd been gratifyingly impressed by the posh private box. She'd worn her best gown, which, sadly, was black, but at least it was fine and she looked bright-eyed and lovely sitting forward in her velvet-upholstered chair, watching raptly, not for a moment realizing that most of Society was, in turn, watching her.

Cas heard the whispers and saw the curious stares. They all knew him, for the Worthingtons knew absolutely everyone. Whether he was liked by them as well was a matter that concerned him not at all. Most people in Society thought the Worthingtons odd in the extreme.

However, it was understood that they should be tolerated for their ancient name and high friends.

Cas knew if Miranda realized that she was on display with one of the most renowned heartbreakers of the past five Seasons, she would want to flee from all those prying eyes.

Such an odd mix, she was; so beautiful, yet so retiring in public. It was as if she feared the world and what it might do to her if she were caught stepping over some invisible boundary, or breaking some unwritten law.

Cas broke laws, written or unwritten, as needed. He didn't steal, or at least, did so rarely, when he felt the need to deprive some undeserving soul of their wealth. He didn't cheat, unless the situation called for it. He didn't lie—well, that was a lie, actually.

He and Poll had been stretching the boundaries of socially acceptable behavior for so long that most people assumed they were mere moments from swinging from the gallows.

It wasn't that severe, truly. A bit of grift, a bit of card playing, a bit of charm, and a lot of nerve went a long way to supporting a young man's lifestyle in London.

He wished Miranda never had to know about all that . . . at least, not yet. Perhaps not until he'd had the opportunity to introduce her to Castor Worthington, inventor—a man of accomplishments, with a Royal Patron.

Usually his reputation preceded him, and made him all the more attractive, especially to those ladies looking to experience life on the undomesticated side. Miranda didn't require a rowdy life. She was starving for *life,* just plain, ordinary, go-to-the-opera life.

Cas leaned back in his seat and enjoyed her rapt profile, happy to oblige.

Afterwards, as they walked down Pall Mall, greeting a

few people and nodding at a few more, Miranda turned to regard him in surprise.

"You know everyone!"

He shrugged. "I am Worthington. We've been around forever. My father likes to claim that our name is as old as Stonehenge. "

She frowned. "I thought names of that time would be names of work, like Tanner and Sawyer and Smith."

"I think he means to be fanciful." He laughed. "And, since I've never met a Worthington who worked, that would leave us out completely!"

She smiled but her brow still wrinkled. "I thought you were an inventor?"

Cas was surprised. Had he mentioned that? Poll had, most likely. "My brother and I tinker endlessly." He wanted to keep the news of Prinny's support to himself until he'd actually gained it, so he grinned as he glossed over his true dreams. "I suppose if we wished, we could open a shop of sorts, toys perhaps, but then we'd have to be there and sell things and count money." He shrugged. "Dull." He swung her into his arms. "Would you step out with a shop-keeper, Mira?"

She smiled shyly up at him. "I would step out with you if you were a tosher down on the docks."

Cas pictured himself poking through the river mud, salvaging the trash and lost items off the ships coming in and out of port and shuddered. "Not me. I prune fiercely."

She gave him a little push as she laughed. Cas was delighted with her spontaneous touch. She'd spent the evening sitting most decorously far from him and even as they strolled, she'd not snuggled even a little, though the night was cool.

He caught at that hand, palm open on his waistcoat and pressed it there. "There you are. I've found you."

She tugged at her hand slightly, casting her gaze about.

A little line of worry appeared between her brows. "Mr. Worthington, please. People are looking."

Cas shook his head with a smile. "Mrs. Talbot, you are a grown woman, a widow, not an unaccompanied miss. The hand stays with me."

She sent him an exasperated glare and tugged her hand hard. Surprised at her force, he allowed her to escape.

"Mira, why are you so afraid?"

She lifted her chin and intentionally misunderstood him. "I am not afraid. You are with me."

He stopped walking and faced her, folding his arms and frowning down at her. "You are afraid of everything. You are afraid that someone will see. You are afraid that someone will—what?—talk about what they see? And then what will happen? The world will crack in two, because a person is telling another person that Mrs. Gideon Talbot let a gentleman take her hand in a deserted park?"

She looked away. "Do not mock me."

He narrowed his eyes at her. "Coward."

She turned on him furiously. "I am no such thing!"

Cas cupped his hands around his mouth and shouted into the night, "Mrs. Gideon Talbot is a coward!"

"Stop that!" She gave him a real push, this time. Two hands in his belly, making him grunt with the force of it.

"I am not a coward! I am a lady!"

He laughed, rubbing at his abdominal muscles with one hand. "Why?"

"What?"

"Why are you a lady? There's no one here but me."

She drew herself up. "I am always a lady."

"You weren't a lady that morning you let me into your bedchamber."

This time when she came at him, he was ready. He caught at her wrists and pulled her close, holding her hands wide. "I think you're a child, hiding out in your playhouse, hoping no one finds you out."

Her eyes flared and he wondered why. Had he struck a nerve?

She went very still. "I am not a coward. I am not a child. I am an independent woman of means."

He was a Worthington. He couldn't resist. "Then prove it." He released her and stepped back. "Go on. Stop being a lady for three minutes entirely."

She stayed where she was, though she let her hands drop to her sides. "I—"

She had no idea what to do, did she? Cas found her inability to create mischief adorable—and a little heartbreaking. *Who frightened the life out of you, Mira?*

Casting a glance down the path, he saw the fountain and had an idea. "A lady would never wade barefoot in a public fountain."

She looked askance at the falling water. "Never."

He knelt before her. Biting her lip, Miranda allowed him to take her foot in his hand.

A big warm hand wrapped about her heel, while the other slid up her ankle, then her calf, then kept going. All the while, his green eyes stayed fixed on hers, promising hot reward for her boldness. Sweet shivers traveled up her spine.

She barely felt her shoe slip from her foot. What she did feel were his warm fingers untying the garter tied just above her knee. With a practiced touch, he rolled the fine-knit stocking down until it fell in a warm coil about her ankle.

Then both her feet and legs were bare beneath her skirts. She felt wickedly naughty already and she'd not stepped toe in the water yet.

At his challenging expression, she turned her back on him and stalked to the fountain. Settling herself most demurely to sit on the edge, she swung her legs over to the other side, keeping a careful hold on her skirts.

The water was icy at first. She felt for the bottom with her feet in the dark and then carefully stood, tottering slightly on the slippery tiles beneath her toes.

"There." She turned to face him triumphantly. "I've done—"

Just like that, her feet slipped on the scummy bottom and she went down, falling facedown into the water.

"Mira!"

Like a cork, she bobbed up at once, spitting mad. He reached for her but she slapped his hands away.

"Look at me! I'm soaked and my dress is ruined and—oh, this water is *cold*!"

He reached for her again, and this time she allowed him to help her out. Her black gown was soaked, though truly that was no loss. Her perfectly pinned hair was a mess of fallen, dripping tangles. She looked as disgruntled and awkward as a wet cat. He tried to keep a straight face; he truly did. Really.

There was no help for it. He laughed so hard, he had to lean his hands on his knees to stay upright.

She scowled all the harder, which sent him off again. Straightening finally, he swiped at his watering eyes and bowed his apology. "Mrs. Talbot, allow me to offer you my coat—"

"Well, bloody well hand it over! I'm freezing!"

He whipped off his surcoat and wrapped it around her. Oh, damn. She was like ice.

The hired hack still waited by the gate to the park. Cas swung her up into his arms, ignoring her scandalized protest, and rushed her back to the carriage.

Once there, he ignored the wide-eyed driver and stuffed her inside.

"Hurry, back to Breton Square!"

While the carriage rattled on, Cas took Miranda's hands in his. Her fingers were icy and her entire body trembled. "Damn it!" He wrapped her more tightly in his coat and pulled her into his lap.

The carriage rolled to a stop and didn't move again. Cas pounded on the small trapdoor above his head. The driver flipped it open.

"What the bloody hell is taking so long?"

"Sorry, sir. It's all them folks leaving the theaters. Can't wedge me way in."

"Damn it!" He settled back down next to Miranda. "I'm sorry, darling. I didn't think." He never did, neither he nor Poll.

She was fully shivering now, her teeth chattering like dice. "It's su—summer. How c—can it be so ch—chilly out?"

Miranda was beginning to feel decidedly odd. She shuddered so hard she felt as if her bones were clacking together. She huddled on Mr. Worthington's lap, wishing she could dig further into his warmth, no longer concerned about proprieties.

He wrapped his arms tightly around her, and took her hands in his again to warm them.

She could scarcely feel her fingers or toes. Without thought, she kicked off her sodden slippers and drew her feet up to his lap as well. He tucked her hands into his waistcoat to warm up and used his to rub at her icy feet.

The heat of his body began to seep through her skin, though she still shivered. She squirmed and turned her face into his neck, for if she could only get closer still . . . .

"Miranda." His voice was tight and strained in her ear.

"Hmm?"

"I—ah—"

She looked up, realizing that she was practically crawling up his chest. "Am I too heavy? Should I move?"

"Don't move!" He held her more tightly. "Please—if you squirm any more, I'm likely to embarrass myself."

Shocked, she went entirely still. She could feel it now, the stiffened organ pressing against her thigh. For several long moments, she hardly dared breathe.

Then, she sneezed, rocking deeply in his arms with the strength of it.

He gasped and his hand fisted around her bare ankles. "Miranda—" His voice was full of dark desire. His touch on her skin felt like fire and need.

Oh my. The seed of curiosity that had never been truly tamped out rose and stretched cat-like within her. She truly couldn't help herself. Pretending to pull her soaked neckline higher, she rotated her bottom in his lap.

There was a small lantern affixed to the inside of the carriage. With a flailing hand, he reached up to turn the key to douse the wick. The interior of the carriage plunged into darkness, lighted only by the streetlamps passing slowly outside.

However, the street was crowded with pedestrians and carriages alike. There were people only a few feet away from them.

The knowledge should have sent Miranda scrambling for the opposite seat. As she lay in the heat and security of Mr. Cas Worthington's arms, she thought she probably ought to ponder her indifference further—but she simply didn't care.

She wanted to be closer to him. Her last proper resistance disappeared when she thought of how he would feel against her, skin to skin, and how his warm hands would feel on her chilled breasts.

She undid the buttons of his waistcoat one by one. "I need to be warmer."

He clenched his eyes shut. "Mira, we'll be back to your house soon enough." Really, it was sweet—but entirely hopeless.

"No, we won't. This crowd will take hours to get through and you know it." She slid her hands beneath the weskit, seeking warmth, seeking strength, seeking him.

She truly was on the verge of being dangerously chilled. It was all in the name of good health. And he felt so good. His big body was hot and hard and she was so blasted cold.

She felt his body shudder beneath her, around her. "Mira." His low voice rumbled into her, setting off vibrations in unexpected places.

Tensing for his rejection, she waited, but he only wrapped his arms more tightly about her and rested his chin on the top of her wet head.

"Burrow in, Mrs. Talbot," he murmured. "I'll keep you safe and warm."

At his concerned tone and his protective embrace, Miranda's eyes abruptly filled. Had anyone ever in her life promised to keep her safe and warm?

And she was, both out of harm's way and no longer cold.

Closing her eyes, she pressed her damp face into his warm neck and let out a deep sigh. His arms tightened about her.

Gratitude filled her. If not for the dousing that forced her to cling to his warmth, she might never have given in to her desire to feel his hard chest once more, to feel cradled safe in his arms.

Most of all, she might never have acknowledged her own secret craving to press her body to his as he rescued her once more.

Her nipples throbbed, as hard as rubies in mingled chill and arousal. However, she'd never known a little chill to ignite the sweet, hot ache that grew between her thighs. It was the scent of him—a mingled perfume of damp wool and clean, aroused male. It was the solidity of his broad body and the strength of his powerful arms wrapped tightly about her. She allowed the melting, quivering awakening to fill her, to expand beneath her skin, Her blood heated, burning away the chill.

Miranda turned her head to rest upon his chest, over his heart. The deep, potent sound of his racing pulse rang through her like a bronze bell.

I want more. Heaven help me, I want it all.

He didn't know it, she was quite sure. The silence and darkness wrapped about them, keeping her secret for her. She could ache for him with no one the wiser.

They rode that way all the way back to Breton Square and home.

Cas left Miranda in the capable hands of her bossy little maid, Tildy, who shooed him from the premises with a hard look for any man who would be foolish enough to give her mistress a chill—and on a night with no rain yet!

Cas left reluctantly, for he knew Miranda was exhausted.

Their adventure was a first for Cas. Oh, he'd nuzzled a few bosoms while on wheels, but no woman had ever ridden quietly in his arms as if he were a shining knight rescuing her from a dragon's lair!

There was something different about her. Was it her eagerness or her naïveté? Except . . . Miranda wasn't naïve! She was a good woman, a kind and intelligent creature . . . with just a touch of naughty wench within. He'd felt her desire in her touch when she sought the warmth of his body. He probably could have seduced her right then and there, if he'd put a little muscle into it.

But he hadn't wanted that. He didn't want to see that

expression on her face, the one he called the day-after look, the one of mingled shock and shame and delight, tainted by the growing realization that he was on his way out the door.

And Miranda would be shocked if she knew him at all—if she knew what it was that he wanted from her.

She'd give it to you anyway. You know she would.

Yes, he did know it. She would submit with the same vulnerable, sweet generosity that she did everything, from dealing with her snippy butler to tolerating old Seymour's haughty puffing.

Cas had been alone for a while now, longer than he would confess to anyone, even Poll. He'd told himself that he was bored with all the women he knew, but in truth he had become very weary of hunting tigers.

Chapter Twelve

The next morning, Miranda received yet another letter from her sister-in-law, Constance Talbot.

"Miranda—

It has come to my attention that you are neglecting your duty to maintain the house in its original condition. In particular, it seems you are being somewhat cavalier with the ancestral treasures held within."

Ancestral treasures? For a moment, Miranda frowned, picturing secret caches of Egyptian booty stolen by early Talbot grave robbers. Then she realized that Constance was referring to the damned dogs!

"Twigg, you are a dead man," Miranda murmured.

"I hope this letter finds you more inclined to see to your responsibilities. I should hate to have to oversee matters myself—"

"Oh, no." Miranda's throat tightened. She'd have to allow it, of course. This was Constance's childhood home. Miranda could hardly ban her from it, as much as the notion might appeal!

Her fury at Twigg's betrayal boiled over, happily concealing the deep anxiety of the possibility of living under Constance's heavy thumb once more.

Striding into the hallway, Miranda let her head fall back. *"Twigg!"*

The butler popped up from whatever realm butlers frequented when not needed. "Yes, madam?"

Miranda regarded him sourly. "This is my house, Twigg. Mine."

Twigg took a step back. "Ah, yes, madam. This is your house."

She glared at him through narrowed lids. "Good. I'm glad we resolved that little question. My house. Not Miss Constance Talbot's house. Gideon—Mr. Talbot—left it to *me*."

Twigg nodded, paling slightly. "Mr. Talbot left it to you."

Miranda pinned the butler with one last furious glare, then turned away. "*My* house," she muttered as she strode away down the hall. "I bloody well *earned* it."

"Yes, madam." Twigg's voice followed her down the hall. "*Your* house."

When Mr. Poll Worthington called on Miranda the next afternoon, she greeted him with a relieved smile. "I am very happy to see you," she told him. "And that you are unaccompanied."

He tilted his head, his smile of greeting fading slightly. "Is Cas giving you any trouble, Mira?"

Miranda shook her head with a small laugh. "No, not trouble. However, this is all a bit . . . confusing. I preferred things the way they were, I suppose."

Her reply eased Poll's tension, yet he could not help but think that "the way things were" had been a little too safe and a little less than satisfying.

Before she was kissed by Cas.

Yet he was surprised and gratified when she trustingly

tucked her hand into his arm and turned to walk him back to her parlor.

Back to tea and conversation.

Poll truly enjoyed Miranda's company, and his admiration for her mind grew by the day, and he certainly found it refreshing that she required him to do more than simply rely upon his charm—but today he'd made other arrangements.

"Miranda," he laughed. "Wait, wait!" He took her hand and led her back down the steps. "Come with me. I'm taking you somewhere special!"

By the way her eyes lighted, he knew he'd been right to draw her out of her safe surroundings at last.

He waited with an expectant smile while she donned her spencer and gathered her gloves and reticule. Tildy was ready with everything, which to Miranda meant that her maid knew more about this afternoon's surprise than she did. This was irritating, yet intriguing.

A hack waited in front of the house. It occurred to Miranda that, aside from her opera-and-fountain adventure of the previous evening, she had left the house very little in the past week. Resolved not to allow herself to continue to wait around for her handsome callers, she laughingly took Mr. Worthington's proffered hand and stepped into the weathered hack.

Poll murmured some complicated directions to the driver, then settled back on the cushions next to her. "As the day is so fine, I told him we'd take the long way round. After so much rain, I thought it would be lovely to take a drive in the air."

Miranda leaned back in the velvet-tufted seat with him, realizing that the world was indeed summer fresh and gleaming.

They drove through Mayfair at a sedate pace until they

turned down a lovely small street lined with gracious old houses set impressively far from the street, though a few had gone a bit shabby with neglect. The hack rolled to a stop before one of them.

Miranda peered out curiously. "Who lives here?"

Mr. Worthington smiled. "I haven't the foggiest."

Miranda frowned at him, then squinted at the distant door. "I believe . . . oh, dear. I do not think they are at home."

Mr. Worthington vaulted lightly to the street and helped her out until she stood beside him, her brow still wrinkled in confusion.

"I don't understand. We are not making calls?"

Mr. Worthington reached behind the seat and tugged free a well-loved woven wicker picnic basket, latched shut.

Then he bowed, gesturing her up the walk of the deserted house.

"Come this way," he whispered, taking her hand and pulling her aside as she automatically made for the front steps. Hand in hand, they crept around the side of the house. Miranda felt like a naughty child, back when a simple scolding was the worst thing she had to worry about.

When they reached the back garden of the place, Miranda sighed in delight. The place was magical, a garden returned to the ownership of the fairies. Flowers bloomed riotously, weeds and exotic blossoms alike. Rampant ivy transformed a pretentious little copy of a Roman ruin into something quite charming. A cherub fountain sat askew, the sculpture looking down as if in contemplation of the green weedy liquid beneath, dotted with water lilies and Miranda would bet not a few frogs!

"Oh, this is wonderful! What an ideal picnic destination." She could not help but notice the privacy as well. Daring Poll!

He kept going through the garden, just when she would have stopped to spread the picnic on a patch of golden sunlit grass gone to hay.

"Oh no," he said, grabbing for her hand and tugging her onward. We aren't there yet."

Mystified and, yes, a little disappointed, Miranda let the wild garden go with one last longing glance and followed him back, back past the neglected kitchen vegetable beds with their tangle of onions gone mad, past the ivy-covered mews, long since cleared of the scent of horse. There was a wall and a gate, which led to the alley, a sort of private drive for the houses on this row, where the driver would exit with the horses and carriage to pull around front for the inhabitants of the house.

Beyond the gate, which Mr. Worthington nonchalantly forced open with a grunt, there was the aforementioned graveled alley and across the drive was a high wall, also green with ivy so old the vines were branches and the branches like great tree trunks. Mr. Worthington grinned at Miranda, his eyes alight with mischief—

And tossed the picnic basket over the wall.

Miranda drew back. "Mr. Worthington, what is on the other side of that wall?"

"A very nice place. You'll adore it."

She examined the wall doubtfully. It had to be more than nine feet high. "The person who built that wall doesn't seem to me to be a person who would be casual about trespassers."

He grinned and lifted one foot to place it on a low, horizontal vine. "It's an easy climb. You can do it, even in skirts."

She took a step back. "I like the garden. Let us have our picnic there."

"What?" He scoffed. "That weedy pit? Wait until you see. I know you love gardens. That's why I thought of this."

"But, Mr. Worthington—" She tilted her head at him, perplexed. "Why do you want to climb someone else's wall?"

He eyed the wall for a moment, then gave a careless shrug. "To me, a wall such as that is like a dare." He turned to bestow a beautiful smile upon her that she could only interpret as having criminal intent. "I dare you, Miranda," he sang teasingly. "Climb the wall. Just to take a peek."

She folded her arms. Despite herself, she was beginning to be curious about the other side of that wall. What if it were no more than another, larger deserted garden, where they might safely while the afternoon away? Or it could be a busy street with shops and she could stroll on his arm for all the world to see.

Or it could be something altogether new and wondrous and she would wonder for the rest of her life if she'd missed something new and wondrous because she wouldn't step up on an ivy vine.

Shooting Mr. Worthington a filthy glare, she dumped her reticule and gloves into his care and took hold of a vine just above her head. She put her foot on the first vine he'd indicated and climbed a foot.

It was all that easy, really. She had to reach down and toss a portion of her skirt over her arm, but as there wasn't a soul in sight, it didn't seem so scandalous at the time.

Soon, vine after vine, step after step, for it was rather like a bushy sort of ladder, her head rose high enough over the top of the wall to see what lay past.

"Oh my stars."

Mr. Worthington was right. The garden behind her was a weedy pit. This—this acreage of flowers and sculpture and emerald lawn and cunning plantings—this was a *garden*!

He popped up next to her on his own vine-ladder and

folded his arms across the top of the wall in satisfaction. "Like it?"

"I—" She couldn't help herself. She clambered up another vine-step, and then another, until she could sit atop the wall with her legs still dangling demurely on the proper side. She absently released her skirt from its tucked captivity and let it fall, forgetting it immediately in her awe. "I don't understand—how could this be in the middle of London and I not know about it?"

Mr. Worthington climbed up to sit atop the wall, dangling his legs on the decidedly illegal side of the wall. "Oh, it's a private garden. The owner doesn't want a lot of people stomping through it."

"But . . . but it's so lovely! The layout, the graceful proportions . . . those marble statues look as if they came from the Parthenon itself!"

Mr. Worthington pursed his lips. "Umm . . ."

Miranda leaned forward, holding on to a thick strand of ivy for balance. "I'm so glad you showed me this, and I do appreciate the sentiment, Mr. Worthington, but this is too grand! I wouldn't dream of violating someone's privacy this way." She caught sight of the picnic basket, lying on its side, still firmly latched, tumbled down the slight hill sloping down from the wall. "Oh dear, your basket! Perhaps if we went to the door of the house and explained, a servant could fetch it for—"

She slipped.

Chapter Thirteen

Clutching at the ropes of ivy did Miranda no good at all, unless it was what gave Mr. Worthington time to grab her wrist. One moment, she was sitting demurely on the wall; the next she was swinging from one wrist in midair, her skirts and her hair and her hat snagging in the bushy ivy that threatened to tear her apart.

"Hold on, Miranda!"

She looked up, struggling to see past her askew bonnet and her snagged hair. Mr. Worthington sat straddling the wall now, holding tight to a thick ivy branch with one hand and holding her by the wrist with the other.

"Find a branch with your feet," he told her. "You're fine, everything is fine. Just feel around for a good thick one."

His soothing, coaxing voice melted the panic from her spine, soothing the air back into her lungs. "Yes, of course, the vines."

A few moments later, she stood quite firmly on a hefty vine and had a good grip on another with her free hand. The only problem was, she couldn't climb up. Her skirts were twisted so tight about her, snagged firmly by the ivy branches all around her, that she couldn't hike them up to step upward.

She could only climb down.

She couldn't help sending Mr. Worthington a foul look. "If I didn't know better, I would think you'd planned this."

He grinned down at her. "You credit me with far more evil genius than I deserve. This is just random good luck as far as I can tell."

Good luck, my shoe! Muttering imprecations all the way down, Miranda descended her vine-ladder until she stood precariously on the small ledge of earth before the slope angled down from the bottom of the wall. "I've made it! You can let go—"

Mr. Worthington released her and jumped down. Of course, he immediately lost his balance on the brief ledge of damp ground, which gave beneath them both.

Miranda might have caught herself if not for her skirts, still twisted about her like stripes on a candy-cane. Mr. Worthington laughed uproariously as he rolled all the way down the hill. Miranda covered her head with her arms and held her breath—and yes, secretly giggled her way down the slope, feeling like a child.

They sprawled simultaneously at the bottom, flung out on the soft, green grass like discarded dolls. Mr. Worthington landed on his back, arms out flung, still laughing. Miranda rolled half across him, lying over his lap.

"A dream come true," Mr. Worthington commented with a breathless chuckle. "This must be heaven."

She slapped at his helpful hands and somehow unwound herself from her ruined, smashed bonnet, her crumpled, muddy, grass-stained skirts, and her tumbled hair, snagged and tangled with torn ivy. Despite the fact that she had never been a more ridiculous mess—no, not even when facedown in a fountain!—she managed to stand with some shred of dignity. Using that smidgen of poise, she gazed contemptuously down at her villainous tormenter.

"This—" She spread her hands grandly. "Is. All. Your. Fault."

It was a priceless moment. He actually started to look a little ashamed of himself.

It was too bad she laughed.

Having now broken the law most thoroughly, Miranda gave into Poll's reasoning that enjoying their picnic anyway couldn't possibly get them into any more trouble. Besides, he pointed out, no servants raced toward them with pitchforks, ready to drive them away. No one seemed to realize they were there at all.

Miranda began to let Poll's charm, lemonade, and cheese and pickle sandwiches ease her fears. It did stand to reason, he reminded her coaxingly, that being caught red-handed picnicking would seem to convince the mysterious owner that they'd not meant any harm by their rude invasion.

The old, clean horse blanket was a welcome shield between them and the damp grass. The sunlight, so missed for the last few days, glowed warm and soothing down on their bumps and bruises. She relaxed enough to lie with her head upon Poll's folded surcoat while he fed her raspberries.

The basket was almost empty of food, for Miranda had rediscovered her appetite recently, which Poll encouraged her to indulge. "You are too thin." He tickled her elbow with a long blade of grass. "Pointy Miranda. Have another Tildy-seedcake, Pointy Miranda."

She did, rebelliously licking her fingers clean of the sweet icing, then relaxing back upon her pillow with a sigh of replete pleasure. Their little glade was tucked between two great evergreens, with the high wall behind them. Before them was visible the uppermost windows ranging the back of a great house, but it was quite far away and Poll managed to quench her fear that anyone could see them from such a distance.

Forgetting about that danger, she tilted her head back and peered up through half-closed eyes at the blue, blue sky of summer, listening to the distant cries of the peacocks strutting about the great lawn.

"Miranda?"

"Hmm?" She rolled her head to regard her companion sleepily. His expression had gone quite serious, his green eyes as dark as the evergreens behind him.

"I wish to address something between us. I feel quite slighted."

Oh. He wanted to "talk"! Miranda blinked herself awake and sat up, curling her feet beneath her skirts and assuming a listening posture.

He watched her, amusement flickering through his serious demeanor. "You are entirely adorable, do you know that?"

Miranda looked down at herself in vague dismay, but she didn't find anything amusing, other than her general ruined disarray, which he shared, and which he had caused, so had no call to be amused by.

Frowning, she looked back up at him. "Which is it—adorable or slighting?"

He laughed softly. "Miranda, you never cease to amaze me with your directness. It is damned refreshing, to always know what you are thinking! So I will return the courtesy."

He tilted his head, regarding her seriously. "You kissed Cas."

"Oh." Miranda folded her hands in her lap. "Yes. Well, he kissed me—but I truly did think it was you, although I ought to have realized something was amiss when he—"

Poll winced and held up a restraining hand. "Please, spare me the excruciating details."

Miranda bit her lip. "Sorry."

"Do you think it is fair that my brother and I fight it out for your attentions when he has such a vast advantage? You have kissed him. You have not kissed me. It is oblig- atory that you rectify the situation before you can truly consider yourself impartial."

Miranda drew back and stared at him. "Mr. Worthing- ton, is this your romantic notion of angling for a kiss?"

He shot her an embarrassed glance, though a grin threatened to break through his somber mien. "I spent all of yesterday considering tactics. I decided upon applied logic." His smile flashed ruefully. "Is it working?"

Her own smile grew slowly. He was, without a doubt, completely endearing. And, despite her resolution not to indulge in any more kissing until she'd decided, she had to admit that he did have a point. Curiosity sank its claws in a little deeper. How could she make a sure judgment unless she had all the facts?

"Mr. Worthington, your reasoning is sound." She licked her lips and leaned closer. "I have heard your appeal," she murmured, "and I have decided to grant your petition."

His eyes flashed green fire and his jaw hardened. "I thank the court for its indulgence."

He leaned in as well, until Miranda could feel the sweet warmth of his breath on her lips. Yes, it was high time she kissed the *right* man!

"Oy!"

At the rough shout, they drew apart quickly to see a fel- low in gardener's gloves and a wide-brimmed hat stomp- ing their way, his features twisted in irritation. "What are you up to there? This be not a bedchamber, you wicked things! Get ye gone!"

Miranda scrambled to her feet, her heart thumping in alarm. Mr. Worthington, however, merely snatched up the basket and blanket in one arm, grabbed her hand with the other, and pulled her away. They ran like naughty children, snickering at their portly pursuer, who clomped after them in his heavy gumboots but fell quickly behind.

In the great house that had seemed oddly familiar to Miranda, two men strolled down an ostentatious and glorious gallery, one with gilded marble pillars and frescoed canopy ceilings.

One was a stout, older fellow dressed in all white with gold trim, but for his garish high-heeled shoes. George IV, Prince Regent and ruler of the British Empire, paused at one of the tall graceful windows to admire his garden. It was an excellent view, for the royal gardeners worked hard to keep it so.

How he longed to be out of doors. Summer was George's favorite time of year—a time of warm days and soft breezes, of lush growth and sweet perfume, of stirring blood and languid laughter, of lovers on a blanket on the grass, of trespassers fleeing the gardeners—

He squinted. "Who is that?"

His Captain of the Guard, a vast-shouldered expressionless force of nature whom George called "Wolfhound" in his head, and occasionally out loud, whipped out a spyglass and trained it on the distant couple. Wolfhound stared for a long moment—long enough for George to wonder if he might be missing something rather good—and then relaxed his giant shoulders and lowered the spyglass.

"No need to worry, Your Majesty." His voice was so deep, it sounded as if it rose from the bottom of a well. "It's only one of *them*. I can't tell which one—you know they both look like trouble to me."

"Ah." George rolled his eyes. "It's best to ignore it. Arrest only encourages them." The Prince Regent leaned one pudgy knee into the embrasure and squinted at the distant fleeing couple. "Yes, but which one?"

The captain lifted his brows. "Sire, I fear I cannot tell you, for I cannot tell them apart even when within arm's reach."

The Prince Regent made a small sound of disappointment. "Can you not? I find them nothing alike, myself. That—" He waved a hand. "—was the harmless one, I think."

The Captain of the Guard nodded. "Yes, Your Majesty. I shall take note. Ah, does that imply that the other one is . . . er . . . dangerous?"

George smiled slightly. "Does it indeed?" He peered one last time out at the landscape, wondering if the fleeing lady was as pretty as they usually were, then resumed his leisurely ramble through St. James's Palace with a sigh. "Spawn of Worthington."

Chapter Fourteen

Dream hands.

Hands both gentle and rough, both giving and demanding.

Hands, hot and tender, moving over my skin. Warm palm smoothing my arms, my shoulders, my throat, fingertips brushing tenderly over my cheekbone, pulling down my hair to veil us both in silken darkness.

I catch at those hands, sliding my touch upward. My fingers follow powerfully built arms, feeling the prickle of manly hair, caressing the bulge of biceps, the furrowed dome of a rippling shoulder.

Then on to a muscular neck, the crisp curl of hair on the back of the neck, the bristling erotic touch of unshaven cheek on mine.

His mouth, hot and sweet on my lips, on my throat, on my temple.

I pull him down atop me, loving his hard weight as he covers me, the way his lean, commanding thighs press my willing ones far apart.

I love him. I love . . . .

A sound like a broken sigh awoke Miranda, and she realized that she'd made it herself.

Rolling over abruptly, she pressed her damp and forlornly ready body down into the feather bed and buried a frustrated sob in her pillow.

Her body, always so obediently detached from any unattainable sexual wishes, was rebelling now. Her sleep each night was plagued with the touch and feel and taste of a man with green eyes and curling brown hair.

She only wished she could be sure which man she dreamed of.

If she knew which man haunted her sleep, then she would know which one she ought to choose, wouldn't she? It would be lovely to have the question decided for her thus.

That tiny, never-entirely-repressed voice spoke in her mind.

Why choose? You could have them both. They are twins. Likely they have learned to share.

Wicked, unworthy voice. Scandalous, depraved voice.

Yet . . . she was so very fond of Poll. On some deep level, she empathized with Cas. They both wanted her. Was she so wrong to wonder how to conduct affairs with two lovers? Would it be so terrible?

Yes. It was terrible. She wanted to kiss two men. Was she truly taking after her scandalous mother after all?

Mama had been beautiful—that glowing, vivacious beauty that had little to do with cheekbones or hair color. Mama *lived*. She'd lived so hard that she made others want to live hard as well.

Miranda was raised by her nurse, but she remembered a few occasions of watching her mother prepare for grand evenings with great fascination, almost as if she were observing an exotic bird preening in a menagerie.

Papa had been no match for his extraordinary, effervescent, self-indulgent wife. Her glittering radiance had kept him in shadow, until he virtually disappeared.

Helplessly worshipping his goddess Elise, subject to her every whim—even to the extent of ignoring her many affairs—Papa had beggared himself to please her. Then, when his own funds ran out, he had beggared the clients whose accounts he managed. His legal practice collapsed from within, and all became public.

Papa had gone to prison. Mama, with her choice of willing devotees, found a new wealthy worshipper and left with him for parts unknown. Word came years later that she had died of a fever in some tropical land.

Miranda imagined that her mother had passed on most attractively. She pictured her pale and beautifully languid end, as her limpid eyes turned beseechingly toward the heavens as she musically sighed her last breath.

Miranda had gone to her grandmother, who never let her forget how easily one's good name could be lost.

I am not like her. I am not.

Yet for the first time she felt a stirring of sympathy for the unfulfilled Elise—vibrant and expansive, wed too young to the wrong man and made wild with resentment at marriage's repressive constraints.

Miranda's grandmother had always blamed Elise for Papa's criminal acts, yet did Society not hold that the husband was the master, if not of his wife, then at least of his own fate?

All the more reason to avoid marriage entirely. Miranda brushed away this tangle of thoughts impatiently. She had two much more pressing problems.

She must choose one or the other.

Or neither.

Her eyes clenched shut against that unbearable notion and she burrowed deeper into the pillow.

She would choose. She would. She just needed a little more time.

And, perhaps, a single decisive dream.

* * *

Cas was finding his increasing obsession with Miranda quite disturbing. He needed a bit of time to think.

Except he couldn't think . . . not of anything but her. Miranda was everywhere.

He paced up and down Bond Street, staring blindly into shops, seeing only the way Miranda's dark, glossy hair fell across her sculpted cheek. He took a stroll along the Serpentine, absently dodging the obnoxious swans that inhabited the park. Her sea-green eyes shimmered at him from the water of the lake.

He strolled Covent Garden, which filled with quiet during the early hours, for the people who brought the theater district to life were still abed and would be long into the day. The white violets being lackadaisically peddled by a yawning flower girl only made him recall the creamy skin of Miranda's fragrant neck.

Mira.

The hour rang in a clock tower somewhere nearby, bringing Cas out of his reverie. It was now Poll's turn.

Cas's feet turned of their own accord, and he went striding back to Breton Square.

The exterior of Miranda's house gave Cas no answers to his questions. It sat there, respectable and stoic, mocking him for his burning curiosity. Was Poll inside the house?

Mira's eyes. Mira's lips. Mira's skin, hair, breasts. The twist of her waist when she turned—

Mira with Poll.

Though he'd told himself he only meant to pass by, Cas stayed, lurking in a doorway a few houses down the square, looking as nonchalant as possible with his jaw tight with tension and his hands fisted in jealous rage.

What was Poll doing to her right now?

Miranda's mouth, opening on a sigh as Poll's kiss deepened. Miranda's body melting against Poll's, her innocent willingness evident in her very suppleness.

This wasn't imagination; it was memory. His imagination simply put Poll's face in the place of his own.

That was excruciatingly laughable. Poll's face. *Their* face, the one and the same.

Cas had always enjoyed their impostor games before, or at least, had not cared. Poll was the one who enjoyed playing Cas. Cas, in his turn, enjoyed the trickery and the intricacies of keeping up with the fibs. He liked the fast talk, the patter that made people's heads spin and used their own doubts to confuse them.

Odd. He couldn't recall ever trying to float one of those chock-full-of-illogic moments past Miranda.

From the first day together, she had won his admiration with her artless honesty. His lies, like the galloping whopper that paraded as his essential civility, were those of omission only. In fact, he had been more honest with her than he'd ever been with anyone other than Poll.

And even then, Cas had for years lied to Poll with such ease that he sometimes worried for his soul.

Poll was the attentive one. Poll liked to cover all the angles before committing to action. Poll liked to assure himself of a lady's attention, sometimes at the cost of common sense.

Yet here Cas skulked, lying in wait before her home, common sense cast to the wind.

The front door opened. Cas drew back into the doorway until only a bit of his forehead and his eyes could be seen, just a faintly lighter smudge in the shadow of the doorway.

They were, of course, fully clothed. This didn't help.

His mad nightmares of lurid decadence could still come true behind closed doors, he had no doubt.

He watched Poll help Miranda into her carriage, and then join her there. Cas's eyes narrowed. He knew perfectly well what two people could get up to in a carriage, right in the middle of the city!

When the carriage pulled away, Cas stepped from his hiding place. A hack was discharging a passenger half a block before him. Without taking a second to reconsider the wisdom of his actions, Cas let out a shout and took off at a run to catch the conveyance.

Poll caught a glimpse of a running fellow out of the corner of his eye as the hack that carried him and Miranda turned onto another street.

Cas.

There was no point in telling himself he was mistaken. One knew one's twin, whether a yard away or a mile.

Cas, lurking outside Miranda's? Waiting for him? Why not greet him, then? Why wait until they were on their way and then catch another hack?

To follow, of course.

Cas was spying on him? Or them? Or was it only Miranda?

In any other bloke, such attentions might indicate deep feelings for the lady in question.

But in Cas?

Poll held the door for Miranda as they entered the orphanage she had told him so much about. He was a little surprised, to tell the truth. It wasn't much of a place, really. Someone had converted an old town house into a residence for dozens of children and a few caretakers.

After accompanying her into the building, he continued

the discussion they'd been having in the carriage. Miranda wasn't telling him something; he could feel it. "But I don't understand how it can be an orphanage in which many of the children are not actually orphans."

Miranda smiled at the young woman in nurse grays who came to take their things. Then she tucked her hand through Poll's arm and guided him through the entrance hall to what once was probably a parlor but was now the office of the headmistress, if that's what one called the matron of an orphanage.

"This is a special place," Miranda began. "These children are from a particular circumstance . . . one in which they are all equal no matter what their origins."

"But their parents have not passed away?"

Miranda bit her lip. "Some have. Some are . . . merely detained elsewhere."

She removed her hand from his arm and greeted the matron. Poll made nice noises—Callie would be proud—but mostly he looked about him, taking the place in. Miranda's reticence had fired up the old Worthington curiosity.

He tried to place what seemed odd about where they were. The place was not ideal for an orphanage in structure, with its large receiving rooms and probably relatively few bedrooms upstairs, so it must have been chosen for some other reason . . . perhaps the location?

Sometimes orphanages were run by churches, or in benefit to the children of the workers of some industry—but there wasn't a prominent church nearby, nor factories, though there were a few warehouses and drapers . . . but other than Newgate Prison, Poll could think of no other landmark nearby.

The prison . . . *detained*, she'd said.

His eyes widened. "These are the children of criminals?"

Miranda hushed him with a hand on his wrist. "We prefer the term 'incarcerated.' "

Poll blinked. "Yes, because they're *criminals*."

Miranda pressed her lips together. "Whatever their parents have done, it is hardly just to hold it against their children."

"Isn't it?" Poll looked around him in alarm. Were any miniature criminals sneaking up on him?

Miranda gave him her shoulder and plainly ignored him while she spoke to the matron. Poll wandered to a window overlooking the side courtyard of the place. Several children were tending what looked to be an old rose garden, gone to weeds long ago. They all worked willingly enough, it seemed. Poll himself never would have stood for it. He'd have been over that wall and off to great adventures, only to come home late and hungry. . . .

But this wasn't home for them, was it? This wasn't a place with an indulgent mother and an exasperatedly affectionate elder sister. This was merely a safe place to stay, until . . . .

Until when? Poll knew enough about the prison system to know that of the people condemned to Newgate, the ones that came out alive—the ones who did not fall prey to violence or disease within—were much changed. What would it be like to wait and wait for your parents or parent, to wait for years, in a place like this one, never knowing if whom you got back would be whom you lost?

Discomfort roiled within him. Poll rubbed the back of his neck. He and Cas broke the law on nearly a daily basis. All small things, of course. Stealing onto palace grounds. Racing through the city on "borrowed" mounts, only to return them happily weary to their stalls, sometimes leaving a mysterious note of thanks. Climbing in and out of windows to reach their ladyloves.

Poll flinched a bit at that thought. He and Cas had

never been caught. The few times they were suspected, they always managed to talk their way free.

Yet what would happen to his own family if he or Cas were ever well and truly convicted of something? It would ruin Ellie and Attie's chances for a good marriage. It wouldn't do Dade any good either. Old family name or not, the Worthington clan didn't have the wealth required to make a little blot like a criminal conviction disappear from the family ledger.

Orion wouldn't care if it did not interfere with his studies. Lysander would only grow more saturnine, if that were possible. Callie . . . God, Poll shuddered to think what Callie would say, she and her scarred husband. Broken and battered the fellow might be, Poll had never mistaken him for anything but dangerous. Dade had confirmed that judgment, telling the tale of how Ren Porter had rescued Callie from a great brute of a kidnapper, downing the giant with only his rage and his bare hands.

As Poll watched the garden, a little girl, hardly more than a toddler, with golden hair and a smudged face, looked up at the window and caught his gaze. She stared at him for a long moment, then ran her wrist under her nose to wipe away the running of it.

The motion reminded Poll forcibly of Attie.

God, what would Attie do if something bad were to happen to him or Poll? They were the only ones in the family who truly understood her. If they went away, she would be left with Ellie's impatient care and Orion's cold tutelage. The effect of Zander's darksomeness didn't even bear thinking about.

It didn't occur to Poll to include his parents in Attie's list of caregivers. Archie and Iris Worthington lived in a world of their own, drifting about Worthington House like colorful ghosts, muttering Shakespearean sonnets or splattering paint on the furnishings, but never, ever taking responsibility for anything.

And what of poor Ellie? If the blight of criminal conviction fell upon the clan, Elektra, no matter how lovely, would be a spinster forever. Everyone knew that delinquency ran in the blood, although he supposed it might skip a generation, for his parents certainly weren't lawless. Odd, yes. Eccentric? They'd invented the word. But he was entirely sure they had never crossed a legal line in their odd, disconnected lives.

The little girl sat abruptly down in the soil she'd been tending, her gaze still locked on his. There was a question in her eyes, and Poll was terribly sure he knew what it was—what every orphan must think a thousand times a day. *Are you going to take me home?*

She reached out one hand, her pudgy fingers twiddling in a wave.

Poll felt a touch on his shoulder and turned to see Miranda smiling at him. "Would you like to meet some of the children?"

Poll frowned at the figure of tragic hope still hunkered down in the garden and shook his head before he had time to think. "No, I'd rather not."

She drew back, clearly disappointed. "Oh. Well." Her brow furrowed, then cleared. She lifted her chin. "I suppose you'd like to be on your way. I'll show you out."

Poll caught at her fingers with his, not caring if the matron saw. "Miranda, wait—"

She turned back, her expression a little wary. Poll smiled down at her. "Don't be so defensive, darling," he teased. "You'd think these little knee-biters were *your* children, the way you protect them!"

He knew he'd said something wrong the moment the words left his lips. Her chin lifted sharply and her eyes flashed.

"They are not my children," she said tightly with a challenge in her eyes. "They are me."

His brows shot up. "Don't be silly. You have nothing in common with the children of criminals—"

She pulled her hand away with a snap. "My father was a thief. An embezzler. He was an attorney in charge of several large trusts. When I was nine years of age, it was discovered that he had stolen every penny from their coffers and spent it on my wayward mother.

"He was caught and sentenced to Newgate. My mother fled the country with one of her lovers. I never saw either of them again."

Poll swallowed. "So you were raised in a place like this?" He found that hard to believe.

She went quite still. "No, though sometimes I might have wished I were. My father's mother took me in. She watched me like a hawk for any signs of criminal tendencies. Every day of my young life I spent living down the transgressions of my parents. I hardly dared sneeze, for she would find fault with the way I tendered my handkerchief."

It explained a great deal. Her shyness, her repression, her extremely poised and proper behavior, at least in public. That husband of hers, Gideon, had likely only made it all worse, conservative old stick that he was.

"Oh, Miranda." He reached for her hand once more, but she stepped away. He smiled coaxingly. "Don't think about it anymore. Let's run off to Hyde Park and loll in the sunshine."

She tugged at the wrists of her gloves, her jaw tense. "These children have never been to Hyde Park." She lifted her gaze to his sharply. "I wonder, would the world stop spinning if, just once, you did something other than play?"

Poll bristled, but only because the truth held a sting.

Miranda lifted her chin. "I think it's time to go." She

turned to the matron, who was practically hiding in a corner so as not to disturb them. "I shall come back another day," she told the woman. "Alone."

Poll did his best to charm his way back into her good graces on the carriage ride home, but Miranda merely bade him good day at her doorstep and did not invite him in.

Poll wondered if Cas were still watching.

His brother must be laughing out loud at the sight of Poll rebuffed at the door.

Chapter Fifteen

When Cas saw Miranda and Poll leave the building, he was torn between continuing his trailing of them and trying to discover what lay within those nondescript walls.

Worthington curiosity won out. Besides, from the distance between them when they left and the way Miranda had disdained Poll's hand on boarding the carriage, there would be no fond kiss good-bye today.

Cas considered a second question. He could continue to lurk, or he could simply walk up and knock on the door. Lurking had done him little good today.

The door opened on a small wren of a woman who peered at him in surprise. "Mr. Worthington! Back so soon?"

Cas nodded smoothly. "I found I simply couldn't go without taking another look."

Her brows rose a bit at that, but she obediently backed away and invited him inside.

Cas walked into the place and turned at once to take a long look around the entrance hall. The place had once been a fine if a bit ostentatious middle-class residence. In another decade, someone, probably a judiciary, had decided to make his home close to work—attending the court sessions at the Old Bailey, no doubt.

Convenient for his work, yes. Conducive to polite living? Perhaps not. Few visitors would wish to brave the surrounding areas by night, nor would anyone with half a brain wish to serve in a house so close to the center of crime and punishment in London.

Except, apparently, the woman before him. Cas lowered his gaze from the baroque cornice-work to contemplate the lady who had answered the door. "Please, tell me more about what you do here."

At first the woman spoke about keeping up the hopes of the children. Children? Cas kept quiet, since evidently he was supposed to know all about the children. He merely nodded, said "Ah" at the appropriate intervals, and tried to follow.

When the woman, who referred to herself as the matron, led him from the entrance into one of the receiving rooms, he saw that it had been converted to a schoolroom. There were books, poor ones, much tattered and used, and slates with chunks of chalk. Pinned on one wall was a map of England that Cas knew full well was at least three decades out of date.

The next room held odd things, like miniature looms and spinning wheels. "This is where we teach the girls their trades," the matron explained. "They'll have a much better time of it if they know they can feed themselves. It makes them not nearly so inclined to turn to—er—well . . ." She faded off, but Cas got her drift. Prostitution was a last resort for many girls who lacked other resources. It might provide survival, but it wiped out any other sort of future.

"What of higher forms of service?" he asked. "What of housemaids or even governesses?"

The matron—damn, was he supposed to know her

name?—stared at him perplexed. "Sir, there isn't no one going to hire a girl what's got criminals in the family to teach their children or shine their silver."

Criminals. These were the children of the inhabitants of Newgate, no doubt. "No, no, I suppose that wouldn't suit."

It did not escape him that the reason for this grim prediction had been caused by people who were not even here. Lawbreakers, and yes, probably a few perfectly innocent ones as well, who were a bit too busy trying to survive the stew within Newgate to worry over much for the welfare of those they'd left behind.

Cas thought uncomfortably about the many times he and Poll had defied the law, pushing their games right to the edge. They'd not been caught, nor ever charged with anything, but the idea that if they had—

Their sisters would be destroyed. Like the girls who worked these looms and spinning wheels in this cheerless room, they would be left with few choices. The icy chill that hardened in his belly like ice was only the first moment of understanding the true consequences of his past actions, but it was a start.

"Mrs. Talbot was one of the fortunate ones," the woman was saying as they left the trades room. "With her grandmother willing to take her in and getting that nice Mr. Talbot to wed her despite her past and all." The woman nodded stoutly. "She's a credit, she is. All the children look up to her so."

Cas stopped midstep. Miranda? He cast his gaze about the place, with its peeling paper and cracking plaster. Miranda had been a child like the ones here?

It seemed impossible, yet at the same time, it made perfect sense. Miranda, so circumspect at all times, unless he was bullying her into doing something outré for his own amusement. Her manner, so quiet, as if every thought must be examined and reexamined and then polished before it was allowed to be uttered, had been honed by a lifetime of trying to live down her family's ruined reputation.

Had old Gideon known? If he had, Cas's estimation of the fellow went up several notches. That had to be why Miranda never spoke ill of him, not even when she let slip something of her old life. Did she still feel grateful to the man?

"Sir, if you'll excuse my impertinence, but what the missus said to you . . . ."

When Cas failed to hide his blank lack of understanding, she gripped the sides of her apron in discomfort. "I'm sorry, sir. I didn't mean to overhear."

"No." Cas really wanted to know, and this woman was as good as a witness to his twin's relationship with Miranda. "Please, go on. I'd like to hear your opinion."

She blinked at that, but stopped wringing her apron so forcefully. "When Mrs. Talbot said, 'I wonder, would the world stop spinning if, just once, you did something other than play?' "

Ouch. The words, though they'd been uttered to Poll, held the same sting for Cas. "Yes?"

She fidgeted, so great was her distress. "Maybe it's not my place to say so, but Mrs. Talbot, she didn't mean anything by it. She's a good woman, real generous-like. And so proper, even after all she's been through. She is an inspiration to these little ones, I'll give you that. Shows them that having their family incarcerated doesn't mean they'll always be looked down on. I shouldn't want—well, ladies can be swayed by what their gentlemen think and all—I shouldn't want her to give up on this place."

Cas looked around at the great, drafty, shabby house and found it admirable, cracking plaster and all. "No," he said quietly. "No, neither would I."

* * *

Home at last. Miranda leaned back on the door she had just allowed Twigg to shut in Mr. Worthington's face and let out a sigh.

She hadn't meant to say anything. She'd only meant to show him the place that meant so much to her. He'd always seemed interested in her stories before—of course, that had been before the explosion in the alleyway, hadn't it?

Had he only pretended interest in order to get closer to her? Or had she thrown too much at him at once? She shook off a tide of combined hurt and regret. She hadn't handled the afternoon well—but then, neither had Mr. Worthington!

Standing before her still, Twigg cleared his throat.

Miranda opened one eye. "Yes, Twigg?" She hoped she was not in for another discussion about the insubordination of her carefully chosen staff. Heavens, she was weary of his insecurities.

But it was not Twigg she was to be dealt now.

"Mr. Seymour, madam. He called while you were out. He asked to wait, but after nearly an hour he took his leave."

Twigg looked a bit sour at the notion of having a visitor to tend to without his employer to view what a good job he was doing. "He left behind a parcel for you. I placed it in the parlor. I hope that is acceptable."

Miranda could not help a weary sigh. "Yes, Twigg, that is acceptable." *Yes, Twigg, you are the finest butler in the history of mankind. You are a genius, a beacon of high servitude, a legend in your own time.*

Knowing that venting her sarcasm would only wound him, she nodded and escaped his hovering by going to the parlor for the parcel herself.

"Oh . . . bother." A few moments later, she sat frowning down at the opened parcel in her lap in consternation. Now, what in heaven's name was she supposed to do about this?

Mr. Seymour, for some odd reason uniquely his own, had purchased her a gown.

What sort of man bought a dress for a woman without consulting her, making sure of her approval? Or even her consent?

The gown itself was fine silk, but it was of such a muddy green that the sheen very nearly looked to be slime. After pondering it for several long moments, it occurred to Miranda that the color had been chosen to match her eyes—if her eyes were the color of pond scum!

Her fingers found a note tucked into the folds. *My dearest Miranda—*

Presumptuous fellow. She had no memory of ascending to a given-name basis with Mr. Seymour.

I hope you accept this trifle in the spirit in which it is meant. I only wish to assist in speeding you from your mourning and back into the sparkling life you deserve.

Well, that was rather dear . . . and if she was not mistaken, precisely the same reason she'd been introduced to the great Lementeur. But that had not been Mr. Seymour's doing. This ugly silken offering assured her of that.

I hope that you will wear it for me soon, and often. I long to sit next to you in your parlor and consider you in my chosen raiment.

"Oh, dear."

It was odd, and inappropriate, considering that they'd only taken tea in this parlor a bare dozen times, and what was more, it seemed rather scheming.

Did Mr. Seymour assume the right to decide her wardrobe with this "offering"?

"Not bloody likely!" After the exquisite silks she'd had to chose from in Lementeur's salon, the gown made her actually shudder. She pushed it aside and stood.

She was most decidedly going to have to do something about Mr. Seymour!

* * *

When Poll returned to Worthington House, he hesitated before entering. He still felt out of sorts and restless from his blunder with Miranda. He knew that if Ellie started in on him, or if Dade gave him that ridiculous look of disappointment—ridiculous since Dade was only a few years the elder!—that he might just end up in Newgate himself!

Therefore, since whom he really had to avoid was Cas, it would be a good idea if he cooled off before he saw anyone. Instead of going inside, he ducked around to the back of the rambling old house by way of the mews and entered the old carriage house. This was where Dade and Callie had banished the twins' workshop when they were twelve and that truly inspiring experiment in lamp oil had taken a sadly wrong turn.

It still seemed like a good idea—a lamp oil in a solid form that would burn in a cake. It wouldn't spill when overturned and there would be vastly fewer fires but it had never quite gelled and there had been a great many fires. If his mood hadn't already been sour, it would have made him smile to remember Callie, barely sixteen, standing in the doorway of their smoking bedchamber, with her foot a-tapping with vexation.

Now it only made him twitch under the cloak of the weight of his family's ever-present . . . well, presence.

The mews consisted of the barnlike structure that held the carriage and the stables where lived the two elderly mounts who had taught all eight Worthington siblings everything they needed to know about lazy, stubborn, intractable mounts. Also residing there, side by side with the ancient nags, much to his evident equine bemusement, was Dade's rather lovely gelding, Icarus.

One really couldn't envy Dade his good fortune for possessing such a creature, for Dade had actually scrimped and saved and worked for him. The acquisition had taken years, what with the family's finances being, ah, unstable.

That was fine for Dade, but Poll still held out the hope that he would win a good horse of his own in a card game or at dice, so why bother scrimping when there were tempting waistcoats to purchase and good-natured barmaids to impress?

Except that he didn't feel like playing cards at the moment and he had lost interest in dandified attire and he hadn't so much as spoken to a barmaid in a month and a half. Was that all he was, in the end—cards and clothes and pretty, forgettable women? Was that all he was ever going to be? Was that all there was to look forward to, year after year of *playing*?

He rubbed a hand over his face, not quite sure what he should do with his unexpectedly serious existence.

I wonder, would the world stop spinning if, just once, you did something other than play?

With this thought roiling through his brain, it was no wonder that he opened the door of the workshop with a kick and shut it with a decided slam.

"Do you mind?" came a voice from one side of the doorway.

Poll turned to see Cas seated on a stool at one of the worktables, surrounded by lanterns and bent close over some sort of intricate drawing.

Once he would have pulled up another stool, eager to hear all about his twin's new idea. At that point, he would usually take over the drawing, for he had a knack for such things.

Instead, Poll turned his back on Cas and strode thoughtfully to the other, second-best workbench, the one with the wobbly leg and the grain so scorched and burned that it was difficult to write legible notes on.

There was nothing on the table, other than dust and the

odd wooden splinter from that unfortunately under-built guillotine trial. They'd be finding those fragments for years, no doubt.

He didn't have a current project of his own, at the moment. The last thing he'd made alone was the jouncing ball toy, and that had been more than six weeks ago. . . .

Yes. Well. He was beginning to see a pattern emerging that he truly didn't feel like facing tonight.

Well, he was here now and he'd be damned if he would leave in order to suit Cas! Just so he would look like he had a purpose and required the workroom just as much as Cas did, he lighted the last lantern and dug out a fresh quill and several sheets of paper.

Bloody hell. Cas had all the ink.

Poll took a deep breath. With infinite patience that practically trembled with rage, Poll put the quill away and found a stub of a pencil that he sharpened carefully with his penknife. It was no more than two inches long. When he wrote, it looked as though he were laying down lines on the paper from his own magical fingertip.

Damn. Damn. Damn.

With his jaw clenched, he commenced to sketch a box. It began as a simple one, just to be doing something, until he imagined that the edge had a graceful double curve and the top was inlaid with ebony and rosewood in a pattern that looked like . . . *ivy.*

Yes. Miranda would remember the ivy.

As he drew out the design, his rage faded, soothed away by his easy skill with the pencil. One part of his mind fiddled with the proportions and the curve and created a clever little secret compartment while another part of mind was lolling with Miranda on the palace lawn on a fine afternoon.

He didn't know if a jewel case was an important contribution to society—definitely not like aiding an orphanage—but it was pretty and it might make Miranda smile at him again.

Or he could allow her to remain upset with him—he could allow Cas the advantage, just this once.

To Poll's knowledge, his brother had never *lurked* for a woman before. Cas didn't lurk, or loiter, or even long. Women longed for Cas, not the other way around.

Yet there Cas had been, lurking outside Miranda's house, following them in the hack—and, if Poll wasn't mistaken, there had been a definite prickle on the back of his neck, the unmistakable sensation of being watched, as he and Miranda left the children's home.

Cas wasn't just competing with Poll. He wasn't simply attending Miranda out of boredom, or the hopes of an easy conquest.

Which meant, what?

Could it be? Could the infamous cocksman Castor Worthington finally have fallen in love?

Poll frowned down at his hands, allowing them to continue the work while his mind went round and round a single question.

If Cas were really in love with Miranda, if his twin had finally found a mate for his troubled soul—

Should he, Poll, stand aside?

On the other side of the workshop, Cas bent over the plans on his worktable and tried to ignore his brother's presence. He'd been working so well, too, before Poll's obnoxious entrance.

Once, having Poll in the room would have been of great benefit. Ideas always became ideas more exciting. Notions became drawings became reality, if not always functionally. Cas loved the process of working with Poll. Poll was the one who made truly fine pieces, for he was infinitely patient—once he was working, anyway—and would spend days perfecting the smallest, most insignificant part.

Cas was more often more interested in power than beauty. As he looked down at the plans of the machine he had come up with, he wondered how he was going to make it look appealing without Poll's help.

He ought not to need Poll for this. It was his idea and his alone. He wanted to do something, anything, to take his mind off Miranda. He was confused by his own actions today; first the avoidance, then the secretive pursuit. He'd never followed a woman in his adult life. He'd rarely even thought about one once he'd left her presence. Miranda had him tied up in twisted ropes of his own feelings and her lovely, generous soul.

She was, quite simply, astonishing. He didn't want her body—well, he did, but he didn't want *only* her body. He wanted to see the world through her cool, deep sea eyes. He wanted to immerse himself in her clean, unsullied soul.

But most of all, for the first time in his life, he wanted to be a different sort of man. He wanted to be the kind of man she deserved.

I wonder, would the world stop spinning if, just once, you did something other than play?

It didn't matter that she'd not said those words to him. He was no different from his brother. They had both forgone serious thinking at about the age of . . . well, always.

Does she believe that this is all I am fit to offer humankind? A handsome place card at a dinner, an amusing companion for an evening of cards, or drinking, or wenching?

It seemed a very small suit to wear, fit for a small man with a small world. It had choked him for some time. He had finally outgrown it, outgrown the need to flee the darkness within him with asinine, shallow pursuits.

Forcing himself to ignore the scratching of Poll's pencil from across the dead silent workshop, Cas rubbed a hand through his hair and narrowed his vision to the next line of his sketch and the next and the next. . . .

Chapter Sixteen

Far above their heads and carefully out of their sight, Attie perched in the rafters of the workshop and watched her dearest brothers split apart at the seams. The workshop was one of her favorite places in the world, as much as her book cave or her under-bed hideout or even Lementeur's Cluttered Cubicle of Coruscation.

She'd sat on those worktables a hundred times over the years, swinging her legs and gently guiding—or sometimes bellowing at the top of her lungs—her brothers to new and greater heights. They never actually credited her ideas as such, but she didn't mind. She had scroll after scroll of her own designs hidden in various nooks and crannies of the house. Someday she would create them all.

She was closer over Poll, so she lay down on her belly on the great beam and hooked her heels together beneath it to keep her balance as she peered at his sketch in the dim light of his single lantern.

It was quite pretty, and Attie always had a great appreciation for a secret compartment . . . but the ivy was boring. Why not a hunting scene? Or better yet, a battle scene! Vikings with broadswords, beheading hapless Britons—that would be much more the thing.

And jewel cases were just jewel cases, in the end. Of course, Miranda would like it, certainly, for she liked good pieces. Attie could tell exactly which pieces Miranda had chosen in her house and exactly which pieces had been there for ages and ages. It was like an Egyptian archeological dig, or like trying to sort out a room in Worthington House. Just layers of people and time and dust and more time.

Once Attie had found a mystery corner of a carpet in an unoccupied servant's room. No one had lived there for years, yet there had been a circular area of white fur embedded into the wool, just as if some large white beast had slept there for months.

The family had never owned a dog for as long as Attie could remember, although there were some cats mousing their way through the jungle of objects filling every room. Sometimes Attie would catch one and hug it until it stopped struggling, obviously deciding that tolerating her would get it freed sooner. They reminded Attie of Ellie that way.

But in that high attic room Attie pictured a secret polar bear, captured by her father on some long ago adventure and concealed there until he could present it to her mother for a grand wedding gift. Attie wasn't sure why she always imagined a wedding, but—white bear, white dress—it made sense, didn't it?

As she pondered the enigma of the great white mystery beast, she had risen to her feet and strolled easily down the beam as it if were a sidewalk and not a ten-inch-wide catwalk above a twenty-foot drop. It was dark, but she didn't need any light. She could, and had, performed cartwheels on these beams, though that had been with Cas and Poll holding a blanket stretched tight beneath her. The fall had been the best part.

Reaching the spot above Cas, she dropped down to

straddle the beam and leaned over, just as she had with Poll.

Cas sat in a great circle of bright light, so she could see his drawing very clearly. He wasn't the draftsman that Poll was, though that was mainly because Poll had more practice. Attie refused to feel any sort of preference for either twin. Such a thing, she felt strongly, was the first step to some great and terrible rift.

A rift like right now. Attie chewed her lip for a moment, feeling the tension in the silence like a tangible barrier down the middle of the room.

Tomorrow she ought to work on the Miranda end of the plan a bit more. It was time this nonsense ended!

"You ought to have more beaus."

Miranda looked at little Attie, who lay upon Miranda's bed with her head hanging off the edge so that their eyes met upside down. It was a rainy afternoon and they'd already had their fill of tea and cakes.

Sometimes Miranda wondered how it was that Attie never visited when her brothers were in attendance. However she managed it, Miranda was grateful that she could be Attie's obviously much-needed friend—and not just her brothers' . . . ah, whatever it was that she was to them.

She watched Attie closely without seeming to. "More beaus? Why would you say that?"

Attie rolled over onto her stomach and propped her chin on her fists. "You're pretty. You're almost as pretty as Elektra. She has scads of beaus, and she's only just out."

Since Elektra, according to her brothers and sister and even Button, was considered entirely breathtaking, Miranda dipped a little sitting curtsy from her perch on her dressing table stool. "Why, thank you, dear child."

Attie scowled. "I mean it. You could have lots and lots of lovers."

Miranda turned, for she'd been having this conversation via her dressing table mirror, to regard the child directly. "Attie! Goodness, what do you know of such things?"

Attie pushed back her tangled mop of hopeless curls and sent Miranda a worldly look. "I know all about it. Mama gave me a book. She said my body is my carriage and I ought to know how to drive it . . . or was it my body is my driver and I'm the carriage?" Attie shrugged. "Mama gets a bit turned about sometimes."

Miranda had heard enough about the elder Worthingtons to understand Attie's meaning. They must be entirely crackers, to let Attie roam the city unescorted—to let Attie leave her room unescorted, especially with her hair and clothing in such a state!

Today Attie wore a too-short, too-tight dress over a pair of boy's pegged knee-length trousers and clunky country riding boots two sizes too large, which had thankfully been left down in the parlor to dry by the fire.

Her hair . . . Miranda despaired of Attie's hair. She wasn't even entirely sure the mess was recoverable, it had been tangled for so long. She'd never so much as breathe mention of a brush, sensing that Attie would withdraw from her at once.

Miranda didn't want Attie to withdraw. She wanted her to come closer, so she allowed her to come and go at will, always ready with sugary tea cakes and a decided lack of censure, no matter how hoydenish she was. Like a lonely wild thing, Attie circled closer by the day.

The little girl missed her married eldest sister, Calliope, with a dreadful ache that Miranda could feel emanating from her in waves. Callie had been as much mother as sister. It was evident that while adored, Elektra was most thoroughly a sister, and Iris Worthington was rather more like a beloved but exasperating pet.

So Miranda set out to inspire little Atalanta by example. Even now, she ran her brush through her own gleaming hair, though it scarcely needed it.

Attie rolled off the bed and wandered over to the dressing table. "If you had a lot of beaus, you could go to balls every night. And carriage rides, and plays, and shooting."

She lifted the lid on Miranda's powder box and bent to sniff it. When she came back up, she had a white spot on the tip of her nose. Miranda smiled as she noticed the divot in her powder.

Moving casually and carefully, she picked up the rabbit fur powder puff and took a matter-of-fact swipe in the general direction of Attie's smidgen.

The fact that Attie didn't duck away or even scowl overmuch encouraged Miranda greatly. However, she had no intention of continuing this inappropriate conversation with a child, driver of her own carriage or not!

Turning on her stool to gaze into Attie's funny little face—heavens, the girl would be a stunner someday!—Miranda smiled kindly but firmly.

"My beau situation is none of your concern, little Miss Atalanta Worthington."

Attie screwed up her face. "Yes, it is."

Miranda tilted her head. "How so?"

Attie tilted her head in the same direction, mirroring Miranda. "If you marry a Worthington, you marry all the Worthingtons. And that is going to be very sticky for you, don't you think?"

Miranda drew back, stunned. "Attie, I have no intention of marrying a Worthington. I will never marry again. I'm sorry that you have been misled."

Attie examined her narrowly for a long moment. The child's odd intensity made Miranda squirm a little inside. Then Attie shrugged. "If you say so. I have to go now." She skipped to the door and then turned back.

"You are beautiful. Beautiful ladies really should have more than two lovers." Then she was gone.

Miranda was left sitting openmouthed. "I don't have any lovers. . . . I really don't. . . ."

Cas couldn't bear it any longer. He'd avoided Miranda for days—and she had not even realized it! It was ridiculous to stay away. He was only punishing himself, not to mention driving his own confusion and need to unmanageable heights!

After assuring himself that, yes, it was "his" night—and that Poll was otherwise occupied with helping Elektra dig through the chaos and madness for a litter of kittens that were keeping the entire household up at night with their yowling so that they could be moved to a nice warm box by the ovens—Cas allowed himself to do more than lurk.

No, the hunt had become a chase, except that Cas was not sure who was the pursued. He felt hounded by thoughts of her, of memories and fantasies still to come. As he neared her house, his pace increased. He actually ran up the stairs to rap on Miranda's polished brass knocker.

The butler took his bloody time answering the door. Cas spent that long moment imagining the scene within.

Miranda, dressed in another drab gown, her hair wound simply at the back of her head. His Mira, turning to greet him with a hesitant smile that made her beautiful.

In his mind, Cas was inside the room in an instant. In his imagination, Miranda was up against the mantelpiece in another instant, being kissed as if she were the last woman on the earth.

He remained frozen on the steps. Even as he fought the desire, and hunger, and aching, tormented longing that whirled in a tempest within him, Cas feared that for him, she just might be precisely that.

The very last woman.

When Twigg opened the door of the house on Breton Square, he found no one there.

On one hand, there is Poll. Darling Poll. He is romantic and playful, coaxing and charming. I feel youthful when I am with him, like a schoolgirl with her first suitor. My attraction to him has an innocence that I never had a chance to know when I was young.

He is someone I can talk to, share my thoughts with, someone who will listen and never belittle my oddest remarks.

When I wake each day, I look forward to seeing him, as I always did, before this mad competition commenced. Now, of course, I never know if he will sweep in with flowers and laughter and flirtation, or pull me along on an adventure and make me feel like a carefree child.

Poll had just about enough of interruptions, just when he was about to get his long-awaited kiss from Miranda!

When a Worthington became frustrated, it was time to duck.

In Poll's case, he'd decided that after genteel courtship and applied logic had failed him, the only thing left was to pull out all the stops. His plan was to sweep Miranda away on a tide of pure unadulterated romance!

Armed with poetry and a handful of stolen blooms from neighboring gardens, Poll waited outside Miranda's, keeping his patience as evening waned and night fell. At last he saw the light of a candle in the window of her bedchamber.

He'd spent his long wait well. Using the light from the sputtering streetlamps, he'd plotted every step of his climb. He knew her window, and he knew from conversing upon the weather that she rarely shut it entirely. Did she enjoy the cool draft stirring across her body, chilling her ivory skin?

He'd best not think on that. Climbing would be hard and dangerous enough without an erection. He'd feel a right fool for dying with newssheets shouting things like ERASED BY ERECTION! or DIS-MEMBERED!

The very real possibility of falling did much to cool his heated blood—there would be plenty of time for *that* once he got up there. He stuffed the bouquet into the front of his weskit and started up.

The climb wasn't so bad. From the railing of the steps, he could reach the ledge at the top of the first-floor window. There was a decorative stone detail over the door that gave his next foothold. Then it was a quick clamber up onto the classical portico over the front door and up to the next story window. The decorative stone ledge below provided his path. Two windows down from that was the one leading into Miranda's boudoir.

Very well, it was hard and terrifying. At any given moment he would not have given great odds of his own survival. He would definitely be leaving by the door, thank you very much.

Sliding his feet along side by side on the narrow ledge, he started to wonder what the bloody hell he was thinking.

Do I love her this much? Or do I just hate to lose?

Both? Poll decided it was both and continued the precarious journey down the ledge. *If I survive this, I promise a long life filled with good acts. I really do.*

At last he reached Miranda's window and leaned gasping on the framing for a long moment. Then, trying to look as though he'd merely dropped in whilst in the neighborhood, he began.

"Miranda!"

Her name came out a bit rough, probably due to the sheer terror lingering in his heart as he contemplated the sheer drop behind him. He cleared his throat and swept the bouquet high.

"Miranda! 'O heaven, O earth, bear witness to this sound—' "

The draperies were pulled back swiftly. The flame of a candle held high blinded Poll instantly. *Oh. I might have thought of that.*

Blind, he clung desperately to the stone frame of the window embrasure. "Ow."

"Cas?"

He blinked rapidly. "No. It is I, Poll."

"Oh, for pity's sake, Poll! You're going to fall to your death! Shift to your left so that I can open the window!"

Poll slid one foot, then the other, thinking that the phrase "dying for love" was just about the stupidest thing he'd ever heard.

The window opened with a creak and he felt a rush of warmed air come from the bedchamber. Blinking, he managed to look past the fading glare in his eyes to see Miranda standing before him in her dressing gown with one hand outstretched to him.

"Let me help you in," she urged. "You idiot."

Poll, who had been quite willing to crawl into her room and lie quivering on the floor for a while, instantly rediscovered his spine.

Instead of putting his hand in hers, he thrust the admittedly less-than-fresh bouquet into her hand.

O heaven, O earth, bear witness to this sound
And crown what I profess with kind event
If I speak true! if hollowly, invert
What best is boded me to mischief!

Poll wobbled a little on the sill. Miranda, who had begun to smile at his antics, gasped and clasped the bouquet close in alarm.

Catching himself, Poll valiantly went on. " 'I / Beyond

all limit of what else i' the world / Do love, prize, honour you.' "

He finished with another flourishing bow, this time leaning into the room, by God!

Miranda looked an adorable combination of worried for his sanity and secretly thrilled. Poll grinned at her. It was a combination he could work with.

"Pray, a kiss for my labors?"

Miranda frowned at him and threw her hands wide in exasperation. "Then will you come in off the windowsill, you idiot?"

Poll wiggled his eyebrows. "Kiss me and find out!"

She made a frustrated noise, tossed her bouquet down on a side table, and advanced on him. Poll grinned in satisfaction—that is, until she fisted both hands in his surcoat and dragged his mouth down to hers, even as she yanked him into the safety of the room!

Chapter Seventeen

Cas knew they imagined themselves invisible, for the room behind them was dimly lit and the hour was very late. He knew his brother had not accounted for the glow of candlelight behind them, nor of the shimmering incandescence of Miranda's beautiful skin. Poll most certainly could not have dreamed that someone might be standing in the park below, someone who happened to be carrying on his person an expandable spyglass.

Through it, Cas saw every smile, every shape her lips formed as she received Poll's ludicrous performance. *I could have recounted Ferdinand's speech to Miranda. I know that damned play backwards!*

He saw Miranda take the flowers. He saw her reach for Poll.

He saw Poll fall upon her for a long kiss, and then another. Then the two of them turned away into the darkness of Miranda's bedchamber.

How he wanted her. Even standing there astonished at his own voyeurism, he wanted her. He wanted to be the one falling hard into her bedchamber. He wanted to be the one she dragged down for a deep kiss.

Cas clenched his eyes shut and his hands into fists.

She had first been Poll's. Cas ought to have known he could not wipe those weeks of advance courtship away from her mind.

He forced himself to turn away. He would not wait, would not watch, would not *know*.

Two steps later, he turned back, unable to leave. The ache for her grew the longer he watched. He was breaking his word being there, was breaking the very law by peering into a lady's bedchamber, yet he stayed.

Poll fell willingly into Miranda's room, his arms already going around her, catching them both before they ended up on the carpet.

We'll get to you later, carpet.

He pulled her close to him and bent his face over hers, his mouth on her soft one.

Hmm. Umm. Well.

It must be his close call with Death on the Cobbles that was interfering. *Get your mind off your own funeral!* He cleared his throat and went in again.

This time she tried harder as well. She parted her lips, although he felt her flinch when he slipped the tip of his tongue between them.

Her body stiffened. Alas, his body, despite the weeks of anticipation, did not.

Er. Ahem.

He pulled away from her and straightened. His mouth felt decidedly odd, his body completely uninvolved, his libido running in the other direction. It was almost as peculiar as if he'd mistakenly kissed Callie or Elektra.

However, he would never upset Miranda by letting on for one moment that he found her anything less than devastating.

Forcing a smile that he feared resembled a manic smirk,

he bowed deeply once more. "Thank you, my lady! I could not have asked for more." She'd tried, poor thing. She'd really given it a go. It wasn't her fault that he had lost all interest in her charms.

"Yes, well . . . you're welcome." She returned his smile with a vaguely bewildered crease between her fine brows. "Ah, it is very late, Poll."

He bent his head. "Of course! Absolutely!" After that alarming revelation, he couldn't get out fast enough, truthfully. "Ah." He gestured at the window. "Shall I—?"

"No, for pity's sake, Poll! No need to take that absurd romantic notion any further!"

Well, no, that was obvious—although not very nice of her to say so. Still, he was deeply relieved to be able to leave like a man and not a monkey!

He politely ignored her swift puzzled touch to her lips as she turned to walk him to the door. A gentleman ought not to notice such things, after all.

Carved into granite stillness by his longing and his jealousy, Cas waited in the dark long after Miranda and Poll had turned from the window and left his view. He waited until he saw his brother leave the house by the front door and trot wearily down the steps.

Cas waited until the last candle went dark, until the last servant went to bed.

The night settled upon the street again and still he waited in a dark so complete that he felt blinded by it.

On the other hand, there is Cas. By turns maddening and breathtaking, he twists my thoughts every moment I am with him. He is exhilarating.

I think of taking him as a lover and the notion thrills and alarms me. Will he overwhelm me with the strength of his need and challenge me to admit the power of my own? He sends my head spinning and my heart leaping and my body—sweet heaven, what he does to my body!

Miranda sat at her dressing table, running her brush through her hair. Even to herself in the mirror, she looked confused.

I do not understand. She closed her eyes briefly. *I fear I have ever understood nothing.*

A kiss was a kiss. One man kissed her and she melted. Another, identical man kissed her and she congealed.

Well, that first kiss was a long while ago. Maybe I've lost whatever aspect that existed then. Perhaps I would not like a kiss from Cas now, either.

Somehow it didn't seem likely.

When a tap came at the bedchamber door, she called, "Come in," without stopping to think.

A heavy tread on her floor made her turn around in surprise. She gasped at the large shadowy form in her dim room . . . then gave a shaky laugh. There was no ready smile, no easy laugh. *Cas.*

Her heart leaped. She pretended to ignore it. "Mr. Worthington, you startled me."

He tossed down his hat and pulled his coat from his shoulders to drape over the chair by the fire. His movements seemed odd, deliberate. A shiver went through her belly at his strangeness. Was he . . . angry?

She stepped back a tiny step and then another one. "Mr. Worthington, why did my manservant not take your hat and coat when you entered the house?"

He slid his gaze away. "I didn't see him."

She swallowed. "You let yourself in? That was a bit presumptuous, perhaps?"

He turned to face her. His handsome features were set,

unsmiling. "Am I wrong?" He moved toward her. "Am I unwelcome?"

There was an edge to his voice. He seemed larger than his brother somehow. He came closer still, slowly stalking her across the carpet. Her back came up against the wall next to the window. He kept coming.

"Mira, I have waited long enough." He reached out and slowly pulled at the belt of her wrapper. "I want to see you."

The heat coming from his large male body was beginning to weaken her knees. Mr. Worthington obviously had a bit of a dark side.

Her heart raced. Her mouth went dry. Terror made her belly shiver—except it wasn't terror at all. She made no move to stop his untying.

When the belt fell away, he slowly slipped the wrapper from her shoulders. It pooled at her feet. She now stood before him in her lacy nightdress. It was a mere wisp of a gown.

She'd received it from Mr. Button last week and had also been given several other things that maidens had no use for and wives needn't bother with. This gown was made for seduction, filmy and fine and barely there. It clung like spiderweb to her skin, leaving nothing to the imagination.

His jaw clenched to see her in it. "You look like a courtesan."

She reveled in his reaction. She inhaled strategically. "Yet I am not for sale." Goodness, she was becoming quite the seductress. How interesting!

He reached out to brush her hair back over her shoulder.

"Mr. Worthington, what are you dong here?"

He twitched slightly, shaking his head as if shaking off a dream. Then he turned away. "My apologies. I don't know what I was thinking. I shouldn't have come."

She stepped forward. "Tell me, sir, what of your mood this evening? I would know what it is that has made you so angry."

He looked down at his hands. "I'm not angry."

She folded her arms. "No, you are furious."

He didn't try to deny it again. Instead, he gazed down at his hands. "Empty," he murmured. "Why didn't I bring flowers, too?"

Miranda went very still. "How did you know Poll brought me flowers?"

Startled, he cast a glance about the room, but she'd not kept the tattered bouquet at all, for it was a strange and uncomfortable reminder of that very odd kiss. Since he could not easily gesture toward the invisible flowers and declare himself merely observant, she knew that he had watched Poll arrive.

She lifted her chin. "Did you see him climb the wall?"

He shot her a glance like green fire. "Yes."

"Ah. Did you see him recite *The Tempest* to me?"

His jaw worked. "Yes, damn it."

"Did you know that I hate that play? Prospero is a bully and Miranda is a twit."

One corner of his mouth twitched. "Such vehemence."

She snorted. "What if your name were Ferdinand? How would you like that?"

He lifted his head to fix her with his eyes like gateways to a deep and dangerous forest. "Then you would have loved me at first sight." Surprise crossed his expression, as if he'd not meant to say any such thing.

Her heart stuttered at the aching depths behind that arrogant facade, clearly visible to her. How could the world not see how he burned, how he writhed within, how he fought back the pain with all his might and mind?

"How do you know that I did not?" The whisper escaped from her lips before she could stop it.

He drew back from her, from that confession, physically stepping back from the words that hung in the air between them.

"No." The word slipped from her mouth in a whisper, a shout from her soul to his. "Stay."

Cas closed his eyes at the word. He was not that man. He did not stay. He never stayed. Miranda would learn soon enough that he only broke hearts, not awakened them.

He would likely destroy her, for she was no jaded Society woman, accustomed to a string of lovers just to interrupt the tedium of the rich and idle. Miranda was good and genuine, a creature of sincerity and decency.

She was doomed if she fell in love with him.

He was damned, for he didn't care. He ached for her as he'd never ached before. Before he could stop himself, he reached for her, his hands closing over her shoulders as he pulled her close to press against his body.

A startled sound escaped her lips before he covered them with his. He fell, hard and spiraling, into the wet, sweet wonder of her mouth.

Miranda's mouth had powers the like of which he'd never known. Kissing Miranda felt like flying, like falling, like spinning out of control and never wishing to land.

Miranda's mind went dark with the shock of her complete and total arousal as his hot mouth took ownership of hers.

A kiss, it seemed, was not simply a kiss, after all.

That was her last coherent thought as Cas pressed her back hard against the carved bedpost and kept her pinned there with his big body as his hands swept over her, spreading, kneading, pulling, and invading as his mouth ravaged hers.

She could only gasp and cling to his weskit as he stripped her nightdress from her, rendering her naked against his clothed body. He held her there, the kiss going on and on, as his fingers slid down between them and found her slit.

No one had ever touched her there but herself. Even her husband had meticulously kept his hands to himself, gingerly positioning himself without touch.

Cas did more than touch. He delved, he stroked, invaded, all the while his tongue and lips took her mouth, nibbling, sucking, driving her onward so forcefully, she fought for breath, fought for sanity, fought to give back to him—until she abruptly melted into him, yielding completely to his skilled and unrelenting stimulation.

She had mounted this runaway stallion with a single word. With her capitulation, she devoted herself to riding him out, taming him, subduing him with her very surrender.

Immediately his urgency slowed. His hands turned to ease and warmth, his mouth gentled, though he still owned her lips and tongue with his.

He allowed her to move away from the cold, rigid bedpost and lay her down upon the bed. At last he pulled his mouth from hers, but only long enough to strip off his clothing.

She watched his body emerge as she lay quivering, unbearably aroused. He was beautifully made, from his narrow hips to his wide, rippling shoulders. His skin gleamed more golden than hers in the candlelight, sunlight to her moonlight, smoldering heat to her cool glow.

His clothing a pile upon the floor, Cas turned back to find Miranda demurely curled up on the coverlet, tugging a fold of it to cover her breasts, her tucked-up legs attempting to hide her furred mound. Cas ached at the sweet shyness of her, though he knew her to be wet and ready for him.

When I am through with you, Mira, you will flaunt your lovely body like the jewel it is.

When I am through with you.

He would be through, probably soon. He would leave her behind, likely devastated and shattered at his betrayal.

He didn't care. He had to have her and he had to have her now.

He wanted to be a gentleman and ready her, to gentle her into her own arousal, but he'd been hard for hours thinking of her.

He rolled her over in one motion, parting her thighs with one knee, spreading her wide open with the other. Wider, until her lips parted in surprise.

"Darling, I—"

He kissed her hard, before she could utter a protest he would have to heed. His erect cock jutting hard forward, it took only a slight motion to center himself in her wet heat. He drove his cock into her, forcing himself slowly into her soft, damp body.

She gasped into his mouth and writhed under him, around him, impaled and helpless as she clung to his shoulders.

Yet she did not stop kissing him, did not pull away to let a breath of protest pass her lips. He loved her so at that moment, loved the depth of her willingness.

He left her lips and raised himself onto his hands, tried to give her a moment to adjust to the length and width of his all-night erection, but she kept twisting and writhing against him. She wanted more, wanted *him*.

The surge of possessive lust had him withdraw sharply and thrust hard yet again. She keened and panted and let her nails bite into the skin of his shoulders. "Please . . . again!" she gasped.

His amazing Mira. He drove himself into her again, then a slow torturous withdrawal that had them both groaning, followed by a single plunging thrust that made them gasp with the intensity.

She turned her head and bit his wrist. "Again," she begged.

He did, again and again and again. The bed shook with the force of his thrusts. She whimpered with each torturously slow withdrawal. Each one was met with her heated, writhing response. She begged for more, pleading with him to go faster but he refused. He wanted to stay inside her forever and he knew that once he reached orgasm, he would have to dress and leave—leave so that Poll could come back in a few hours.

He kissed her hard, silencing her. She whimpered into his mouth and dug her nails into his skin. On the next deep, hard thrust, she came, hot and tight and throbbing around him—

Need swelled within Cas. He could not bear such need. The only way he knew to conquer it was to conquer her.

She wasn't passive. No, she was an eager and ardent participant in her own transformation. Once sweet and naïve, she was now a wild creature in his hands.

Yet he had yet to reach the limits of her openness, of her honesty. What she wanted, she did not hide. Instead, she reached for it, for him, with her arms open and that smile in her eyes.

And he could not get enough.

There must be an end. She must have a limit, a rule, a distance that she would not journey. Cas knew if he met that distance, then his obsession with her would ease and wane.

He felt the urge to push her onward. He wanted to press her, even as he stood in awe of her, even as he feared that wonder within him. If her open being had no walls, no bottom, no limits—might he simply fall forever?

She sighed, inhaling as another shudder racked her body. Her eyelids fluttered as she rolled her head on the pillow. Then she opened her eyes of endless sea and stared at him in wonder.

Her smile ruined him.

He moved over her, into her, feeling her body give before his. With one hand he wrapped her braid around his fist until her head dropped back, exposing her long neck. He took a small bite of that neck, worrying her with his teeth until she sighed a whimper.

Hovering over her lips, his fist tight in her hair, he growled, "Mrs. Talbot, we have only begun."

She turned to warm wax in his hands. Her acquiescence whispered across his lips in a wordless sigh.

It disturbed him. Memory seared him, the sight of her pulling Poll through the window. Madness burned hot through his blood to think of her in Poll's hands.

The window . . . it was a dark and unworthy thought, to put her on display, to claim her before the world. Yet he could not help himself. He lifted her damp, quivering body into his arms and carried her across the room, ignoring her sound of inquiry.

When he pinned her to the window, feeling her shiver at the chilly glass, feeling her tremble at her wicked exposure—he thought surely then that she would draw back from him. Miranda was a lady, a respectable woman regarded well, if indifferently, by Society.

If even one person outside saw her, she would be an instant scandal. The thought of this ought to have made her pull away, to refuse him.

Miranda was no more. Her mind was lost in the wild storm of sensation and emotion pouring into her body from Cas, from his hands, from his scarred and lonely heart, from his body, from the slick hardness of his cock inside her.

Her eyes were open, but she did not see the night city stretching out before her. She had no thought of the park or the square, or of passing strangers that might have business there in the middle of the night.

There was no one in the world but Cas. Cas within her, behind her, around her.

His need overwhelmed her, carrying her own off in the pounding tide of his yearning, his lost, dark craving for her.

Beautiful, pitiless, furious Cas. Lost, aching, wounded Cas.

She knew nothing about the cause of the gaping tear she felt in his heart. She only knew the sensation of being the recipient of that wicked, storm-tossed desire—and knew it for the desperate grasp of a drowning man that it was.

Cas drove Miranda onward, but she continued to absorb his worst, to receive each deep plunge of his cock as if it were a caress.

So lost in the aching sweetness of her hot, willing body, he ignored the fear, turned his back on the terror that, perhaps, just perhaps, he was not fooling her one little bit.

She had three orgasms while he kept her there, taking her on and on, harder and harder, until the power of his thrust vibrated into the glass itself. *See, world? Mine!*

She took his wicked torment until he couldn't bear it. Though he longed to make it last, his orgasm ripped through him, tearing a roar of satisfaction from his throat all unwilling as he thought of her waiting in the window, looking across the park—

At him.

He exploded into her with a pagan shout of ecstasy. Then her knees gave and she slid down the glass in a quivering puddle of hoarse and perspiring female. When he lifted her into his arms he could feel how the window had chilled the front of her body. Her breasts were tight and cold and her belly and hands too.

He placed her in her bed, alone. *I am not the man who stays.*

Yet she clung to him when he left her, holding his wrist, calling him by name.

Cas.

His name reminded him, chilled him, and strengthened his resolve. He pulled away from her, even fled her, striding naked from her bedchamber with his clothes in his hands.

He'd almost stayed in those sweet, willing arms. He'd almost forgotten the game, almost betrayed himself unforgivably.

He'd almost not cared.

Two men. One light, one dark. One rough, one smooth. To be surrounded by such wealth of possibilities, after all my years of airless, loveless despair.

A dangerous choice lies before me.

Yet I have already chosen, have I not?

Chapter Eighteen

Poll had raided the larder early in the morning for a hurried breakfast. He had not slept well at all. He had gone to bed last night trying to think of some new and fascinating way to end his courtship of Miranda.

The old method, the one that never failed—breaking the lady's heart with some act of intentional betrayal that would lead the lovely thing to order him out of her sight forever—wouldn't do this time.

This was no Society jade he dealt with, not a woman who would secretly enjoy the drama and spectacle of a torrid end to a tepid affair. Sweet, ethical Miranda had done nothing to deserve such treatment and the thought of upsetting her actually made Poll's stomach hurt.

So he wouldn't say a word, or give any sign that he didn't want her after all. At least, not until he figured out how to let her down so easily that she scarcely noticed it.

With one hand on a pie plate containing Philpott's very good berry pie—although not as good as Callie's!—a small dish of clotted cream caught Poll's eye.

She'd so enjoyed that day they'd sneaked onto the palace grounds.

Ah. The very thing. A silly gesture, a carpet picnic

designed to entertain Miranda, to make her laugh, to distract her from the fact that he didn't actually want her. He grimaced at the memory of the kiss.

After arriving at Miranda's, he wondered if Cas had given up as well. Casual questioning of the butler, Twigg, had left him certain that his twin had not visited Miranda in days.

"This is my apology for barging in on you last night!" he declared when Tildy, delighted by the romantic notion, let him into the missus's bedchamber with his basket of God-I'm-sorry-but-I'm-done.

First he spread the same horse blanket he'd used on the palace lawn before the fire; then he unpacked his array of tasty morsels.

Poll completed his preparations with a smile, then turned to her with a theatrical bow and an outstretched hand. "If it please my lady?"

Miranda gazed down at the playful breakfast picnic in dismay, her cheeks flaming with shame. Oh, how was she to tell him?

She was not sorry for the astounding experience of the night before. Every moment had been a revelation. Of Cas, of herself, of a world of sensuality and passion that she'd only vaguely imagined.

Even the way he'd left—in full naked flight!—told her more than he'd dared to say.

No, she had no regrets about such a wondrous night. Instead, she was deeply ashamed of her fickleness that had led such a fine and good man as Poll to believe in her affections, when all the time she'd been harboring strong, undeniable feelings for his brother.

She'd simply been too afraid, or perhaps naïve, or constrained by what she thought she ought to want, to understand that wasn't how the heart worked.

She raised her damp, pained eyes to meet Poll's.

"I fear that I have chosen, sir."

Poll knew at once. Miranda looked to be in agony. He decided to spare her any further pain. "You've chosen Cas," he said bluntly.

She nodded miserably. "He came to me last night, after you'd gone. It was . . . he was . . . ."

Poll sighed. It never failed. Bloody Cas. "Irresistible?"

Miranda nodded, her attention fixed back on the carpet.

Poll shook his head with a small, rueful laugh. He stepped closer and reached for her hand. He caught her smaller fist in his and smoothed her fingers open. "Miranda." He dropped a kiss on her downcast brow. "I cannot say that it doesn't sting, dear one, but in truth I knew last night at your window that you and I were not meant to be."

She lifted her gaze to his, relief in her eyes. "That awkward kiss?"

He snorted. "That awful, unfulfilling, cringe-worthy kiss. And the one after that was even worse."

She pressed her lips together, trying not to smile. "Pray, Poll, be not shy. Tell me your true opinion."

He laughed and pulled her close in a warm, brotherly hug. "You are a genuine Original, Miranda Talbot." His arms tightened about her as she leaned against him, limp with obvious relief. "I am glad it was I who rescued you on that street, for you are a treasure indeed. I will take you as sister with all happiness."

At those words, she drew back slightly to raise her eyes to his. "Sister? I—he—I do not know if Cas shares my feelings. I'd thought . . ." She shook off that dream. "But is it best not to build cloud castles, don't you think? He has made no sign of devotion, other than . . . well . . . his desire." She shook her head once more.. "I thought I knew last night. I thought I felt so much more—"

Poll smiled. "Miranda, I know my twin better than

anyone on this earth. I have never seen him like this. His heart is engaged, trust in that. Whether or not he knows what to do about that, or even if he wishes it, only time will tell."

Hope had begun to bloom in her sea green eyes, but the light slowly faded in confusion. "He does not *wish* to love me?"

Poll struggled to find the words to explain something he had only the vaguest appreciation of. "A long time ago, something—or someone—happened to him. We were young men, barely past boyhood. I know there was a woman, but he was very secretive about her. It was the first secret he ever kept from me. She wounded him deeply. I don't know much more, and ought not to tell it anyway, but I can attest that from that day forward, he was not the same Cas. She broke him, in some way that I thought would never heal, never change, until I saw the way he looked at you."

"I love him," Miranda stated firmly. She smiled. "There. I said it. Right out loud, to boot!" She pressed her hands to her throat in wonder. "I have made my decision. I cannot wait to tell him!"

"No!" Poll hadn't meant to shout, but the protest came from a place of such surety that he could not help it.

She flinched and stepped back from him. "Poll, you claimed to be resolved to my choice!"

He shook his head hurriedly. "No, that isn't the problem. Cas . . ." He rubbed a hand over the back of his neck, trying to decipher what had been sheer instinct. Then he had it. He weighed his words for a moment. "He will flee you."

She frowned. "But you say he loves me. Why would he flee love?"

He tilted his head. "Why do you flee marriage?"

Folding her arms, she glanced away. "That is another

matter entirely. For a woman to give up her independence thus—you have no idea how easy it is for a man to abuse such power!"

He held out his hands. "Do you think a woman does not have power over a man? Cas is turning himself inside out right now, trying to deny the very fact that you rule over his heart!"

Understanding dawned. She pressed her palms together at her midriff. "Oh. Oh . . . *bother.*"

She was far too civilized for her own good. Poll sighed at the twinge of affection that washed over him. She might not be the woman for him, but he hoped that someday, that faceless future woman might bear a rather astonishing resemblance to Mrs. Talbot.

Back to the question at hand. "I propose that we continue our 'courtship' for now. I fear that if I withdraw, Cas will use my defection as an excuse to end his own pursuit of you."

An air of distraction had taken over her expression. "Poll?"

"Yes?"

"Do you think if Cas saw me looking particularly fine—say, at the Marquis of Wyndham's Midsummer Ball—that he might find himself more inclined to want to love me?"

Poll frowned. "Well, it couldn't hurt. Er, how fine?"

She smiled slightly. "I have made a particular friend of Lementeur."

Poll whistled, impressed. "If you've somehow won that fellow over, I rather doubt the Prince Regent himself could resist you. In fact, never mind. Avoid Prinny. He always did have an eye for the ladies. But Wyndham's ball is perfect timing. That might do it—to see you at the ball with all the inevitable admirers, it might push Cas to admit his heart. Here is the bargain. If you keep seeing me, and do not tell Cas the truth of your feelings, I shall make sure he attends and then I shall dance you right off your feet!"

Miranda frowned. "Bargain? I suppose . . . if you truly think it will work."

"It will work." He grinned. "As long as I stay in the wager, he will feel obligated to continue, despite his inner fears. He would *never* simply let me win!"

Miranda narrowed her eyes. "Wager?"

Oops. "Ah . . . well . . . I suppose I left that part out, didn't I?"

She tilted her head and regarded him rather like the way Attie regarded a poisonous insect—wondering whether to keep him alive or stick a pin in him and call it a day.

"Let me guess . . . the first one to become my lover? No, for then Cas would have already won, correct?"

Poll sighed. "Salt in the wound, Miranda?"

Her expression continued to be unsympathetic to his not-so-greatly disappointed heart. "So what great milestone must be reached in order to win?"

"Er . . . well, it seemed like a good idea at the time, you understand . . . ."

"Poll."

With a sigh, he gave in. "The prize would go to the one who convinced you to accept a proposal of marriage."

Frowning, she drew back. Poor Miranda, even the very word made her flinch!

"But I will never marry again!"

Poll nodded. "Well, yes, *I* knew that." He shrugged. "It was merely a ploy to buy time. I'd hoped that Cas would lose interest and move on, the way he always has in the past."

She gazed at him with her lips parted in mingled admiration and irritation. "You cheated!"

He quirked a proud smile. "But, of course! *You* were at stake."

"Worthingtons!" She frowned at him but her scolding expression didn't quite stick. "Mad, the lot of you!"

It was not until Poll had seated Miranda upon her horse blanket and plied her with what he now realized was an exceedingly odd breakfast—pickles—what had he been thinking?—that he truly relaxed and began to enjoy her company.

Miranda eyed her pickle with a wrinkled brow. "Is this a usual part of a Worthington House breakfast?"

Poll laughed and started in on a long, convoluted tale involving Attie, pickles, and Elektra's pet monkey. "Although the monkey only lasted a week before Elektra decided she'd rather just keep three-year-old Attie as a pet. More dangerous, but slightly less likely to fling poo—"

He kept Miranda laughing. It was good to see her at ease again. This double courtship had nearly ruined a perfectly good friendship!

Any pangs of anything else could most certainly be buried deep. It wasn't as though he still wanted Miranda, really. What he wanted was a Miranda of his very own, he realized as he amused her by staging *The Tempest* with the blanket as the island and a pickle as Prospero—or Prospickle-O, as the warty green thing was promptly dubbed.

What he felt, and what he hid from her, was the loss of the dream of thinking he might have found the one—The One—and that the search that begins in adolescence might actually be over for him.

Lucky Cas, to have stumbled upon the dream of love in a stinking London alley! Foolish Cas, if he allowed his own fears to ruin it for him now.

Miranda clapped as Prospickle-O recited his final speech, exhorting his audience to send him on his way by thrumming their bellies. Then she reached out, plucked the miniature actor from his stage and popped him into her mouth.

"Pickles," she murmured around her mouthful of briny Shakespearean, "make a perfectly marvelous breakfast."

Poll did not laugh. In fact, his easy smile had disappeared the moment Miranda had leaned across the picnic blanket and outstretched her arm.

On the pale ivory skin of her upper arm, Poll clearly saw the marks of a large hand held too tightly. The skin was merely pink, not black and blue, yet clearly some force had been applied.

Miranda gazed at him innocently as she munched, her eyebrows raised in a question.

Fury swept Poll. What the hell kind of game was Cas playing? If he loved her, how could he hurt her?

If he didn't love her, why didn't he just leave her the hell alone?

Miranda blinked as her playmate went instantly as still and icy as stone. Then she felt him slip away, though he yet sat across from her. He'd gone away from her, although he'd been laughing softly with her only a moment before. She'd never seen him so withdrawn.

Untangling himself from his untidy sprawl with rigid care, he left her there on the floor. He rang for her maid and ordered her a pot of tea, then walked away from her with nothing more than a brief hesitant moment at the door, where it seemed he'd almost turned back to tell her something.

Then he was gone.

Miranda was left staring down at her half-eaten pickle and wondering what she'd done wrong.

Chapter Nineteen

"You rotter!"

Cas looked up from his morning newssheet—the one he was not reading, for the words simply swam into memories of sea green eyes and sweet moans of desire—just in time to see Poll's fist headed for his jaw.

Ow. That was all he had time to think before the blow sent him out of his chair and splayed on the carpet of the breakfast room.

He was back on his feet in a split second, dabbing at his lip with the back of his wrist, his hands already fisted. Rage at his brother roiled up from some white-hot place within him.

Poll had just come from Miranda's. What had he done while there?

He could do no worse than you.

Cas's vision reddened. Fists were good. Cudgels would work, too.

Weapons were in short supply about Worthington House, due to a regrettable incident last year between Attie and Callie's new husband, Sir Lawrence, so Cas was going to have to beat the hell out of Poll with his bare hands.

His fingers curled more tightly as a snarling smile lifted a corner of his lips. *Looking forward to it.*

Poll stood before him, pale with fury. "You are an animal!"

Cas flinched, but he didn't let Poll see it. Last night had been unbelievable. It had perhaps been the most intimate moment of his life. He'd never before been with a woman who wasn't frightened by his intensity. That was why his dalliances never lasted long, why his lovers were swiftly exchanged for the one after, and the one after that. When he felt the darkness welling up, he walked away rather than subject himself to their shocked rejection.

When Miranda turned herself over to him so trustingly, it had expanded something within him. He'd been freed, and yet at the same moment, held more closely than ever. Deep within her warmth, in the sweet cavern of her, he'd at last been allowed to be his true self. He'd felt closer to her than he'd ever felt to anyone outside his own family.

More so, for none of them truly knew of that flawed and injured part of him. Even to his family, he kept up the facade of the jokester, the carefree lad-about-town. To hear Poll judge him so went directly to that hidden, lonely place, piercing Cas like a knife.

So he let his snarling smile widen. "Oh, she liked it. A lot. She actually *thanked* me afterward. What are you doing wrong that you aren't getting thanked?"

It was Poll's turn to flinch. Pain and jealousy and old boyhood hurts shone from his eyes. Cas knew that it had always bothered Poll that when people finally did manage to tell them apart, they usually seemed to prefer Cas's company to his, though Cas seemed to give not a whit for their time.

Poll didn't understand it, so he continued to be winning and charming and courteous in an effort to win others over.

Cas could have cynically explained it to him, but not in a way that Poll's whole and loving spirit could comprehend. Like dogs that followed after humans who mistreated them, ordinary people longed to please—and if someone appeared harder to please, they longed all the harder to do so. A little arrogance, a little disdain, and one suddenly became someone such people wanted to win approval from.

It meant nothing. It was a shallow win. In the end, people usually tended to gravitate back to Poll, for his friendship was of the generous and warm variety. Yet the damage had already been done with Poll. He saw himself as someone less preferable.

Now, Poll glared at him with loathing in his eyes. "You hurt her. I saw the marks myself!"

Cas didn't show a single shred of reaction, although inside him he turned to ice. He'd always held back—always feared to release the wildness within him. He'd worried that he might someday harm someone—

Not her. Oh, God. Not sensitive, gentle Miranda!

Self-loathing ripped at him with claws honed in the exquisite satisfaction he'd felt last night—felt even as he'd hurt her!

"If I thought you loved her, I'd let her make her own decision," Poll growled, swearing. "Do you? Do you have anything in your heart but ice?"

Cas flinched, but he did not speak. Better ice than fire. Fire would reduce him to ashes, until there was nothing left but emptiness when it was over.

"No?" Poll advanced upon him. "Then you do not deserve her. You're done," he pronounced, his tone a growl. "Finished. She's mine now. I'll not allow you to ever go near her again!"

"No." The word was ripped from Cas's throat before he could take a thought, even as his body assumed an ag-

gressive crouch. He would be more careful. He would hold back. He would do anything he had to do, fight his way through Poll, *anything* to see her again, to touch her again, to have her again!

Poll snarled, his jaw rigid, his eyes narrowed. It struck Cas—just before Poll's fist once again impacted his face—that for the first time in his life, he couldn't tell his twin's face from his own.

Breaking glass and broken furniture noises wouldn't normally cause much consternation in the Worthington household. Philpott might mutter an amusing obscenity without pausing in her task. Iris might dreamily lift her head to listen for cries for help, then hearing none, might drift back to dabbing the finishing touches on *Shakespeare with Ostrich* or perhaps her latest work, *Shakespeare with Platypus*.

Archie might look up from the piles of Elizabethan documents on his desk, blinking myopically as he, too, listened for signs of rescue needed—or, depending on what he had just discovered on the topic of Shakespeare's true gender, he might not.

Attie always ran toward sounds of chaos. Ellie usually ran away. Orion was often the cause of the chaos. Lysander tended to react to anything resembling cannon fire, but ignored anything less. Dade would typically let out a deep sigh of resignation, then troop dutifully through the house to determine the estimated cost of repairs.

Not this time.

This time it was the never-before-heard bestial howls of rage that brought them all running. Dade was last, nearly tripping over Attie, who huddled in the cluttered hallway with her hands over her ears. Ellie shot Dade a look of horror as he approached and stepped around their dithering father and handkerchief-waving mother, who kept pronouncing, "The Wrestling Match! It's the Wrestling Match!"

Ellie grabbed Dade's hand and tugged him along. "They're fighting! I mean to say, really, *truly* fighting!"

Dade glanced around at his other brothers. Orion nodded. "It's true." Lysander looked as if he'd give anything to be anywhere else.

"Bloody hell," Dade muttered. He pushed open the door of the smoking room, but was immediately thrown backwards when a large, solid body crashed into it from the other direction. Orion caught him and gave him a helpful shove back at the door.

This time Dade kicked it open. *"What in the seven levels of hell is going on?"*

Cas and Poll ignored him completely, too wrapped up in rage and violence to realize they had an audience. It took all four men to pull them apart and pin them down separately.

Ellie and Iris helped by dashing cold water into their faces. Dade, dripping now, wished his mother had better aim. The water did the trick, shocking the twins from their mindless rage back into actual human speech. Poll came out of it first, sputtering and sitting up, pushing his brothers' piniong hands away. "I'm fine! I'm calm! Get off!"

Cas was not so inclined to break out of his fury.

Dade allowed Poll to stand, backing away slowly, ready to tackle him should he make a move at the still-pinned Cas.

Iris pattered forward with another container of water, this one a vase still full of flowers. Poll intercepted her. "Allow me." He pulled the flowers free and unceremoniously doused his twin further, causing Cas to sputter and choke on his epithets. Poll dropped the dripping flowers upon his twin's chest, tossed the empty vase to Dade, then turned and walked from the room.

Dade watched him go with a frown. Then he returned to where Lysander and Orion still held the snarling, spitting Cas to the floor. "Sit on him until he's human again."

Then he turned to contemplate the only person present who didn't seem surprised by the fight. "Attie, what say the two of us stroll down to the kitchen for a snack?"

Attie wrapped her chilled hands about the mug of hot chocolate that Philpott had made for her—she didn't really like the bitter cocoa, but Attie made it a policy to always refuse Philpott's offer of tea.

Dade had seated himself across the battle-scarred kitchen worktable from her, but she fixed her eyes on the spot where she had spent an entire day scraping at the wood with a sharpened spoon. She had been trying to ascertain how long it would take to escape from a locked cabin aboard a pirate ship—but that had been forever ago when she was still a child.

Dade cleared his throat significantly. Attie scowled at him through lowered brows. She didn't want to tell, but she did worry so, and it was a bit gratifying that everyone else was finally worried with her.

They all perched behind Dade like birds on a clothesline, watching her with sharp, intelligent eyes, just waiting to hear what she had to say—unlike most people, who would be talking, or lecturing, and not bothering to listen to an almost-thirteen-year-old girl.

The fierce love and need she felt for them all welled up painfully within her, making her scowl all the more ferociously.

Iris smiled brightly at Attie's intensity. "Just tell us, dear. Tell us why the boys are reenacting the wrestling match between Charles and Orlando from *As You Like It*, Act One, Scene Two."

A blurred sort of dismay traveled across Iris's dear,

vague features. "They've never before showed signs of having a talent for the stage, you know. They were very convincing."

Mama, Attie decided, could make an exploding workroom into a fireworks display. Most people thought that her mother was a bit fluffy in the mind, but Attie knew that Iris had a will of iron—for no one could be so consistently optimistic unless they worked hard at it every moment of every day.

Ellie, on the other hand, watched Attie narrowly, as if expecting nothing better than a lie to emerge from her lips.

Which was entirely unfair. Attie made it a policy never to lie more than five times in any given day—and she'd already used them all up!

Orion stood a little apart from the others, like the bird who always sits on the end. Attie knew better. She knew that Orion could have gone to University and that he could still be welcome in the house of any prominent scholar as assistant or protégé.

Orion said that he didn't want to be bothered with thinking another scholar's thoughts—not when his own were so vastly more interesting, but Attie knew how much he worried for her parents and Lysander especially. Orion and Lysander had been close as boys, almost as close as Cas and Poll.

Lysander—poor Zander!—gazed at her darkly. Lysander didn't care for strife.

But there was no help for it. Attie again met Dade's encouraging eyes. Strife was about to erupt but good.

"Cas and Poll are fighting over a lover!" she blurted.

Iris brightened. "Oh, my. How romantic! Is she fantastically beautiful like Helen of Troy?"

Dade nodded. "So it's not all that serious, then. One of them will lose interest soon and things will go back to normal."

Attie shook her head violently, which meant that she then had to push back a wad of tangled mop from her face. "It is serious. They're in love! They've been seeing her for weeks! Poll for almost two whole months!"

Everyone gaped at that. None could remember any lover holding one of the twins for an entire month.

Ellie looked thoughtful. "It must be her fault, then. She's playing them against each other."

Dade shook his head. "They're far too to clever to fall for that sort of romantic intrigue."

Ellie scoffed. "Do be serious. They're *men.*"

Even Orion had to lift a brow in agreement with that statement.

Attie nodded miserably. "She's pretty, too. And smart. And, even though I'm positive she's evil, she's rather nice."

Ellie stepped forward. "What? You've seen her? They introduced you to this strumpet? Oh, when I get my hands on those—"

Attie rolled her eyes, though she was secretly pleased by Ellie's protectiveness. "Of course not. I went on reconnaissance."

"Ellie!" Dade didn't turn around, but kept his attention on Attie. "Ellie, settle down."

Ellie settled, still seething.

Dade reached across the table and took Attie's cold little hand in his big warm one. "Tell us about her, pet."

Attie did so, telling the whole unvarnished truth, too, since she had already fulfilled her quota of fibs for the day.

She told them about Miranda Talbot—

"Ah, Miranda!" Archie was fair to swooning. "Prospero's daughter, Miranda! 'Is she the goddess that hath sever'd us, / And brought us thus together?'"

"*The Tempest,* Act 5, Scene 1," Iris added brightly.

—and about her nice face and her ugly gowns and how

she didn't seem to think there was anything at all wrong with having two lovers at once—

"I'll bet she doesn't," Ellie snarled.

—and how she talked to Attie like a person.

They all nodded their understanding of that, for it was a common grievance among the Worthingtons that the rest of the world found them rather disconcertingly odd and behaved accordingly.

Then Attie told them about the plan she had cooked up with Mr. Button and Cabot—

Iris clapped her hands and exclaimed, "A plot twist!"

Ellie looked smug at the mention of a Lementeur wardrobe refurbishment.

—and how as soon as Miranda went to Lord Wyndham's ball, the problem would be solved.

Orion nodded sagely. "Not a bad plan. Not bad at all."

Attie blushed furiously at such high praise, and scowled horribly at the entire clan, exquisitely relieved that she wasn't going to have to kill anyone after all.

Chapter Twenty

By the time Poll made it up three floors to his bedchamber, he no longer felt particularly homicidal toward Cas.

If anyone knew that Cas was inwardly writhing in pain, it was Poll. For so many years, he'd watched helplessly from the outside while Cas wrestled with his secret demons. He'd pried deeper once, only to cause his twin to pull further within himself. He'd not asked again.

The loyalty of twinship had kept Cas's secret anyway. It was a good thing that Dade was busy running Worthington House; otherwise, even loyal Poll would not have been able to fool his eldest brother for long. Dade was always on watch for deception. Paranoid bastard. It was enough to make one *want* to lie. Well, lie *more*.

Poll knew both Orion and Lysander believed that nothing untoward had occurred in Cas's youth. Neither of them was much inclined to romantic pursuits. Orion was as controlled as a machine, disdaining any and all emotions, while Lysander, once returned from battle, kept far as possible from destabilizing influences.

So Poll alone had kept watch on Cas, helpless to alleviate his brother's pain, able only to distract and entertain—

which, if anyone had known, would have done a lot to explain some of their wilder adventures.

Distraction had worked, mostly. Now, however, after all these years of secrets, Poll found himself very nearly gleeful.

Cas would go to Miranda at once, Poll was sure. Nothing would stop his twin now. He, Poll, would stay away for the moment. He didn't want to admit to himself how much the thought of seeing them together still stung.

Miranda was meant for Cas. This courtship charade would simply ensure it.

On his way to his bedchamber to change out of his soaked, bloody clothing, Poll felt the swelling beneath his eye and smiled. He hadn't had the chance to do half the damage to Cas that he would have wished. They were too equally matched.

So why did Miranda prefer Cas? Better not to ask that question. Better to wonder why did he, having known her longer, having courted her longer, feel so little passion for such a lovely woman?

There was no point in trying to fathom the mysteries of romance. Why did anyone fall in love?

Instead he sat up by his fire, fully dressed, merely biding his time. Thinking of the marks left on her fair skin, he thought he ought to check on her after Cas was well and gone.

He finally admitted to himself that he was a little worried about her. He had never seen Cas so enraged. He feared that if Miranda thought she would be visited by a gentle and courteous lover, she had perhaps best think twice.

Cas walked the streets of Mayfair until the day waned and he continued until midnight was not far off. If asked, he couldn't have said where he'd been. The hours ran together into misty rain and sputtering streetlights and furtive shadows in the growing gloom.

It didn't matter where he went. The problem was, Miranda was somewhere else.

When he found himself outside Miranda's front door in the deep night he knew for certain that he was a madman. She wouldn't even be awake, much less ready to see callers.

There was a tangle inside him. Desire. Darkness.

Dread.

Cas tried to force himself to turn around and walk away into the mist. Poll was right about him. He was no good for the endearing creature sleeping in the house before him.

She should know that. He ought not to disappear without confessing the truth to her. The fact that this allowed him to feed his aching need to see her again did not escape him. He simply didn't care.

In the end, it was quite simple for Cas to sneak around to the tradesman entrance and let himself into the door.

There were stirrings in the kitchen, and he heard a quick light tread above him in the house, but he saw no one as he made his way to Miranda's room.

The room was cold and quiet. The bed was fully made, untouched by sleepers of any kind. Casting a glance about the room, he found her. She sat slumped at the dressing table, her head down on one crooked arm and the other hand wrapped about the handle of silver hairbrush.

She wore the filmy wrapper that he liked.

Waiting for me.

If he woke her, would she cringe from him? Would she gaze at him mistrustfully?

He couldn't resist touching her even so. Her dark waving hair flowed down over her one bared shoulder. Wisps of it drifted over her lips, moving with every exhalation.

He reached his fingertips out to sweep those stray strands of silk back behind her ear. She was curled up, her shoulders hunched against the chill of the room.

First Cas built up the fire, digging out the best coals from the ash and arranging fresh ones around the hottest ones. As the room warmed, he wiped his hands on the towel by the pitcher and bowl, then he knelt beside her seated form.

He took her hand, as icy as it was, and opened it against his cheek. He held it there, letting her palm take in the day's growth of beard and his warmth.

He took her cold feet onto his lap and warmed them with his palms as he watched her face. She shifted slightly and a brief play of emotions marched across her sleeping features: surprise, consternation, sensual enjoyment.

Her feet were like ice, her hands as well, when he took them in his and chafed them so gently. Like the night in the carriage. The ache of memory was no worse than he deserved.

He slipped his hands beneath her, lifting her at her knees and one arm under her shoulders. She turned into his warmth at once, nuzzling her cool cheek into his neck and draping one arm up over his neck.

He lifted her easily and walked slowly toward the bed, cradling her soft body against his.

She looked so weary. Her face was pale, except where her cheek was creased by the fabric of her sleeve. Bluish shadows showed in the early morning light. She looked like an exhausted temptress in that barely there wrapper.

He wanted her, suddenly and fully, the way she always made him feel. His erection strained at his trousers. She was soft and pliant and entirely asleep. He longed to lay her down on the bed and enter her sleeping body, to have her wake with him already inside her.

He didn't want Poll to have her any longer. He wanted

her all to himself. For the first time in his life, he had no desire to share with his twin.

For the first time in his life, he was willing to fight his twin to the death for something he wanted.

Of course, he didn't really want Poll dead. Not entirely dead. He wanted him gone. Far away. Far, far from his lovely Mira.

Quickly, before he could do something regrettable to her yielding and delicious form, he slid her between her covers. Then he tucked her in, all around, until only her face showed in the large bed.

Miranda roused in the dim, predawn light to find her fire-side chair had been pulled to her bed, like a sickbed vigil. She stared blurrily at the dark figure of the large, broad-shouldered man draped uncomfortably in her dainty flowered-chintz seat.

"You are here."

He looked up at once, his gaze concerned—and a little careful. He seemed almost apologetic as he leaned forward to take her outstretched hand.

"Hello. Are you warm enough yet?"

She was quite exquisitely warm and comfortable. "No, I'm freezing." She shivered and gave his hand a little tug. He took the hint and climbed in next to her fully clothed, although he did remove his boots.

He pulled her close. "Is that better?"

She tucked her face and hands into his chest, as she had done that chilly night in the carriage. "It will be." It was.

"I found you sitting up at your dressing table, freezing. Why would you do such a thing with a nice warm bed so close by?"

"I was waiting for you. I worried this morning when Poll left. He seemed so angry at you. I didn't want to go to bed in case one of you came back."

He hadn't come, out of shame. Poll had not come, probably out of the anger that she sensed. They'd both spun about in their own minds, full of fury and selfish sulking, leaving her to wait and wait.

He kissed her brow. "I'm sorry. That anger was not directed toward you." That was the truth. "I am . . . I am so sorry I hurt you. That was not easy for me to hear." More fragments of truth for her.

She snuggled closer. "I am quite well, you know."

He'd been too wild with her. Yet even now he felt that wildness stirring within him.

He must be careful. No matter what, he must remain in control. Miranda tugged at his waistcoat, reminding him of her presence and pulling him back from the war within him.

"Are you listening? I am not harmed, just a bit sore."

He stroked a strand of silken hair back from her face and nodded, seeming satisfied with her response. Then he rose to pace the room once. That didn't seem to help, for he walked to the foot of the bed and sat there, gazing at the floor darkly.

Miranda slid out from beneath the covers and lowered her feet to the floor. It too was warm. She padded around the bed to frown down at him, one arm wrapped about the bedpost.

"What troubles you, Cas?"

He ran a hand through his hair. "I am not like Poll," he muttered.

She almost smiled. "Yes, I've noticed. I like you the way you are."

He shook off her words. "Poll is whole. He could make you happy—"

Miranda opened her mouth to tell him of the ludicrous kiss, then remembered that she had been instructed not to. She bit her lip instead as Cas hunched his shoulders, leaning his elbows on his knees.

"I'm not that sort of man." The words came hard but Cas forced himself to straighten and meet her eyes. "I cannot . . . I cannot open to you. I . . ." He gazed into her sea green eyes and knew she did not understand. "If I were to—to fall in love, I should have to be open, to trust and share, bring that into the light. I can't."

"I don't understand." Her look was simple and direct. "I want to understand. What does that mean to you, to be open?"

"To be open means to be helpless before someone. Naked, with no lies or stories or boundaries between you. I was open once—open and young and naïve and so, so unwise."

"Oh." She looked thoughtful. "I wish I could be unwise. I have spend my entire life being prudent. I have been careful since I was a child. Careful of every word I say, every move I make. I dress carefully, I speak carefully."

"You sleep carefully." He smiled slightly. "You sleep as if someone is watching."

Her lips quirked. "Apparently, someone is watching."

"Just tonight. What of all the other nights of your life?"

She released the anchor of the bedpost and advanced upon him, moving slowly until she stood between his open knees. She reached a tentative hand to stroke his hair back from his temple. He didn't pull away, although his eyes dropped from hers. "There was one time I wasn't careful," she said softly. "I was not careful last night. I forgot to be, the moment you touched me.

Lifting his eyes, he gazed back at her, knowing what she wanted him to say, what shone in her eyes like hope but he would not lie, not to her.

"I did not forget." He shook his head at her disappointment. "Mira. I cannot. My heart, what . . . what is inside my heart—" *No.* "I cannot!" The dread grew within him. He wanted to stand up, to stride around the room, to shake off his rising turmoil. Her body blocked his way—and he knew if he reached out to move her, then he would touch her. If he touched her, he would never let her go.

So he flexed his jaw and stared over her shoulder, for he could not meet her deep-sea gaze. "I wish I could make you understand. It isn't as though I do not look around me and see others with their hearts alight, with their hopes and dreams written on their faces. But I cannot. I cannot *unknow* what I know."

"What is it that you think you know?" Her voice was a breath of a whisper that stirred his hair.

He closed his eyes against the need that surged into his chest. "None of it is true. What people think is love is simply desire meeting desire. Loneliness meeting loneliness, at its best. Madness meeting madness, at its worst."

He forced himself to meet her gaze then. He looked into her eyes and told the truth to a woman for the first time in more than ten years. "There is no such thing as love."

"I see." She lifted her chin. "Then I suppose I must settle for unwise."

Chapter Twenty-one

Miranda stepped closer, moving his thighs wide, and settled her hands lightly upon his shoulders. Curiosity was wide-awake with hunter's gaze unblinking. "Show me how to be unwise, Cas. Teach me."

"You do not wish to learn what I know."

She considered him for a long moment, then dared. "Should I ask Poll to teach me what he knows, then?"

His entire body went tight beneath her perceptive hands. Ah. If the muscle in his jaw flexed any harder, she feared he might break his teeth.

"You are very beautiful, especially in that wicked excuse for a wrapper," he noted. "That translucent silk shows everything."

She could not help glancing down at herself. Arousing his interest had been her only intention in donning it.

He went on thoughtfully. "I think you would make an admirable harem slave, with a bit of training."

She swallowed. "Training?" She lifted her head to catch his gaze and she saw it.

The fire, like glowing coals deep in the jungle green of his eyes.

He wanted to burn with her.

A shuddering thrill raced through her, straight to her lower belly. Good. She wanted to combust with him. She wanted to scorch him right back. This, then, must be something new for him to teach her. She was an excellent student, so she lifted her chin and slowly untied the closure of the barely there dressing gown. She let it slip down off her shoulders to pool around her feet. "Train me."

His narrowed gaze was shadowed. "I will not stop once begun. You will want me to stop, but you will wish in vain. You must embark knowing this."

Heat pooled between her thighs. "I understand."

"No, you don't. But you will." He reached his hands to toy with her breasts. He took the heavy weight of them in his hands and squeezed gently, pushing them high. "Lovely Mira." Then he slid his fingertips to her nipples and tweaked them until they surpassed their already pointed state.

He did not stop there. When her nipples were pink and rigid, he took them in his fingertips and squeezed them, twisting slowly. A whimper of surprise escaped Miranda.

He squeezed harder, just for an instant. "Mira, do you like this?"

She nodded. She did like it, for the sweet, hot tingle afterward was like a reward for enduring the pain. He twisted again, slowly but ruthlessly, until she gasped aloud.

"Are they throbbing, Mira? Can you feel your heartbeat in your nipples?"

She shook her head, not understanding but willing to learn.

So he showed her. She stood utterly still as he took her to the edge of pain, over and over again, until her pink nipples became red and swollen and she felt the hot pulse of her heart in each of them.

The wickedness of his torture, the look of banked heat in his eyes as he watched her gasp and writhe for

him, the naughtiness of standing before him naked while he sat before her clothed had Miranda's thighs wet with arousal.

"You did very well. Do you like this now?" He brushed his palms over her sore nipples, barely touching. She gasped and quivered at the rich rush of sensation.

"Oh yes," she breathed.

"Now you'll feel everything," he told her mysteriously.

He slid his hands down to grasp her small waist and pulled her into his lap.

Miranda found herself lying across Mr. Worthington's thighs, not in a friendly, faceup, "let me kiss you for hours" way—but in a facedown, "you'll never steal from the cookie jar again!" way.

"But—"

In a swift moment, he caught at her hands and pinned them behind her, one large hand wrapping easily around both her wrists. With no way to hold herself up, she was forced to lie with her face in the coverlet. Her hair fell about her, blocking her vision. Her throbbing nipples rubbed against the nubby wool of her coverlet, a fresh torture.

"Cas, I don't believe I—"

His open hand came down upon her bare bottom, a light slap that stole her words with shock.

"I do not wish you to speak without permission, Mira."

Alarm traced through her. She swallowed hard. "I—"

Slap. Then, *slap!*

That one stung a bit. She gasped.

"Do you understand?"

She opened her mouth to reply, then thought better of it and nodded. She hoped he could see it under all her hair.

Slap.

"When I ask you a question, I expect a swift and ready answer, Mira."

She blinked back the heat behind her eyes. Don't speak! Speak! "I understand!"

"You enjoyed displaying yourself in the window while I took you from behind."

It wasn't a question, yet it made her uncomfortable. She tried to squirm, but he merely pressed his hand holding her wrists down against the small of her back and she was pinned completely still.

His hard hand came down upon her bottom again, much harder. She bit back a yelp of surprise at the force of it, not sure if she cared for this new direction much at all. Yet the deep rich tingle left behind by his palm was like the "training" of her nipples, and made her squirm slightly on his lap. He must have realized this, for he caressed her bottom with gentle circles of his hand, soothing away the sting.

"You've enjoyed the wicked things we've done, haven't you, Mira?"

She bit her lip, not sure how he wished her to answer. The slap of his hand on her bottom brought the truth from her in a gasp. "Yes!" She buried her face in the coverlet.

"Say it out loud."

She turned her face and spoke the truth through the fall of her hair. "Yes . . . I've liked the . . . the wicked things we've done."

"Enough to want more, I should imagine. More and more." He didn't seem to require an answer. His fingertips trailed thoughtfully over her buttocks, outlining each globe, slipping down into the crease between, then up again.

"You'll allow me to do anything to you, won't you? Anything I wish?"

She held her breath as his hand circled and soothed. Anything? Would she truly?

"Mira? Answer the question."

Still she hesitated.

Slap.

She gasped. "Yes! Yes, I'll let you do anything you wish to me!"

"You're a wicked wanton creature, aren't you, Mira?" His palm, hot as flame on her sensitized bottom, circled around and around the most tender section of her skin. "Say it. Tell me what you are."

When she hesitated again, even knowing what would come from her pause, she realized that she wanted this. She indeed liked it, thrilled to being pinioned there, naked and helpless on his lap, while he, still fully clothed, held her there.

Master and slave.

Owner and willing, eager object of his desire.

Slap. Slap! Harder than ever before.

She cried out loud this time, then gasped out, "Yes! Yes, I'm a wicked, wanton creature!" Then, more softly, "I'm *your* wicked wanton creature."

"Mine." His circling soothing hand slipped down, down between her thighs, touching her, sliding along her labia. "You're wet for me. You want this, don't you?"

He slid a long finger deep into her, penetrating her slowly while she squirmed on his lap. Miranda flushed hotly. Yes, she wanted it. She liked being pinned down, held safe while he stroked into her, while he took her down into herself, into her own darkness, allowing her to enjoy what she ought not to enjoy, what should be wrong to enjoy.

He'd warned her of the dangers of such a journey, yet she trusted him, especially after his confession to her. This was play—wicked, deviant play, but play nonetheless.

And it was the very wickedness of the game that made her all the wetter.

I think I may have a talent for being wicked.

He thrust that long finger in again, deeper. She panted, helpless in his grasp, helpless to do anything but allow the sweet invasion.

This time when he withdrew that slick finger, soaked with her arousal, he used it to wet her clitoris. It throbbed at his touch, already swollen, already sensitive. She wanted to roll her hips, to move into that touch but she could not move. His grip on her wrists was not painful, but it was without mercy or quarter. He was in control and he meant for her to stay pinned.

With a shuddering sigh, she released into her imprisonment. The training would continue. She wanted it to continue. She ached for it to continue. The wicked, wanton creature inside her was dying to see where her master/lover would take her next.

He touched her softly, making tiny circles now, stroking her clitoris until she began to gasp and tremble and moan. Fast and faster still, until she came close to that sweet height, that cliff that she longed to willingly fling herself from to fall so sweetly—

Abruptly, he stopped, slipping his wet fingers away from her clitoris.

The spanking commenced once more. She was not permitted to speak so she whimpered and moaned and gasped as he "trained" her until her lip ached for being bitten and her bottom burned like fire.

He stopped, just as she thought she might just break her silence and beg him to cease.

His hand, hot from striking her flesh, rubbed softly over her sore skin, soothing and stroking, circling wider and wider until his hand slipped between her thighs once more.

She nearly wept with relief as his fingers lingered at the slippery gate to her vagina.

Slowly he penetrated her again, thrusting his longest finger deep, again and again, taking her high once more.

Then it was two fingers, thick and knobby, twisting within her, taking her breath away with the spin of sensation. Helplessly she could only toss her head on the coverlet, for he held her so firmly, she could not even buck into that wonderful, invading hand. She could not change its relentless pace as it forced her high again, higher, and yet higher—

He stopped, his hand slipping from her slowly.

"Nooo!"

He went very still. "What was that? Do you defy me, Mira?"

Oh no. *Oh yes.* She caught at her lip with her teeth, holding silent, waiting. The hand lifted. She began to shiver with anticipation and, yes, a tiny bit of fear. Her clitoris throbbed. Her labia swelled and pulsed hot with every beat of her heart. She wanted . . . wanted . . . .

He spanked her hard, so very hard, three times in quick succession.

She came.

Immediately that hand moved, his sure fingers reaching between her thighs for her clitoris, stroking swiftly. At once, her orgasm doubled in intensity, carrying her up in a hot relentless rise, no sweet release allowed. He forced her to the height again at once, his touch implacable and merciless. She cried out wordless protest, even as she came again and again.

At last, he stopped. She lay limply across his lap, gasping and, yes, even sobbing into the coverlet, her eyes wet.

Through the haze of jolting aftershocks, she was astonished at herself. Why did she weep? Pain? No, her body didn't hurt, not really. Her bottom stung fiercely, her skin tight and hot, and her nipples were sore and aching, but these weren't tears of pain or debasement either. She didn't feel abused. She felt *free.* He freed her when he dominated her so. He freed her from doubt, from worry that she ought not to be doing what she was doing. When she handed him her will, she also handed him responsibility for what happened next.

It wasn't a lifelong decision. It was a mere moment out of time—a brief moment when the decisions were his, where the intention was his, where she was could relax into being the simple sexual creature he required her to be.

Open.

What a beautiful relief.

He released his grasp about her wrists, and her arms slid down so that she dangled limply across him, sated, so sweetly calm deep down within her soul.

His large hands stroked gently down her naked back over her stinging bottom, down her damp, parted thighs. She allowed herself a moment to simply breathe, to simply be. A gift.

She wanted to return that gift. With trembling arms beneath her for support, she pushed herself upright. He aided her, strong arms lifting her to sit on his lap. She shivered at the sensation of his broadcloth trousers against the naked, throbbing sensitized skin of her bottom. He held her close, burying his face in her hair. She felt his rigid erection against her hip, trapped hard and tight inside his trousers. He shook as he held her, trembling with lust withheld. Withheld while he'd satisfied her over and over again.

She wanted him, too. The spike of sudden lust surprised her. Had she not been entirely satisfied just a few moments ago? She swarmed into him, enjoying the feel of his clothing on her skin, his surcoat that rubbed rough on her aching nipples and the still-fastened buttons of his weskit that felt cold against her skin. Naked against clothed. The contrast was delightful.

It gave her an idea.

Could she manage it? Miranda tested her limbs surreptitiously. Yes, she felt stronger already. Perhaps it was time for her to take charge after all. Wouldn't he like a moment of sweet relief?

So she wrapped her arms about his neck and brought him in for a long, hot, wet kiss. She had never kissed as the aggressor before and she found she liked the power of driving her tongue between his lips, of pressing in close. She wrapped both arms around his neck, holding *him* in place.

Using his shoulders for leverage, she opened her legs and sat astride him, facing him. This had the added benefit of forcing her aching, rigid nipples into the silk of his weskit, and letting her labia press against the massive bulge in his trousers.

His arms came about her at once, gripping her bottom and pulling her in tight.

She lifted her mouth from his. "No," she commanded in a whisper. "Don't touch me. Not at all."

He hesitated. Then with a last squeeze of her reddened buttocks that made her gasp, he put his hands on the bed, leaning back on them a little, giving her room.

She kissed him as she'd always longed to kiss him— fully, with abandon and lust, kissing as a man kissed, demanding and invading. She dug her fingers into his hair and tugged hard as she assaulted his mouth.

His erection swelled impossibly further.

She writhed on him, letting the buttons and wool and silk dig into her flesh, loving the hard bite of the metal on her skin.

"My God," he gasped against her mouth. "Mira, I need you!"

She lifted her head, frowning down at him, their faces dim and secret behind the curtain of her hair. "Say it," she demanded. "Beg."

His eyes dark and burning, his jaw tight with strain, he

gasped the words. "Please, Mira! Please, let me take you. I need you now!"

She kissed him once more, a hot slippery battle of tongues and nibbling teeth.

Then she lifted her head. "No."

He gaped up at her in disbelief. She smiled, a wicked vixen's smile that came from some place she'd never before explored. "*I'm* going to take *you.*"

He let out a long shuddering breath. "Oh, damn!"

Her questing fingers found the buttons of his trousers. Though she fumbled a bit in her lust, soon she had him freed, falling hot and thick and so very hard in her hands. She squeezed once, a little harder than she ought, just to let him understand that this time, he was her creature.

He moaned aloud, letting his head fall back in surrender. Good.

She moved in, holding his straining cock with one hand, the other braced on his wide shoulder. She was so wet, so very past ready. She pressed the thick blunt tip of him into her and stayed there a moment, rolling it slightly, wetting it. Using her own slippery desire, she slid her hand up and down the length of him, slicking the satin iron of him, making him ready. Then she drove herself down onto him, piercing herself deep with his thickness in a single rich beautiful slide of pleasure/pain. He cried out, a wordless growl. She felt his body shift as if he meant to reach for her. She pulled his head up with her fingers tight in the curls of his hair and gazed commandingly into his eyes.

"Stay," she ordered. He stayed.

Rising upon him, she used her thighs gripped tight around his hips, used her hands on his muscled shoulders, used the arch of her back. She rode him, rising and falling in a sweet hot mimicry of a gallop. He was her stallion now.

She drove him onward until she could no longer fight her own orgasm. She wanted to wait, to make him come, but her desire to command faded and her desire to reach completion rose. She rode him on and on, galloping hard toward her own satisfaction until she convulsed, arching back, keening out her bliss in a high animal howl. She felt herself quiver around his thickness, throbbing even more tightly within her.

It was more than he could bear. With a roar he broke his willing chains of obedience. Wrapping his arms tight about her waist, he held her still as he thrust upward into her hard, once, twice, thrice. She felt him come inside her as she hung shivering in his grasp, each of his shuddering moans translated to the thick throbbing of him inside her, giving her further deep, sweet tremors of satisfaction.

Gasping, dizzy, trembling with exhaustion, she found herself pulled close. He tucked her hot face into his neck, leaning her limp body on the solid support of his wide chest.

Still impaled upon him, still naked against his clothed form, she shuddered rhythmically to his heartbeat, echoed in the throbbing of his thick cock inside her as her own tempest faded softly away.

Chapter Twenty-two

Cas brought a fresh cloth from the washing bowl, wetted with cool water, to the bed. He drew back the covers and cleansed her with tender hands. Roused, she rolled her head to smile at him, lifting one languid hand to push back her tousled hair.

"Thank you," she murmured sleepily. "You always take such good care of me."

Cas could only watch her as her lids fell once more and her smile relaxed into a pout of sleep. While she lay there on her side, partially curled, still naked, he looked upon his handiwork.

Her bottom glowed red. He could see the distinct imprint of his hand in at least two areas. Her nipples were still rigid and deep pink. He imagined her wincing slightly the next time she dressed, feeling him all over her sensitized body. His pulse quickened at the mere thought.

He was entirely astonished at himself. He'd never struck a woman in his life, yet he'd pinned her down and spanked her again and again. True, he'd meant it as play in the beginning, or perhaps a test, to discern the depth of her alleged willingness.

Or punishment, for her allowing Poll to touch her when she belonged to *him*.

He did not wish to believe that of himself but the notion would not fade—nor would the arousal it gave him.

He'd not supposed even for a moment that she would permit it, that she would allow matters to go so far—that she would trust him so much that she would allow him to enact his deepest, most private fantasy upon her willing flesh.

The actual experience had been everything he could have hoped it would be. The feel of her flesh quivering, the sound of his hand on her sweet round bottom, the noises she had made, whimpers of pain and pleasure and aching, wordless protest. She had liked it as much as he had. He'd made her so wet and hot inside, so ready.

He'd stolen her orgasms like a thief, forcing her to give them over and over again, savoring her submission, savoring her sweet helpless lust. He'd wanted to flip her over then and there, spread her legs and drive himself into her, but he'd still been fully clothed.

Clever, naughty Mira to have come up with such a wickedly satisfying solution to his dilemma.

He'd been so proud of her as she rode him. She'd been extraordinary, hot and glowing with power, taking him as he'd imagined taking her. She was so beautiful—and so very, very animal.

Perhaps as much of an animal as he had become.

Miranda did not sleep, although she let Cas tend her as if she did.

His touch was as careful and tender as it had previously been dominant and unyielding. Allowing him to perform such intimate cleansing was one of the easiest and hardest things she had ever done.

Her trust was absolute. She knew him, knew with every drop of blood in her veins that he loved her, that he would never harm her.

What she didn't understand was how she knew it.

Nor could she reconcile the arrogant, rude man whom she'd initially disliked with this fierce and tender lover.

At last he put away the cloth and lay down beside her, pulling her to his chest so that her head tucked beneath his chin. The sigh that came from him was the sigh of a man coming home.

Miranda was silent for a moment, tracing the circles of his waistcoat buttons with one finger. Then she could keep her curiosity at bay no longer. "May I ask you a question, Cas?"

He smiled. "Of course."

She gave a tiny snort. "There is no 'of course' about it. The two of you almost always turn my questions aside with a jest or a fascinating tale of the Wild Worthingtons."

Cas had no doubt that she was right, about both him and Poll. It was mostly habit, for two young bachelors with dubious means had to remain as entertaining as possible, if they wished to be invited back.

Habit for Poll and, for him, part of his mask.

A viper of uneasiness commenced to twine in his belly, but he only nodded. "Go on," he teased.

She hesitated for a moment, then lifted her gaze to his. "There is something I wish to know and if you cannot answer, then don't. I only want the truth."

He went still at her seriousness. "I will answer, if I can."

She ran light fingers down the buttons of his waistcoat. "What happened with that woman?"

She felt him smile against her hair. "She was almost blown up in an alleyway."

She tugged assertively on his weskit. "Answer or don't, but do not pretend that I am not asking what I am asking."

"Ah." He didn't wish to tell her and yet, he longed to be as honest with her as she was with him. She had given him a gift with her beautiful, constant truth. He had taken it all without a single confession of his own.

"It is not a pretty story."

She merely watched him, waiting. Those eyes were fathoms deep.

He inhaled and spoke, before he stopped himself forever. "When I was still a boy, barely fifteen, I was so sure that I was already a man. I wanted all the rights and privileges of one, to be sure.

"My . . . another young man I knew was taken by an older woman as her lover. She was good-hearted and lusty and he had a roaring good time with her. He told me everything and I was most envious of his fun. I thought to myself that I should do the same.

"There was a lady I had seen many times, for she lived near our home. She had always fascinated me. I decided that she was the one I wished to learn from. I looked for her, and arranged to be in places where she might appear.

"I don't know why I focused on her, except that of course she was very attractive. I think she was perhaps forty, but her figure was as slim as a girl's and in her black gowns she seemed haunting and mysterious."

"Black gowns?"

He looked down at her. "Yes, she was a widow."

"Like me."

He didn't quite know how to answer that, so he merely tucked her closer into his body and continued his story.

"She was not inclined to take notice of me at first, but I grew bolder and more persistent. I was man-sized and gangly, all hands and feet, but women had been giving me admiring glances for a while, so I decided that her lack of interest was not because of my looks."

She gave a low laugh. "No, I should say not."

He smiled at her, a quick flash of white teeth in the dimness, but it faded quickly as he went on.

"The lady was the widow of a very powerful and wealthy lord. When I finally penetrated her defenses, I learned that she had been squeezed out of the family home by her husband's grown children, the heir and his brothers. Her husband had left her with nothing of her own but a tiny pittance. That was why she lived in our vicinity, which is quite respectable but not where the wealthy and powerful usually gravitate.

"I could feel something in her. I don't know if I saw it in her eyes or felt it radiating out through her skin, but she had a restlessness—"

"Like me."

He dropped a kiss down on the tip of her nose, then shook his head. "No, not at all like you. Quite the opposite. I thought it was passion. I took her shadows for loneliness and hunger and sexual need, like yours, like my own. It was not those.

"It was rage. A towering and vindictive rage toward all men. And she found her first willing victim in me."

Miranda withdrew slightly to gaze up at him. "What did she do to you?"

"Everything." He closed his eyes briefly. "She did everything to me."

He felt her fingertips on his cheek, his temple, stroking through his hair.

"Tell me," she whispered.

He dropped his face into her neck, shaking his head, using her scent and her warmth to keep himself here, in her arms, in this moment and not in the past.

"You know a bit already. There are things I have done with you."

She nodded thoughtfully. "Wild things. The naughty harem girl."

He chuckled at her apt label, at her sweetness and her shimmering, unique honesty. "Yes."

She narrowed her eyes thoughtfully. "Dangerous things, like the window."

He smiled, his blood stirring at the memory. "I do apologize for the window. That was . . . unsafe."

"Why do you like to do those things, if you did not like what she did to you?"

"Oh, but I did like what she did, for the most part. I couldn't stay away from her. I was in her thrall and I had no desire to break that wicked bond. She knew that. She made me prove my usefulness again and again—with her, with her decadent friends."

Miranda's eyes widened. "Oh. Poll said nothing about that."

Cas shook his head. "I'm sure he doesn't know it all. I allowed such treatment because I imagined myself in love. I thought she loved me. I thought she was testing my love— that I could prove my loyalty by obeying her every wish."

He let out a sigh. "Power corrupts, they say. It corrupted her. It amused her to push my slavish devotion to its limits. She would cry and wail and say that I did not love her enough, until I would beg her for a chance, any chance, to prove my heart. Then she would push me away, telling me that if I came back to her, then she would know that I truly loved her."

He smiled slightly, an expression so devoid of joy that Miranda's heart flinched to see it. "I told myself that our love was special, that it could not be defined by the usual boundaries—and, since I am a Worthington, those usual boundaries were quite flexible to begin with—but even I had to see what I had become—"

Miranda's arms tightened about him.

"A plaything," he said flatly. "A puppet on a string, dancing madly for my lover, my adored puppeteer. I was nothing to her but a way to pay off her gambling debts. I was nothing but a dupe."

Miranda shook her head. "You were but fifteen. Think a moment. That is only a few short years older than Attie is now. If, in two years, Attie fell into the hands of someone malignant, would she be the one to blame?"

Cas shook his head and moved back, stepping away from the clemency that she offered. "I—she—"

The words were jumbling in his mind.

Miranda slipped toward him, her palms on his chest, her fingers tightening around his lapels. "You were not yet a man," she murmured. "You were scarcely more than a child, vulnerable and easily influenced. She was a woman too corrupted by her own degradation to see that."

"I lost control completely. I spiraled down to a place of true darkness—"

She shivered. "I don't want to go there."

"I have no wish to revisit it myself. But I cannot deny that the journey changed me—that because of it, I want more than just sweet, soft, romantic lovemaking." He looked down into her sea green eyes and wished he could submerge in her so that she could truly understand. "I need the fire," he confessed softly. "I *need* to burn."

She bit her lip, thinking. "I like it when you burn, by and large. I like being swept up in your storm." She ducked her head. "I wish I were bold enough to sweep you up in mine."

He tipped a finger beneath her chin and lifted her gaze to meet his. "Miranda," he said seriously. "You already have."

She tried to smile at him, but she was overtaken by a most enormous yawn. Mortified, she clapped a hand over her mouth.

He laughed out loud and she was glad to see the shadows gone from his eyes. He bent to kiss her. She tried to wind her arms about his neck for a deep, long one, but he ducked away after only a single, sweet buss and left the bed.

"You, pretty creature, need to sleep." He tucked her back in like a child.

She wanted to disagree, to talk him into staying, or possibly seduce him into staying, but the yawns would not stop. Finally, she waved him out with watering eyes, unable to do more than roll over onto her side in her exhaustion.

As her eyes fell closed as if weighted, and the darkness of sleep crept up around the edges of her mind, Miranda's thoughts skidded sideways.

I am not the woman I was.

I do not mind so much. The old Miranda seems dry as a husk in memory—a woman so empty that she scarcely needed to breathe.

I breathe now. I pant, I moan, I shamelessly scream out my orgasms until my throat is rendered hoarse. My blood pumps through my veins, my skin tingles, my body aches with lust and satisfaction and athletic overuse.

The old Miranda is dead. I am Mira, the woman Miranda was never allowed to be.

I have a lover. A lover who believes I am also attracted to his brother. So in his mind, I have two lovers?

And don't forget Mr. Seymour.

She did keep forgetting Mr. Seymour.

In another part of Mayfair, in a drafty terraced house whose walls did little to keep out the damp from the nearby river, a woman sat with several shawls wrapped about her shoulders.

Even in early summer, the house was too deep in the shadow of larger ones to get much sun. The nearby Fleet

River emitted a constant, chilling fog in the mornings that wormed its way through every crack and open seam of her "snug little hideaway."

The weasel-faced land agent had lied about that, too, of course. God had a plan for the liars in the world, and Miss Constance Talbot hoped He wouldn't forget the man who had sold her this dank hole with glowing letters of description that had raised bucolic images of flower gardening and cozy privacy and at last the immersion into her own affairs and only her own affairs!

Now she sat in stiff, chilled fury while that groveling bit of rubbish whom her brother had—for some reason that would forever escape Constance—married and left everything to, sat high and dry in Mayfair, living in *her* house!

Constance fumed. She just knew Miranda was up to something with that fellow, the smarmy one with the brown hair and the too-easy smile and the green eyes— eyes that made an old woman think of spring and flowers and the whisper of warm breezes across young, soft skin.

Men. Men couldn't be trusted. Just look at Gideon, the old fool. To have married so late, to such a young creature, whose family had fallen so far beneath the solid respectability of the Talbots.

That the awkward child had grown into a pretty woman only made Constance the more furious. Thin and clunkfooted, young Miranda had been properly cowed by Constance's vaster experience and confidence.

She'd kept the young girl properly in line, until that day when the will was read. Constance had kept meticulous track of Gideon's last wishes, although she'd pressed her lips tight as the lawyer rattled off Gideon's valuables as gifts—gifts for servants, no less!—when they ought to have remained in the family, as had been the Talbot custom for generations.

No Talbot ever gave away their wealth to the undeserving!

And when the lawyer had read the disposition of the house on Breton Square, Constance had seen Miranda's head come up, like a puppet on a string, her muddy eyes widening in realization.

The power went with the keys.

Constance's keys, which she'd been forced to turn over to Miranda like a thief.

Her subsequent decision to quit the house had been an attempt to force Miranda to admit that she couldn't get by without her.

Unfortunately, that had backfired.

Not for long, by God. Not for very damned long.

Opening her book of accounts, she withdrew a folded letter that she had read more than a dozen times and read it once more. Her informant, reporting from the premises of Talbot House itself, thought there might be something untoward going on with Miranda and that green-eyed fellow.

It wasn't much to go on, but it was a start.

Her home would belong to her once more. It was only a matter of time.

Chapter Twenty-three

"It is so nice of, ah, *all* of you to come."

Miranda sat opposite her guests in the parlor, with her hands folded in her lap and her posture perfect. On the sofa opposite her, lined up in ascending order of height and possibly descending order of ferocity, were Atalanta, Elektra, and Orion Worthington.

If she was not mistaken, she was under examination.

She did not mind the inspection, for she was enormously curious about the rest of the Worthingtons. So, despite her long list of frantic preparations for the Marquis of Wyndham's ball the following night, she set aside her list of Lementeur's detailed instructions and met with her callers in the parlor.

"Mama and Papa wanted to come as well, but we wouldn't allow it." Elektra was quite matter-of-fact about ordering her parents about, Miranda thought.

Attie nodded. "Papa would only quote at you, and then Mama would footnote. Prospero's daughter, you know. He's going on and on about it."

Miranda smiled. Something she understood. "Yes, I believe my mother was quite an aficionado of Shakespeare."

Elektra tilted her head. "Believe?"

Attie leaned over, cupped her hand around Ellie's ear, and whispered loudly enough for Twigg to hear where he hovered in the hallway, *"Orphan!"*

Electra's expression took on a glazed instant of envy. Just a flash, however. It was not the first time Miranda had run across that particular response from people, but Elektra managed to hide it well and move on. While her parents sounded as though they were a considerable amount of work, they also seemed to be loved and appreciated for who they were.

Mr. Orion Worthington, who looked very little like *her* Mr. Worthingtons, other than being handsome and tall and rather delicious in a soulful and poetic fashion, merely looked at Miranda with neither sympathy or envy.

Miranda looked down at her hands and then back up at the three invaders—er, *guests*. "The tea should be here at any moment."

The tea had best be there in less than a moment, or she would find herself a new butler!

From behind her, Twigg cleared his throat. "Tea, madam."

Miranda did not close her eyes in relief. She was rather proud of that fact. "Attie, will you pour?"

Elektra twitched at that, as if inclined to leap between Attie and the teapot, protecting the china with her very life.

Attie, however, did a fine job. There was only a little slosh in Orion's saucer and she forgot to put a gingersnap on Elektra's plate, but Miranda smiled approvingly at her little friend as she sat back down.

Elektra and Orion stared at their sibling with frank astonishment, then turned their impressed gazes upon Miranda.

Miranda simply sipped her tea with a small smile.

She'd never taught Attie a thing. She'd known the child was brilliant and had merely poured precisely and serenely for her once on that rainy afternoon. She'd known Attie hadn't missed a thing.

"Mr. Worthington—" Goodness, it felt strange to call another man that! "I have been told that you are a scholar of the animal kingdom. I would love to know more about your findings on the migration patterns of the crested tit."

Orion set down his tea and expounded succinctly and briefly on his research. Miranda asked a few questions that she was pleased to think sounded not-too-idiotic. Orion, upon making his final point, turned to his sisters and stated, "She is quite intelligent."

Now it was Attie's and Elektra's turn to regard their brother with slack-jawed surprise, and then turned blinking befuddled expressions upon Miranda.

Miranda simply sipped her tea. *I believe I may pass this test.*

Elektra, who seemed to give Attie full competition in the ferocity finals, set upon Miranda at once. The latest gossip—thank heaven for Mr. Button!—the latest novels and plays—thank goodness for Poll!—and even the current mood in Parliament—score one for Mr. Seymour!

Miranda passed with apparently high marks, for the three of them leaned back a bit from their offensive postures and regarded her in meditative silence for a moment.

"I told you," Attie whispered, loudly enough for Twigg to hear in the hallway.

Miranda set down her tea. "Now that the examinations are over, is there anything else I may assist you with?"

Elektra tilted her head at the faint challenge in Miranda's tone. "You're even-tempered as well. I should have broken something over someone's head by now."

"Probably mine," Attie muttered.

Orion abruptly stood. "Thank you for the tea, Mrs. Talbot." Before Miranda could respond, he turned and strode from the room, no doubt nearly running over Twigg in the hallway.

Elektra, who seemed to find nothing unusual about her brother's abrupt departure, turned to her little sister. "Attie, go with Rion."

A fearsome scowl commenced formation. Miranda cleared her throat. "Atalanta, your sister and I wish to discuss shoes and hair, now that there are no men in the room."

At the very thought, Attie sagged with incipient boredom. She grudgingly slid off the sofa, trudging after her brother.

Elektra smiled conspiratorially at Miranda, her expression tinged with respect. When Attie suspiciously slowed her pace further, hoping to overhear some adult conversation, Elektra began with, "Don't you think the new heel height is ridiculous? I shan't be able to dance in them at all!"

Miranda nodded. "Outrageous. Why, I shall be as tall as my partners!"

Miranda could practically feel Attie rolling her eyes as she sped up to race out the front door after Orion.

Then Elektra turned to Miranda. "Out with it!"

Miranda raised a brow. "Out with what, pray tell?"

"How did you do it? How did you get Attie to pour tea without requiring three hours of cleaning afterward?" Elektra gestured at the perfectly unharmed tea set in disbelief.

Miranda smiled. "Why, I asked her to."

An impatient frown crossed Elektra's brow; then it faded and Miranda could see that the young woman was truly considering her words. "You asked."

Miranda nodded. "There are so many of you and she is so much younger. I think it is all she can do to not be trampled in the herd. She feels she must fight, fight to be noticed, to be heard." *To be loved,* but Miranda couldn't say that. Besides, she could see the affection Elektra had for her wayward sibling. It was a great deal to ask of an eighteen-year-old woman to mother a child not hers. Poor Elektra didn't seem to have much opportunity to simply be a girl with Attie and all those brothers.

"I have always wished for siblings," Miranda said shyly. "I have been told your family is a mad lot, but still I envy you your closeness."

Ellie looked away with a shrug, but Miranda could see her expression soften. "'Tis bedlam, that's what it is."

Elektra glanced around the silent parlor and tilted her head to listen to the complete absence of noise in Miranda's house. "In contrast, it is so peaceful here."

Miranda tilted her head to listen, too. "Yes, it is a quiet house," she said sadly. "I have often wished for more humanity within it."

Elektra snorted. "I'm up to the tip of my nose in humanity. I should be happy to share!"

Miranda smiled, something inside her warming at the very concept of sharing the Worthingtons. "My dear, do not make promises unless you intend to keep them."

Elektra drew back slightly at that, and considered her own hands in her lap, unconsciously mirroring Miranda. Then she looked back up with a new light in her eyes. "Mrs. Talbot, I don't think I'd mind at all."

Miranda blushed and made herself busy with the tea tray. Elektra, who despite Mr. Worthington's contention that she could make a saint into a shrew in a week's time, seemed to be a sensible and sensitive young woman, delicately changed the subject.

"I must tell you about my new gown! I'm terribly excited, for there's a marvelous ball coming up—"

After a moment, Miranda realized that Elektra was speaking of the Marquis of Wyndham's ball. She longed to join in on the girl's excited plans, but she'd promised Mr. Button not to say a word!

However, it was nice to know that tomorrow night she might have a friend in the hall.

Button held up his latest creation to the morning light from the window and peered closely at a beaded detail on the bodice. It was, of course, perfect. He smiled.

Miranda would be the second most beautiful woman at tomorrow night's ball. Button felt that to be fair, since Lady Wyndham was a dear friend and a natural redhead, to boot—an opportunity not to passed up, creatively speaking.

This was very good, for Attie had informed him that matters between the twins had become strained to the point of actual violence. There was not a moment to lose in the quest to provide adequately handsome and wealthy distraction for Miranda's seeking heart.

The door to Button's sanctuary opened. Without turning around, he felt Cabot come into the room. Cabot, ever-present, even when Button was all alone. Beautiful, untouchable Cabot.

Button pasted on a cheery grin and whirled, flipping the gown out in an elegant swirl. "Well, what do you think?"

This was an important question. Cabot's taste was unerringly elegant, his judgment severely, ruthlessly stylish. Button, on the other hand tended to overdo, just a touch, on the delightful dramatic possibilities in every outfit.

Button created freely, confident that Cabot would edit him flawlessly.

Cabot eyed the gown. "This is for Miranda?"

Button nodded. They had all become quite familiar, referring to her as Miranda. Once past her initial—but considerable!—reserve, she was delightfully friendly and warm.

Cabot walked around Button slowly, then the other way. At a twirl of the younger man's finger, Button flipped the gown to reveal the back.

Cabot pursed his lips slightly. Button glanced down at the gown. "What? Too much? Or too little?"

Cabot shook his head. "It is perfect."

A smile creased Button's puckish features. "I know."

Cabot took the gown from him to pack it carefully in layers of tissue for the journey to Miranda's house. As he opened the door, Button remembered. "Ah, Cabot, how did your little reconnaissance mission go?"

Cabot halted with one arm braced high on the door to keep the gown from touching the floor and his torso twisted back toward Button. It was an unbearably romantic pose, made all the more dazzling by Cabot's complete lack of awareness. Button concealed the way his breath caught at his assistant's unearthly beauty, his effort assisted by years of practice.

Cabot reported dutifully. "The Worthingtons Squared are most definitely expected to attend Mrs. Blythe's Midsummer Madness orgy tonight instead of the Marquis of Wyndham's ball. They confirmed many weeks ago." He paused. "The young ladies present were very happy to hear it. The young men were slightly annoyed."

"Ah, youth." Button smiled. "I'm surprised you did not get an invitation in the post."

Cabot regarded him evenly. "Mrs. Blythe invited me personally."

Smiling through the twinge in his chest, Button nodded. "Well, of course. You've been a very popular guest in the past."

Cabot's face became as expressionless as marble. "That was a very long time ago, sir." Then he spun on his heel and left the office.

Button, sans witnesses, set aside his perpetually energetic demeanor for a moment and sagged wearily into his chair. *Cabot*.

Always there. Always gorgeous. Always at his right hand, presciently aware of his every need. Always waiting for him to notice.

What on earth was he going to do about Cabot?

Miranda rolled over in her warm, sumptuous bed and snuggled deeply into her pillows. She cracked her eyelids just enough to verify the hour by the light coming in the window.

The room was still dark. Marvelous. She had hours left to sleep. Her body had had two days alone to recover from her athletics with Cas, but she thought she might never catch up on her sleep!

The next time she opened her eyes, her room was still very dim, yet she could tell she'd slept many hours. She sat up and looked again at the window.

The draperies were tightly drawn, when she knew perfectly well she'd left them open. "Tildy!"

As if magically conjured, Tildy entered the bedchamber with a breakfast tray that also held a steaming pitcher of water for washing.

"Don't you fuss, missus. That dressmaker bloke gave me strict instructions that you weren't to have black sacks under your eyes and see there, you don't!"

Miranda relaxed a bit when she saw the time on her mantel clock, for it was still early afternoon and yet more when she saw in her looking-glass that she indeed looked most refreshed.

She ate sparingly, however, for the butterflies in her belly refused to rest. Both of her Mr. Worthingtons meant to attend this evening, along with their sister and parents. She could not wait to see Cas's expression when she stood before him in her delicious, new Lementeur creation!

Lementeur!

"Tildy, hurry! Mr. Button will be here in less than an hour and I still haven't had my bath!"

Would Cas think she was beautiful? Would he realize that she was a woman he could possibly . . . *love*?

Chapter
Twenty-four

Cas rummaged in Poll's wardrobe for a decent silk weskit. A man had to keep up appearances, especially at a do like Wyndham's ball.

He wished Miranda could accompany him, but Poll had reminded him that an occasion of this magnitude came with sartorial expectations—expectations that a woman still wearing her drab, half-mourning gowns could not meet.

If he'd thought of it in time, he would have had Button whip something up for her—something green or perhaps blue. Wispy and flowing and serene.

"I saw it this morning when I went to pick up my dress," came Elektra's excited voice in the hallway. Her distinctive step—half authoritative stride, half childish skip, as if she hadn't the patience to actually walk anywhere—sounded down the boards of the hall, coming toward Poll's room.

"Will it suit her, do you think?" Poll's voice.

Cas grabbed three possible weskits and thrust them behind his back, whirling to stand innocently next to the swiftly shut wardrobe. He didn't want Poll to—

"Miranda is going to be the most beautiful woman at

Wyndham's," gushed Ellie, coming closer. "The plot is going marvelously. Cas won't know what hit him—"

Ellie turned into the doorway of Poll's room and stopped short. "Oh."

Poll stumbled to a halt behind her. "Ellie, do watch where you—" His eyes widened. "Oh."

Cas straightened, forgetting his casual pose, letting the weskits fall to the floor behind him. "What plot?" A chill twined in the center of his gut.

"Cas!" Ellie assessed his frozen face and swallowed hard. "I—oh, bother!" Giving up on trying to out-Worthington a Worthington, she simply turned and fled, dashing around Poll before he could do more than raise a hand in protest at her desertion.

Cas breathed in and out. Again. Poll watched him like a rabbit before a fox.

At last, Cas unfroze his lips enough to speak. "What. Plot?"

Poll gave him a sickly grin that faded quickly. "It isn't so much a plot as—well, Attie got it into her head, you know how Attie can be—"

Cas felt the ice spread, hardening his belly, spreading upward and out.

Poll ran his fingers through his head. "She got Button to give Miranda a new wardrobe, all that sort of stuff—thinking that if Miranda had some rich beaus to choose from that she would lose interest in us poor, bedraggled Worthingtons."

Cas tilted his head. "I find it hard to see where you fit in there—being one of the poor, bedraggled ones."

Poll shrugged. "I came in later—actually, just recently, really—"

"Poll."

"I'm not really courting Miranda!" Poll blurted. Then

he ran a hand over his face. "I'm glad to get that one out, actually. It's bloody hard to keep anything from you—"

"You're lying." The ice was turning to stone, like walls around him, a labyrinth, turning him this way and that, tricking him. "I saw you kissing her, in her window."

Poll threw out his hands. "I know! A bloody awkward kiss it was, too!" He had the nerve to beam at Cas. "Just awful, like laying one on Aunt Clemmie!"

"You were putting on an act?" He felt raw. "You knew I was there?" No secrets in the dark for him, then. He felt foolish, thinking himself private when all the world seemed to be watching.

Poll rolled his eyes. "No, not then, actually, but I did catch you outside the house and then at the children's home—"

Cas flinched. He'd looked the fool truly, then, hadn't he?

"And Miranda told me she thought you cared for her. From the sound of it, I thought so, too—"

Ice. "Miranda told you?" Stone.

Poll opened his eyes wide in protest. "It isn't like that! It's only that I know that after what that Quinton woman did to you when we were lads—"

The blow was nearly physical, so much so that Cas stepped back and away from that truth. "You know—you knew all this time?"

Naked. He was stripped, raw and naked before the world, thinking himself clothed, thinking his secrets safe, his darkness hidden deep inside. All the while it had been sitting on display in the middle of the street with its hands over his eyes.

The hot slide of fury, a knife to cut through the shadows with. "You." He stared at Poll, feeling shame and pain and hatred boiling up from deep and long ago. "Anyone but you! You set me up—you and Miranda, manipulating me, twisting and turning me—"

Poll paled. "No. No, Cas. Not like that. I just—I simply couldn't allow you to ruin it—I knew you'd let her get away, just like you've walked away from every chance of happiness you've ever had!" Poll took a step forward, one hand reaching out. "Cas, you need Miranda. You need love. If you lose her, you'll just be emptier than ever—"

Too much truth. Too raw. Too open.

Cas spun from it, from the look of pity and love and Poll's eyes, from the knowledge that once again he'd been moved about like a pawn on the chessboard, thinking himself a free man, all the while naked and blind.

"No." He turned away from Poll, away from Miranda, away from all of it. *"No. I am no one's puppet! Do you hear me? I will not dangle from your strings!"*

He left Poll there, pale and shaken.

Miranda poured the tea and smiled at Mr. Seymour, trying to conceal her exasperation. There was so much to do and so little time left!

Of course, she ought to have realized that he would keep to his regular—one might almost say "mechanical"— calling schedule. A brief note in yesterday's post about her unavailability would have freed up her afternoon nicely!

As it was, she could scarcely tell him so now. She only hoped he would drink his tea quickly, recite his usual newsy tidbits, eat a bit of cake—and then leave!

Mr. Seymour took the tea with his usual gravity. "I am most glad to see you are well, Mrs. Talbot. It distressed me greatly when you were abed."

I will not turn his words into innuendo just to keep from nodding off. I will not.

Instead, she decided to put the bothersome call to good use. Standing, she moved across the parlor. "Mr. Seymour, while I must thank you for this very thoughtful offering—" She took the box containing the dress from a shelf by the door and held it before her. "—I now find myself in an uncomfortable position. I do not wish to offend you, but I cannot accept this gift."

He blinked and then he flushed oddly. "I am confused, Mrs. Talbot. I had hoped . . . but it seems that you are not interested in my pursuit of you after all."

"I apologize for that, good sir. I ought to have made my feelings clear sooner. I was merely distracted—" One could certainly say that truthfully. "—by some unrelated concerns, which have now come to a close."

With sudden and strange urgency, he reached for her hand. "If I may be so bold, Mrs. Talbot, I implore you to consider my suit one last time. I know I am not the most exciting of fellows but I do like to believe I am a solid contender for any lady's hand. You should think on this, before it is too late—" He went down upon his knee at once. There was no mistaking the pose or the gleam in his eye. "Mrs. Talbot, I am your humblest servant and I long for your good company for the rest of my life. Will you be my wife?"

One had to give him points for boldness, and she never thought she would say that about Mr. Seymour.

Pulling her hand from his damp grip, Miranda inhaled. "Mr. Seymour, please stop. You have been a fine friend to me, but I am not interested in your suit. And I shall not alter my feelings."

Mr. Seymour cleared his throat. Slowly he released her hands. "Mrs. Talbot, I am disconcerted." He stared at her with bulging eyes unblinking.

Then, as he started to recover from his surprise, she saw it. She saw the thing that had been lurking behind the polite mask and the well rehearsed newsy tidbits.

There was no mistaking the gleam of vindictive fury

in his eyes. She knew it. She recognized it at once. It had been the gleam in her grandmother's eyes, and in Constance's.

A curl of his lip resembled a snarl. She leaned away from his scornful countenance. "Mr. Seymour, it seems it is time for you to leave."

He drew back, his face gone blank with surprise for an instant. It was a relief to see the sneaky little reptile that was his true self scurry back behind his bland camouflage.

Miranda stood and strolled to the door of the parlor, where she turned to assess him evenly. "Twigg will show you out, sir."

With that she turned and left the room, her thoughts already turning to her room upstairs, where waited Mr. Button, Attie, Cabot, and an enticing pile of boxes marked with a distinctive looping *L.*

I am going to a ball! With Cas!

Her feet fairly danced her up the stairs, with not a single stumbled step.

Cas snapped his cravat about his neck and began to tie it in short, sharp jerks.

Through his open door, he could hear his father reciting. " 'We are such stuff / As dreams are made on, and our little life / Is rounded with a sleep.' "

Involuntarily, Cas's well-trained memory provided the footnote—in Iris's voice, of course—*The Tempest,* Act 4, Scene 1.

Miranda.

Ah, so his parents were in on the scheme.

What of the post-boy? How about the fellow who delivered the produce? Would he walk down the street and see knowing amusement in every face?

His cravat tore from the fury of his tying. The damned Gordian knot he was attempting to tie resisted his best effort—not that he cared. He wasn't going to Wyndham's ball, to wait on bloody Miranda like a pet! No, he was going to Mrs. Blythe's Midsummer Madness orgy, and he was going to plow Lily *and* Dilly *and* any other female who held still long enough!

After all, it was what he was best at. What he'd been born for, according to the lovely, filthy Lady Quinton. How had she described him, all those years ago—a great cock with a trivial man attached?

There was no point in trying to be anything else. There was no point in trying to keep the Prince Regent's bargain, no point in wishing he were something he was not.

No point in wanting to be *more*.

He had assumed that Poll would no longer be interested in Mrs. Blythe's entertainments, that he would go dance attendance upon Miranda at Wyndham's, but he'd learned an hour ago that Poll had every intention of accompanying him.

Cas had looked around the table at his wide-eyed expectant family and declined to fight about it.

Not that a rousing fight wouldn't do him good.

He stripped off the mangled cravat and grabbed his last pressed one. Glaring at it in the mirror, he pointed a finger. "You will tie correctly or you will undergo the dreaded iron torture."

"You can't torture it. It's mine."

Cas turned to see Poll in his doorway, wearing pegged knee trousers and a fine white shirt. At Cas's hard look, Poll shrugged irritably.

"Mama forced me to rig out. You'd better, too. She said it isn't respectful to Mrs. Blythe to go underdressed."

Cas didn't reply.

Poll wrinkled his brow. "Do you suppose she understands who Mrs. Blythe actually is?"

Cas—who once would have joined him in a highly

entertaining rant on the various, hilarious, and incorrect perceptions of Iris Worthington toward Mrs. Blythe, notorious madam and happy corruptor of innocent youth— merely stared at his twin flatly.

"Cas, you shouldn't do this. Go to Wyndham's with me. See Miranda. She'll make you forget all about this—"

Cas growled. Poll held up both hands. "Fine. All right. But don't betray her, Cas—you know what she's been through—"

"Get. Out."

Poll gave up. "I need my cream jacquard weskit."

Cas turned away. "Not here."

"You borrowed it, last October, and I haven't seen it since."

Cas's fists clenched, promptly ruining the press of the cravat. With a growl, he stripped it off and threw it at his twin. Then he went to his wardrobe and gathered half a dozen weskits into his arms.

Depositing the entire pile over Poll's head was childish but satisfying. As a seething Poll bent to gather them up again, Cas snatched up his first wrinkled cravat and turned back to the mirror. Another time he might have asked Philpott to press it again. However, the flustered housekeeper was already overwhelmed with preparing everyone else in the family for the fancy do at Lord Wyndham's.

In the mirror, he watched as Poll carefully smoothed the weskits and turned slowly to leave the room. He would not lose control. He would not slip in the slightest manner.

For if he did, he was rather afraid of what he might do to the man who used to be his best friend.

Chapter Twenty-five

In the mistress's bedchamber in the house on Breton Square, Attie was having a marvelous time, unpacking and dumping Button's boxes of pretties as fast as Cabot could follow behind her busy fingers and set them aright.

One day she would likely bother with all the ribbons and corsets and powder and go to balls and such—but in the meantime, putting Miranda together would do. It was very much like building a suspension bridge out of candles and string. Everything had to go together in the right order or, like that ill-fated construction, Miranda might list to port and not be able to hold up under the weight of Attie's wooden horse and cart that Poll had made for her when she was just a child.

So there was no call for the strain in Miranda's voice when she turned from the mirror to help Tildy rescue the long blue-green hair ribbons from Attie's fingers, which were truly only a tiny bit sticky.

"Attie, I don't believe Mr. Seymour stayed long enough to eat his tea cakes. If Twigg is being his usual dubiously efficient self, they will still be downstairs in the parlor."

Attie's eyes narrowed. She knew perfectly well she was being ousted from the proceedings. Still, tea cakes.

"What kind are they?"

Miranda frowned, thinking back. "Almond and poppy seed, I believe."

Tildy nodded helpfully. "Yes, missus. And Cook put on some of those little ginger biscuits from yesterday, too."

Cabot perked up. "Far too good for the likes of Mr. Seymour." He looked at Attie. "I call rights on the biscuits."

Attie folded her arms. "Fine. I'll go, but only because I feel like it." She flounced from the room, followed by Cabot.

As she left, she heard Miranda breathe a sigh of relief. "I do love that child, but I am as nervous as a cat as it is!"

Cabot smiled down at Attie as they went down the stairs, just a quirk of his perfect lips. "I heard it. You cannot deny it now."

"I know. I can't help being lovable." Attie grumbled. "She's all right—and she can be friends with Ellie, if she likes. It would do Ellie's vanity good to have someone around who is nearly as pretty as she is."

Cabot tilted his head, considering. "But not friends with Cas and Poll?"

Attie wrapped her arms about herself and followed Cabot into the parlor, dragging her feet a little. "I suppose it isn't Miranda's fault, how those two carry on—but they never fought before she came along and now they're fighting all over again!"

Cabot listened intently as he munched a ginger biscuit—despite his claiming them all, he ate only one to keep her company, she knew—and Attie allowed herself a full confessional, the kind of thing she kept from her family at all costs.

"(Sniff) And Ellie said that Cas's face was the color of ice—except that ice doesn't have a color, but that's Ellie for you—and (sniff) she didn't know what they said because she lost her nerve—Ellie!—and she ran for it!" She poked miserably at the tea cake on her saucer. She was so distraught, she'd eaten only four-fifths of it. She'd barely been able to choke down the first one at all. "But Philpott told me that neither Cas nor Poll are going to Wyndham's now—and they won't even see Miranda get all those new beaus, because they're both going to that party at the House of Pleasure—"

Cabot choked on his biscuit. "Attie! How do you know about that place?"

Attie chewed, absently finishing her second cake after all. "Mama told me. She said it's like a garden, full of flowers, that gentlemen come and pluck whenever they need to relax—although I've never known Cas and Poll to be all that interested in botany. Orion, perhaps, but— Cabot, are you quite all right?"

She banged Cabot on the back, most helpfully, she thought. He had no call to wave her off like that. And then he sort of covered his face with his handkerchief for a moment. If it were anyone other than Cabot, she might have suspected him of laughing at her.

But Cabot never laughed.

Poor Cabot.

A sound came from the doorway, the clearing of a male throat. Attie turned. It was that Twigg fellow, the one who looked like he didn't know whether to cross the street or go home. That's what Philpott called it when someone couldn't make up his mind about what to do, except that Twigg always looked like that, in Attie's opinion.

"If the young miss is finished with the tea tray?" Twigg looked at Attie for permission, but not at Cabot. Cabot was no better than a tradesman, it was plain on Twigg's face, and ought not to sit about in parlors with young ladies eating the household's ginger biscuits.

Which wasn't fair, really, for Cabot had only had one.

Someone sneezed, a man sneeze, but it wasn't Cabot or Twigg.

Twigg looked up, his face growing quite sharp and suspicious. Cabot and Twigg looked at each other. Twigg shook his head, quick and short. Cabot rose to his feet and joined Twigg as he started toward the other door in the room, the one that led to Miranda's little library, her "reading room" as she called it. Attie liked it for its deep windowsills with cushions upon them, although Miranda's books were mostly old Mr. Talbot's stuffy history books, but for the ones that Poll had given her.

Cabot waved Attie back to her seat, which of course she didn't return to, and he and Twigg crept carefully up to the door, Attie right on their heels. She might not be very big, but she could trip anyone, fast and dirty—and did it really matter *how* someone hit the floor, as long as they did so?

But when they pushed open the door, it was only old Seymour, sitting at a table with a book open before him, apparently lost in his reading.

When the door opened, he looked up, blinking. "Oh dear. I fear I've lost track of time. I just meant to check for a volume I lent Mrs. Talbot some weeks back, for I wished to search in the footnotes—" He drew back when he saw the two men staring at him and Attie scowling at him from between. He snapped the book shut and stood, pulling his dignity about him sternly.

"I must go. My, it grows late. Please beg Mrs. Talbot's pardon for me." More of that, blah-blah, heavens the man was a bore, and then he left with the book under his arm, mostly hidden, but Attie was short enough to read the binding.

She sneered as old Seymour let Twigg show him out. "He didn't give that book to Miranda," she told Cabot. "Poll did. Sneaky old sneak-thief!"

*   *   *

Miranda clapped her hands as Button opened the final, largest box—which Cabot had earlier secured against Attie's curious, sticky fingers—and lifted the exquisite creation from it, flicking away the folds in the fabric with an expressive gesture.

"Oh, Button! For me?"

Miranda stepped forward to touch it, although she nearly drew her hand back like a child tempted by breakables. Which was ridiculous, for she would not only wear it on her skin, but she would also dance and whirl in it tonight.

Abruptly, she couldn't wait!

It was crafted in the most beautiful shade of Turkish-blue silk, with a pattern in sapphire blue and emerald green glass beads twining sensually up one side and branching across the bodice like vines growing up a statue of a goddess. A wide sapphire velvet ribbon banded the high waist, and Button displayed a daintier version that would go about her neck, holding a single, perfect pearl pendant in a teardrop that she could already imagine would rest perfectly in the hollow of her throat.

Then she noticed some other details. The gown streamed down from the waistline in a sleek column. It lacked the fullness in the skirts that Miranda had become accustomed to in the demure and practical gowns Constance had ordered for her.

There would be no striding about in this glorious creation. *I shall have to drift like a ghost!*

Button climbed onto a ready chair and held the gown over her head. She dived upward into it, for he did not wish to pool it on the floor for her to step into.

"It will crease, darling. In fact, from this moment onward, you probably ought not to sit, other than the carriage ride. Of course, if you could manage to lie flat?

Miranda frowned. "It is a ball. May I dance?"

From his perch, Button pondered her for a long moment. "You ought to manage a waltz well enough. Mind you, no country reels."

Miranda's brows went up. She had intended sarcasm.

Button clambered down from his place on the chair and moved behind her to fasten her up the back. She twisted a bit, wishing to see more in the mirror.

Button gave her bottom a little spank. "Be still."

Miranda blinked at that. Goodness, the world certainly made free with her bottom lately.

She held her breath as he turned her toward the mirror at last. "Oh."

She was beautiful. There was no denying it, no demurring, no waving off of compliments. She was absolutely gorgeous. "I had no idea," she murmured in astonishment.

What a simply magical gown. What a strange and magical little man, this Liar.

"You'll notice the new waistline," he went on. "It is a classical line, very Greco-Roman, but the band around is much wider, thus lowering the waist by a few inches. It adds a certain elegance, don't you think?"

Miranda bit her lip. Her body seemed terribly well defined in this gown. In fact, she was quite sure her bosom had never been so plentiful!

The gown was beyond her wildest dreams, however. "The new low waistline," Miranda murmured. "I've truly fallen out of mode, haven't I? When did that happen?"

Button, who was still behind her, fastening what was likely number twenty-five of the fifty buttons, straightened to smile angelically over her shoulder into the mirror.

"Tomorrow."

Miranda went still. It suddenly occurred to her that for someone who had always preferred to stand on the sidelines and observe, she was about to become very, very visible.

To think she might, under Button's patronage, be one of those astonishing women who set the mode of the day!

Button seemed to think such a thing routine. Of course, he would. He was the great Lementeur. Still buttoning, he recited a list of all his favorite clients—"Women," he told her, "who changed the path of our history. After that," he added, "creating a new bodice line is an amusing little game.

"You shall be one of those, I think," he murmured as he took a tiny stitch somewhere in the back with the threaded needle that he'd kept thrust into the lapel of his perfectly fitted silk surcoat. "If you wish, you could quite easily fix the attention of a viscount, or even a duke."

Miranda blinked; then a short laugh of disbelief burst from her lips. "Oh, no. Oh, Button, that's . . ." *Impossible.*

There is only one man's attention I wish to fix.

And for the first time she really believed she could— his attention and his heart. Her beautiful, darkly shining Cas.

She suddenly felt light and joyous, ready to show the world that she was so much more than simply her inexcusable parents' child, more than her repressive husband's widow.

I am Mira. I am beautiful, and brave, and invincible . . . and in love. I have nothing to fear.

The past is in the past. At last.

A slow smile spread over her face, her body, and her soul. With her fingertips to her lips, she gazed in wonder at herself in the mirror.

Mr. Button watched the joy infuse her features, and his anxious face creased into a puckish grin. "Ah! This is good, then?"

Miranda made a small sound of disbelief. "Good? It

is astonishing! Wondrous!" She lifted her chin, her joy
bubbling out of her in a lilting chuckle. "You need not
worry over wrinkles from the carriage, dear Button! I do
believe I could fly to Wyndham's ball!"

A short time later, the lovely Mrs. Talbot left the house on
Breton Square with a smile on her pretty face. Button was
as proud as any papa, or mother duck watching her hatch-
ling take to the water.

Swim, my dear!

Oh, when he got his hands about the throats of those
two rotters! Really, to spin their wily web around a perfectly nice creature like Miranda!

There would be no more of that now. Miranda would
go to the ball, advertise his genius and her own beauty
while he took a well-deserved celebration with his Cabi-
net.

Really, the world had no idea of the intricacy involved
in launching a legendary beauty! As if one could simply
be born fabulous!

Button helped Miranda into the rented carriage and
gave the driver directions to Lord Wyndham's grand house
in Grosvenor Square.

Once the carriage was lost among the hordes of others
heading out to their entertainments, Button turned to re-
enter Miranda's house to gather his tools and saw Cabot
stepping out with the already packed cases in his capable
hands, along with Button's hat and coat and gloves. Cabot
stopped, lifting his head, looking for Button.

Button's throat tightened. That jawline . . . just devastating. Then, as he always must, Button pushed Cabot's
incandescent—naturally born!—appeal to the back of his
consciousness and forced himself to see only the useful
assistant, who was now striding toward him. "Cabot,
you're a godsend!"

Cabot looked down at him calmly. "No one sent me. I am never far."

Later, at Worthington House—which had never been so quiet!—the three conspirators, Button, Cabot, and Attie, sat down at the kitchen table and lifted their hot chocolates high.

Cabot glanced askance at the inattentive Philpott rocking in her chair by the ovens. Attie dismissed his concerns with a wave of the lemon biscuit in her hand, which Philpott had prepared for the sole purpose of cajoling another very fine bonnet from the great Lementeur.

"Don't mind Phillie. She's on her second pot of tea. I could chase a cobra about the kitchen and she'd never notice."

Cabot slid his gaze toward Attie. "Tell me that never happened."

Attie only smiled.

Button tapped the kitchen table impatiently with the head of his entirely-for-striking-a-fashionable-pose walking stick. "Attention, if you please! We have a dire emergency of the Cas and Poll variety!"

Attie stopped in mid-chew, a frown skewering her brow. "Mmph-phy?"

"Emergency?" Cabot translated for Button. "The plan came off swimmingly. Miranda has never been more beautiful. What could go wrong now?"

Button paused for dramatic effect. "Miranda is *in love*."

Attie's jaw dropped, crumbs and all. Cabot let out a long breath.

"Oh damn." That was Cabot, who never cursed.

"Oh my." That was Attie, who often cursed. "Are you sure?"

Button nodded, obviously much gratified by their shock and amazement. "I told her she could easily angle for a duke. She only smiled dreamily."

"So you believe we are too late." Cabot, who disliked sweets, absently took a lemon biscuit and bit into it. When he noticed, he handed it to Attie, bite-mark and all.

She dug in at once, for Attie always did think best while chewing. Or hanging upside down. She'd learned long ago not to mix the two.

Button spread his hands. "My worry, exactly!" He ran his fingers distractedly through his thinning hair, disarranging it madly. "And now I've made her one of the most beautiful women in London! What are we going to do?"

Cabot reached out, but didn't quite touch Button's hand where it lay on the tabletop. "Sir, there is nothing we can do tonight—and Miranda is safely in the hands of Lady Wyndham, with the twins safely occupied at Mrs. Blythe's."

Attie nodded. "Ellie and I managed to keep them away from Miranda all day. We can keep it going a little longer, I think."

Button let out a breath, then mustered up a smile. "Yes. There is time to think of some solution."

In thanks, he reached out to put a hand over Attie's smaller one and Cabot's larger one. It was a gesture of relief and friendship. There was no reason to imagine that he felt Cabot's hand vibrate slightly beneath his.

No reason at all.

Chapter Twenty-six

Since Miranda had never been terribly in the know with Society gossip, Button had given her a few clues about the stunning redhead who greeted her in the grand hall of Wyndham House.

"Lady Alicia, Marchioness of Wyndham. Fallen woman, such a scandal, married very well anyway. No one in Society remembers her past. I know that because they say so every time they mention her. Don't tell anyone, but she has saved the British Empire at least twice— and goodness knows the trouble she saved our future citizens! Don't let the fact that she is petite and curvaceous fool you. That ginger hair comes with a temper. She killed the most dangerous man in the world with the very knife with which *he* had just stabbed *her*! It's a wonderful story, which I can't possibly tell you, because it is a state secret. In addition, she has the most marvelous taste in bonnets. You should see what she can do with a veil!"

Miranda looked a few inches down at the ridiculously beguiling creature who stood smiling at her in welcome. Lady Alicia's Lementeur gown was in a rich bronze that made her hair look like flame. The beading swept down over her from one shoulder, making her look as though she stood among green branches. Her gown also sported the "new" waistline.

Her bosom looked even better than Miranda's.

Lady Alicia didn't look like a killer. Or a fallen woman.

Then again, I don't look like a woman who is secretly having a wildly wicked affair. Miranda looked down at herself in the fitted bronze gown that did miraculous things for her middling bosom. *Or perhaps I do.*

Miranda adored Mr. Button, and Mr. Button adored Lady Alicia. That was all Miranda needed to know about her. She smiled back at her hostess in delight.

"Button has told me so much about you!" they said simultaneously.

They both laughed. Lady Alicia smiled at her conspiratorially. "Button has perhaps told me a bit *too* much about you! Tell me, are Worthington men as delicious as they look?"

"Exceptionally scrumptious." Miranda quirked a brow. "And how fares your stab wound, my lady? Have you saved the nation lately?"

"I like you!" Lady Alicia giggled. "Mutual blackmail guarantees mutual silence!"

She tucked her arm through Miranda's and walked her into the ballroom, glancing down at their similar gowns. "Button thinks of everything. We look quite well matched, don't we?"

Miranda agreed. "We are most appetizing. I fully intend to systematically break hearts all evening long."

Lady Alicia snickered. "Come, then! Let us make grown men weep!"

Miranda wasn't sure whether it was Lady Alicia's patronage or the Lementeur gown, but by the end of the first hour, Mrs. Gideon Talbot was officially declared a devastating Original.

By the end of the second hour, she could scarcely move for the circle of new suitors about her. Even Mr. Seymour lurked nearby, though he could not possibly have mistaken her refusal for anything but definitive. She saw him eyeing her gown sourly.

However, she refused to allow anyone's bitterness to ruin her evening!

By the end of the third hour, she'd had three spontaneous offers of marriage from young men barely old enough to shave. One of them did actually weep, just as Lady Alicia had predicted. A few older, married fellows had dropped barely veiled hints that she'd make a wonderful mistress, and she'd received one forthright offer from a distinguished silver-haired gentleman for a single night in her arms: a very fine house on the edge of Mayfair, furnishings negotiable.

She knew the street well. It was an extremely pretty house. She smiled. "Very tempting, my lord, but I fear I am well claimed already."

This response set up a clamor to know who the lucky bastard was, but Miranda only smiled mysteriously and accepted the next offer to waltz. However, as she danced, she could not help but keep her eye out for a certain tall brown-haired man.

The only thing that would make her triumph complete would be if Cas could see her transformation. Unfortunately, there was as yet no sign of a single Worthington.

Damn it.

Cas strolled through Mrs. Blythe's Midsummer Madness ball and tried to remember why he'd once found this sort of thing so exciting.

So there's somewhere you'd rather be tonight?

No. No there was not. This was precisely where he belonged.

After all, it was another outstanding orgy. This year's theme was "Country Faire." Stalls lined the ballroom, with signs above them proclaiming SHOOT THE BASKET or STRONGMAN COMPETITION.

The activities were, of course, not something one would ever see in public. Cas, for one, would never think of bobbing for apples in quite the same way again.

He paused curiously at a booth where pretty young women and young men were dressed as dolls, with matching dresses and suits and faces painted with bow lips and round pink cheeks. He tilted his head, trying to figure out what the game might possibly be.

The sign above said only HIT THE MARK!

As he watched, a portly gent was blindfolded and spun round and round. As he turned about, Cas saw more of the bloke than he really wished.

"Oh!" His brows flew up. "Ninepins!"

Sure enough, the man rushed forward and ran directly into the line of "pins." There was much blushing and ribbing when he found the last one still standing was a young man, but he allowed the "pin" to take his hand and lead him into one of the small private tents anyway.

Cas turned away with a shake of his head. He wondered if the young man's name was "Mark." Fortunately for all concerned, the events that occurred at Blythe's remained at Blythe's.

All around him, men and women were enjoying thrills and satisfaction. In contrast, Cas felt hollow. There was an ache in his chest. All he wanted, all he could *feel,* was Miranda.

I am not a puppet on her string.
I am my own man.

From the corner of his eye, he saw Poll strolling past the ninepins and stopping to gawk in surprise. Poll. Like a shadow Cas could not shake.

Like a spy.

Cas reached down and tested his fury. Yes, it was still there, still sick and roiling and black. Enough fury for a lifetime.

Enough to get him laid at least three times before he thought of Miranda again!

Enjoy the show, Poll!

Poll saw Cas throw a glare over his shoulder at him, then watched as Cas strode purposefully toward two beautiful blond women.

Lily and Dilly, on the prowl.

Unfortunately for the fellows trying to chat them up at the moment, they saw Cas coming and turned their backs on their companions, lifting their smiles up to Cas's sardonically smiling face like flowers to the sun.

The two men, younger than most at the event, were strapping fellows still in their prime, although getting a bit thick about the middles. Poll well knew that blokes like that could really pack a punch if they wished.

From the looks on their disappointed faces as they watched Cas walk away with an arm about each twin, they wished.

Damn it, Cas, if you're so damn determined to misbehave, can you not at least pick on some smaller, older fellows? Blind and creaky, doddering, even?

Sure enough, he saw Cas glance back over his shoulder at the fuming duo and laugh shortly. Then his gaze sought and met Poll's.

Twins hardly needed to speak to communicate. Poll knew precisely what Cas wanted to say.

I do as I please. No one controls me—not even you, brother!

Poll sighed. "Too bloody right no one controls you," he muttered to Cas from across the room. "Not even yourself, apparently!"

Poll reached a long arm to snatch a drink off a tray carried by a girl dressed as a barefoot country milkmaid—one in dire need of a needle and thread!—and tossed it back without even looking at it.

The whiskey hit his throat like a hammer. He wiped his mouth on his sleeve and tossed the glass to the milkmaid, who caught it with one hand. Poll barely noticed that the movement caused her tattered bodice to fail in its duty. His focus was entirely on his brother, and in keeping his furious twin from self-destruction or, worse, from breaking Miranda's heart!

Miranda whirled in yet another waltz, this time in the arms of a tall, handsome man who might have once seemed quite pleasing to her. Lord Something. Lord Fowler? No, Foley!

She was relieved that she would be able to bid her partner a polite good-bye despite the fact that he had yet to look her in the eye, obviously preferring the view somewhat lower.

Bosoms were for peeking at, not for staring! Such behavior showed a certain lack of self-control, or perhaps an infantile obsession, neither of which tendencies made her interested in becoming more closely acquainted.

She turned her smile down by several candlepower and added a tinge of entirely false regret. "Oh my! I've been danced off my feet! I believe I ought to sit this one out. I'm terribly sorry," she lied.

"Please, do not wait upon me. There are so many lovely

ladies who have yet to dance. There." She pointed out the most bosomy of all the adult women. "She hasn't had a partner for an hour!" She gave him a little push, then turned and fled while he leered.

Not even the attentions of unworthy men could upset her tonight! She felt shimmering and light as she moved about the floor, as if her body weighed nothing, buoyed skyward by exhilaration.

So this is what happiness feels like.

A servant in the stylish forest green livery of Wyndham House bowed to Miranda.

"A message for you, Mrs. Talbot."

Miranda widened her eyes, then took it from him eagerly. The smile she gave the man made him draw in his breath. She turned aside, unfolding the note.

Miranda—

She smiled. It was in Poll's cramped hand. As she read on, however, her smile faded.

I need you. Cas has been wounded in a brawl. Please, come at once!

Her heart went still with fear. Her hand shaking, she read on.

There was an address next, one nearly a half mile off.

I dare not ask anyone else. Please, tell no one!

Miranda swallowed, her dry throat catching tightly. Wildly, she looked about the room and found the liveried man. His face brightened as she neared him, but when he saw her expression, he came to instant alertness.

"Madam, how may I serve you?"

"Please, who gave this to you?"

He blinked. "It came to the door, madam. A runner boy brought it and said it was for you. Is there anything I may assist you with?"

"No. Yes! I need a carriage!"

"Lord Wyndham has several prepared. He would wish for you to take one. I shall have it brought around the front, madam."

Miranda nodded and turned away. She must go at once.

The front hall would be reached by going up the grand curving stair at the end of the ballroom. Miranda tried to move quickly, but found the way blocked. Hurriedly she dodged the lady with the ridiculously puffed sleeves, and sidestepped a servant with a tray of champagne flutes.

Keeping her eye on her escape route, she dipped and spun her way through the dancers.

I look as if I've lost my partner. He is somewhere else, hurt and in trouble.

She was agasp by the time she made it across the ballroom. Picking up her skirts, she ran lightly up the winding stair that led to the great double doors at the top.

Three steps up, she encountered a familiar lady coming down.

"Oh, good evening, Mrs. Teagarden." She was a friend of Constance's, someone in fact that Constance had always longed to impress. Miranda had no such intention, but her lifelong habit of good manners forced her to slow and nod in greeting. "You are looking most stylish this evening."

The woman's stole looked as if she'd forgotten and brought one of her many cats instead. Perhaps it had died of old age on the journey and she'd thrown it over her shoulder for a later burial?

"Oh, it's you." Mrs. Teagarden blinked at her in surprise. "But I thought you'd been run out of London!"

Miranda shook her head, confused but unwilling to take a single moment to untangle the dowager's meaning. She brushed past Mrs. Teagarden, heading upstream, dodging ladies and gentlemen and servants alike.

Just before the hall, she paused for a moment, pressing

her hand to the stitch in her side. The corset that enabled her to fit into her dress made her lungs fail to fill completely and her head swam a bit, although perhaps that was because her very blood had turned to ice.

Lightheaded with fear, she pressed her cool hands to her hot cheeks and made for the hall beyond the doors.

She must get to Cas!

Chapter
Twenty-seven

Upstairs at last, Miranda rushed through the milling guests, some still arriving and doffing their wraps amid helpful servants.

A familiar face swam through Miranda's distracted vision.

Elektra Worthington! And that must be their mother, Iris, as well. Miranda hurried forward as more Worthingtons entered the hall.

There was that fair-haired brother, what was his name? Yes, Daedalus. Such an odd name to saddle a son with. Of course, all the names in that family were a mouthful . . . Elektra, Daedalus, Atalanta.

"Miranda!" Elektra beamed at her. Miranda found herself noticing the girl's incredible beauty, even in her preoccupied state. "Mama, this is Mrs. Gideon Talbot! Miranda, this is my mother, Iris Worthington."

Miranda almost threw herself on Elektra, ready to share her worry, then remembered that Poll had said to tell no one. Not even his family—Cas's family?

Tell no one.

If he'd felt able to turn to his family, would he not have called upon his parents, or at least his brothers?

No, whatever had happened, it was clear to Miranda that she must not breathe a word.

She rushed past Elektra and Mrs. Worthington with only a nod. "So sorry. I will call, soon, but I *must* go—"

Elektra helped her mother remove her best, if slightly tatty, velvet cape—all the while watching Miranda Talbot, the world's most serene and even-tempered woman, flee the house in a white-faced panic.

"Mother, something is afoot." She frowned. "I smell a fracas brewing."

Iris peered dreamily up at the chandeliers. "Yes, my dear. Aren't those crystals lovely? They shimmer like fairy wings, casting rainbows about the room.."

Elektra patted her mother's arm absently. "Yes, Mama. Like fairy wings." For all she knew, her mother knew exactly whereof she spoke. It must be lovely to live in dreams. Unfortunately, someone had to be practical in Worthington House.

Where the bloody hell was Dade? Oh, there, bringing Papa in from the front steps where he'd been distracted by the grand ornate knocker on the door to Wyndham House.

"It's Perseus, you see," Archie was telling Dade. "Just marvelous! I know it appears at first glance to be a simple Medusa, but if you look closely, there is the hand of Perseus, clasping the snakes—"

Elektra caught Dade's eye across the hall and lifted her chin and rolled her eyes. *Trouble.*

Dade narrowed his and did a swift head count in the hallway. Everyone was accounted for but Attie and the twins. *Who?*

Elektra smirked and held up two fingers.

Who the bloody hell do you think?

Dade towed Archie closer. "How do you know?"

Elektra explained Miranda's unusual departure. "Who else would Miranda get all atwitter about? It has to be Cas or Poll."

"Or Cas and Poll," Dade finished grimly.

"You know where they are tonight," Elektra said meaningfully. "She . . . she wouldn't go *there,* would she?"

Dade frowned. "No. No, she wouldn't. Would she?"

Wyndham's driver exchanged a shocked glance with the liveried servant when Miranda recited the address she'd been given.

"Ah . . . madam, are you sure that is where you wish to go?"

Miranda, who by this time was nearly on fire with urgency, snapped uncharacteristically. "Of course, I'm sure. Now, let us go or let me find another conveyance!"

The servant looked up at the driver. "Wait for her," he instructed the man. "Er, *outside.*"

The driver nodded silently, but gave Miranda another strange look as the servant helped her into the carriage.

"Are you sure you won't let me send a footman along, madam?"

Tell no one. Miranda shook her head at the reasonable and somewhat tempting offer. "I shall be fine with the driver." Whatever Poll's secret was, he would not be betrayed by her!

The man looked worried, but shut the door and gave it a knock to signal the driver to roll on.

Traffic was not yet heavy, for the worst had been earlier and would be again later, when the various events broke up for the evening, but Miranda felt as though the carriage traveled on the back of a turtle. She fretted at every slowing of the wheels, and nearly burst into tears when a tipped cart held the carriage traffic back for half a block whilst it was righted.

At last the driver stopped before a large house on a street Miranda had never visited.

She didn't wait for him to jump down to take her hand, but slipped out of the carriage and ran up the steps.

The fellow at the door hardly even looked at her, but simply opened the door as if he saw disheveled, out-of-breath ladies every day.

Miranda ran into the front hall and then stopped, her mouth dropping open. A half-dozen ladies . . . er, women were dashing to and fro, carrying trays and looking as if they'd been dressed by someone who wished them all to catch a chill!

Apparently disheveled and breathless were quite the norm.

Miranda might be a bit unworldly, but one did not need to be a whore to recognize a whorehouse when one saw it.

A spectacularly underdressed woman approached her. "Blimey, it's about bloody time! I'm overrun! It ain't just you, is it, lovey? You've brought along a dozen friends, I hope?"

Belatedly, Miranda realized that the girl was dressed as a sort of milkmaid, if milkmaids were prone to going about with their bosom released for an airing.

She pulled her shocked gaze up to the woman's face. "I'm—I'm looking for Mr. Worthington. I need to find him at once."

The woman rolled her eyes. "Don't we all, pet? Lily and Dilly snapped up those two months back. Twins for twins, I suppose, eh?"

So Miranda was in the right place.

The outré location at least explained the "tell no one" portion of the message. Poll would hardly want his poor mother to know that he and Cas had come to a place of ill repute!

But why were they in a place like this when she'd been expecting them at Wyndham's ball?

Miranda threw off her cape and tossed it to the milk-maid. "I am here to see Mr. Worthington," she commanded. "Show me to him, now!"

The girl gaped at the stylish gown and the pearls and Miranda's no-nonsense lady-of-the-house expression and, despite her earlier cheekiness, curtsied, her generous breasts bobbing cheerfully. "Yes, miss. Right away, miss."

Miranda followed the woman into the house and down into yet another ballroom. She could see from the top of the stairs that this one was laid out in some sort of bazaar or faire.

"There." The girl stood at the railing and pointed. "That's 'im, ain't it?"

Miranda looked down the steps to an area partitioned off by bales of hay—really, some people carried a theme a bit far. Hay in a ballroom?—where she saw a familiar brown-haired fellow sitting on a velvet-lined nook carved out of the stack of bales.

Well, it was a Worthington, to be sure, but was it Cas or Poll? The fellow didn't look wounded, yet, Poll wouldn't be lolling about if Cas were severely injured?

As Miranda watched, a buxom blonde, who wore a baker's apron and a smile, approached him with a glass in each hand. She handed him a drink even as she settled herself to sit . . . on his lap!

It could be Poll. It was probably Poll.

Please let it be Poll!

"Miranda?"

Even just hearing his voice, Miranda knew the man behind her was Poll, not Cas. There wasn't a trace of self-mockery in his tones. He called her Miranda, not Mira. Poll.

Which meant that the man below her, the one with the beautiful half-naked woman squirming on his lap—

Cas.

She could not tear her gaze away as Cas reached up to slide his hands over the woman's bare shoulders—

Poll took hold of her arm and tugged her about to look at him. "Miranda, what are you doing here?"

"You sent—" Her throat closed. Mutely, she held out the note—the blasted note, in Poll's handwriting, the note that he clearly had not sent, that he had no idea about—

Poll glanced down at the note and his jaw hardened. "This is a ruse, Miranda. Someone wanted you to come here to witness, er, that!"

Miranda closed her eyes, unwilling to see Cas and the beautiful whore again.

Poll pulled her away from the railing. "We have to get you out of here at once!"

"Y—yes," she stammered. "Please, get me away from this place!"

Poll put his arm about her to guide her back to the doors that led into the front hallway of the whorehouse.

Suddenly, a heavy hand landed on her arm and stopped her short. She clung to Poll, who perforce stopped as well.

The man who had detained her scowled down at Poll. "Not this one," he growled. "You got the twins. I'm taking this one."

"Not me." Poll grabbed the fellow's wrist and pulled his hand from Miranda. "Back off, you bounder!"

The man took exception to Poll taking exception. A brief tug-of-war resulted, until the silk of Miranda's gown gave way at the shoulder. The abrupt sound of tearing gave both men pause, their grips slackening enough for Miranda to twist away.

Poll, much less drunk, much more angry, reacted first, taking a mighty swing at the mountainous fellow's jaw.

The blow connected, but the man only rocked backward slightly, too numbed by drink to feel much at all.

Miranda watched breathlessly as Poll ducked from a ham-fisted blow, only to be struck so hard by the other fist in the belly that she heard the thick impact of it standing two yards away.

With a gasp, Poll spun back, into Miranda. She felt herself miss a step and shrieked, twisting desperately, recalling the long fall down to the ballroom beneath!

The railing caught her at the waist and she bent over it, almost losing her balance, but her hands scrabbled at the ironwork and her fingers found purchase. She had a swift, intense impression of Cas's face below her, turned upward and staring in utter shock as she dangled half over the ballroom floor.

Someone, Poll, grabbed her by the waist and dragged her upright again, away from the dangers of gravity and hard marble floors far, far below.

Looking back, Miranda could honestly say that it wasn't so much the fight between Poll and the aggressive stranger as it was the ensuing brawl.

Actually, it wasn't so much the brawl as it was the lanterns that fell onto the bales of hay when the roiling mass of fighting men—and some women!—tumbled into them.

Although, to be truthful, it wasn't so much the fire as it was the way that the swiftly expanding flames drove everyone from the house into the street.

Everyone, male and female, old and young, dressed and undressed—and truly, one hadn't lived until one had seen the retreating naked arses of a dozen stately older gentlemen flowing before one like a pasty, waggling river. . . .

However, for Miranda, the ultimate moment was when she and Poll dragged Cas's barely conscious form—he'd taken exception to the way the first ham-fisted fellow had torn Miranda's gown. The aforementioned fellow took exception to Cas taking exception, of course, et cetera, et cetera—out of the burning whorehouse into the smoky, riotous street, where scantily clad milkmaids and farmer's daughters bounced and jiggled in squealing alarm—really, the country faire theme was ruinously overdone!—and Miranda found herself brought up short by the shocked gasp emitted from the darkened confines of an expensive carriage stopped by all the fracas.

"Miranda?"

Miranda looked up into the familiar face of that crony of Constance's—and Society Gossip Extraordinaire. "Oh. Good evening, Mrs. Teagarden."

It was a nightmare, born of every one of Miranda's worst fears.

No. It was much, much worse than a nightmare, for Miranda was completely, sickeningly awake.

"Miranda?"

"Miranda, dear, please speak to us."

Miranda could hear her name, and realized she'd been hearing it for some time. She opened her eyes and turned her head to see an older woman with loads of lovely silver hair piled on top of her head gazing at her with pale blue eyes.

The woman's identity swam reluctantly out of Miranda's memory. "Mrs. Worthington?"

The lady smiled sweetly at her. "Yes, dear."

A man with wild silver curls bent into her field of vision. "And who am I, Miranda? Who am I?"

Miranda blinked. "I don't know."

He turned to Iris Worthington with a worried frown. "Is she injured as well? Did she strike her head in the brawl?"

"No, Archie. Poll swears that she took not a single blow."

Miranda shook her head. It was a bad idea. She pressed a hand to her brow. "I don't know you, sir, because we have n . . . not yet been introduced."

Whatever was the matter with her? She lifted her head to look about her, but she did not know where she was. It was a small chamber, rather like a billiards room, though there were no tables set up. It was, however, filled most bizarrely with the luridly painted wooden slats, parts of the set of . . . a carnival?

A carved and gaudily dabbed flying carousel horse gazed back at Miranda, its arched neck and flat, black eyes accusing. *Fool.*

Her hands clenched on fistfuls of silk. She looked down her own hands where they lay draped across her lap. Turkish-blue silk. Mustn't sit in this gown. Well, she wasn't sitting; she was lying down in the billiards room with no table and a self-righteous carnival horse.

How had she come here? Oh, yes. The fire. Cas's knock to the head. A silent, appalled journey through the dark streets in Lord Wyndham's carriage to this house.

She would not have left an injured cur in the street, so she could hardly abandon Cas when she had conveyance at hand.

The last she remembered, she'd sat down next to a sleeping Attie while she waited for the physician to finish examining Cas—

Then, in a rush that flooded her mind and body with heat and fury, she remembered.

Two identical men, playing with her, toying with her like two hounds tussling over a bone. Bargains and betrayals. She turned accusing eyes on her companions. "Worthingtons!"

"I fear our sons have behaved very badly toward you," Iris agreed.

Archie nodded sadly. "By foul play, as thou say'st, were we heaved thence."

"*The Tempest,* Act One, Scene Two," Iris said to Miranda, her voice soft with sympathy. "Doesn't Archie make a fine Prospero?"

Miranda stared at the woman. "What?" She sat up, easing away from Iris's hands that attempted to soothe.

As she moved, she felt something rain down onto the backs of her hands, like grains of sand. She looked down to find that a portion of the beading of her gown had been torn from its stitches on her shoulder and was even now spilling from its threads.

Her first impulse was to clutch at the trickling beads to stop the ruination of the beautiful work—but what did it matter now? The night was over. The torn, smoky— and yes, that was blood!—ruined gown had done its part to make of her as public a fool as anyone could ever wish.

She lifted her gaze to fix the elder Worthingtons with eyes filled with fury. "What"—she bit out—"did I ever do to your family to deserve such wicked trickery?"

Standing, she found with bitter relief that she swayed only a little. She pushed away Iris's and Archie's helping hands, knowing that they were only trying to be kind, knowing that they couldn't help their foolishness and their terrible example to their offspring that the world and those who dwelt in it were nothing but toys for the breaking—

Fury sharpened her mind and hurried her step. Pulling away, she ran from the room and from the cluttered, fascinating squalor of Worthington House.

She could not flee them fast enough, these Worthingtons!

She didn't wish to vent her fury at those poor fools anyway.

There was someone else who made a much more suitable target.

Chapter Twenty-eight

Miranda helped herself out of her borrowed-for-so-long-it-might-be-considered-stolen carriage before her driver had time to descend from his seat. She spared not a moment of sympathy for Wyndham's poor beleaguered driver. She picked up her skirts and strode to the discreetly set door on the most desirable shopping street in London.

And pounded on the door with both fists.

"Are you in there? You . . . you *schemer*!"

She pounded and kept pounding, until the door was unlocked and thrown open by a furious and half-dressed Cabot.

Now, normally a half-dressed Cabot would be enough to stop any woman, and not a few men, in their tracks, but it took Miranda only a moment to remember to inhale, such was her rage.

She pushed past Cabot into the dark shop. "Where is he? I want to see that—that manipulative, mendacious—"

Cabot stared down at her. "Well, he isn't here with *me*!"

The young man sounded rather regretful about that, but Miranda fought back the twinge of sympathy she felt and spun about to glare at him.

"Cabot, you take me to that—that *Liar,* right now!"

Cabot held up both hands and backed away a step. "Mrs. Talbot, I'm sure that whatever happened—"

Miranda advanced on him, sneering. "Whatever happened? Whatever happened? Did you know that tonight I was lured away from my unveiling to a brothel? Rushing to rescue them, mind you, only to find them having the time of their lives?" The pretty blonde, draped across Cas's body as he smiled up at her—

She gasped, her chest tightening, the pain leaking in past the rage she had armored herself with, and then she released a single, rending sob.

Cabot took a step forward, but before Miranda gave in to her understandable feminine curiosity about precisely how Cabot meant to comfort her, she flung herself away from him to pace the shop.

"Where is he? Where does he live? I'm going to find him. You can't stop me. Someone, somewhere, knows his address!"

Cabot nodded in resignation. "I will take you, but you must give me a moment to—"

"No!" Miranda grabbed Cabot's hand, dragged him from the shop and all but lifted him bodily into her waiting carriage.

The driver pretended not to see his temporary mistress kidnapping a bare-chested young god from a dark shop. He did a creditable job of it, too.

It was not far, mere blocks, to a pretty, tree-shaded street lined with neat terraced houses. One was of them was painted mauve.

Miranda didn't need to be told which one was Button's.

Once again, she picked up two fistfuls of skirt and stomped her way up the steps. Cabot had to bodily thrust himself between her and his master's door.

"I have a key." He opened the door and she followed him into the house. He stopped at a door that led into a dark parlor. "Stay here. I will alert his staff to wake him and bring us all a pot of tea. Doesn't tea sound nice?"

He was treating her like a dangerous idiot and perhaps she was—"But I don't want any bloody tea!" she shrieked.

"Well, *he* does, so you'll drink it or you won't get to speak to him tonight!"

Frustrated by the logic of that answer, Miranda turned away to pace the dark, chilled parlor.

Someone bustled in with a coal scuttle and lighted the fire. Someone else slipped in to light candlesticks about the room. They both avoided Miranda as if she were a tigress loose in the center of the room.

Like that tigress, Miranda paced back and forth, her fury barely leashed, from the window to the figurine-encrusted mantel. They were lovely, graceful little shepherdesses, not mournful-eyed spaniels. Miranda hissed at them in loathing anyway.

Button came down, tying the belt of his dressing gown as he hurried into the room. "Cabot, what—!"

Miranda turned to see the little man gaping at his half-dressed assistant. He didn't even notice her.

She regretted the figurine that went flying toward Button as soon as it left her hand. Fortunately, it was snatched from the air an instant before impact by Cabot, who then walked over to her, carefully returned the little shepherdess to her empty spot, and then took Miranda by the shoulders.

"Breathe."

He had the loveliest eyes.

Miranda breathed.

It was terrible mistake. The moment her fury slipped, the pain came flooding over the wall like a river after a storm.

She pressed both hands to her heart and backed away from Cabot with another gasp. She felt both men help her to a chair, easing her down onto a throne of cream velvet and rosewood. She could see the grain of the wood through heightened vision as the pain stole her breath.

The lovely woman, draped over his body—

His hands—his hands that had brought her back to life!—his hands on the woman's bare, pale skin—

She couldn't breathe around the agony in her heart. It tightened about her, feeding her broken sobs, growing tighter and tighter. *A fool, a fool, I'm such a fool.*

She'd not been enough woman for him, she'd been too naïve, too restrained, too repressed—a boring little widow, untutored and tentative—he'd wanted more, of course he'd wanted more!—once again she hadn't been good enough—

Cabot held something under her nose. The sharp tang of the vinaigrette pierced the graying fog, and Miranda was once again in control. She leaned back in the chair with both hands gripping the arms tightly and closed her eyes. *Breathe. Breathe.*

She heard Button's gentle voice. "Miranda, dearest, I'm sure there is some reasonable explanation for—"

"For leaving me behind to consort with beautiful demireps?" Her grief switched back to rage so quickly it left her breathless once again. "For brawling? For burning down Mrs. Blythe's House of Pleasure?" *For making me into the biggest fool ever known!*

Button blinked, then looked at Cabot, who nodded. "The driver confirmed it. The gossips will tattle for *years.*"

Gossip. Years. The words rang distantly in Miranda's mind. She knew she ought to care, but all she could see were his hands touching someone Not Her.

Cas.

She would not weep. Castor Worthington would not make her weep. She wouldn't allow it.

With her eyes fixed desperately on Button's kindly ones, she breathed. *In. Out. In. Out.*

At last her body began to relax. Air became air again.

Miranda let them ply her with tea and biscuits, consuming them numbly, for they tasted of sawdust.

Finally, she turned her attention on Button. "I would give anything to get out of this bloody gown," she told him, her voice flat and empty of feeling.

In seconds Button had a maid bringing in a nightdress and soft wrapper and slippers.

She allowed the girl to strip her of the scorched, torn gown on the spot, while Button and Cabot conferred on the other side of the room. What did it matter?

When she was cradled in the softness of fine wool and silk, although cut in a masculine style, with her slipper-clad feet pulled up next to her on the chair, a freshly steaming cup of tea in her hand, Miranda felt a fraction less miserable, on the outside anyway.

The Turkish-blue gown was whisked out of her sight.

Button and Cabot moved chairs closer and sat down facing her. From somewhere Cabot had acquired a shirt that more or less fit him and Button had taken a moment to dress.

Their normality offended her. She'd preferred the chaotic state of emergency. Miranda turned her face from them and fixed her eyes on the fire.

"How could you allow them to do this?" she asked, her voice dull. "How could you all just *watch*?"

Button edged closer, holding out one hand helplessly. "Miranda, until earlier this evening . . . last evening . . . I thought you liked them both."

That surprised her out of her cold place for a moment. She turned to gaze at him. "You thought I was the sort of woman to trade off twin brothers as if changing my shoes?"

He rubbed at the back of his neck. "Well, that was a bit of a problem for me, I admit. I knew that there was something odd."

Miranda snorted. "I should say so!"

Cabot intervened for Button. "Mrs. Talbot, the Worthingtons are very well known in London. Their oddness is common knowledge. The twins have been given a sobriquet, the Double Devils. They are known womanizers and—"

Button held up a hand. "You're not helping, Cabot."

Miranda looked down at her teacup. "Womanizers." Was that what she had been? A piece in a game? A wager, Poll had told her. Wagers and bargains and conspiracies.

I wish I had never met the Worthingtons.

Button's jaw was hard. "Until last evening I would have sworn there was no true harm in them. Now, I am not so sure of that."

Miranda let out a short, bitter bark of laughter. "Harm." She closed her eyes against the cheerful flickering of the coals and tried not to let the pain sweep her away again. "I feel most definitely harmed."

"I—" Button hesitated. "I have made it worse in my attempt to find you more appropriate suitors. At one time, you were invisible enough that you might have simply slipped away unnoticed from the fire, anonymous until the stories faded. No one would have likely cared. Until last night."

Miranda turned her face from him. "As of last night, I am an Original. As of last night, all of Society will watch my every move." She let out a long breath. "Button, I don't think I can survive much more of your help."

Cabot stirred. "Mrs. Talbot, that isn't fair—"

Button hushed him. "It *is* my fault that I didn't investigate my own instinct that something was not as it should be. Neither Miss Atalanta nor I truly believed you were an evil seductress, bent on shattering the bond between brothers—"

Miranda made a tiny sound of pain. "Attie, as well?"

"—And I certainly ought to have remembered how the twins used to play their careless games with people." He sighed. "I never would have thought *this* of them. Never."

"Oh heavens!" Miranda opened her eyes to send him a look of exhausted horror. "Cas. I thought myself in love with—but that Cas doesn't exist, does he? I am in love with a mirage."

Her breath came faster. "He is gone, as surely as if he had died—yet how can I mourn losing him? He is nothing but a bit of trickery, a shell game!" She grabbed Button's hand. "It hurts so that I will never see him again—even as I loathe the man who deceived me!" Real tears flowed at last.

Button wrapped his arms about her and let her weep. Cabot looked at him with alarm at the force of Miranda's sobs, but Button reassured his assistant with a nod. Fury and rage and pain might be dangerous, but true grief was something that would help heal Miranda's wounds.

If anything ever could.

It lacked but an hour before dawn when Cabot closed the door of the room where he'd settled Miranda and sent Button's little housemaid back to her usual duties. He found his master still in the parlor, sitting before the fire, gazing thoughtfully into the glow of the coals.

Button looked up as he entered. "Is she sleeping at last?"

Cabot nodded. "I put her in the yellow room."

Button leaned forward to rest his elbows on his knees. Dropping his head, he rubbed both hands over his face wearily.

Cabot ached for him. "You should try to get some sleep. I can manage your morning appointments."

Button raised his head and smiled slightly. "Ah, to be young. You've had even less sleep than I."

Pain laced through Cabot, a needle he'd felt too many times to count. "Don't do that," he said with an edge to his tone.

Button widened his eyes. "Don't do what, pray tell?"

"Don't take advantage of every opportunity to mention how young I am, or how young you are not." He needed to stop. He needed to stop talking right now!

Button stared at him warily. "Cabot, I—"

"Stop." Cabot astonished himself by striding across the room and dropping to his knees next to Button's chair, his hands gripping the rosewood arm until his knuckles went white. "*You are not an age.* You simply are, as I simply am, and age is what we make of it." A wild desperation would not allow him to shut his mouth. "Sometimes I would even swear that you are the youth and I am the elder!"

Button was pulling back, leaning back in the chair, regarding him with that terrifying expression on his face, the one Cabot had seen years before, the one that had kept him from saying these things for so damned long.

The expression that said, *I should send you away.*

Icy fear did what self-control could not. Cabot dropped his forehead to rest on his rigid knuckles and stopped talking, biting his cheek so hard, he tasted blood. *Breathe,* he'd told Miranda, as if he knew what he was speaking of, as if he had any idea how to survive an impossible love.

Breathe.

He felt Button stir, then inhale as if to speak.

Cabot flinched. "Don't say it." His voice felt like shards of glass in his throat. "Don't."

Before he could hear the terrifying words, he leaped to his feet and strode from the room, his long legs outracing the sound of Button's voice.

Button leaned back into the cushions, his heart pounding. The hand that had hovered over Cabot's shining head, not daring to touch, fell to the arm of the chair.

It was a good thing that Cabot had left the room before he'd given in to temptation.

It was a good thing.

It was.

Chapter Twenty-nine

In her drafty little house in her unfashionable neighborhood, Constance sat drinking her morning cup of tea and reading the London scandal sheets piled next to her plate. She'd sent that lazy slattern of a maid out all over the city to find them.

Constance cackled with glee at the description of the brothel in flames and fairly swooned with pleasure when the gossips described the "disheveled" and "indecent" condition of a "certain Wicked Widow" who was named after Prospero's daughter.

Usually, Constance didn't hold with plays and theaters and other useless fripperies, but even she knew that Miranda had been named after some wanton stage creature by her no-better-than-she-should-be mother!

Oh, it was all coming along just as she'd planned, except even better!

All had come to fruition, better than Constance's wildest dreams. Since Miranda had done nothing to blackmail, despite Constance's well-placed spy, Constance had been forced to grow resourceful and create a trap.

Of course, only idiotic Miranda would take a simple

indiscreet appearance at a place of ill repute and turn it into a roaring public scandal!

Of course, it didn't reflect well upon the Talbots, but the family name could withstand it.

After all, Miranda had only married into it. She wasn't born a Talbot. She'd been one of those . . . what was their name? Oh yes, such a story in the day. It would help to remind Society that Miranda wasn't really a Talbot after all. It was too bad the tale couldn't come out all over again.

Unless, of course, it did.

Constance drank her tea, an uncharacteristic smile creasing her round face. Such a lovely morning

It was only too bad that Gideon couldn't know that his wise older sister had been right all along—it would serve the idiot right for leaving everything to Miranda in his will.

Her teacup clanked onto its saucer. Constance gazed straight ahead, unholy joy rising within her.

The will!

Miranda sat in the small, sunny morning room where she managed her accounts. It had once been draped in stuffy brocade and was dark as a cupboard. When her sister-in-law had taken her own little house, Miranda had stripped the draperies and removed the heavy, carved furnishings that hadn't been attractive even when new.

It was a welcoming room now, with its polished wood and the pale blue figured-paper on the walls. Her desk was delicate and feminine. It was the first new piece she had purchased and it was still her favorite.

Today she felt no pleasure in the pretty room, or in her view of the verdant garden. There was no solace to be found in flowers or foliage or in balancing her accounts. She'd once taken pleasure in it, in her independence and her good management.

Her mind could make no sense of the columns. The numbers swam before her, blurring, becoming the shadows and lights of a man's muscled chest or shimmering glints she saw behind her eyelids when she exploded into orgasm.

Her body didn't understand the shattered heart or the tormented mind. It longed for what it used to have: the ecstasy, the satiation. It hummed and throbbed, driving her to sexual restlessness, as if she weren't miserable enough.

The ache in her heart, however, rang constant and hollow, a black bell tolling with every beat of her pulse. The humiliation and the anger welled and exhausted themselves in a recurring cycle, but the pain itself, the Cas-shaped hole in her soul, the powerful void where love had dwelt, that simply echoed on and on.

A tap on her door snapped her out of her dark thoughts. "Come!"

Twigg entered the room with a letter on a tray. "The post, madam."

Miranda glanced at the salver without interest.

"And madam? That family came again, a great lot of them this time. Even the little one was with them at the door."

Miranda shrank back. "Was he—they—?"

"No, madam. There was no sign of them. That upstart tailor and his little friend were here as well."

Miranda sighed. "Mr. Button and Mr. Cabot, please, Twigg." Simply because Cabot had failed to soothe Twigg's insecurities! The butler's prickly defensiveness felt like spikes to Miranda's raw nerves.

Twigg looked at her with a face suddenly lacking in expression. "There's a letter from Herself." He held out the salver once more.

Miranda recognized the thick, old-fashioned stationery that Constance favored. Her spidery script on the address was unmistakable. Since she was quite sure that she could not feel any worse today, Miranda did not delay opening Constance's missive.

She could not have been more wrong.

Miranda,
I write you incensed and indignant!
   It seems that my worst suspicions about you have been correct after all, and that you are too ill-born and ignorant of your advantages to properly appreciate the respectable circumstances my brother provided for you.
   Therefore, I am forced to abandon my retirement and return forthwith to the home of my family to defend its honor, if I must, with my last breath!
   Be prepared, Miranda! You will not succeed in ruining the Talbot name!

There was no closing, friendly or otherwise. The letter was simply signed with a large swooping *C* that made Miranda think of a butcher's meat hook. It had been written with such indignant force that the thick paper had taken a deep scratch from the quill.

The paper was quivering. Miranda realized that her hands were shaking with reaction and rage. She let the letter fall to the desk, where it lay, radiating accusation.

Decadent mischief?

That her brief exploration into freedom could be seen in such a revolting and dissolute light made her feel ill. All her life had been an ongoing attempt to live down her family's past. She'd always been so careful, so watchful. Until little more than a month ago, she had guarded her own behavior like a warden guards a dangerous prisoner—

For she'd known, hadn't she? Just as Constance had

sensed, Miranda had always known that there lived a mutinous rebel within her.

It was only then that the most sinister line of the entire vicious letter rose to her attention.

Therefore, I am forced to abandon my retirement and return forthwith to the home of my family to defend its honor, if I must, with my last breath!

Constance was coming home.

Poll left Worthington House behind him, taking long strides through the thick summer air. It wasn't a nice day at all.

There was a nasty damp coming off the river Thames, seeping into every corner and crevice, leaching unwelcome through Poll's clothing. It was midday and everyone had their coals burning, throwing more soot into the air, which came down and stuck to the damp.

Being out in putrid weather was still better than being inside Worthington House. The trenchant disapproval within made Poll feel like he was wading through a foot of sticky mud. He deserved that blame, for everything had been fine until he interfered with Miranda!

Miranda. He closed his eyes against the sudden aching surge of guilt that welled up in his chest. It was unbearable, spiky and twisting inside him, making him feel foul and decayed—

No. He sent his thoughts sideways, away from the memories of her, away from the imaginings of what she must think of him now.

He pulled his collar tight against the damp. The coldest summer in years, that's what people had been saying, but until today, Poll hadn't noticed.

A hot lance of shame went through him. Both he and

Cas, laughing it up, two jolly lads, making sure everyone was having a good time, especially them.

Anything to avoid thinking about the serious state of their family. The family had been skating on the edge of destruction for years. This past year had been both better and worse—better because there had been enough to eat. Worse because without Callie's sane and practical presence, the clashing personalities had begun a downward spiral that led nowhere good.

Meanwhile, he and Cas played dirty tricks on innocent women.

He hadn't yet finished the jewelry case. He supposed he might as well. He'd worked so hard on the ivy, inlaying the leaves with ebony and mother-of-pearl, as shadow and light. It was some of his most beautiful work ever.

Cas had been hard at work on something as well, but Poll refused to give in to curiosity and give Cas the satisfaction of knowing that Poll gave a rat's rump about what he was up to.

He missed his twin.

Poll walked along the Serpentine. The swans were huddled on the bank, their heads tucked under their wings. Poll hated them, hated their legendary monogamy most of all. Orion had once informed the family—he'd been about thirteen at the time—that he didn't believe in marriage, that if man was meant to be monogamous, then he would be unable to be anything else, just like the swan.

Cas had promptly agreed. Poll had frowned and shaken his head. Even at the age of nine, he'd known he wanted it all. The girl, the marriage, the home and family.

Attie had been a fussy infant then and Callie a girl of sixteen, tending the baby as if it were her own. Ellie had been about six and had mimicked Zander and Cas and Poll when they'd taken exception to Orion's new and serious bent.

The ridicule had been a bit fierce, now that he thought about it. Rion had become more and more grave in response, until they'd driven the fun right out of him and he'd become the cool man of thought he was now.

Poll wished he were more of a man of thought. He wouldn't be in this pickle now, aching inside as he walked through the coldest summer in decades.

Poor Miranda.

He'd loved bringing her out of her shell, loved watching her learn to believe in herself, to speak her mind, to gleam like mother-of-pearl, to allow herself shades of light and dark, to be true to her own desires and rebel against anyone who thought she ought to blend herself back into invisibility.

He and Cas had done that for her—and then he and Cas had ruined it all. Miranda likely would never believe in anything, now that her trust had been so betrayed.

Widows were fair game; everyone knew that. Except, Miranda wasn't like the other widows Poll had known. She didn't know anything of the world. He'd seen it immediately, that she didn't know how to protect her heart, yet he pursued her anyway, drawing Cas in as well.

Why hadn't he taken one look at her wary, naïve eyes and politely bid her good day?

Cas shut the damned book he'd been holding up before his eyes for an hour. It didn't matter if it were open or not. The words were blurs, the sentences meaningless jumbles of words. He'd been gazing blindly at it, instead seeing Miranda's wide, shocked eyes.

Castor Worthington, beloved son of Iris and Archimedes Worthington, beloved sibling to Dade, Callie, Rion, Zander, Ellie, Attie—and formerly Pollux—was hiding in the library because he was completely and most thoroughly in the bog house.

Even Attie was off limits to him. Every time he entered the room, Elektra would stand and sweep majestically out of it, sweeping Attie protectively into her wake. While it was nice to see those two becoming close at last—and nice to see Attie's hair brushed, even if those odd braids weren't strictly à la mode—he felt like a pile of horse apples every time.

He was still being fed and no one had locked him entirely out of the house yet, but neither had a single member of his family spoken a word to him or Poll for nearly a week.

He missed them. He even missed Poll, though he would not admit that even under torture!

As for Miranda, the ache was quite physical, radiating out from somewhere in his chest until his entire body hurt with longing for her. Miranda, rolling naked in bed, turning toward him with a soft smile, reaching for him, kissing him as he kissed her back with a driving, hot rise from sweetness to wildness.

He loved to bring her lust on hard, to push her focus down into her body, to make her feel everything he did to her, to make her burn as he did—

Had burned. Past tense.

His thoughts skittered away from Miranda. He could not think of her without recalling the way she had frozen, staring at him, her face growing paler and paler, her lips parted as if to ask, or beg for someone to tell her it wasn't true.

The problem was, it was true. It was all true.

Miranda. God, hadn't she looked beautiful? She'd seemed like a magical being, a goddess in the form of an exquisite blue-green lance, so elegant and slender, her breasts pressed high and proud, her marvelous hair piled luxuriously on her head and twined with shimmering beads.

He remembered the beads. Strange how little details became so clear. When she'd dragged him home with Poll, he lost his balance for the millionth time in the front hall of Worthington House. Tiny beads had spilled there in the hall, gritting under Cas's boots like sand on the stone.

Orion and Zander had carried him into the small parlor. Iris had called for tea and whiskey. He didn't recall much after that, although there were three stitches in his scalp that implied he was lucky to remember anything at all.

Lucky to remember that it was over. Miranda—that glaze of shock in her eyes, that submerged betrayal in her sea green eyes, the way she'd flinched, her body half twisting away, her hands pressed to her belly as if she felt ill.

Why hadn't he run from a woman ready to love— aching to love? Why hadn't he dashed away in the opposite direction? Because, despite his heartless exterior, he wasn't heartless at all. Because he ached for that love as well.

And for a brief, wonderful while, he'd had that love, he'd basked in the full force of Miranda's open, shining heart—and then he'd shattered it.

He could not let that be the last moment they had together. He could not let it live on in time, etched in forever.

Chapter Thirty

I dreamed of him last night, after crying myself to sleep yet again. He reached for me in my sleep, pulling me into the warmth of him. I was so cold and so alone. He felt like sunlight after an ice storm.

His fingertips ran over her damp cheek. "Why are you crying?" he asked her.

She couldn't remember. All she knew was the permanent ache in her chest was fading now that he was there. She stroked her open palm down his hard, naked chest, savoring the rigid muscle and the skin that felt so different from hers. Her fingertips caught at the curly hair sprinkling the plates of muscle and he twitched, laughing softly at her.

"I am real. I am here."

Somewhere in her mind she knew she was dreaming, that he was not real, that he was not there. She shut that knowledge off, forgetting to remember, and wrapped her arms about his neck so she could press her body to his all the way down to her toes.

His heat enveloped her, melting away the last chill and

she relaxed sensually into his hard body. He stroked his large, warm hands down her back to cup her buttocks and pull her tight to him. His thick erection pressed into her soft belly, lying between them, ready to connect them.

Mouth on mouth, chest on breast, belly to belly they lay. His big hand dived into her hair to hold her for his deep, demanding kiss.

He flexed his hips to stroke his cock against her belly slowly, dragging the hot, satin-iron length of it up and down. "Are you ready for me?"

He took one hand from her breast and ran it down her side and over her hip to stroke between her thighs, touching, circling, spreading her wetness to her clitoris, making her moan in response. "Are you ready for me?"

"Yes," she sighed.

He took her then, entering her slowly, carefully, as she arched, quivering, impaled upon him, held safe in his arms, his hot hands on her skin, his hot mouth on her mouth, kissing, being kissed, being impaled by him, by her beautiful, wicked man.

"I love you," she gasped to him. "Oh, how I love you!"

I awoke gasping in a powerful orgasm, shuddering, aching and throbbing, my heart pounding. As I caught my breath and recalled my situation, I realized that it was still true. Despite the betrayal, I am still in love with Castor Worthington.

I would do anything not to be.

Miranda ought to have known that Constance would never easily give up the house on Breton Square. However, she had not suspected that Mr. Seymour was Constance's spy all along.

When she came out of her hidey-hole—er, her office, to find the front hallway filled with Constance's bags and trunks and self, with Mr. Seymour in tow, Miranda blinked, then immediately turned to her dismayed butler.

"My deepest apologies, Twigg. Your service has been impeccable and your loyalty complete. I should not have suspected you."

Then she took a deep breath and walked slowly forward to confront her "guests."

A few moments later, after Constance had abused most of Miranda's new staff into instant hatred while her things were moved into her old bedchamber, Constance, Mr. Seymour, and Miranda sat in an uneasy silence in the parlor.

Miranda had a feeling that Twigg was going to take a very long time with the tea today.

Constance brushed aside Miranda's attempt at politeness. "Don't you play hostess in my house, Miranda!"

Miranda felt her nails bite into her palms, though she knew she showed no other sign of her annoyance. "Constance, you will always be welcome here, but as Gideon's widow, this property belongs to me." To be truthful, it was a bit unfair that Constance had been excluded, but the will had been Gideon's to write, not Miranda's.

Constance had an alarmingly sure gleam in her eyes. "We'll see about that, won't we?"

Mr. Seymour turned his head to regard Miranda as well. She realized that Mr. Seymour was now more than merely Constance's informant. The two of them had banded together in their envy and greed. Miranda's belly chilled as she gazed back at them.

She was outnumbered.

And with the weapons that she herself had handed them in her imprudent search for love, she was most certainly outgunned.

"Dear Mr. Seymour has been such a help to me. He's such a fine young man, don't you think? Of course, he's entirely respectable and above reproach—that sort of man isn't really your cup of tea, is it, Miranda?"

Miranda lifted her chin. "You are quite correct there, Constance. Mr. Seymour is most assuredly not my cup of tea."

Seymour's expression soured, but Constance never lost her smug glint. "I asked Mr. Seymour to keep an eye on proceedings in this house," she explained with a saintly demeanor. "I knew it would only be a matter of time before you fell back into your old ways."

Miranda frowned in puzzlement. "I have no old ways. I wed Gideon when I was but nineteen years."

Constance lifted her lip in a sneer, forgetting for a moment to be saintly. "Your family's ways, then. Bad blood always tells, Miranda. You have very bad blood!"

"So you have never hesitated to remind me." Miranda worked her jaw. "Constance, I beg of you, get to the blasted point!"

Constance shot her a knowing glance and Miranda regretted the vulgarity—but honestly, the woman was enough to try the good nature of an angel!

"I arranged for Mr. Seymour to be well compensated for his efforts, should they come to fruition. I had planned—that is, we had planned—to *persuade* you to agree to a financial arrangement, Miranda, wherein Mr. Seymour and I kept our silence in exchange for the house and certain supplemental benefits."

"How prettily you describe blackmail, Constance." Miranda realized that she was shaking with fury. "But the spectacle was quite public. How do you blackmail a woman with no secrets? You have nothing with which to bend me to your will."

Constance smiled and Miranda's hot fury chilled to fear.

"Oh, but dearest Miranda, there is no longer any need

to . . . ah, *persuade* you. Surely you recall the scandal clause in Gideon's last will and testament?"

Scandal clause? Miranda quickly cast her mind back— that reading had been so very long and dreary—all those stock pins.

Ah. Yes. In the event of Miranda causing a scandal that would somehow impact or diminish the name of Talbot in social circles, her inheritance—the house, Gideon's prudent investments—would be rescinded. All would go to his sister, Constance, instead, and Miranda would be evicted with only what she could carry.

At the time, Miranda had found the notion vaguely amusing. Imagine her, a scandal?

Only now she need imagine nothing. She was every bit the tawdriest scandal of the Season!

Nothing. That was what she was left with.

Nothing but painful memory and the clothes she wore.

If only I dared, I might be the most blissful of women— although tiresome good sense rushes to assure me I might well be the unhappiest, with a lifetime of regret ahead of me and only sweet memories behind.

She had inscribed those words in her diary more than a month before. Miranda pressed her fingertips to her forehead. *How prescient of me.*

Had it only been a few days ago that she'd thought herself that "most blissful of women?" How odd, to go from having everything to having nothing.

Constance's smile became sharp, bringing to Miranda's mind the nasty dagger shape of shark teeth. "I encouraged the inclusion of that clause," Constance boasted, "although even Gideon saw the sense of it, once I reminded him of your poor father's predicament with that unruly mother of yours." Constance made it sound as though nine-year-old Miranda ought to have been able to leash her wayward mother's ways.

In her shock, Miranda had entirely forgotten Mr. Seymour's presence. Now, it was his significant clearing of his throat that drew her stunned attention.

He smiled spitefully. "I'll wager you'll remember me now."

Chapter Thirty-one

Attie stood in the hallway outside the parlor, listening very intently to the evil within.

When she had arrived at Miranda's, lonely for someone to talk to—or, in her case, to think at while scowling fiercely—she had seen the strange carriage sitting before the house. She had slipped around to the back and tapped on the kitchen door instead.

Tildy had let her in and sent her to wait for the missus in her little morning room.

Attie never waited for anyone if there was something more interesting to do—like spy.

Twigg turned the corner and spotted her. When he opened his mouth to admonish her, she waved him silent and grabbed his hand to pull him against the wall next to her.

"It's bad," she whispered soundlessly, which she was perfectly capable of. She just liked to annoy people by whisper-shouting their secrets. "They've got her cornered. The old cow wants the house and the jackal-man wants the money."

Twigg's frown deepened. "We'll all be out, then." His soundless whisper was as practiced as Attie's. "They'll not want any of the loyal staff. They'd know we'd know what they did."

Attie bit her lip. "It's a rotten mess, all right. But I think I know just who to call to help clean it up."

Miranda stood before her open wardrobe, gazing with vast apathy at the dreary assortment of mourning and half-mourning gowns. The only lovely thing she had ever possessed was the Turkish-blue silk that had lived so briefly on her skin before being torn and scorched and tainted by betrayal. She'd left it at Button's without a thought, undoubtedly to be destroyed.

Everything she gazed at now had been of Constance's choosing—much like the contents of the house itself. At this very moment, heavy, oppressive draperies were being rescued from the attic and rehung, blocking out the light. The process was overseen by a glum Twigg, who had survived the staff purge by virtue of having been originally hired by the sainted Gideon himself. The heavy carved furniture that Miranda had cleared out had been carried down from the attic and once more crowded the house, pressing the life from it. She had no doubt that the little china spaniels had invaded once more.

It was as if Miranda had never happened at all.

Spurning the gossamer nightdress and wrapper that reminded her too forcefully of nights best forgotten, Miranda packed a sensible batiste gown, a staid flannel wrapper, the plainest and therefore least ugly of her lavender gowns—and her diary.

She contemplated the leather-bound book for a long moment before placing it into the satchel. It was full of protest and powerless wrath and silly, secret nonsense dreams about one or the other of the Worthington rogues.

Her own gullibility made her flinch, but she resolutely placed the diary deep into her bag, for it was clear that she could not trust her own sense. Since her wonderful adventure had been a lie, and the punishment for stepping outside the boundaries had been breathtakingly severe, she would not risk doing so again.

The diary, full of such thoughtless idiocy that Miranda cringed from it, would ensure that she never forgot this lesson.

Swiftly, Miranda fastened the straps of the old leather satchel—the only item, other than the then-blank diary, still remaining from her arrival in this house as a young bride—and stalked from the swirl of rich, vicious memories contained in the mistress's bedchamber of the house on Breton Square.

Poll entered the workshop to find Attie hard at work on some project involving a dining room chair placed next to a hanging curtain that was strung from the rafters with clothesline.

"Ellie said you needed my help with something?" Poll felt oddly tentative around his little sister, but she'd been so odd the last few days, as if she knew about Miranda.

Which was impossible, of course. While the family might be open about many things, he truly didn't think any one of his siblings would wish to involve Attie in the sordid knowledge of what he and Cas had done.

However, now Attie smirked at him with a light of delighted mischief in her eyes. "I've invented the best trick—wait until you see it! Only I can't test it, because I'm not heavy enough to release the spring I put in the seat. Sit down and put your hands on the arms, like this." She demonstrated, which put Poll's mind somewhat at ease. The chair did not respond to her weight at all.

The trick probably didn't even work. Most good tricks took weeks to get right, and Attie had been out here only for an afternoon.

Eager to get back into Attie's good graces, so at least someone in his family might be speaking to him, Poll moved to the chair to take Attie's place. As he began to lower himself gingerly into the seat, he hesitated.

"Do you hear that?"

There was a strange noise coming from somewhere. *Squeak-squeak.* Attie shrugged. "Rats. I'll bring some of the cats outside for a few days. They'll love it. Sit!"

Poll sat. Nothing happened. He turned his head to look at her. "I think it needs a bit more work, pet—"

Attie had her hand on a rope. As he watched her, she yanked it hard.

Spring-loaded clamps sprang from beneath the arms of the chair to arch around his wrists and pin them to the wood.

"Ouch!" It didn't hurt that bad, but—"Attie, that's marvelous, but these are quite tight—"

She pulled another rope and the curtain fell. With horror, Poll saw a mirror image of himself in the chair—except that the other man was most thoroughly gagged with a length of sprigged muslin.

Cas rolled his eyes and rocked his body violently in the sturdy chair. *Squeak-squeak. Squeak-squeak-squeak!*

"I see." Poll nodded. "Yes, I am an idiot. Obviously, so are you." He turned to glare at Attie. "What is this about? We haven't lifted a finger against you for weeks. Pax, remember?" He'd never slept so well. Apparently the peace was over.

"It is about me."

Cas and Poll turned their heads to see a spare figure outlined in the open carriage door of the workshop.

Button stepped fastidiously into the workshop, weaving his way carefully through the piles and cupboards and random mechanical parts that lay on the floor.

Poll turned to Attie. "You could have just told us Button wanted to see us."

Attie regarded Cas and Poll with a sad scowl. Poll had to admit that disappointing Attie disturbed him more than he'd ever dreamed it would.

"Yes, I could have just told you—or I could have done something much, much worse."

It was true. Poll felt Cas shudder slightly at his side.

Attie went on. "So if I were you, I'd take the lesson as well deserved and shut up about it." She had another length of sprigged muslin in her hands.

In an instant, he was gagged just as Cas was. They never should have taught her those instantly looping knots!

Button paced slowly back and forth before the twins and their Spanish Inquisition chairs. "And what of you two? Would you leave a member of your family out in the cold?"

Poll shook his head no. He saw Cas do the same.

"Right. A *Worthington* would never be left alone in the world, disgraced and driven from her home." Button spread his hands. Then he walked around behind the chairs and gave both brothers an idiot slap on the backs of their respective thick skulls.

"Mmph!" Poll twisted his head to glare at the man.

Cas, however stared at the dressmaker with dawning horror in his eyes. Poll frowned at his twin, confused. Then—

Oh, God. Miranda.

Button crossed back in front of them again with his hands behind his back. He regarded them with his head tilted to one side. "I can see you have questions. I shall attempt to address them."

He held out his hand and counted off one finger. "Is Miranda in desperate trouble? Yes, she is."

Poll turned to glare belligerently at Cas, only to find Cas glaring right back.

This time it was Attie who delivered a pair of idiot slaps.

"This is no longer about the two of you." Button bent slightly and frowned into their faces with narrowed eyes, his usually mischievous face etched in hard lines that gave credence to Iris's hints that her old friend used to be a dangerous spy.

"Because of your irresponsible little games, a lovely woman has been robbed of her fortune, her home, and her reputation! When are you two going to realize that you cannot play games with people's lives!"

Cas and Poll and Attie shared a look. Now was not the time to point out how odd that was, coming from Button.

"This is all your fault!" He straightened and glared at them. "Fix this at once!"

Poll glanced at his twin to see Cas's expression shadowed with a similar sickened cast. Cas stared back at him, queasy shame emanating from every pore. Poll knew he looked the same.

Button let out a sigh. "Finally." He waved a hand at Attie. "Release them."

Attie did something to the back of each chair and the clamps released. Cas and Poll quickly disengaged themselves, tossing the muslin gag strips to the hay-speckled floor as they ran from the carriage house and toward Miranda.

Button walked to the large doorway and gazed out at the fine summer day.

Miss Atalanta had done amazingly well. Much better than the dress rehearsal, in fact.

When she came to stand next to him, he smiled gently down at her. "Such a lovely plan. The only thing I don't understand is how you made those chairs so quickly."

"I didn't. Orion did."

Button nodded. "Well, that explains why they worked the first time."

"Oh, we practiced on Ellie. I've been locking her up for hours. It was great fun."

Miranda stepped from the door of her house—Constance's house—with a cool nod at an obviously distressed Twigg.

She had little enough breath to face the world outside, but she spared some to turn to the unhappy butler for a moment. "This was not your fault," she told him. "You did try to warn me."

Every one of the man's efforts to resist commands that might anger Constance was now seen in a clearer light. He'd been trying to protect her, to keep her from pushing her spiteful sister-in-law to enact drastic measures.

"Of course, I didn't listen." Miranda felt numb, too defeated to even sense pain. "I wish you well, Twigg. You are a paragon of service, you truly are."

The man sniffed. The familiar sound struck Miranda's ear discordantly. She suddenly could not wait to see the last of the house that had been her home for more than a dozen years.

Leaving Twigg, she walked slowly down the steps. Turn left? Turn right?

Her vision suddenly blurred. Right or left? The decision seemed impossible to make. Her numbness was abruptly swept away by a chill wash of fear. People lied, and plotted, and showed her smiling faces that hid profound betrayal. The world was not safe, no matter if she chose right or if she chose left!

So when a dainty white-lacquered carriage, drawn by a matching pair of snow-white horses, pulled up before her and a gracious Cabot leaned out to reach his hand to take hers, Miranda did the only thing she could do.

She stepped forward.

* * *

The clock chimed in the hall of Button's pretty little house. Miranda sat rigidly on the settee next to Mr. Button while he and Cabot discussed arrangements for a small but respectably located set of rooms just outside Mayfair proper.

She'd be fortunate to get them, even tiny and inconvenient as they were. No one wanted to let to the Wicked Widow, even when offered favor by the great Lementeur!

It had been all over the scandal sheets yesterday evening. As Miranda and Cabot had ridden in the sweetly well-sprung conveyance across Mayfair, they had heard it shouted out from every street corner, as the newsboys had hawked their latest edition to a fascinated public.

The Wicked Widow's Corrupt Past!
The Wicked Widow's Wicked Pedigree!

And Miranda's personal favorite, *Wicked, Wickeder, Wickedest Widow!*

She'd thought that particular newsboy ought to receive hazard pay for that tongue-twister.

Every moment of her life had been spent making sure that no one recalled her parents' scandal. She'd learned to speak softly, move slowly, contain her wayward thoughts. She'd hidden her true self under layers of perfect behavior. She'd done everything right.

Until a green-eyed man had gazed down at her with hunger in his eyes. Until that man had touched her until she burned alive.

Now she sat, so motionless that her flesh chilled. Moving hurt too much. Breathing hurt too much.

Cas.

The clock kept chiming. Miranda shivered at the sweet, relentless ringing. Another hour of her life had passed. Only a few hundred thousand to go.

Chapter Thirty-two

In the attic chamber of Worthington House, Cas gazed at his brother calmly.

Poll scowled back. "Why do you want it? What good is it?"

"I'm going to get evidence on who sent it. I'm going to prove that Constance Talbot is guilty of blackmail . . . or at least, guilty of something! Blackmail is against the law, but like all blackmailers, Constance thought Miranda would never accuse her because then her own secrets would come out. But Miranda can now!"

Poll gazed at him for a long moment, then pulled a small folded paper from his pocket. He gazed down at it unhappily. "It actually does look a bit like my handwriting."

Cas snorted. "Well, since we know it is not, we can assume it is a forgery."

Poll nodded and handed it over to Cas. "Yes, that is certain." He shook his head. "I would never have done that to Miranda. God, her face when she saw you holding Lily—"

"When she saw me pushing Lily off my lap, you mean."

Poll shrugged. "I'm fairly sure she missed that part.

She was being assaulted right about then by that bloke you angered by monopolizing the twins."

Cas stood quite still and let Poll take his shots. It was all true.

Yes, someone else had tricked Miranda into going to the brothel, but it wouldn't have happened if Cas hadn't insisted on going there in the first place. If he'd been at the Ball as he'd promised his sister and Poll, then even if someone had given Miranda such a note, she would merely have turned to him—because he would have been, should have been, right by her side.

The simple deception Miranda and Poll had enacted upon him now seemed so trivial. Cas honestly didn't remember why he'd felt so angry, unless it was that he'd finally allowed himself to be angry about past betrayals, letting them sour the present.

At any rate, he'd been the reason Miranda had been hurt. He'd been used like a weapon against her, shot out of a Cas-created cannon, directly into her innocent, open heart.

Poll ought not to have tricked him. Miranda ought not to have gone along with his brother's mad scheme.

Cas would never forget her face.

He'd been laughing at Lily, rejecting her ninth or tenth playful attempt to clamber onto him in some way. He'd taken her by the shoulders and given her a little shake to emphasize his refusal.

And out of the corner of his eye he'd seen a streak of brilliant blue-green silk high above him, a trick of the light on gleaming satin that drew his eye instantly to the upper landing of the stairs.

Miranda—just turning away from him, her face pale, her eyes wide, her lips parted in horror, or disgust, Cas wasn't sure.

Then, a scuffle. He couldn't see it all. He'd dumped

Lily aside without a thought and ran to where he could observe, just in time to see Miranda nearly fall over the railing. His only thought had been to catch her, but someone, probably Poll, had snatched her back from certain death.

For that alone he could forgive Poll any amount of brotherly meddling.

At that point, he'd run up the stairs to tackle the ridiculously large fellow who was pinning Poll down and punching him. It was a good thing the man had been so drunk, for if those blows had landed with any accuracy or force, Poll might well be dead.

Miranda had stood right there, tugging on the brute's shoulder and screaming into his ear, pulling his hair and generally making a nuisance of herself, but the man had been too intoxicated to do more than brush her off like a buzzing insect.

Cas had caught her against his chest. Turning her head, she'd looked into his face, then twisted away from him, shrinking from his touch as if he were more of a monster than the ruffian who had shoved her.

He'd done it to himself, of course.

No, he'd done it to her.

Now he meant to repair the damage. Somehow.

At first Cas tried to find proof in the physical evidence. He carefully examined the note itself—but it was scrawled on ordinary foolscap in the sort of ink that half of England kept in bottles on their desks.

Not in reality would he discover that it was some exotic paper made from fibers only obtainable in the depths of Africa, written on with ink concocted from berries only grown in the heights of the Andes.

That sort of nonsense was for tawdry novels, like the ones that Elektra hid from Attie—not that it did any good.

The note itself being useless, the only thing left was to investigate the people.

"Honestly, Cas!" Elektra stared at him in exasperation in the mirror as she sorted hair ribbons at her vanity table. "I didn't tell anyone *your* plans! I was far too busy getting ready for *my* evening. Some of us actually went to Wyndham's ball, you know!"

"Cas." Dade gazed at him flatly from his seat behind the desk in his study. "You went to an orgy. That is hardly information that I would wish to share with anyone."

"What orgy?" Orion blinked at him when Cas cornered him in his laboratory, which was really the second kitchen, but no one would dare cook edibles in it any longer—not after the episode with the cobra venom!

Cas didn't bother questioning Lysander. All secrets were safe with Zander, for Zander never spoke at all, except to Mama and sometimes Attie.

Oh. Oh, no.

Attie.

Cas banged on Miranda's—er, Constance's front door— *damn it, not for bloody long!*—until Twigg opened it.

"Good afternoon, sir," the butler greeted Cas stiffly. "I regret to inform you that I have instructions regarding . . . er, certain callers."

"Fine," Cas snapped, "for I came to see *you*."

Twigg hesitated, then leaned closer to Cas. "Come to the tradesman's entrance in five minutes," he murmured. Then he straightened to his haughty butler best. "Sir, if you do not remove yourself, I shall have you forcibly removed!"

Cas nodded shortly and turned away from the door. Five minutes later, he waited outside the delivery door off the kitchens, down several steps from street level.

Twigg joined him there and let him in. "No danger of

Cook saying a word," he assured Cas. "She preferred the young madam as well."

Twigg led Cas into a small room off the main kitchen that he recognized as the butler's pantry, primarily by the familiar scent of spirits of turpentine—except in this house it was used to clean silver, no doubt, not paint brushes.

Twigg closed the door and stood at attention. "Have no worry, sir. Miss Constance will not bestir herself to enter here, now that she has counted the silver for the week."

From the harried expression on the fellow's face, Cas guessed that Constance had found fault with the state of the plate.

"Twigg—"

"Have you seen her?" Twigg burst out. "We're all terribly worried, sir! Not a peep after that tailor fellow kidnapped her right off the street!"

"Button is a good friend, Twigg. She is safe with him." Cas swept away Twigg's concern with one hand. "I came here to investigate an incident. Attie told me that you witnessed Mr. Seymour stealing about the place on the day of the Wyndhams' ball. What can you tell me about it?"

Twigg blinked. "Oh, that Seymour fellow! I've seen his sort before. Like wool moths, eating holes in everything whilst you aren't looking!"

"Er, yes." Cas supposed moths would be quite a bother to a butler. "Is it true that Mr. Seymour stayed in the house after Mrs. Talbot had asked him to go? And then when he left, he took a book?"

Actually, what Attie had said was more in the vein of "the old donkey's arse nicked Miranda's *Kubla Kahn*!" A book that Poll informed Cas had contained a rather long inscription—Poll did tend to wax romantic—in, yes, Poll's usual hand.

Twigg pursed his lips. "Oh, I should say so! Hours

later, it was. He took that book of verse that the other Mr. Worthington gave her. I ought not to have allowed it, but he claimed it belonged to him. It was only later when I was sorting the books that I noticed it missing. A bad business, that Mr. Seymour. Lurking like that, sitting in the little library, scribbling away, using up the mistress's paper and ink on a bunch of nonsense words."

"What words?" Cas swallowed back his urgency when he saw Twigg flinch. He was alarming the help! "Do you recall what the words said?"

"Well, no." Twigg sniffed. "I didn't *read* them. That would be inappropriate."

Cas sagged in disappointment. So close.

"Although I suppose it would not be so very indiscreet if you read them. After all, Mr. Seymour did toss them into the grate. I only kept them, you understand, should the mistress wonder if one of the staff was making off with all that fine paper."

Cas snapped to attention. "You kept them?"

Twigg nodded earnestly. "Every one. Habit, I suppose. The elder madam is most particular. She wants accounting of every single thing in the house."

A grin slowly grew on Cas's face. *Constance, you miserly wretch, you've done it now!*

Chapter Thirty-three

Miranda sat in Button's parlor, the one with the sweet-faced shepherdesses arranged on the mantel, and read her diary.

She had vowed to do it every day, so that she might not forget. She dared not let her thoughts veer into sweet memory, nor to gaze into the coals and imagine a pair of green eyes that burned like peat fire.

So, to keep her wayward thoughts in line, she kept the leather-bound diary with her, to open whenever she weakened into kindly thoughts of Cas.

There was no need to read the entire work. There was nothing useful in the dreary accountings of her marriage to Gideon, or in the hopeful burbling of a newly independent widow.

No, there was really only one page she needed to read. She read it over and over again, her soul flinching every time.

Cabot entered the parlor. "There's a Worthington to see you," he said blandly.

Attie. "Oh, all right, Cabot." Miranda realized that she couldn't turn the child away yet again. None of this madness was Attie's fault. It wasn't the littlest Worthington's responsibility that her brothers were—were—blasted *arses!*

"Miranda."

The deep voice caught at her heart like a tangle of fishhooks, dragging it up from the depths of numbness. Her gaze rose to meet the summer green of Cas's eyes.

An arse. In the flesh.

She hadn't realized she'd said it aloud until Cas snorted a laugh and bowed. "At your service," he said with a small hopeful smile.

Miranda stayed very still and gazed at him. It had not been a jest. She had not intended to make him laugh, a fact he seemed to realize as the hope faded from his expression.

He cleared his throat. "Mira, ah, Mrs. Talbot, I came here to inform you that I have secured proof that Mr. Seymour was the creator of the note that, ah, led you astray."

She tilted her head. "It did not lead me astray. It led me to you. I shall write to Mr. Seymour at once to thank him for his helpfulness. I might never have known the truth otherwise. Certainly I would not have had it from a Worthington."

Cas flinched. "Miranda—"

She held up a hand. "Don't. I saw you in a brothel, in the arms of a whore."

Cas swore. "Lily is actually a good sort, if you must know. She was only pretending to—an orgy is a lot of work for a girl! If she pretended to be seducing me, she could rest a bit!"

Miranda's eyebrows rose. "A malingering ladybird. Will wonders never cease?"

He stepped forward. "The point is the note! I can prove that Constance and Seymour conspired to ruin you! You can bring charges against them, for blackmail at the least!"

She shook her head. "You don't seem to understand,

Mr. Worthington." She stood, clasping the diary before her bosom like a shield. "I. Don't. Care."

She couldn't even look at him without seeing Lily draped across his lap. She closed her eyes and turned away. "Constance and Seymour only ruined my reputation. You ruined *me*." Her throat threatened to close. She would not weep in front of him!

Tightening her belly against the tremble that threatened her, she went on. "The only thing I ever did to you was to keep a secret. I did not tell you that I loved you."

Cas's breath left him. *Loved*. Past tense.

Oh, I thought I hurt before. I was so very wrong.

She turned back to him in a swift motion that spoke of urgent bravery in the face of fear. In a quick gesture, she flipped the book in her hands open. It fell to a page as if it had fallen open to it many times before.

As she read to him, her soft voice had a flat thread of steel in it that he'd never heard before.

"All through my childhood and beyond, I have never truly felt secure. With my father's imprisonment and my mother's death, I learned that nothing is permanent, that no one stays. I learned that the world is full of danger and damage and selfishness—and that I could trust no one completely.

"Until now. Until him. For the first time in my memory, I know what it means to trust. When I am with my lover—" She choked up, then forced the words through her tangled throat. *"—for the first time in my life, I feel safe."*

Cas would not have surprised to look down to find the carpet soaked in his blood. There didn't seem to be any left in his heart, for each beat was painful and aching and empty.

Oh, Mira. I did this to you.

She was broken, like a lovely young filly turned into a shivering wreck by abusive hands.

My hands.

She closed the diary with a snap and lifted her flat sea green gaze to his. "I will not defend myself. I am a scandal. Unlike you, apparently, I know that scandal never goes away."

He had to try, just once more. "You can't quit now! The fight has just begun!"

She turned away again. Her shoulders sagged. "Mr. Worthington, my fight began when I was nine years old. I am too tired to fight anymore. Go away."

Cas was surprised when the Prince Regent agreed to see him right away. When he was guided to yet another luxurious retiring room padded in velvet and silk, he only paced restlessly, no longer interested in the trappings of royalty.

Shortly, the portly Prinny sailed into the room, clad in yellow silk, trimmed in snowy white. He looked like a large tropical fruit. "Ah, Worthington! How nice of you to come to allow me to gloat!"

Belatedly, Cas recalled the bargain he'd made with the Prince Regent to go thirty days without a scandal, a record now most thoroughly lost. "Gloat away, Your Highness."

Prinny smirked and ambled across the room to a brilliantly cut crystal decanter. He lifted it in offering to Cas with his brows raised.

Cas bowed. "No, thank you, Your Highness, though I am honored."

The Prince Regent blinked at his formality. "What has you so stuffed, Worthington? You're not sore about losing our little wager, are you? You did much better than I imagined, you know. What was that, nearly three weeks?"

"Was that all?" Cas asked faintly. Three weeks, three minutes, three hundred years. Time had turned into a silvery liquid in Miranda's presence—moments timeless and forever, yet running through his fingers: uncatchable, unabiding, unforgettable.

"Well, it's over now, at any rate." The Prince Regent settled into a chair. "You'll have to perform some other feat of strength, I suppose." He laughed and pointed skyward. "Go fetch me a golden fleece, Jason!"

Chuckling, he took a healthy sip of the brandy and leaned back with a sigh. "Worthingtons! Always good for a laugh!"

Cas held his temper carefully. "Your Highness, respectfully, I did not come here to amuse you. I came to beg you to address a grave injustice, done to a woman who deserves better!"

Quickly, Cas explained the situation to the Prince Regent, emphasizing his own fault, Constance's conniving, and Miranda's extreme innocence. He brought forth the scribbled practice sheets, the newssheets with Constance's accounting of Miranda's parents. "It is all so unfair! Please, Your Highness, you must help her!"

Prinny yawned. "Why should I?"

Cas gaped at him. "Because it is an injustice!" He thought quickly. "Because Mrs. Talbot is a loyal subject, a respectable woman—and because the Scandal Clause is a terrible notion. You wouldn't want that to become a regular practice, would you? Think of all the widows who would be forced to lock their knees!"

"Don't preach policy to me, whelp." The Prince Regent gazed at him impatiently. "*You* made this mess. *You* clean it up!"

Cas turned away, thrusting his hands through his hair. "I would if I only knew how!"

Prinny seemed to take pity on him. "I know what it's like to get it all wrong," he said quietly. "To do nothing but harm when you meant only the best."

Cas knew the Prince Regent was thinking of his

youthful marriage to his beloved Maria Fitzherbert, which had been declared invalid so that he could make a later state marriage.

The Prince Regent stood and poured himself another brandy. He lifted the hand with the glass and pointed one finger at Cas. "You're the problem, you know. Not Poll. You're the worst tomcat in London. The best thing you can do is to leave her alone. Leave her in peace. Hell, leave England!" He waved a hand, carelessly splashing the brandy on his blinding white silk weskit. "With you out of sight, there will then be half as many opportunities for people to be reminded of her notoriety."

Cas went very still. "Yes. I could travel out to the West Indies for a time. I shall come back, when they forget."

"Ha!" Prinny tossed the newssheet back at him with the retelling of Miranda's scandalous parents. "*They* never forget." He sighed. "Ever."

"No, I'll go—if it will save her. If I leave, will you help her?"

The Prince Regent swallowed the brandy he'd been swishing in his mouth. "You'd really leave England?"

Cas didn't even hesitate—not with the image of broken Miranda locked behind his eyes. "I will board a ship at first light if it means she will regain what I have cost her!"

For a moment, the Prince Regent looked envious. Then he snorted. "Fine," he agreed, clearly disbelieving. He raised his glass in vow. "When that ship leaves the harbor, I will overturn the will." He scowled as he lifted his glass to his lips. "Bloody 'Scandal Clause'! We wouldn't want that to become a regular practice, would We? There wouldn't be a willing widow left in all of England!"

The Prince Regent was fond of his widows.

Chapter Thirty-four

Miranda sat blankly, staring at nothing. Nowhere to go. Nothing to do. How had she filled her days before the Worthingtons struck?

Then she remembered. She turned to Button and Cabot. "I fear I must go. I am quite late for a meeting with the matron at the orphanage."

"Of course," Button added thoughtfully as she stood to leave, "it will do you good."

Miranda made some garbled reply and left the house as if she'd been shot from a cannon. It was not a visit she looked forward to. She had no choice but to inform the matron that she could no longer assist the efforts of the home financially. Indeed, any further association with her would only taint the very results they wished to achieve.

The silence on the ride in the carriage, at first relatively peaceful, soon made her remember when she'd clung to Cas, wet to the skin and freezing and how he'd warmed her.

How he had kept her safe.

Hot, silent tears dripped onto her folded hands as she stared blindly out the small square window, lost in memory.

When Miranda arrived at the children's home, her

heart still lay so heavy in her chest that it seemed only natural that she would find the matron in tears as well.

Then she shook off her melancholy and peered more closely at Matron Beetles. "Oh, dear, is something wrong? Is it one of the children?"

"Yes! I mean, no, not one of them—oh, Mrs. Talbot, I've made such a mess of things! And the children are so hungry!"

That last fact snapped Miranda from her dolor as nothing else would have. "How can they be hungry? I have made sure that everything they need is delivered right to your door!"

Matron Beetles dried her eyes with her handkerchief and returned it to the pocket of her starched pinafore. Then she stood before Miranda with her shoulders slumped in shame.

"I suppose naught will do but to show you."

She led Miranda down a dark servant stair to the kitchens. On one of the wide, worn tables there, someone had deposited several large baskets covered in cheap burlap.

"This is the bread delivery, missus."

Miranda drew back. "It doesn't smell like fresh bread." Reaching over, she whisked the burlap aside to see rather ordinary looking loaves. They were brown and fairly even. When she looked at Matron Beetles curiously, the woman picked up a loaf with one hand and tapped it on the table. A loud knocking noise resulted.

"Stale!" Miranda frowned. "As hard as rocks! But when was this delivered?"

"This morning, just before noon. Late it was, late it has been, ever since . . ." Matron Beetles shook her head. "That's not the worst of it, missus. Stale I can work with. Cook could make a pudding with egg and currants, or we could make a bit of goose stuffing or some such. But . . ."

She pulled off the top lay of loaves one by one to reveal the next layer of black crusts and loaves edged in round, greenish patches. Miranda gasped. "Burned! And moldy as well!"

Furiously, she turned on Matron Beetles. "Why did you not inform me at once that the baker is cheating you?"

The woman paled and twisted her hands together. "After the first time, I thought I could persuade the baker to make it right. He scoffed at me, he did. He said that he'd found out what sort of children we kept here. He told me that if I dared to tell the authorities that he would tell them he'd caught one of my charges stealing from him and have the child locked away. 'Who do you think they'll believe?' he said. 'An upstanding tradesman or a bunch of infant thieves?'

"I told him we would take our custom elsewhere and he said he would just tell the world if I did." The matron looked down at the carpet, her round features miserable. "I was afraid he'd make good his threat, missus. Word could get out, you see. People would take objection to the house, sayin' the children ought to be put away with their parents, not left free to do mischief."

Rage burned hot within Miranda. She knew firsthand the prejudice that Matron Beetles spoke of. She'd hoped to keep the primary mission of the home secret, which would hopefully allow some of the children a clean slate when they ventured out into the world. An "orphan" from a blandly respectable school might find honest work where a prisoner's child would not.

It was a shame to build lives on lies, but how else when the truth would ruin them all?

She flinched from the obvious correlation to her own current difficulty and focused her fury on the perfect target.

"Let us go speak to this baker, shall we?"

* * *

The greedy baker's name was Malden. Miranda recalled it on the walk of more than three blocks, and also recalled how piteously the man had bemoaned the fate of the poor orphans last spring and had professed his desire to help.

"I'll be sure to throw in a bit extra, just a few cakes now and then, missus. It'll do me heart good to see them wee ones fattened up a bit. Wouldn't want them to be getting sickly come winter, would we?"

From the perspective of her greater experience in the foibles of man, Miranda now recalled the gleam of avarice in the fellow's eyes, which at the time she had taken for a friendly twinkle.

Heavens, she had been so credulous. If nothing else, she'd gained a more realistic perspective on human nature along with her other battle scars.

The bakery still appeared wholesome and honest, with its handsome wooden shelves and cases behind the counter filled with decadent buns and pastries.

Miranda strolled in, looking for all the world like a lady in search of a popover.

Malden stepped smartly up to serve her. He was a short, burly fellow with bushy . . . well, everything. Among the bushiness, his bright blue eyes gleamed like cold little stones.

Wiping his big hands on his apron, he regarded Miranda without recognition. Of course, she looked very little like the drab and serious housewife with whom he had originally bargained. In a swiftly borrowed Lementeur gown and a stunning bonnet, decorated and sent to her yesterday by Lady Wyndham in a supportive gesture, she looked ruthlessly stylish and very, very rich.

More lies, in a world built on lies.

She smiled sweetly at the baker. He ogled back. It didn't hurt that she had removed her lace from her neckline and had given her bosom a nice plumping by bending over in the Button's office and rearranging matters, aided by Cabot's loan of two bath sponges.

She blinked vapidly at him. "What a pretty shop. What pretty breads! I think I'll take them all."

The baker smiled, not quite sure if she were joking or simply idiotic. She leaned forward over the counter—or rather, her bosom leaned forward—as she held out one gloved hand. "Will one of these do?"

Her palm was full of guineas, hastily borrowed from Button, who apparently kept them in jam jars, rolling about amid buttons and thimbles. A single guinea would buy a bakery full of bread, for weeks. Tucked in amongst the gleaming gold coins was a dull copper penny.

The fellow swallowed. "One of them might just about cover it. I suppose I'll allow it, since you are such a fine and lovely lady." He leered.

Flirting? Ugh!

Miranda clapped her hands with silly glee. Her conspiratorial bosom jiggled. The baker took the coin she dropped into his hand without so much as glancing at it.

"Children!" she called over her shoulder. "Do come in and help yourselves!"

In an instant, the shop was filled to bursting with children. Like locusts they descended—rather loud, rowdy locusts, swarming madly and voraciously as they filled their hands and pockets and pinafores and arms with bread and scones and buns and sticky sweet iced cakes and then ran out again, shrieking and giggling. There was nothing left but crumbs and a single, trampled loaf in the middle of the floor.

The entire event had taken place in less than ninety seconds. It had been positively *Worthingtonian*.

The baker looked shaken, but his fist simply tightened about the coin and he gave Miranda an obsequious bow.

"That's precious generous of you, madam, given them urchins a treat like that. I would've rather delivered it all, for they've made a bit of mess in me shop." Then he shrugged. "Still, I suppose the gold will cover it."

Miranda smiled at him. "Gold? Did I say anything about gold?"

The baker opened his fist and examined the coin with a frown. It was the round copper penny.

"But . . . but . . ."

"You must be more attentive, sir." Miranda shrugged. "I can't imagine why you thought I gave you gold. Don't you know the difference between a guinea and a penny?" She smiled at her little rhyme, righteousness burning in her veins.

The man finally found his voice. "You robbed me! I'll have the law on you, I will!"

Miranda straightened and smiled with sugary ferocity.

"Oh, do. I wonder who the magistrate will believe: a lady or a cheating tradesman?"

Defying the baker gave Miranda courage. Her heart beat faster. Her lungs filled with air.

I remember this.

She'd found it once already. She'd been living quietly, if one could call it living, hoping that if she held on long enough, someone would rescue her.

Well, someone did. She did, with the help of her lover and her friend, who taught her how to speak and fight for herself.

She'd been wrong to blame Cas for everything that had happened. She'd knowingly stepped out from beneath the umbrella of propriety into the dicey rain—because she'd wanted more.

He'd certainly given that to her. He'd given her excitement, and passion, and dreams the like of which she'd never dared to dream.

The fact that her heart could break was the chance she had taken. She loved him.

She would not undo that love, even though he had so obviously not returned it. That deep and whirling maelstrom had made a woman out of a repressed girl. It had filled her, expanded her, shown her a world that glowed and shimmered and breathed. She refused to unsee that world.

I will never live under anyone's thumb again. I will never again be afraid. I will be scandalous but free.

She smiled. She wanted to tell someone what she had realized—someone who would understand the dizzying intoxicating freedom that fizzed through her blood.

She wanted to share it with her family.

The Worthingtons.

Chapter Thirty-five

Miranda arrived at Worthington House with her heart bursting, ready to share her brilliant new understanding with everyone, up to and including Cas. She knew that seeing him would be painful, but she was not angry—not any longer. He'd not kept promises, for he'd not made any.

Her love for him would never fade, even were it not fed by his affections. However, there was no reason to deny herself of Poll's friendship, and Attie's stubborn loyalty, and Elektra's bright and vivacious company, or even Iris's dreamy insight!

However, Worthington House was as sad and drear a place as Miranda had ever seen. Philpott opened the door for Miranda, and answered her greeting with a sob. Tossing her apron over her face, she scuttled from the entrance hall as if she'd seen a ghost.

A pale and furious Attie sat on the bottom stair, staring hard at Miranda.

"I don't hate you," Attie said firmly.

Miranda nodded cautiously in greeting. "Nor do I dislike you."

The child had made a real attempt to dress properly today. Her frock was quite nice, if a bit long and a bit loose in the bodice. She wore proper stockings and shoes, though she'd managed to tear a ladder into her stockings already and her shoes looked a little tight.

Her hair was the most astounding transformation. Attie saw her staring and raised her fingers to touch her elaborate hairstyle.

"Ellie asked if she could practice braiding on me. I liked the way it looked so I've been practicing, too." Braids, indeed. There were perhaps seven or eight of them, sprouting from all areas of her head like a palm, or perhaps the legs of an octopus. Each glossy, perfect braid was tied off with a different substance. Ribbon, twine, clothesline, wire, sprung springs—it seemed that Attie had raided the infamous workshop Miranda had heard so much about.

Miranda hadn't the slightest urge to chuckle. She was much too moved by the words "Ellie asked." It seemed that the lovely Elektra had actually been listening.

Attie's little freckled face screwed up into a hideous grimace. Miranda thought with some alarm that the child was either going to sneeze or possibly combust.

"I didn't mean to do it!"

Miranda's first response was, "Of course, you didn't!" Then she thought perhaps she ought to clarify. "Ah . . . what precisely do you think you didn't mean to do?"

Attie knuckled her eyes for a moment. Miranda saw the tiny child still lurking just under the worldly-wise skin.

"I didn't mean to make you notorious! I just thought that if you had lots of beaus that you wouldn't make Cas and Poll fight—because they were fighting and they've never fought before—not since they were my age and Dade had to sit on them to make them stop—"

This was obviously a story Attie relished and to be frank, Miranda was a bit curious to hear more, but she stopped Attie with a gentle hand on her bony little shoulder.

"Attie, you didn't make me notorious. Someone tricked me into going someplace I shouldn't have gone, and someone who shouldn't have seen me there did see me there and then they only told the simple truth—so it was really my own doing that I ended up notorious."

She rather liked that word. She rolled it around in her mind while she waited for Attie's response.

Notorious.

The Notorious Miranda Talbot.

And then, because she was in the privacy of her own mind and it was no one's business what she dreamed of—

The Notorious Miranda Worthington.

"So there," she told Attie. "Now, you've nothing to cry over at all."

Attie's face started to crumple once again. "Yes, I do! I do! Because Cas is *gone!*"

Miranda went very still. "Gone? Where has he gone?"

Attie laid her head down on her arms that were crossed over her bent knees. She said something damp and muffled that Miranda was quite horribly certain translated as "The West Indies."

"Attie," she said slowly. "I need to speak to Poll."

Miranda found Poll easily enough. At first she wasn't quite sure. When the stout housekeeper in voluminous striped muslin showed Miranda to the jumbled workshop, she saw the brooding figure leaning one elbow on the table, his jaw hard and his eyes narrowed as he stared unseeing at the coals in the iron stove.

She had at first glance taken him for Castor. Then, as he raised his gaze to see her enter, the flash of sweetness in his smile identified him as Pollux.

Miranda stood opposite Poll at the worktable and leaned both fists on the scarred and burned—and she wasn't sure what that violent scarlet stain was but it was probably best to avoid touching it—tabletop.

"Poll, you must tell me everything—and don't you dare edit it for my tender ears. I am a grown woman. I can handle anything."

So he told her everything—all about Cas's big dream, and his bargain with the Prince Regent.

Miranda pressed her fingertips to her lips. "Oh. Oh dear." It seemed she wasn't the only one who'd lost something on the night of the Wyndhams' ball!

Poll told her of Cas's anger at being manipulated—

"Well," she reminded him, "I did tell you I didn't care for the plan."

Poll nodded, then went on to explain the orgy and Lily—and Dilly—who actually did sound like good sorts if one could overcome the whole prostitution obstacle.

"Do you really believe that Cas didn't dally with Lily—or Dilly—" Miranda shook her head. So many flower names!

Poll gave her an exasperated glance. "Cas might not tell me everything, but he would never *lie*. Not to me."

Miranda drew back at his vehemence. "Oh." Biting her lip, she decided to believe him, for *he* had never lied to *her*. "So you believe that Cas's, er, overreaction was because he does love me?"

"Love you?" Poll shook his head, laughing sadly. "Miranda, Cas is tearing himself, all of us, into tiny little pieces—and it's all for you!"

"Me?" *I don't believe you, my friend.* "I don't understand. Poll, where is he? Why is everyone acting like he's gone away forever?"

He shook his head again, sadly this time. "That was the bargain he made, you see. The Prince Regent promised to intercede on your behalf—to negate the Scandal

Clause by Royal Order—if Cas took himself off. Permanently. The Prince Regent said that the scandal would never die as long as Cas remained visible in the eyes of Society."

Miranda couldn't breathe. Her chest was far too full of her expanding heart to engage in something as tedious as breathing! "He did that? Truly?"

Poll dropped his head into his hands. "God, you're stubborn. How did someone so sweet and gentle become so stubborn?" He lifted his head and glared at her. "Yes. He. Did. That. For. *You*."

Miranda straightened and gazed down at Poll primly. Joy spiked within her like luminous crystals quickly growing. "There's no need to be surly, Pollux." She tugged her spencer straight and pulled at the fingertips of her gloves, arranging them properly. "Now, where is this ship?"

Chapter Thirty-six

It was a big ship, and the rough men serving upon it eyed Miranda with grim concern as she crossed the plank and made her way through coils of thick, tarred rope and mysterious wrapped bundles. *Do not fear. I am not traveling today. You won't have to fetch me lemonade or carry my parasol on walks about the deck.* Not that a little coddling would go so amiss, but she was there for only one reason.

Cas.

So as to hurry her on a bit, one of the sailors briskly showed her down to the small corridor of staterooms for those people brave enough to call themselves passengers.

The rather hairy, certainly smelly, man tapped at one door, rumbled out a slurred and accented string of words that had to run through Miranda's mind twice before decanting to "Your missus is here to see you."

Miranda hurried to correct the man, but the door was already opening. The sailor cast Miranda a rotten-toothed grin of farewell and thudded back up the narrow, ladder-like stairs toward the deck.

Cas, taller and darker somehow—not to mention just plain delicious—stood in the tiny hole of a doorway, staring at her.

"Miranda, what are you doing here?" Then his astonishment changed to alarm. "Mira, you ought not to be here. If Prinny learns of it—" He shook off the rest of his words. "I am not good for you. You should not associate with me."

"It's lovely to see you as well, Mr. Worthington." Miranda folded her arms. "Aren't you going to invite me in?"

He hesitated. She could actually sense the tumbling thoughts, the spinning gears inside his mind. With a slight smile, she gave him a hint. "If I am in your cabin, I am much less likely to be spied lurking outside it."

He reached out a hand to hers and tugged her inside. Even she had to duck to go through the low-hung doorway.

Cas closed the door behind him, thinking quickly. *She's here! She's here, with me! And that is not hatred in her eyes!*

However, there was no need for such hope to rise in his heart. Prinny would not care to have Cas fail again. There would be no more chances.

His ship would be departing soon. It was good that he should leave her, erase himself from her life, from the gossip. It was also good that he would not be here, living less than a mile from her. He was no coward, but even he could not bear such torture.

Miranda started to speak, then stopped, her nerves showing in the tremor in her voice.

Flustered, she pressed her gloved fingertips to her lips— and Cas was lost.

In two strides he took her into his arms. She squeaked slightly, then relaxed as he kissed her.

Oh, how he kissed her! So softly, so tenderly. He tried to give her his very soul in that kiss. It was nothing like his old, raging self. He still wanted the fire, but just being near her fair to burned him to death.

The desperation was gone, he realized as he lifted his mouth from hers. He had already let her go.

He did not need to grasp or cling to her. He did not need to possess her—it was enough, almost, just to know that she was in the world and that she would be well.

It was no more than he deserved. Cas smiled around the spike in his heart. Good. The sooner she forgot him, the sooner the damage he had done to her would heal, and the sooner sweet Miranda would be whole again.

After all, he was willing to die for her, either swiftly or slowly, day by endless day, for the rest of his life.

Cas suddenly realized that Miranda stood in his arms, her hands upon him, claiming him.

Loving him? Present tense?

He gazed down at her, his throat tight. He tried to swallow but his mouth had gone dry with aching, impossible hope.

"Mira—"

She stroked her fingertips over his beard-roughened jaw. "Have I ever told you how much I like the way you say my name, as if you see right through the proper exterior to the woman within?"

His heart was thudding. "Mira, I must leave. If I go, the Prince Regent has offered to overthrow the Scandal Clause in Gideon's will. If Prinny comes down on your side, most of Society will follow along."

She drew back. "No! No more blasted bargains! We will not bargain away our happiness ever again!" Then she gentled once more. He felt the tingle of her fingers lacing through the hair on the back of his neck. "Besides, how can I pass up a man who would trample his own heart to make me happy?"

He tried very hard to push her away, he truly did. "But your inheritance—the house on Breton Square? Your reputation?" The fact that he shifted her not an inch said a great deal about her determination—or his complete inability to resist her.

She laughed and twined her arms about his neck. "I don't care, Cas. I don't need anyone else to tell me that I am a good woman . . . not as long as you think so."

"You are not a good woman. You are an angel." He ran a tender fingertip down her soft cheek. "I love you," he said for the first time.

Miranda tilted her head back to look into his eyes. Surprise lighted the deep-sea green, and then, slowly, the shock transmuted into joy, like lead into gold.

And he was the alchemist who put it there. Perhaps he was an inventor after all, for he'd invented a new man, just for her. Pride and stunning, knee-weakening gratitude overwhelmed him.

"One more bargain, my beautiful Mira."

Her head began to shake before he could continue. "No."

Cas chuckled. "I think you'll like this one." With the fingers of one hand he stroked her fallen hair back behind her ear. "Here are my terms." He kissed the tip of her nose. "I propose that you, Mrs. Gideon Talbot, will marry me and become a Worthington in truth."

Her smile crept past her disapproval. "I suppose I should hear you out," she agreed cautiously.

"Thank you." A kiss for each eye. "In turn, you, soon-to-be Mrs. Castor Worthington, will receive protestations of my undying love every day for the rest of your life."

She nodded. "Go on."

"More? Very well. In addition, there will be episodes of spontaneous tempest-making in our bedchamber, at your discretion."

She blushed. "Your proposal grows interesting. I should like to hear more."

He grinned down at her. "You bargain like a Worthington already. All right, I will invent something absolutely, incredibly *useful* to assist your school."

Nodding, she tightened her arms about his neck. "That would be most welcome."

Cas began to worry. He had nothing, therefore he had nothing to offer her. He drew back and gazed down at her seriously. "I fear I cannot offer you a new house. We shall have to live with my family—"

Her eyes brightened yet more. "Sold!"

A small laugh burst from Cas. If he'd only known that the bedlam of Worthington House would be a selling point!

She lifted her chin. "I will not stop once begun. You may want me to stop, but you will wish in vain. You must embark knowing this."

Cas swallowed hard. *Damn.* "I understand."

"Very well. Your bargain is acceptable to me." She grinned, dimpling. "That means yes."

"Yes," he murmured as he pulled her hard to him.

Mine.

He kissed her again, softly, then harder and harder still.

She kissed him back, matching his intensity. Cas could feel the fire, banked and contained, knowing she would meet his heat with her own flames. He also felt the warmth, soothing and uplifting, her love and acceptance smoothing over all the rough edges.

He'd never before realized that love could be more powerful than the ache of the past.

Epilogue

Miranda stood before the looking glass in the bedroom she shared with Cas. They had been given two small chambers on a mostly unused floor of the grand old house, and Orion had set about making it one large, convenient chamber.

The plaster still smelled of lime and there was a place where the floors rose to a peak, just where the wall between used to be, but other than that, one might never know it had been two rooms.

She turned this way and that, using the morning sunlight to hopefully cast a shadow across her hips, pressing her chemise down over her small belly, trying to see what an observer would see. "Tell me," she said over her shoulder. "Am I an expectant mother or just a woman a bit too fond of her lemon tea cakes?"

"Both." Cas was at his dressing table, brushing soap over his face in preparation for shaving.

There was no such thing as privacy in this house, Miranda had learned.

She loved it, every shabby, ancient, creaking square foot of it.

It was full of things, of books and music and inventions and costumes and people—people who loved her, who loved Cas, and who loved her child. Though there was still pain and some things would never be the same, the Worthingtons swelled to surround the two—three—of them.

Miranda had never been so happy in any of her three former homes.

Yet, she missed Poll. They all did, of course. Poll's family tangibly ached.

There had been no stopping him, however. "If there's more to life than play," he'd told her with a smile and a shake of his head, "then I intend to go find it."

As for Miranda, she knew she would miss her dearest friend. She'd confessed this to Cas, and he'd held her while she cried for that loss. She knew he hurt for the loss of his twin like he might hurt for a missing limb.

Poll had left the house the day that she and Cas were wed. Miranda knew Poll had done it for her, that he still felt he owed her something for the game in which she'd been a pawn. She wished she could tell him that the gifts he and his brother had both given her far outweighed the pain they'd caused, but he'd quietly disappeared sometime after the ceremony and only Iris received the occasional note to reassure his mother of his continued existence.

Cas spent every day in the workshop. So far he'd invented a corking device that Miranda had promptly put to use in the children's home. Dr. Philpott's Evening Tonic was doing very nicely in the shops and the school might even make a profit in a few months! With or without royal patronage, Cas meant to gain a name as a serious inventor.

Later, dressed and still annoyingly slender, Miranda trotted down the stairs in search of a hearty breakfast. The rare queasiness she had suffered for the first few months had now disappeared altogether and she couldn't seem to stop eating.

Eggs, she thought with delight. And those creamy vegetables that Philpott made especially for her—although Philpott claimed not to like her at all and it was only the baby Worthington that made her presence tolerable—even as she sneaked Miranda another lemon tea cake.

At the bottom of the stairs, Miranda stopped and cocked her head. Was that—?

Sniffle.

Yes. Attie.

Miranda knew that the infamous Book Cave existed somewhere in this hall, so she walked slowly, half-crouching, listening for the next—

Sniffle.

It came from right in front of her. Miranda sat down on the floor, which all the Worthingtons did as a matter of course, and patting her belly, began to sing a little song.

"O merry maids do come afore, and let thy feet be dancing."

Sniffle. "You can't sing that song to the baby. It's bawdy."

It was, very. It wasn't about dancing at all. "The baby doesn't know that."

"I did." Attie crawled halfway out of her Book Cave and sat scowling sorrowfully at Miranda. "I knew everything. I remember being born."

Miranda couldn't remember a thing before the age of four or five, but she only nodded. Attie was special. Perhaps her child would be special as well.

"Then the baby knows you are crying. He's probably wondering why."

Attie rubbed her wrist beneath her nose and gazed at Miranda pityingly. "She's a girl. Thalia."

Miranda went quite still. "I think I like that name. Thalia is a muse, is she not?"

Attie nodded. "She's going to have your hair, and

Papa's green eyes. She's going to be taller than you. She's going to be gentle, like Poll, not fierce, like Cas and I."

A chill ran up Miranda's spine. Sometimes Attie was a little extra odd. Miranda just patted her belly again. "Then, Thalia would very much like to know why you are crying."

Attie just crumpled, then and there. Miranda scrambled on her knees across a wall of books to wrap the girl in her arms as she cried.

"No m—matter what I d—do, they k—keep leaving!"

Miranda nodded. Her own eyes began to leak, perhaps because of the pregnancy, or perhaps because Attie's pain pierced Miranda's bliss, straight to the place in her heart where the child she'd once been had wailed nearly the same words so long ago.

"Oh, pet, I know—"

Pounding footsteps came toward them. Miranda was very glad she was half in the safety of the Book Cave when Lysander came rushing down the hall. He stared wildly at them both.

"Hurry! Gather in the study!"

"What?" Miranda's heart stuttered. Lysander never spoke. "What is wrong!"

"It's Elektra! We have to do something about Elektra!"

"Elektra," Miranda gasped. "Is she hurt?"

"No!" Lysander ran anxious hands through his thick shaggy hair. "She's kidnapped an earl!"